Happiness rushed th
she saw Caleb on the porch steps behind
her.

Stop it! He was meant to be her twin sister's match and her way to happiness, not Annie's.

"Looks like you didn't get your laundry done earlier in the week."

"These are your cousin's and her *boppli*'s clothes."

"I didn't mean to dump this extra work on you, Annie. If you'd rather, I can pay you for taking care of my cousin and her *boppli* and find someone else to work with me at the bakery."

"No!"

His eyes widened at her vehemence.

She told herself to be cautious or she'd give away her true reason for accepting his job offer. Working with Caleb would be Annie's best opportunity to gently shove him and her sister toward each other.

"I want to work with you at the bakery," she replied as if it were the most important oath she could take.

And it was, because what she did while in Caleb's company could mean the difference between healing her sister's heart or not.

But what would it do to hers?

Jo Ann Brown has always loved stories with happily-ever-after endings. A former military officer, she is thrilled to have the chance to write stories about people falling in love. She is also a photographer and travels with her husband of more than thirty years to places where she can snap pictures. They have three children and live in Florida. Drop her a note at joannbrownbooks.com.

Cheryl Williford and her veteran husband, Henry, live in South Texas, where they've raised three children and numerous foster children alongside a menagerie of rescued cats, dogs and hamsters. Her love for writing began in a literature class, and now her characters keep her grabbing for paper and pen. She is a member of her local ACFW and CWA chapters, and is a seamstress, watercolorist and loving grandmother.

JO ANN BROWN

The Amish Bachelor's Baby

&

CHERYL WILLIFORD

Their Convenient Amish Marriage

LOVE INSPIRED

INSPIRATIONAL ROMANCE

LOVE INSPIRED®
INSPIRATIONAL ROMANCE

Recycling programs
for this product may
not exist in your area.

ISBN-13: 978-1-335-22985-4

The Amish Bachelor's Baby and
Their Convenient Amish Marriage

Copyright © 2020 by Harlequin Books S.A.

The Amish Bachelor's Baby
First published in 2019. This edition published in 2020.
Copyright © 2019 by Jo Ann Ferguson

Their Convenient Amish Marriage
First published in 2019. This edition published in 2020.
Copyright © 2019 by Cheryl Williford

This edition published by arrangement with Harlequin Books S.A.

For questions and comments about the quality of this book,
please contact us at CustomerService@Harlequin.com.

Harlequin Enterprises ULC
22 Adelaide St. West, 40th Floor
Toronto, Ontario M5H 4E3, Canada
www.Harlequin.com

Printed in U.S.A.

CONTENTS

THE AMISH BACHELOR'S BABY

Jo Ann Brown

For Mike Freeman,
a superstar real estate agent…
with a fabulous sense of humor.
Thanks for everything!

This is my commandment,
That ye love one another, as I have loved you.
—*John* 15:12

Chapter One

Harmony Creek Hollow, New York

"**D**on't you dare eat those socks!"

Annie Wagler leaped off the back porch as the sock carousel soared on a gust and headed toward the pen where her twin sister's goats were watching her bring in the laundry. The plastic circle, which was over twelve inches in diameter, had been clipped to the clothesline. As she'd reached for it, the wind swept it away.

Snow crunched beneath her boots, and she ducked under the clothes that hung, frozen hard, on the line. She despised bringing in laundry during the winter and having to hang the clothing over an air-dryer rack inside until it thawed. She hated everything to do with laundry: washing it, hanging it, bringing it in and folding it, ironing it and mending it. Every part of the process was more difficult in the cold.

Pulling her black wool shawl closer, she ran toward the fenced-in area where Leanna's goats roamed. She wasn't sure why they'd want to be outside on such a frigid day, but they were clumped together near where Leanna would feed them later. Annie sometimes wondered if the goats were one part hair, hooves and eyes, and three parts stomach. They never seemed to be full.

And they would consider the cotton and wool socks a treat.

Annie yanked open the gate, making sure it was latched behind her before she ran to collect the sock carousel. She had to push curious goats aside in order to reach it. One goat was already bending to sample the airborne windfall.

"Socks are for feet, not for filling your bottomless stomachs," Annie scolded as she scooped up the socks that would have to be washed again.

The goats, in various patterns of white, black and brown, gave her both disgusted and hopeful glances. She wasn't sure why her identical twin, Leanna, liked the creatures, especially the stinky male.

Leanna had established a business selling milk and had begun experimenting with recipes for soap. Her twin hoped to sell bars at the Salem farmers market, about three miles southwest of their farm, when it reopened in the spring. As shy as her twin was, Annie wasn't sure how Leanna would handle interacting with customers.

They were mirror twins. Annie was right-handed, and Leanna left-handed. The cowlick that kept Annie's black hair from lying on her right temple was identical to Leanna's on the other side. They had matching birthmarks on their elbows, but on opposite arms. Their personalities were distinct, too. While Leanna seldom spoke up, Annie found it impossible to keep her opinions to herself.

How many times had she wished she was circumspect like her twin? For certain, too many times to count. Instead, she'd inherited her *grossmammi*'s plain-spoken ways.

Annie edged toward the gate, leaning forward so the socks were on the other side of the fence. She needed to finish bringing in the laundry so she could help her *grossmammi* and Leanna with supper. Her younger siblings were always hungry after school and work. She'd hoped their older brother, who lived past the barn, would bring his wife and *kinder* tonight, but his six-year-old son, Junior, was sick.

Keeping the sock carousel out of the goats' reach, she stretched to open the gate. One of the kids, a brown-and-white one her twin called Puddle, butted her, trying to get her attention.

Annie looked at the little goat. "If you weren't so cute, you'd be annoying, ain't so?"

"Do they talk to you when you talk to them?" asked a voice far deeper than her own.

In amazement, she looked up…and up…and up. Caleb Hartz was almost a foot taller than she was. Beneath his black broad-brimmed hat, his blond hair fell into eyes the color of early-summer grass. He had a ready smile and an easy, contagious enthusiasm.

And he was the man Leanna had her eye on.

Her sister hadn't said anything about being attracted to him, but Annie couldn't help noticing how tongue-tied Leanna was when he was nearby. He hadn't seemed to notice, and maybe Annie would have missed her sister's reactions if Annie didn't find herself a bit giddy when Caleb spoke to her. Before Caleb's sister, Miriam, had mentioned that Leanna seemed intrigued by her brother, Annie had been thinking...

No, it didn't matter. If Leanna had set her heart on him, Annie should remind him how *wunderbaar* her sister was. She'd do anything to have her sister happy again.

"Gute nammidaag," Annie said as she came out of the pen, being careful no goat slipped past her.

"Is it still afternoon?" He glanced toward the western horizon, where the sun touched the mountaintops.

"Barely," she laughed. "I've been catching up with chores before working on supper. Would you like to eat with us this evening?"

"Danki, but no." Caleb clasped his hands behind him.

Annie was puzzled. Why was he uncomfortable? Usually he chatted with everyone. While he traveled from church district to church district in several states, he'd met with each of the families now living in Harmony Creek Hollow and convinced them to join him in the new community in northern New York.

"What can we do for you?" she asked when he didn't add anything else.

"I wanted to talk to you about a project I'm getting started on."

Curiosity distracted her from how the icy wind sliced through her shawl, coat and bonnet. "What project?"

"I'm opening a bakery."

"You are?" She couldn't keep the surprise out of her voice.

A *bakery*? Amish men, as a rule, didn't spend much time in the kitchen, other than to eat. Their focus was on learning farm skills or being apprenticed to a trade.

"Ja," he said, then grimaced at another blast of frigid air. His coat was closed to the collar, where a scarf was edged with frost from his breath. "I stopped by to see if you'd be interested in working for me. The bakery will be out on the main road south of the turn-off for Harmony Creek Hollow."

She set the sock carousel on a barrel. "You want to hire me? To work in your bakery?"

"I've had some success selling bread and baked goods at the farmers market in Salem. Having a shop will allow me to sell year-round, but I can't be there every day and do my work at the farm." He shivered again, and she guessed he was eager for a quick answer so he could return to his buggy. "Miriam told me you'd do a *gut* job for me."

His sister, Miriam, was one of Annie's best friends, a member of what they jokingly called the Harmony Creek Spinsters' Club. Miriam hadn't mentioned anything about Caleb starting a business.

"It sounds intriguing," Annie said. "What would you expect me to do?"

"Tend the shop and handle customers. There would be some light cleaning."

"Will you expect me to do any baking? I'd want several days' warning if you're going to want me to do that."

He frowned, surprising her. It'd been a reasonable

request, as she'd have to rearrange her household obligations around any extra baking. Asking Leanna would be silly. Her sister could burn air, and things that were supposed to be soft came out crunchy and vice versa. Nobody could quilt as beautifully as her twin, but the simplest tasks in the kitchen seemed to stump her.

"You've got a lot of questions," he said.

Don't ask too many questions. Don't make suggestions. She doubted Caleb would treat her as her former boyfriend had, deriding her ideas until he found one he liked so much he claimed it for his own.

His frown faded. "I may need you to help with baking sometimes."

"Will you expect me to do a daily accounting of sales?"

"*Ja.* Aren't you curious how much I'm paying you?"

She rubbed her chin with a gloved finger. "I assume it'll be a fair wage." She smiled. "You're not the sort of a man who'd take advantage of a neighbor."

His wind-buffed cheeks seemed to grow redder, and she realized her compliment had embarrassed him.

Apologizing would cause him more discomfort, so she said, "*Ja,* I'd be interested in the job."

"Then it's yours." His shoulders relaxed. "If you've got time now, I'll give you a tour of the bakery, and we can talk more about what I'd need you to do."

"*Gut.*" The wind buffeted her, almost knocking her from her feet as she reached to keep the sock carousel from sailing away again.

"Steady there." Caleb's broad hands curved along her shoulders, keeping her on her feet.

Sensation flowed out from his palms and riveted

her, as sweet as maple syrup and, at the same time, as alarming as a fire siren.

"Danki," she managed to whisper, but she wasn't sure he heard her as the wind rose again. It made her breathing sound strange.

"Are you okay?" he asked.

When she nodded, he lifted his hands away and the warmth vanished. The day seemed colder than before.

Somehow, she mumbled that she needed to let her twin know where she was going. He wrapped his arms around himself as another blast of wind struck them.

"Hurry…anna…" The wind swallowed the rest of his words as she rushed toward the house.

She halted in midstep.

Anna?

Had Caleb thought he was talking to her twin? She'd clear everything up on their way to the bakery. She wanted the job. It was an answer to so many prayers, for God to let her find a way to help her sister be happy again, happy as Leanna had been before the man she loved married someone else without telling her.

Leanna was attracted to Caleb, and he'd be a fine match for her. Outgoing where her twin was quiet. A well-respected, handsome man whose *gut* looks would be the perfect foil for her twin's. But Leanna would be too shy to let Caleb know she was interested in him. That was where Annie could help.

God, danki *for giving me this chance to bring joy back to Leanna's life. I won't waste this opportunity You've brought to me.*

As she was sending up her grateful prayer and rushing to the house, she reminded herself of one vital thing. She must be careful not to let her own attraction to Caleb grow while they worked together.

That might be the hardest part of the job.

One task down, a hundred to go…before he started tomorrow's list.

Caleb glanced at the lead-gray sky as he moved closer to the heat box on the buggy's floor, shifting his feet under the wool blanket there. The clouds overhead were low. Snow threatened, and the dampness in the air added another layer of cold. He hoped the Wagler twin wouldn't remain in the house much longer. If he wanted to get home before the storm began, the trip to the bakery would have to be a quick one.

He hadn't been sure when he went over to the Wagler farm if he'd get a *ja* or a no to his job offer. He had to have someone to help at the bakery.

But is she Annie or Leanna?

He hadn't been sure which twin he was talking to. His usual way of telling them apart was that Annie talked more than Leanna, but without both being present, he hadn't known. Not that it mattered. He had to have someone help at the bakery because he had his farmwork, as well.

After almost two years of traveling and recruiting families for the Harmony Creek settlement, he finally could make his dream of opening a bakery come true. He'd turned over the community's leadership when the *Leit* ordained a minister and a deacon. It'd been the first service of the new year, and the right time to begin building the permanent leadership of their district.

He smiled in spite of the frigid wind as he glanced

toward the white two-story farmhouse. Miriam had suggested he ask a Wagler twin to work for him. It had been a *gut* idea. The Wagler twins made heads—plain and *Englisch*—turn wherever they went. Not only were they identical with their sleek black hair, but they were lovely. The gentle curves of their cheekbones contrasted with their pert noses. Most important, they seemed to accept everyone as they were, not wanting to change them or belittle their dreams as Verba Tice had his.

His hands tightened on the reins, and his horse looked back as if to ask what was wrong. Caleb grimaced. It was stupid to think about the woman who'd ridiculed him. Verba was in Lancaster County, and he was far away. And…

He pushed the thoughts from his head as the back door opened and a bundled-up woman emerged. Her shawl flapped behind her as she hurried—with care, because there were slippery spots everywhere—to the buggy. He slid the door on the passenger side open, and she climbed in, closing it behind her. The momentary slap of wind had been as sharp as a paring knife.

"Sorry to be so long," she said from behind a thick blue scarf. "My *grossmammi* asked me to get some canned fruit from the cellar."

"It's fine." Which twin was sitting beside him? Too late, he realized he should have asked straightaway by the goats' pen.

How could he ask now?

Giving his brown horse, Dusty, a gentle slap of the reins, he turned the buggy and headed toward the road. He tried to think of something that would lead to a clue about which Wagler twin was half-hidden behind the scarf. He didn't want to talk about the weather. It was a grim subject in the midst of a March cold snap. What if he talked about the April auction to support the local volunteer fire department? The *Englisch* firefighters found it amusing when the plain volunteers called it a mud sale. He wondered if the ground would thaw enough to let the event live up to its name.

"Caleb?"

He wanted to cheer when she broke the silence. *"Ja?"*

"You know I'm *Annie* Wagler, ain't so?"

"Ja." He did now.

"I wanted to make sure, because people mix us up, and I didn't want you to think you had to give me the job if you'd intended to hire Leanna."

She *was* plainspoken. He prayed that would be *gut* in his shop, because he wasn't going to renege on his offer. It could be embarrassing for her, and him, and the thought of the humiliation he'd endured at Verba's hands stung.

And one thing hadn't changed: he needed help at the bakery. It shouldn't matter which twin worked for him.

Who are you trying to fool? nagged a tiny voice inside his head. The one that spoke up when he was trying to ignore his own thoughts.

Like thoughts of how right it had felt to put his hands on Annie's shoulders as he kept her from falling in the barnyard. He didn't want to recall how his heart had beat faster when her blue-green eyes had gazed up at him.

He must keep a barrier between him and any attractive woman. Getting beguiled as he had with Verba, who'd claimed to love him before she tried to change everything about him, would be stupid.

"Do you and your sister try to confuse people on purpose?" Caleb asked to force his thoughts aside.

"We did when we were *kinder*. Once we realized people couldn't tell us apart, we took advantage of it at school. I was better at arithmetic and Leanna excelled in spelling, so sometimes I'd go to the teacher to do Leanna's math problems as well as my own. She'd do the same with spelling."

"You cheated?"

"Not on written tests or desk work. Just when the teacher wasn't paying attention."

He laughed, "The other scholars never tattled on you?"

"They wouldn't get any of *Grossmammi*'s delicious cookies if they did."

"I didn't realize we had a pair of criminal masterminds in our midst."

"Very retired criminal masterminds." She smiled. "Our nice, neat plan didn't last long. A new teacher came when we were in fourth grade, and she kept much better track of us. Our days of posing as each other came to a quick end."

"So you had to learn to spell on your own?"

"And Leanna did her arithmetic problems. She realized she had a real aptitude for it and surpassed me the following year." Annie hesitated, then said, "I'm sure the whole thing was my idea. Leanna always went along with me."

He glanced at her. She was regarding him as if

willing him to accept her words. He wondered why it mattered to her. For a moment, he sensed she was struggling with something big.

Again, he shut down his thoughts. Annie was his employee, and it'd be better to keep some distance between them.

"So you're now the better speller?" Caleb asked, glad his tone was light.

She laughed, "I don't know. We haven't had a spelling bee in a long time."

"Maybe we should have one. I read somewhere that *Englisch* pioneers used to hold spelling bees for entertainment." He gave her a grin. "Something we could do in our spare time."

"When we get some."

Miriam had told him how much fun she had with the Wagler twins, but he hadn't known Annie possessed a dry sense of humor. She wasn't trying to flirt with him, either, and he'd heard several of the community's bachelors saying Leanna was eager to marry. Maybe asking Annie instead of her twin hadn't been such a mistake after all.

When they reached the main road, Caleb held Dusty back. Traffic sped past. Most cars were headed to ski resorts in Vermont, and the drivers couldn't wait to reach the slopes. Local drivers complained tourists drove along the uneven, twisting country roads as if they were interstates.

Two minutes passed before Caleb felt safe to move onto the road. They didn't have to go far before he signaled a left turn. He held his breath as a car zipped by him, heading east, but he was able to make the turn before another vehicle, traveling as fast, roared toward Salem.

"Everyone's in a hurry," Annie said as she turned her head to watch the car vanish over abandoned railroad tracks.

"I hope they slow down before they get hurt." Pulling into the asphalt parking area behind the building where ghosts of painted lines were visible, he said, "Here we are."

"Your bakery is going to be here?"

"Ja." He was still amazed he'd been able to buy the building in October.

It had served as a supply depot for the railroad until the mid-1960s. The parking area and the pair of picture windows on the front were perfect for the shop he had in mind. Its wide eaves protected the doors. The building needed painting, but that had to wait for the weather to warm. As a few stray snowflakes wafted toward the ground, he couldn't help imagining how it'd look in May, when he planned to open.

"Why a bakery?" she asked.

"My *grossmammi* taught me to bake when I was young, and I enjoyed it." He didn't add he'd been recovering from an extended illness and had been too weak to play outside.

She glanced at him, and he suspected she wanted him to explain further. He didn't.

Walls. Keep up the walls, he reminded himself. Getting close was a one-way ticket to getting hurt again. He wasn't going to do something that *dumm* again.

Not ever.

* * *

The wind tore at Annie's coat and shawl when Caleb opened the door on his side and got out. When she reached for her door, he called to her. She had to strain to hear his voice over the wild wind.

"Head inside. Don't wait for me." He grabbed a wool blanket off the floor. "I'll tie up Dusty. I want to put this over him to keep him warm while I give you the nickel tour."

She nodded, but she wasn't sure if he saw the motion because he'd already turned to lash his horse to a hitching rail. The building would provide a windbreak for the horse.

After hurrying through the back door, she paused to cup her hands and blow on them. She wore heavy gloves, but her fingers felt as if they'd already frozen.

It was dusky inside. Large boxes were stacked throughout the cramped space. She wondered what was in them. Not supplies, because the room didn't look ready for use. Paint hung in loose strips between the pair of windows to her left.

She stood on tiptoe to look for writing on the closest box. She halted when she heard a quiet thump.

It came from beyond the crates. She peered around them. A door led into another room.

Was someone there?

Should she get Caleb?

A soft sound, like a gurgle or a gasp, was barely louder than her heartbeat. If someone was in trouble in the other room, she shouldn't hesitate.

God, guide me.

She took a single step toward the other room, keeping her hand on the wall and trying to avoid the big crates. Her eyes widened when she saw a silhouette backlit by a large window. She edged forward, then froze as a board creaked beneath her right foot.

The silhouette whirled. Something struck the floor. A flashlight! It splashed light around the space. A young woman was highlighted before she turned to rush past Annie.

"Wait!" Annie cried.

A *boppli*'s cry echoed through the building.

"Stop!" came a shout from behind Annie.

Caleb!

"There's someone here," she called as she spun, hoping to cut off the woman's escape.

She ran forward at the sound of two bodies hitting each other.

Caleb yelled, "Turn on the lights."

"Lights?"

"Switch…on the wall…by the door." He sounded as if he was struggling with someone.

She flipped the switch and gasped when she saw the person trying to escape from Caleb.

It was a teenage girl, holding a *boppli*. Blonde and cute, the girl had eyes the same dark green as Caleb's. The *boppli* held a bright blue bear close to his cheek and squinted at them in the bright light.

Annie started to ask a question, but Caleb beat her to it when he asked, "Becky Sue? What are you doing *here*?"

Chapter Two

Becky Sue?

Caleb knew this girl and the *boppli*?

Annie wondered why she was surprised. Caleb knew everyone who came to Harmony Creek Hollow. Was this young woman part of a new family joining their settlement? There was one empty farmstead along the twisting road beside the creek.

Annie faltered when she saw the shock on Caleb's face. His green eyes were open so wide she could see white around the irises, and his mouth gaped.

Then she remembered what he'd said after calling the girl by name.

What are you doing here?

He wasn't shocked to see Becky Sue. He was shocked she was in his bakery.

What was going on?

As if she'd asked that aloud, Caleb said in a taut tone, "Annie, this is my cousin, Becky Sue Hartz. She and her family have a farm a couple of districts away from where Miriam and I grew up." He closed his mouth, and his jaw worked with strong emotions.

The girl shared Caleb's coloring and his height. Annie wondered how alike they were in other ways.

Stepping forward with a smile, she tried to ignore the thick tension in the air. "I'm Annie Wagler. I should have guessed you were related to Caleb. You look alike."

"Hi, Annie." Becky Sue's eyes kept cutting toward Caleb. Her expression announced she expected to be berated at any second.

Why? For being in the bakery? It wasn't as if she'd broken in. The door had been unlocked. However, even if Becky Sue had jimmied a window and climbed in, her cousin would have forgiven her.

"And who is this cutie?" Annie tapped the nose of the little boy in the girl's arms, and he chuckled in a surprisingly deep tone.

For a moment, Becky Sue lost her hunted look and gave Annie a tentative smile. "This is Joey. He's my son."

Her son? The girl didn't look like much more than a *kind* herself. If Annie had to speculate, she would have guessed Becky Sue was sixteen or seventeen. At the most. The little boy, who had her flaxen hair, appeared to be almost a year old.

Shutting her mouth when she realized it had gaped open as Caleb's was, Annie struggled to keep her smile from falling away. Though it wasn't common, some plain girls got pregnant before marriage as *Englisch* ones did. Or had Becky Sue been a very young bride?

As if she'd cued Caleb, he asked, "Is your husband with you?"

Becky Sue raised her chin in a pose of defiance. A weak one, because her lips trembled, and Annie guessed she was trying to keep from crying.

"No," the girl replied, "because I don't have a husband. Just a son." When Caleb opened his mouth again, she hurried to add, "I'm not a widow, though that would be convenient for everyone, ain't so?"

"Everyone?" He frowned. "Do your parents know where you are?"

"Ja." When he continued to give her a stern look, she relented enough to say, "They know I left home."

"But not where you're going?"

She didn't answer.

"Where *are* you going?" Caleb persisted.

Again the girl was silent, her chin jutting out to show she wasn't going to let him intimidate her. Though the girl was terrified. Her shoulders shook, and her eyes glistened with unshed tears.

Knowing she should keep quiet because the matter was between Caleb and the girl, Annie couldn't halt herself from saying, "I'm sure you and Joey would like something warm to eat. It's cold here, ain't so? Though I was here last winter, I can't get used to it. Caleb, we need to get these two something warm to eat."

Caleb aimed his frown in her direction. She pretended she hadn't seen it. Didn't he understand they wouldn't get any information if the conversation dissolved into the two of them firing recriminations at each other? Once the girl and her *boppli* weren't cold and hungry—and exhausted, because Joey was knuckling his eyes with tiny fists and dark crescents shadowed his *mamm*'s eyes—Becky Sue might be willing to come clean about why she and her son were so far away from home.

But Annie's comments were ignored as Becky Sue said, "I told you, Caleb. I left home, and I'm—we're not going back."

"And you decided to come to Harmony Creek Hollow?" Annie asked, earning another scowl from Caleb.

"I heard about the new settlement." Though she answered Annie's question, she glared at her cousin. "I didn't know this was the one you were involved with, Caleb. If I had—"

"Well, isn't it a *wunderbaar* coincidence, Becky Sue?" Annie hurried to ask. "And your timing is perfect."

"It is?" Becky Sue seemed overwhelmed by Annie.

Gut! That was what Annie wanted. If the girl stopped thinking about defying Caleb, she might relax enough to reveal a smidgen of the truth; then Annie and Caleb could figure out what was going on.

No! Not Annie and Caleb. She shouldn't use their names together in her thoughts. *She* had to keep *her* focus on helping Caleb see what a *wunderbaar* wife Leanna would make him.

Wishing she could think of a way to bring her twin into the conversation, Annie said, "Your timing is great because Caleb was giving me a tour of his bakery."

"Bakery?" Hope sprang into the girl's voice. "I didn't see any food around here. Do you have some?"

"I've got soup in a thermos in the buggy." Caleb's

face eased from its frown. "I meant to eat it for lunch, but I got busy and forgot."

"Wasn't that a blessing?" Annie hoped her laugh didn't sound as forced to them as it did to her.

"It probably won't be hot," Caleb said.

Annie frowned. Didn't he realize his cousin might be so hungry she wouldn't care what temperature the soup was? "We can heat it up."

He shook his head. "The stove isn't connected. Nothing is yet. The gas company is supposed to have someone come later this week."

Annie made a quick motion with her fingers toward the door. Did he understand that she hoped, when he was gone, Becky Sue would open up to her? Sometimes it was easier to speak to a stranger.

The *boppli* wiggled in Becky Sue's arms and began crying. While the girl's attention was diverted, Annie gestured again to Caleb. He gave her a curt nod, but his frown returned as he headed for the door. If he disliked her idea, why was he going along with it?

Focus, she told herself.

Pasting on a smile, Annie held out her arms to Becky Sue. "Do you want me to hold him while you have something to eat?"

"No, I can do it myself." Her sharp voice suggested she'd made the argument a lot already.

With Becky Sue's parents? Other members of her family? Joey's *daed*? The girl had said she wasn't a widow, but where was the *boppli*'s *daed*?

Wanting to draw Becky Sue out without making the conversation feel like an interrogation, Annie began to talk about the weather again. Her attempts to convince the girl to join in were futile. Becky Sue refused to be lured into talking. Instead she stared at some spot over Annie's head as she bounced her son on her hip in an effort to calm him.

But Annie wasn't going to waste the opportunity. There was one topic any *mamm* would find hard to ignore. "Becky Sue, do you have enough supplies for your *boppli*?"

Her face crumbling as her defiance sifted away, Becky Sue shook her head. "I've only got one clean diaper left for him."

"Do you have bottles, or is he drinking from a cup?"

"I had a bottle." She stared at the floor. "It got lost a couple of days ago."

"My sister-in-law has a little one not too much older than Joey. I'm sure she or someone else will have extra diapers and bottles you can borrow."

Bright tears clung to Becky Sue's lashes but didn't fall. The girl's strong will astonished Annie. It was also a warning that Becky Sue, unless she decided to cooperate, would continue to avoid answering their questions.

"Gut," the girl replied.

"I know it's none of my business, but are you planning to stay here?"

"You're right. It's not any of your business." A flush rose up Becky Sue's cheeks, and Annie guessed she usually wasn't prickly. In a subdued tone, she added, "I don't know if I'm staying in Harmony Creek Hollow...beyond tonight."

"I'm glad you don't plan to go any farther tonight. It's going to be cold."

"I didn't expect the weather to be so bad."

"None of us did."

Annie watched as the girl began to relax. Becky Sue was willing to talk about trite topics, but the mere hint of any question that delved into why she was in Caleb's bakery made her close up tighter than a miser's wallet.

A few admiring queries about Joey brought a torrent of words from the girl, but they halted when the door opened and Caleb walked in. Annie kept her frustrated sigh to herself as she searched for a chair Caleb said was among the boxes.

Somehow they were going to have to convince the mulish girl to let them help. Becky Sue must be honest with them about what had brought her to northern New York. Annie prayed for inspiration about how to persuade her to trust them.

Not having any ideas on how to solve a problem was a novel sensation.

And it was one she didn't like a bit.

While Becky Sue sat on the floor and began to feed her son small bites of the vegetable soup from the thermos, Caleb watched in silence. The same silence had greeted him when he came into the bakery. He'd heard Annie talking to his cousin, but Becky Sue had cut herself off in the middle of a word the moment she saw him.

Annie edged closer and offered him a kind smile. He was startled at the thought of how comforting it was to have her there. She was focused on what must be done instead of thinking about the implications of his cousin announcing the *boppli* was her son.

But the situation was taking its toll on her, as well. Lines of worry gouged her forehead. She was as upset as he was about his cousin.

"I'm sorry," he murmured.

"For what?" she returned as softly.

"Putting you in the middle of this mess. When I asked you to work for me, I didn't think we'd find my cousin hiding here." He gulped, then forced himself to continue. "Here with a *boppli*."

"You didn't know she was pregnant, ain't so?"

He moved out of the front room. When Becky Sue glanced at them with suspicion, he made sure no emotion was visible on his face. The *boppli* chirped his impatience, and she went back to feeding her son.

Standing where he could watch them, he leaned toward Annie. A whiff of some sweet fragrance, something that offered a tantalizing hint of spring, drifted from her hair. He hadn't thought of Annie Wagler as sweet. She was the forthright one, the one who spoke her mind. But standing close to her, he realized he might have been wrong to dismiss her as all business. She had a feminine side to her.

A very intriguing one.

"Caleb?" she prompted, and he realized he hadn't answered her.

Folding his arms over his coat, he said, "Nobody mentioned anything about Becky Sue having a *kind*."

"But you've got to let her family know she's here. She…"

Annie's voice trailed off, and Caleb looked over his shoulder to see Becky Sue getting to her feet. Annie didn't want his cousin to know they'd been talking about contacting Becky Sue's parents. A wise decision, because making the girl more intractable wouldn't gain them anything.

He realized Annie had guessed the same thing because she strolled into the front room and began asking how Becky Sue and Joey had liked their impromptu picnic.

The girl looked at her coat that was splattered with soup. "He liked it more than you'd guess from the spots on me. I should wash this out before the stains set."

Making sure his tone was conversational, Caleb pointed into the kitchen area and to the right. "The bathroom is through that door."

Becky Sue glanced at her drowsy son and hesitated.

Annie held out her hands. "I'll watch him while you wash up."

"Danki," the girl said as she placed the *boppli* in Annie's arms.

Becky Sue took one step, then paused. She half turned and appraised how Annie cuddled the little boy. Satisfied, she hurried into the bathroom and closed the door.

Annie began to walk the floor to soothe the uneasy *boppli*. He calmed in her arms when she paced from one end of the kitchen to the other. As he stretched out a small hand to touch her face, she said, "This may be the first moment she's had alone since they left home. I can't imagine having to take care of a *boppli* on my own while traveling aimlessly."

"What makes you think she's being aimless?"

"It seems as if she's thought more about running away than running to a specific place."

Caleb nodded at Annie's insightful remark. "We've got to figure out what to do."

"What's to figure out? She has to have a place to stay while you—" She gave a glance at the closed bathroom door. "While you make a few calls."

He was grateful she chose her words with care. If they spooked Becky Sue, she might take off again.

"That's true, but, Annie, I live by myself. I can't have her under my roof with nobody else there."

Puzzlement threaded across her brow. "Why not? She's your cousin."

"She's my second cousin."

Comprehension raced through Annie's worried eyes. Marriage between second cousins wasn't uncommon among plain folks. He had two friends who'd made such matches.

"Won't Miriam take them?" she asked, adjusting the *boppli*'s head as it wobbled at the same time he began to snore.

"Under normal circumstances, but she has caught whatever bug has made so many of her scholars sick. When I stopped by earlier today, the whole family was barely able to get on their feet. She won't want to pass along the germs."

"Then there's only one solution."

"What's that?"

"She can stay at our house."

To say he was shocked would have been an understatement. "But they're not your problem."

She gave him a frown he guessed had daunted many others. He squared his shoulders before she realized how successful her expression nearly had been.

"Caleb, Becky Sue and Joey aren't a problem. Becky Sue is a girl *with* a problem. Not that this little one should be called a problem, either." Her face softened when she gazed at the sleeping *boppli* in her arms and rocked him.

He almost gasped, as he had when he recognized his cousin among the boxes in the bakery's kitchen. The unguarded warmth on Annie's face offered a view of her he'd never seen before. He wondered how many had, because she hid this gentle softness behind a quick wit and sharp tongue. He was discovering many aspects of her today. He couldn't help being curious about what else she kept concealed.

"We've got plenty of room in our house," she went on, her voice rising and falling with the motion of her arms as she rocked the *kind*. "There will always be someone there to help Becky Sue."

He couldn't argue. The twins' younger sister, Juanita, was in her final year of school. In addition, Annie's *grossmammi* and younger brother lived with them.

At that thought, he said, "You've already got your hands full."

"True, so we won't notice another couple of people in our house. Let us help you, Caleb. You've worked hard building our community, and doing this will give our family a chance to repay you."

Guilt suffused him, but he couldn't think of another solution. It seemed Becky Sue had already decided she could trust Annie. Now he must show he trusted her, too.

The bathroom door opened and Becky Sue emerged.

When Annie asked her to stay with the Wagler family, she made the invitation sound spontaneous.

Caleb held his breath until his cousin said, *"Danki."*

"Get your things," he replied. "I turned the heater on in the buggy when I got the thermos. It's as warm in there as it's going to be, so bundle up. I'll stop by later and check on you."

"You aren't coming with us?" Becky Sue asked suspiciously.

"No. I've got work to do." Turning to Annie, he said with the best smile he could manage, "You taking them tonight will let me keep my work on schedule."

"Gut," Annie replied, as if the timetable for the bakery was the most important thing on their minds.

As soon as Becky Sue went into the front room, Caleb lowered his voice and said, *"Danki* for taking her home with you. Now I'll have the chance to contact her family."

"Do they have access to a phone?"

"I'm pretty sure they do. If not, I can try calling the store that's not far from where they live. The *Englisch* owner will deliver emergency messages." He couldn't keep from arching his brows. "I don't know what would constitute more of an emergency than a missing *kind* and *kins-kind.*"

"You know the number?"

"The phone here at the bakery is for dealing with vendors, but I've let a couple of our neighbors use it, and at least one of them mentioned calling the store. The number should be stored in the phone's list of outgoing calls."

Becky Sue returned with a pair of torn and dirty

grocery bags in one hand. The girl carried a bright blue-and-yellow blanket in the other. Stains on it suggested she and her *boppli* had slept rough since leaving their home.

Joey woke as Annie was wrapping the blanket around him. He took one look at Caleb and began to cry at a volume Caleb hadn't imagined a little boy could make.

As Annie cooed to console him, she handed him to his *mamm*. She finished winding the blanket around him at the same time as she herded Becky Sue out of the bakery.

Caleb went to a window and watched them leave in his buggy. He went to the phone he kept on top of the rickety cabinet that must be as old as the building. He'd planned to start tearing the cupboard out after giving Annie a tour of the bakery. He wondered when he'd have time to finish.

Soon, he told himself. He'd set a date at the beginning of May to open the bakery. He'd already purchased ads in the local newspaper and the swap magazine delivered to every household in the area because his customers from the farmers market had been so insistent he inform them as soon as the bakery opened its doors.

Picking up the phone, he frowned when he began clicking through the list of outgoing calls. Someone had made a call about ten minutes before he and Annie had arrived. He had no doubt it was Becky Sue.

The number wasn't a Lancaster County one. It had a different area code, one he didn't recognize. He wasn't sure where 319 was, but he'd ask someone at the fire department where he was a volunteer firefighter to look it up for him.

But that had to wait. For now...

He found the number for the small store and punched it in. This wouldn't be an easy call.

Chapter Three

As Annie had expected, her arrival with Becky Sue and the *boppli* in tow threw the Wagler house into an uproar. The moment they walked in, her two sisters stopped their preparations for supper and came over to greet their unexpected guests. The family's new puppy, Penny, who was a hound and Irish setter mix Annie's younger brother had brought home the previous week, barked and bounced as if she had springs for legs.

Annie's efforts to catch Penny were worthless. The copper-colored pup was too eager to greet the newcomers to listen. Little Joey seemed as excited as the puppy. Becky Sue had to wrap him in both arms to keep him from escaping.

Annie pulled off her coat and tossed it over a nearby chair. She finally was able to grab Penny by the scruff. The puppy wore a mournful expression when Annie shut her in the laundry room. She hoped Penny would calm down at the sight of her dish filled with kibble.

Annie returned to the kitchen and looked around. A bolt of concern riveted her. *Grossmammi* Inez wasn't in the rocking chair by the living room door. Her *gross-mammi* had lived with them for a year after Annie's *daed* died from a long illness. When Annie's *mamm* married her late husband's cousin and had two more *kinder*, Annie had used any excuse to visit her *grossmammi*.

The elderly woman had taken them in a second time after *Mamm* and her second husband, a hardworking man who'd been a loving *daed* to his stepchildren, were killed in a bus accident when Kenny was a toddler. Though she couldn't do as much as she once had, *Grossmammi* Inez supervised the kitchen she considered her domain.

"She's resting," Leanna said before she shot a smile at Becky Sue and introduced herself.

Annie nodded, glad her twin knew what was on her mind. However, her uneasiness didn't ebb. Her *grossmammi* sometimes took a nap, but Annie couldn't recall her ever staying in bed while meal preparations were underway.

Her attention was drawn to her guests when Becky Sue asked, "You are twins, ain't so?" The teenager stared, wide-eyed, at Leanna before facing Annie. "You look exactly alike."

Leanna said with a faint smile, "I'm a quarter inch taller."

"Really?"

Leanna lifted her right foot. "Only when I'm wearing these sneakers."

Everyone, including Becky Sue, laughed, and Annie wanted to hug her twin for putting the girl at ease.

"I've never met girl twins before," Becky Sue said.

"There were two pairs of boy twins in my school, but no girls."

"No?" Annie laughed again. "Well, now you have."

Before Becky Sue could reply, Annie's younger sister, Juanita, edged around Leanna. She was a gangly fourteen-year-old who was already three inches taller than the twins and still growing, though Annie doubted she'd ever challenge Becky Sue's height. Juanita's light brown hair was so tightly curled it popped out around her *kapp* in hundreds of tiny coils. It was the bane of Juanita's existence, and nothing she'd tried had straightened it enough to keep the strands in place.

"Can I hold him?" Juanita held out her arms to the *boppli.*

Annie smiled at her younger sister. Juanita wavered between being a *kind* herself and becoming a young woman. It was shocking to realize Becky Sue couldn't have been much older than Juanita when she became pregnant. Annie's sister hadn't begun to attend youth events yet, preferring to spend time with girls her own age. They seemed more interested in besting the boys at sports than flirting.

"This is my sister Juanita," she explained to Becky Sue. "We've got two brothers, as well. Lyndon is married and lives next door, and Kenny, who's twelve, should be out in the barn milking with him. You'll meet him at supper."

Juanita cuddled Joey, who reached up to touch her face as he had Annie's. Becky Sue took off her coat and hung it up by the door as she scanned the large kitchen with cabinets along one wall and the refrigerator and stove on another.

Standing by the large table in the center, Annie smiled at her younger sister, who loved all young things. She delighted in taking care of the farm's animals, other than Leanna's goats and the dairy cows. She tended to the chickens, ducks and geese as well as the pigs and two sheep.

When Joey began fussing, Annie urged her sisters to return to making supper while she took Becky Sue upstairs and got her and the *boppli* settled. The extra bed was in Annie's room, but if Becky Sue was bothered by the arrangement, she didn't mention it. Annie cleared out the deepest drawer in her dresser and folded a quilt in it. Tucking a sheet around the quilt, she added a small blanket on top to make a bed for Joey. She urged her guests to rest while she went to help her sisters finish supper.

Annie asked Juanita to run next door to ask their sister-in-law if they could borrow some diapers and a couple of bottles for the *boppli*. Her younger sister was always happy for any excuse to visit her nephews and nieces.

Leanna didn't pause chopping vegetables for the stew simmering on the gas stove. Not that her twin would do any actual cooking. Juanita was already a more competent cook.

Hanging up the coat she'd draped over the kitchen chair, Annie went to the stove and checked the beef stew. She halted, her fingers inches from the spoon, as she wondered if Caleb would be joining them for supper. He'd said something about coming over after he called Becky Sue's parents.

"We need to set extra plates on the table," Annie said as she stirred the stew so it didn't stick.

"More than one?" Leanna looked up from the trio of carrots she had left to chop.

"Caleb said he'd stop over." Annie dropped her voice to a whisper to explain why he'd remained behind at the bakery. "It'll be a *gut* opportunity for us to get to know him better."

Her twin set down the knife and walked away from the counter. Taking the broom from its corner, she began to sweep the kitchen floor. "Why were you at the bakery today?"

"Caleb wants an assistant to help with getting it ready and to wait on customers when it opens. He asked me, though he thought he was asking you." She told Leanna about the conversation by the goats' pen. "If you'd like to take the job instead, I'm sure he'd agree."

Leanna stopped sweeping. "I've already got a job."

That was true. Leanna cleaned for several *Englisch* neighbors. She could have a house sparkling in less time than it took Annie to do a load of wash.

"This would be different." Her answer sounded lame even to Annie, but somehow she had to convince her sister to be honest about her feelings for Caleb.

Leanna was generous and kind and, other than her inability to cook and bake, something that shouldn't be as important to a man who owned a bakery, would make Caleb a *wunderbaar* wife. It was a fabulous plan, even if it broke Annie's own heart.

Frustration battered her. Why couldn't those two see what was obvious to Annie? Leanna and Caleb could make each other happy as husband and wife. Of that, she was certain.

Because you believe you *would be happy with him as his wife.*

Annie wished her conscience would remain silent. It was true she'd imagined walking out with Caleb before she noticed how her sister reacted each time he was near.

God, make me Your instrument in bringing happiness to Leanna, she prayed as she had so many times since her sister's heart was broken.

"It doesn't matter," Leanna said, "whether the job is different or not. I wouldn't have time to work for Caleb. This morning, I agreed to clean Mrs. Duchamps's house twice a week."

Annie recognized the name of one of the few *Englischers* who lived along the meandering creek. Mrs. Duchamps had worked at the bank in Salem most of her adult life as well as taking care of her late husband during the years when he was ill. Having no *kinder* of her own, it was no surprise Mrs. Duchamps had hired Leanna to help.

"I didn't know you were looking for more houses to clean."

Leanna smiled. "I enjoy the work, so why not? And we could use the money. Kenny is growing so fast it seems as if he needs new shoes every other month. This works out for the best because I wouldn't want to work at Caleb's bakery." She began sweeping again. "Don't you think it's odd he wants to start a bakery at the same time he's trying to keep his farm going?"

"Not really." Annie recalled the light beaming from

his eyes when he spoke about his plans for the bakery. It was a chance to make his dream a reality.

"Then it's a *gut* thing he asked you instead of me." Leanna shuddered. "I don't know what I'd say to his customers, and I'd get so nervous I'd end up dropping a tray of cookies."

"You navigate among your goats without stumbling. Even when you're milking them."

Leanna laughed, "Having them crowd around me hides a lot of my clumsiness. Besides, I'm sure you're going to have *wunderbaar* ideas to help Caleb."

"Maybe. Maybe not." Annie began to chop the rest of the carrots.

"You never used to hesitate sharing your ideas, Annie. I wish I had half of the ones you have."

"Ideas come when they come."

Ideas did always pop into her head. She used to speak them without hesitation, but that was before she'd started walking out with Rolan Plank three years ago. They hadn't lasted long as a couple. After a month, he'd started to scold her for speaking up. He chided her for what he'd called her silly ideas. Yet, after he'd dumped her, he'd taken one of her so-called silly ideas and let everyone think it was his own.

"Either way," Leanna said, "I'm glad you're working for Caleb instead of me."

"But you could have had a chance to get to know him better."

"True, but I'm sure you'll share many stories about your time with him." Leanna paused for a long moment, then added, "I didn't think we'd still be talking about jobs now. I assumed I'd be a wife and *mamm,* but that hasn't happened."

"It will when—"

"Don't tell me it's God's will whether I marry or not." Her twin kept moving, each motion sure and calm in comparison with her voice. "I've heard that too many times."

Annie paid no attention to her sister's words. Only to her heartbroken tone, and Annie's heart broke, as well. Her sister had fallen hard for Gabriel Miller before they moved from Lancaster County, but Gabriel had wedded someone else. In retrospect, Annie wasn't sure he'd been aware of Leanna's feelings. As far as Annie knew, her sister hadn't told him. Instead, she'd decided to let him pursue her as the heroes did the heroines in the romance novels Leanna loved to read.

In the months since they'd arrived at the settlement in Harmony Creek Hollow, her sister had begun to emerge from her self-imposed isolation. Being a member of the Harmony Creek Spinsters' Club with two of their friends had helped. Now their friends Miriam and Sarah were married. In fact, there had been three weddings at the end of the year, and while Leanna was thrilled for her friends, each ceremony had been a reminder of what she wanted and didn't have: a husband and a family of her own.

Annie scooped up the chopped carrots and dropped them into the stew. When Caleb had offered her the job—even if it'd appeared to be a mistake—God had opened a door for her to help her sister. She ignored the familiar twinge in her own heart as she tried to convince herself that persuading Caleb to walk out with her twin sister would be the best idea she'd ever had.

How was it possible the evening was growing colder by the second? Each breath Caleb took seemed to be more glacial than the one before. He hadn't thought it could get any more bitter, but with the sun setting, the very air felt as if it'd turned to ice. He guessed by the time he'd left the bakery, got home and milked his cows, the mercury must have dropped to ten degrees below zero. It would be worse by the time he got up in the morning. The idea of heading into his comfortable house and calling it a day had been tempting, but he couldn't cede his responsibility for his cousin and her *kind* to Annie. He'd told her he'd stop by, and he couldn't renege on the promise.

As he led Dusty toward the Waglers' barn so the horse could get out of the cold, Caleb glanced at the goats' pen. It was empty, and he guessed the goats were huddling inside their shed.

Smart goats. He smiled at the two words he'd never thought he would put together.

Caleb's shoulders ached by the time he walked to the house. Trying to halt the shivers rippling over him was foolish, because he couldn't relax against the cold. His body refused to keep from trying to keep the polar wind at bay.

He climbed up onto the porch and rapped on the door. The faint call from inside was all the invitation he needed to open it.

Taking one step inside the mudroom connecting the kitchen to the porch, he was almost bowled over by a reddish-brown ball of fur. A sharp command from the table didn't stop the excited puppy from welcoming him.

Kenny rushed into the mudroom to collect the dog. Caleb smiled his thanks to the dark-haired boy before shrugging off his coat. Watching Kenny try to get the puppy to behave with little success, Caleb wondered if the boy's shoulders grew broader every day. Kenny wasn't going to be tall, but he was going to be a sturdy adult. Hard work in the barn was giving him the strength of a man twice his age.

Caleb set his coat, scarf, gloves and hat on a chair by the door because the pegs were filled. He turned to walk into the kitchen and then stopped as he took in the sight of the families gathered around the table. Two families. The Waglers—Annie and her twin, as well as her *grossmammi*, sister and younger brother, who was sliding into his chair, holding on to the puppy— and two members of the Hartz family: his cousin and her son.

Yet they could have been a single family. No one acted disconcerted. One twin held Joey on her lap and offered him bites of her food while his cousin sat on the opposite side of the table between a girl close to her age and the other twin.

But which twin was which? He was embarrassed that he wasn't sure.

His discomfort was overtaken by distress. He hadn't been able to reach Becky Sue's parents. He'd waited by the phone at the bakery for an hour, hoping for a call back. He'd left after that because his dairy herd got uncomfortable when he delayed the milking.

"*Komm* in…and join us," Inez said, motioning to him.

The elderly woman was shorter than the twins, and though her hair was gray and thinning, she had the same blue-green eyes. It was more than a physical resemblance, because she said what she thought, exactly as Annie did.

"*Komm*…in, Caleb," Inez urged again when he didn't move. She paused often as if having to catch her breath. "Sit…so we…can thank God…for our food… before…everything…is cold."

He entered the kitchen, which smelled of beef gravy and freshly baked bread. When his stomach rumbled, a reminder he'd skipped lunch, he was glad he was far enough away from the table so nobody would hear it. "You could have eaten without me."

"See?" piped up Kenny. "I told you he'd be okay with it."

"But… I wasn't." Inez's tone brooked no argument, and the boy didn't give her any as he bent to soothe the puppy, who was lunging to escape so it could greet Caleb as he neared the table. "Hurry. Join…us before hunger…makes Kenny forget…his manners again."

When the twin holding Joey—Caleb was almost certain she was Annie—flashed him a quick smile, he dampened his own. He admired how Inez spoke her mind. Not that she ever was cruel or critical of anyone, though she denounced what she saw as absurd ideas. She, as one of his fellow firefighters was fond of saying, called it as she saw it.

The only empty chair was at the end of the table. He sat there and nodded when Inez asked him to lead grace. He was the oldest man present, and it was his duty. As he bowed his head, his thoughts refused to focus on his gratitude for God guiding his young cousin to the bakery where she could be found. He was too aware of both twins sitting at the table.

If he mistook one for the other...

Annie had given him an easy way to avoid admitting he hadn't realized which twin he was asking to work for him, but he couldn't depend on that happening again.

He cleared his throat to signal the end of grace. As he raised his head, he was startled by an abrupt yearning he hadn't expected. A yearning for a life where he could sit with a family of his own at day's end. Several of his friends had married in November and December and stepped into the next phase of their lives. He was moving forward as well, but not in the same direction. Was he missing his chance to have a family?

There wasn't time for such thoughts. Between the farm and the bakery, he had too much work to do every day. The responsibilities of a family would require more of his nonexistent time. He'd made his choice, and he shouldn't second-guess himself.

Caleb took the bowl of fragrant stew. He spooned some onto his plate, then more when urged by Inez, who told him in her no-nonsense voice not to worry if he emptied the bowl because there was extra on the stove. When he sampled it, he was glad he'd listened to the old woman.

He focused on eating as conversation went on around him. He looked up when Inez spoke.

"Leanna...pass the basket...of rolls...to Caleb." Inez

gave him a wink as she spoke with her usual interruptions. Seeing how the twins glanced at her, he wondered what her pauses to take a breath meant. "I've… never met a…man who doesn't…have room for…another roll…or two."

"Especially with apple butter," he replied as he waited to see which twin did as her *grossmammi* had asked. When it wasn't the one holding Joey, he was relieved. He'd guessed Annie was the twin bouncing the little boy on her knee and keeping Joey entertained with pieces of soft carrot she'd fished out of her stew. He watched, amazed at how she kept the *kind* fed while she ate her own supper. He was beginning to wonder if Annie was *gut* at everything she did. She'd handled the touchy situation with Becky Sue with a skill he didn't possess.

"I'm not as out of practice as I thought," Annie said with a laugh. Was she trying to put him at ease for staring? That she might be able to discern his thoughts was disquieting. "I used to feed Kenny this way when he was little."

Kenny grumbled something, and Caleb swallowed his chuckle. No boy on the verge of becoming a teenager wanted to be reminded about such things.

As the meal went on and Caleb had another generous serving of the delicious stew, laughter came from the Waglers. But Becky Sue was reticent, and every movement she made displayed exhaustion. He wondered when—and where—she'd last slept.

A quick prayer of gratitude for their food, their families and for shelter from the cold night ended the meal. Leanna offered to help Becky Sue upstairs so she could rest, and Inez took the *boppli* into the living room to rock him until he became sleepy. Kenny wandered off somewhere with the puppy he called Penny.

Annie began to clear the table, carrying the dishes to the white farmhouse sink. "Did you get in touch with Becky Sue's parents?"

"No answer yet."

"As soon as they get the message, they'll call. I can't imagine how happy they'll be to discover their daughter and *kins-kind* are safe with you."

"With you, actually."

"We're happy to help." When he picked up his dishes, she said, "You don't have to clear the table. I know you've had a long day."

"No longer than yours."

"But I didn't have to milk," she laughed. "Lyndon, Kenny and Leanna milk every day, and Juanita will help sometimes. I always try to find somewhere else to be."

"Why? There's something *wunderbaar* about being in a warm barn and spending time with animals willing to share their bounty with us." He set the dishes by the sink. "For me, it's one of the clearest symbols of God's gifts to us."

She turned on the water and squirted dish detergent into the sink. "That's a much nicer way of looking at milking."

"But not your way?"

"Definitely not." She chuckled as she reached for the dishrag.

"You may have your mind changed one of these days."

"Don't hold your breath."

He smiled. Trust Annie Wagler not to withhold her opinion! It was one of the reasons his sister liked her, and working together at the bakery was going to be interesting. At least he wouldn't have to try to guess what she was thinking.

"So you prefer spending time with a *boppli* who spits up on you rather than a nice, clean cow who gives you milk?"

"Spits up?" She glanced at the spots of orange on her black apron. "I didn't notice. Oh, well. It'll wash out," she laughed. "Joey should be glad he wanted to sit on my lap rather than Leanna's."

"Why?" He was curious how the little boy had figured out which twin was which. And a bit envious of the *kind*'s intuitive ability.

"Leanna prefers *boppli* goats to *boppli* humans because she spent most of her teen years babysitting for an *Englisch* family who had a ton of rules about their *kinder*. They insisted she carry the *boppli* in some sort of contraption that wrapped around her shoulders. Half the time when she came home, she was covered with formula because they believed she should feed the *boppli* in the getup."

"That's enough to put anyone off from *kinder*."

Annie flinched, surprising him before she went to the table to collect more dishes. "She won't feel that way about her own *bopplin*. She'll be a *wunderbaar mamm*, I know."

"But you'll never like milking?"

"Never!" She carried the other dishes to the sink.

"Don't you know you should never say never?"

"That sounds like a challenge."

"It might be."

"It's one you're guaranteed to lose. Cows and I agree we're better off having as little to do with each other as possible."

"You're going to make me prove that you're wrong."

"About what?" asked Inez as she came into the kitchen. She set Joey on the floor and pressed one hand to her chest. An odd wheezing sound came from her, and she sat in the closest chair.

Annie rushed to her side. "Are you okay, *Grossmammi*?"

"I guess I'm not as young as I used to be." She glanced at the *boppli*, who dropped to his belly. "Chasing a young one is a task for someone with fewer years on her than me. So, what you are going to prove our Annie wrong about, Caleb?"

"That milking is a pleasant chore," he replied, though he wondered how Inez had failed so fast.

Beside her chair, Annie looked worried, but she kept her voice light. "*That* is something he'll never prove to me. *Grossmammi*, I can finish up if you want to go to bed."

He thought Inez would protest it was too early, but she didn't. Coming to her feet, she said, "A *gut* idea. These old bones need extra rest to keep up with a *boppli*." Before he could say he'd make other arrangements for Becky Sue, she added, "Caleb, we're glad to have your cousin and her *kind* stay with us." She wagged a gnarled finger at him. "Such things should go unsaid among neighbors, ain't so?"

Again, as he bade Inez a *gut nacht*, he was discomfited at how the Wagler women seemed to gauge his thoughts.

At the very moment Inez closed the door to her bedroom beyond the kitchen, Joey began to crawl toward them on his belly. Caleb bent to pick up the little fellow, but froze when Joey let out a shriek. The *boppli* clenched his fists close to his sides as his face became a vivid red.

"What's wrong?" Caleb asked as he reached again for the *kind*.

With a screech that rang in Caleb's ears, Joey cringed away.

Annie scooped up the *boppli* and held him close as she murmured. Joey's heartrending screams dissolved into soft, gulping sobs as he buried his face in her neck. She patted his back and made soothing sounds into his hair. When the *boppli* softened against her, she looked over his head toward Caleb.

Sympathy battled with dismay in her expressive eyes. Caleb had never guessed a mere look could convey such intense emotion. Or maybe it was as simple as the fact he felt sorry for the toddler, too.

Becky Sue burst into the kitchen, wearing a borrowed robe over a nightgown too short for her. Her hair was half-braided and her *kapp* was missing. "What's wrong with Joey?"

"I think he's overtired," Annie said. "*Bopplin* get strange notions in their heads when they're Joey's age. Some don't like men. Others fear dogs or cats or tiny bugs."

"Do you know why he's scared of men?" Caleb didn't want to admit how relieved he was Joey's antipathy wasn't aimed solely at him, because he'd always got along well with *kinder.*

Becky Sue shrugged. Or she tried to, but her shoulders must have been as stiff as his had been outside in the cold, because they curtailed the motion. Instead of answering him further, she hefted her son and walked away.

Caleb watched her climb the stairs at the front of the house and vanish along with the *boppli.* Her lack of answer told him plenty. She was hiding even more than he'd guessed.

Chapter Four

The soft chirp from the makeshift crib beneath the dormer window woke Annie two days later. Though the sun hadn't risen yet, she guessed it must be after 5:00 a.m. because lights glowed in the barn. Her brothers were already milking. They'd be ready for breakfast when they were done, so she should get started on her day.

She glanced at the extra bed between her and the window. Becky Sue was burrowed beneath the blankets, her knees drawn up under her and her rear end in the air, as if she were no older than her son who'd been in the same position when Annie checked on him last night.

The two had settled into the Waglers' home more easily than Annie had dared to hope. Last night, *Grossmammi* Inez had come into the bedroom to bid them a *gut nacht* and had asked pointed questions about Becky Sue's trip north. Their guest refused to share where she'd stayed during her journey from Lancaster County or how she'd traveled. While *Grossmammi* Inez didn't push, neither did she hide her annoyance. However, nobody asked why the girl said nothing about Joey's *daed*. It was as if the man didn't exist.

Becky Sue would learn keeping such secrets was futile in a household run by *Grossmammi* Inez. The elderly woman wouldn't be denied getting her way. She'd astounded everyone in the family when she announced she wanted to move with Annie and her siblings to New York. No arguments would persuade *Grossmammi* Inez to remain in the *dawdi haus*, where they had lived with her youngest son and daughter-in-law and their eight *kinder*. This drafty old farmhouse was now home, and Annie was glad they had enough room for Becky Sue and Joey.

Last night, when Caleb had again joined them for supper, Leanna hadn't said more than a handful of words, but Annie had seen her twin glance at him. Had he noticed, as well?

Annie chided herself. Why had she talked about Leanna staying away from other folks' *kinder*? She had to be cautious. Caleb might have mistaken her jest for the truth. If he wanted a family, why would he marry a woman who'd had her fill of *kinder*?

With a soft groan, Annie asked God to help her curb her tongue. By His bringing Caleb's cousin into their lives, He was offering Annie a chance to find the perfect way to open Caleb's and Leanna's eyes to what a great match they'd be. She couldn't mess that up.

She must remember that when the interrupted tour of the bakery resumed. It'd been postponed for a few days because of extra work Caleb had at his farm, so Annie had used the time to figure out some ways to point out, while he showed her around his bakery, Leanna's attributes.

Working to find joy and love for her sister was the best way to make herself happy, too. She had to believe that.

If only Caleb's face didn't keep wafting through her mind along with the sound of his voice when he spoke of his bakery. She inserted Leanna into the image each time his face reappeared. Once she became accustomed to thinking of Caleb and Leanna as a unit, Annie would be able to squash her attraction to him.

That was how it worked, ain't so?

Pushing aside her thoughts as well as her blankets when Joey began to make soft sounds again, Annie rose and went to where the *boppli* was sitting up in the deep drawer. He regarded her, wide-eyed. She doubted he understood when she leaned close to him and put her finger to her lips. When he copied her motion and gave her a grin revealing his four tiny teeth, she hurried to dress.

Annie twisted her hair into place and secured it with the ease of a lifetime of practice and set her *kapp* on top of it. Joey continued to make cheerful sounds, each one making her move faster so Becky Sue could sleep.

Edging around the other bed, Annie scooped the *boppli* up. He needed to be changed, so before leaving the room, she grabbed clean clothes from the basket delivered by her sister-in-law. Annie closed the door behind them.

The little boy tugged at Annie's *kapp* strings as she carried him downstairs. Getting a towel from the bathroom, she spread it on the floor. She changed him and tossed the dirty clothes into the washer. Once breakfast was over, she'd do laundry for him and Becky Sue.

She grimaced as she thought of hanging clothes out on another freezing morning, but Becky Sue was too tall for any clothing in the house.

She was surprised when Joey began to pull himself on his belly across the floor. At his age, he should be crawling on hands and knees. Instead, he seemed content to belly crawl to where she'd left his blue teddy bear.

When the door opened and her brothers entered, Annie had Joey on her lap and was feeding him cereal and pieces of toast.

Lyndon's eyes lit up at the sight of the *boppli*. He was a doting *daed* who spent every moment he could with his own *kinder*.

"No!" Annie put up one hand to keep her brother away.

"Sorry." He looked at his barn coat that was worn and stained everywhere. "Rhoda keeps telling me I need to wash before I hug the *kinder* so she doesn't have to clean them up."

"It's not that. My little friend here is scared of men. He's thrown a hissy fit every time Caleb comes too close to him."

"But he likes me," Kenny announced as he reached for a piece of toast in the middle of the table.

"Goes to show there's no accounting for taste, ain't so?" teased Lyndon.

Kenny stuck out his tongue and grimaced, bringing a laugh from his siblings.

Cold billowed off her brothers, and Annie got up,

balancing Joey on one hip, to pour *kaffi* for Lyndon as her older brother continued to joke with Kenny. She hurried to the table when Joey began to fuss. Handing him another piece of toast, she set the cup by Lyndon's right hand.

The food she put in front of her brothers vanished. They downed the oatmeal, toast and bacon she'd had waiting for them. She listened to their banter while her sisters made bleary-eyed entrances into the kitchen. Juanita offered to make eggs for anyone who wanted them, and Lyndon and Kenny raised their hands. They seemed to have bottomless pits inside them, because neither ever passed up food.

Grossmammi Inez was the last to rise, something that once would have been unthinkable. She smiled when Juanita placed scrambled eggs and toast in front of her. Leanna poured a cup of *kaffi* and set it next to her *grossmammi*'s plate.

"A soul could get accustomed to such service," the elderly woman said with a smile.

Annie laughed along with her siblings, but was bothered by the uneven pace of her *grossmammi*'s breathing. *Grossmammi* Inez insisted it was the aftereffects of the cold she'd had before Christmas. Annie hadn't argued, but was beginning to fear it was something more serious because *Grossmammi* Inez seemed to be getting worse rather than better.

Joey pushed away her hand holding another piece of toast topped with apple butter.

"Done, sweetie?" Annie asked Joey as she'd heard Becky Sue do at the end of each meal.

He nodded so seriously Lyndon chuckled.

Putting the *boppli* on the towel with a handful of the blocks sent over from her brother's house, she went to the sink to wash off her sticky hands. She filled a bowl with oatmeal for herself and carried it to the table. Adding brown sugar and cream skimmed off the top of the milk Kenny brought in every day from the barn, she kept an eye on the *boppli* as she bent her head to thank God for her food, her home and her family.

And for a little boy who was chewing on one of the blocks as if he could gnaw off one side of it. He held it near his face, ran his fingers over it and then put another section in his mouth as if he thought it might have a different taste.

I'm going to need a lot of help with this, Lord, she added before she raised her head again.

Lots and lots of help.

"No goats trying to eat your laundry today?"

At the question, Annie looked over her shoulder. A pulse of happiness rushed through her when she saw Caleb on the porch steps behind her. She didn't try to pretend it was because she could postpone hanging clothes while she spoke to him and found out what was in the small white box he held. Seeing his smile set off a low, long rumble within her, as if a distant thunderstorm hid on the other side of the mountains.

Stop it! He was meant to be Leanna's match and her way to happiness, not Annie's. How could Annie be content if her sister was lost in her grief at Gabriel Miller's betrayal?

"No wind today," she replied. "That means I don't have to chase the sock carousel across the yard."

"Looks like you didn't get your laundry done earlier in the week."

"These are the clothes Becky Sue and Joey had with them."

He came to stand beside her on the porch. "I didn't mean to dump this extra work on you, Annie." He paused, and she could tell he was giving consideration to a thought he'd been wrestling with. "Look. I know I offered you a job at the bakery, but if you'd rather, I can pay you for taking care of my cousin and her *boppli* and find someone else to help me at the bakery."

"No!"

His eyes widened at her vehemence.

Telling herself to be cautious or she'd give away her true reason for accepting his job offer, she reached for another tiny garment in the basket. At supper last night, Leanna had said less than a half-dozen words to Caleb. She hadn't greeted him, but she'd wished him *gut nacht*, and she'd told him *danki* when he passed something to her at the table.

Yet each time he spoke to her twin, Leanna flushed. Annie wondered how anyone could fail to see her sister had feelings for Caleb. They needed a gentle shove toward each other. Working with Caleb would be Annie's best opportunity to do that before he found someone else to wed.

"I want to work with you at the bakery," she replied as if it were the most important oath she could take.

And it was, because what she did while in Caleb's company could mean the difference between healing her sister's heart or not.

* * *

Caleb searched Annie's face, wanting to be sure she was being honest with him. Not that he had any reason to doubt her because she was the most forthright person in Harmony Creek Hollow. He wouldn't have to worry about her manipulating him as Verba had when she tried to convince him to follow her plans for them.

Verba had hated the idea he'd have a business where he wouldn't be around the farm all the time. He'd seen that as a sign she loved him and preferred they spent time together. But as their courtship had gone on, he'd begun to believe that what he'd considered affection was, instead, a determination to mold him into what she deemed would be the perfect husband.

Why was he thinking of Verba? Or marriage? He must concentrate on the reason that had brought him to the Waglers' farm beneath the hills lifting toward the Green Mountains a few miles to the east.

He looked at Annie. A faint wisp of wind tugged at her *kapp* strings beneath her black bonnet while it played with the edges of the shawl she'd secured around herself in two places with clothespins. Her cheeks were almost as red as the sky at sunset, but her eyes, which seemed to vary in color between green and blue, were warm.

"Are you certain you want to take on both jobs?" He hoped she was. Trying to find someone else for the bakery could set back his plans and he'd miss the opening day he'd be announcing in the ads he'd ordered.

"*Ja*, Caleb. I gave you my word I'd take the job at the bakery, and it's not as if I'm alone in helping Becky Sue and Joey."

"Miriam hopes to be on her feet by the end of the week, and she'll be glad to have them come to her house."

"A house that's undergoing so much renovation isn't the best place for a little *boppli* who puts everything in his mouth." She hooked another clothespin onto a small garment.

"You sound as if you want them to stay here."

"*Grossmammi* Inez has mentioned several times in the last couple of days how nice it is to have someone around while Juanita and Kenny are at school."

"Leanna—"

"Has jobs of her own. She cleans houses for some of our *Englisch* neighbors."

"I didn't know that." Again he thanked God for leading him to the correct twin to ask for help at the bakery.

Annie bent to pick up the empty laundry basket. Straightening, she grabbed the clothesline near the pulley on the porch post and pushed the clothing along its length toward a huge maple tree. She grimaced and braced her feet as she tried to give the line a bigger shove outward from the house.

"Let me help," he said.

"*Danki.*" She handed him the empty basket and grasped the line with both hands.

He stared at the laundry basket, then laughed.

She paused and asked, "What's funny?"

"You. Me. I thought you'd let me push the clothes out for you."

"Oh." The color on her cheeks deepened.

He hadn't intended to put her to the blush with his comment. For a moment he was as flustered. He hadn't imagined candid Annie Wagler was ever embarrassed. He had to wonder what other assumptions he had of her that would be overturned in the weeks to come.

He began to apologize, but she cut him off. Motioning him toward the line, she stepped back as she told him that she'd appreciate his pushing the clothes out another few inches.

Feeling like the world's biggest *dummkopf*, he handed her the empty basket and pushed the line out as she'd asked.

"Would you like to come in and have something warm to drink?" Her *gut* spirits seemed to revive themselves when she added with twinkling eyes, "It's the least I can do when you've helped so much."

"Hey, I pushed the last of the clothes clear of the eaves."

"Something for which we'll be forever grateful." She edged past him and opened the door. "I doubt we'll ever be able to repay you for this, Caleb."

He laughed, the cold air searing his throat. *This* was the Annie he knew, and he hoped she would continue to be irrepressible when she worked at the bakery with him. Laughing would make the time pass faster and the hard work more fun.

Caleb was still chuckling after he'd hung up his coat in the mudroom. He watched as Annie set the laundry basket by the washing machine.

"Inez, it's always a pleasure to see you," he said when he went into the kitchen and set his white box, which was full of cookies, on the counter.

"Aren't you a charmer today?" She motioned at the chair next to hers.

He looked around before he took another step.

"Becky Sue and Joey are resting upstairs," Inez said, as if he'd announced his thoughts aloud. "You won't upset the *boppli* when he can't see you. Sit and tell me the news while it's quiet."

Caleb smiled, not at her words but at how Annie rolled her eyes out of her *grossmammi*'s view. He wanted to assure them he understood the importance of patience when dealing with Joey. He needed the same forbearance when speaking with Becky Sue, who changed the subject or ignored his questions whenever he spoke to her.

He settled himself into the chair while Annie made and served fragrant hot chocolate to the three of them. Inez kept up a steady chatter of the latest tidings. Though she'd asked him for news, she had more than he did. Not just from their settlement, but from families beyond Harmony Creek.

"You are as full of information as *The Budget*," Caleb said between sips of delicious hot chocolate.

"Much of it comes from the circle letter Annie has kept going for almost ten years. Her cousins are scattered from here to Colorado."

He looked toward where Annie was by the counter. "I was hoping to work at the bakery tomorrow. Will you be able to come?"

"Ja." She opened a cupboard door, blocking his view of her face. "Are you starting early?"

"By seven."

"I'll be there."

"No, I meant I'd pick you up at around seven."

She turned, and he saw her astonishment. "You

don't have to pick me up. It's not a long walk to the bakery."

"It's close to a mile, a long distance in this cold. I don't mind."

"Say *danki* to Caleb, Annie," said her *grossmammi* before she could reply. "You'll do neither of you any *gut* if you take a chill and sicken as I did last month."

"*Danki*, Caleb. Leanna will be happy she doesn't have to worry about me." She came to the table and held out a plate of the oatmeal-raisin cookies Caleb had brought with him along with some snickerdoodles. "Leanna worries about us. Her heart is big, and she always has room for one more."

He nodded as he took a snickerdoodle, then a second one as Inez raised her snowy brows. He'd sampled cookies from the Waglers' house before, and they always were delicious. A quick bite told him these were better than he remembered.

"Astounding!" He finished the cookie. "Is that molasses I taste?"

"*Ja.*" Annie sat facing him. "I've tried making cookies with molasses and with honey. I like the molasses version best. I like using variations in old cookbooks."

"Both honey and molasses are *gut* ideas."

"Our Annie always has ideas," Inez interjected with a smile. "Most of them are *gut*."

Reaching for another cookie, he replied, "If your other ideas are as tasty as this one, Annie, I hope you'll share them."

A pretty flush warmed Annie's cheeks again, and he realized his request had pleased her. Knowing he'd brought a soft smile to her pleased *him*. More than it should for a man who didn't want to get involved with a woman. He'd have to be on his guard, but later…after he'd learned the recipe from her. The cookies would be a popular addition at his bakery once it was open.

Chapter Five

Except for the bone-gnawing cold, the day was perfect. No clouds marred the bright blue sky. Sunshine glistened on the snow along the mountains, turning each into a huge multifaceted diamond. The creek was almost silent as it ran between the thickening sheets of ice reaching out from both banks. Traffic was busy on the main road. Again Caleb had to wait before it was safe to pull out.

As he steered his buggy around the tall snowbanks and into the parking lot of his bakery, Caleb wondered how everything could be the same as the last time he'd brought Annie to the old railroad depot…and how everything could be so different. He glanced at where she sat next to him.

Her face was shadowed by her black bonnet, but he could see enough to know she was as anxious as he was. Maybe more, because she was dealing with Becky Sue and Joey. This morning, when he'd stopped to give Annie a ride, he'd seen only the back of Becky Sue as she rushed out of the kitchen.

"We're not going to find someone else lurking in the bakery," he said.

"Promise?" She gave him a faint smile. "Leanna is helping take care of Joey today, but she won't be able to most days. The people she cleans for depend on her, and she doesn't want to let them down."

"I'd like to say *ja*, that I promise no surprises at the bakery."

"But stranger things have happened."

"Stranger than finding my cousin with a *boppli* in my bakery? I hope not!"

When she chuckled, he relaxed. He couldn't say why he'd felt on edge as they approached the old depot building. He didn't expect anyone would be inside. He'd installed locks on both doors. But he couldn't push aside his uneasiness. He hoped Annie would see something he hadn't. Something—anything!—to give them a clue why the girl had run away.

Annie had used the word *coincidence*, but Caleb wasn't ready to accept that the encounter had been accidental. Becky Sue had chosen to come north. She'd admitted she knew about a new settlement but asserted she hadn't known it was the one he organized. That didn't add up.

Maybe if he had a chance to talk—really talk, one-on-one—with his cousin, he'd be able to get to the bottom of the tangle of half-truths and evasions Becky Sue used to keep him from learning why she'd left home. But his cousin was careful never to be alone with him.

Not that he could get within a foot of her when she carried her son, because Joey became hysterical each time he came near. He didn't want to accuse Becky

Sue of using her son as a shield to prevent Caleb from talking with her, but it sure felt that way.

Again he wanted to apologize to Annie for saddling her with his cousin and her *boppli*. He didn't, knowing Annie would push aside his words as she had before. Each time she spoke of being glad to help another member of the *Leit*, guilt rushed through him. He'd given her and her family a huge responsibility, which they'd accepted. In the meantime, he hadn't managed to get in touch with Becky Sue's parents. He'd left messages twice a day. The answering machine he'd hooked up in the bakery hadn't been activated once.

"Here we are," he said as he stopped the buggy by the hitching rail.

"You've got a sign." She pointed to the simple plank he'd painted with Hartz Bakery. Underneath that, it said Not Open Sundays.

He planned to add the hours of operation later and edge it with strips of wood. Once the frost left the ground, he'd set it in place in front of the bakery. "Figured it was something I could do now."

"*Gut* idea." Annie opened the door on her side before he could reach for his.

Stepping out, he threw the warmed blanket over Dusty. He patted his horse before motioning for Annie to follow him to the door. By the time he reached it, his fingers were stiff with the cold. He fumbled with the key. The new lock didn't seem to want to open, but he finally unlocked it and threw the door open. He stepped aside so Annie could go in first.

When he heard her sigh with pleasure as she stepped into the kitchen, he hurried after her and switched on the lights. They showed the dust and dirt, as well as the water stains on the ceiling. No matter. By the time the bakery opened, every inch of the building would have been cleaned and painted. He wanted to impress the health inspector with the cleanliness of his bakery.

The temperature inside was around fifty degrees but felt as balmy as summer in comparison with the outdoors. He unbuttoned his coat, letting the warmth banish the chill seeping through him. He recoiled when an elbow almost hit his chest, and he realized Annie was unwinding her scarf. She must not realize how close they stood to each other.

He couldn't be unaware of her, however. There was something about her that drew his eyes whenever she was nearby. She was so full of life, always looking on the best side of every situation.

Why hadn't one of the single men in the settlement asked her to walk out with him? Were they focused, as Caleb was, on establishing a toehold in the hollow? No, that wasn't true. They'd had three weddings last fall, and he'd heard rumors of other relationships or seen people pairing off to share a ride or a walk home after church services.

But he'd never heard Annie's name mentioned or seen her leave with anyone other than her family. It shocked him that he'd taken such notice of her without his realizing.

Caleb shed his coat and hung it and his black wool hat on a rack where aprons and towels would be stored. He took her thick shawl and coat and placed them next to his. He tossed his gloves on the lone cupboard set against the wall. The rest of the storage units remained in boxes, waiting for him to install them.

Annie untied her bonnet and set it on top of a cardboard box as high as her waist. Looking around, she said, "You're going to have more cupboards than every kitchen combined along Harmony Creek."

"I bought the appliances and cupboards from the owner of Summerhays Stables, who'd planned to renovate the family's kitchen. When they put an ad in *The Penny Pincher*, I jumped at the chance."

Annie didn't seem as surprised as he'd been at the high-end quality of the gas stove and ovens as well as the massive refrigerator and matching freezer that would take up almost half of the large room. Like his sister, Annie counted Sarah Kuhns as a *gut* friend. Sarah had worked as a nanny in the Summerhayses' home until the end of the year, so Annie knew how fancy the *Englischers*' house was.

Caleb was astonished by how self-conscious he was to show Annie around the kitchen. So far, he'd fixed broken windows and cleaned out debris. Once cabinets were installed over the concrete floor and the appliances set in their proper places, he planned to paint the fly-speckled walls. With a new furnace in the cellar, it was no longer so damp and cold the paint would peel off the walls almost as soon as he put it up.

What would Annie think of his future shop? Would she come to see it as he did, with ovens heating the space and wondrous-smelling goodies waiting in simple glass cases out front? Could she imagine, as he did, a day when the bakery would be crowded with eager customers?

He discovered he was holding his breath in anticipation of her reaction and forced himself to draw air in and out.

"You've done a lot of thinking about this," Annie said.

"I have."

"I can't wait for Leanna to see it. She says our kitchen would be easier to work in if we got rid of the appliances, which are older than we are."

He smiled, glad she could envision what he'd planned. "I dream big, I guess."

"There's no sin in that. The *gut* Lord gave us the ability to find the best ways to walk the path He's given us." Without a pause, she asked, "What sort of counters are you planning to use here in the kitchen?"

As he explained why he'd chosen quartz over marble for the area where bread would be kneaded and dough rolled out, he was delighted to have such a responsive audience. She asked questions, some he hadn't considered, and he thought of Inez's comment about how Annie had lots of ideas.

He again urged her to share them. Changes to his bakery would be fine as long as she didn't try to change him, too. He'd had enough of that with Verba.

"*Komm* into the front room," Caleb said, motioning to the other room. "It's where customers will be served."

She paused in the doorway and rapped her knuckles against the wall. At the hollow sound, she said, "You might want to consider a pass-through window here. Your customers could speak to whoever's in the kitchen. That would allow for special requests or questions about ingredients. So many people must be careful about allergies or gluten."

"I like that idea, though I'd have to make sure the kitchen was kept extra neat and tidy."

"If you don't want customers to see bowls filled with dough or bread rising, you could put bifold shutters on the window." She moved so she could appraise the wall. "Add a sign saying whether the baker is available, and you'll have customers who feel free to ask questions."

"Watch your step," he warned when she turned to follow him to the center of the customer area.

It was a little larger than the kitchen, but unlike the concrete in the other room, this space had wide, dusty floorboards. He grimaced at several that had warped to the point the nails had popped, making the floor treacherous to anyone not paying attention to where they walked.

"Those boards look as if they're trying to escape," Annie said.

"From what I've been told, this building has been empty for more than ten years since the feed store that was in here closed."

"What's that?" she asked, pointing to a square cut into the floor.

"It leads to the cellar. Nothing there but cobwebs. There were mice, but I think they're gone."

He expected her to shudder, as most women did when mice were mentioned. She simply nodded and walked to the large front windows. Each had a checkerboard of wooden mullions.

"Did you have to replace any of these?" she asked.

"About a half-dozen panes. The yard out front was

overgrown. Kids with mischief on their minds wouldn't risk the briars to get close enough to break many windows. I finished getting rid of the last thorn thickets the day before the first hard frost hit." He leaned a shoulder against the wall where a poster for some old-fashioned power tool was flaking into oblivion. "I didn't want to come over here that day, but if I hadn't, I would have had to wait until spring to finish digging them up. That could have meant opening later than the first week of May."

"Your customers wouldn't have wanted to walk through an obstacle course of bushes." She toed another loose board. "Have you considered painting this floor? A simple pale tan. It wouldn't show dirt as much as a dark floor, and the paint would seal in any splinters, so you don't have to worry about little ones getting hurt if they're on their hands and knees."

"That's a *gut* idea."

She gave him a cheeky grin. "I try to have only *gut* ideas."

Not quite sure how to reply, he continued with his tour. "The display cases will be here by the door."

"What about over there?" she asked, pointing to the other side of the room.

Caleb shrugged. "I'm not sure. Maybe a display rack or something else. I haven't given it much thought."

"How about putting small tables and chairs there?"

"I hadn't thought about that."

"You should be able to find something. They don't have to match. What do the *Englischers* call the style with mismatched furniture? Leanna was talking about it the other day because one of the houses she cleans is decorated that way. Shabby something or other," she laughed. "Oh, I remember. Shabby chic. Didn't you have some small tables in the barn when you and Miriam lived there before your house was ready?"

"*Ja.* They'd have to be refinished before they could be used."

"Paint them instead. It's quicker and will add color to this space."

"Let me think about it. Having the tables and chairs will be *gut* in case someone wants to sit while they're waiting."

She frowned in thought. "Have you considered selling *kaffi*, too?"

"No."

"You should. *Englischers* like to have a cup when they're enjoying a sweet roll or a muffin. Plain folks do, too, from what I've seen at the farmers market and the hardware store. You've got enough parking space outside to let people linger here. They might buy more when they see what other people order. It's like free publicity, because nothing helps sell sweets like someone taking a bite and saying, 'That's delicious.'" She looked up at the ceiling where the beams laced together in a simple square pattern. "If you don't mind, I'd like to get Leanna's opinion on flavors of *kaffi*. She knows a lot about them because she's tried many different ones."

"All right."

"How about free samples? Have you considered that?"

"Samples of what?"

"You could have a product of the day. Maybe you decide to make apple-cider doughnuts. You could put the doughnut holes out as a free sample. If they go fast, you can make apple-cider doughnut holes the next day and sell them. You could expand your products."

"I could." Caleb's head reeled.

Inez had been right. Annie had lots of ideas. He wondered how anyone else would ever be expected to keep up with her rapid-fire thinking.

But she wasn't finished. Facing him, she asked, "Do you think your customers will be tourists or local folks?"

"I'm hoping to have both."

He wondered if she'd heard him as she surveyed the room again, her gaze lingering on the far wall. Walking over to it, she stretched out her arms as far as they could go.

Again he was amazed by how small she was. Her personality was so massive she seemed taller than he was. But she was shorter—the right height, if he were to draw her to his chest, that he could place his cheek against the top of her *kapp*. His heart thudded as he imagined how she'd feel in his arms.

"This wall is wide enough you could display a queen-sized quilt." She turned to him and smiled, her turquoise eyes alight with excitement. "Some shops in Pennsylvania take quilts on consignment."

"I know, but I'm not familiar with how it works."

"The shopkeepers in our area would keep thirty percent of what the quilt sells for, which could be a tidy sum when *Englischers* will spend close to a thousand dollars for homemade quilts."

"Do you quilt?" He tried to figure how she'd find

time to work at his bakery, take care of her family—
and his—and make quilts.

"I can, but I'm not great at it. However, Leanna is a
clever seamstress and has a *gut* eye for the colors and
patterns tourists look for." She smiled. "I'm grateful
to her for doing most of our mending, as well. She can
repair a rip and make it appear as if there never was
any damage. Right now, she's finishing up a quilt she
plans to donate to the mud sale for the fire department."

"I thought she preferred to spend her time with her
goats."

"She enjoys them, especially feeding and milking
the does."

"Speaking of milking, don't think I've forgotten the
challenge you gave me."

"What challenge?"

"To convince you that you could like spending time
doing barn chores."

She laughed, "That's not going to happen. Ask
Leanna. She already agrees with you."

He didn't listen as she continued. How many times
had she mentioned her sister's name, lauding Leanna's
skills and kindness? Was this her way of trying to convince him he'd been wrong not to accept Annie's offer
to step aside when he'd hired her? No, she'd been insistent she wanted the job and her twin had other work.

Maybe he was imagining how often she brought
Leanna's name into the conversation. He had enough
complications on his hands. He didn't need more.

Annie looked at Caleb, who had stopped responding to her suggestions. Had she overstepped herself

by mentioning Leanna as she shared ideas? Today had been the first chance she'd had to keep her twin in the conversation.

He'd been asking questions, and she'd thought her plan was working, but he'd become silent. She could see he was deep in thought. She halted what she was about to say next about having handiwork for sale in the bakery. Clamping her teeth over her lower lip, she struggled to hush the many ideas bouncing through her brain like helium balloons.

She didn't want to appear pushy by making too many suggestions. However, he'd invited her to share her ideas. Probably he hadn't realized how many she had. She had to learn to temper the number she offered at one time.

God, there must be a reason You put so many ideas in my head. Are You trying to help me help others, or are You giving me these ideas as a way to teach me a lesson? Do You want me to learn to hold my tongue, or do You want me to give voice to Your inspiration?

Since she'd been old enough to realize not everyone blurted out idea after idea in an effort to find a solution, she'd been asking those questions. The answers hadn't come to her. Ignoring her thoughts had made her miserable, though she'd been extra careful after being betrayed by her former boyfriend. Since then, she'd tried to limit what she said. She should have guessed the opportunity to give voice to them today would overwhelm Caleb.

"Of course," she said into the silence, "the bakery is yours, and you can do what you think best."

"I appreciate your suggestions, but let me think

about them to see how they fit in with my plans." Not giving her a chance to respond, he added, "There's one more place to see. The utility room."

"It's not in the cellar, is it?"

His smile returned. "No. If the bakery's business grows, I may look into using the cellar, but not until it's clean. That'll be a huge job."

"I'm not volunteering to do it."

"Me neither," he laughed and motioned for her to follow him into the kitchen.

Caleb had a lighthearted side to him she hadn't seen often. His sister laughed and joked with her three friends in the Harmony Creek Spinsters' Club, but Caleb had had to deal with many important issues before he turned the leadership of the settlement over to their ordained leaders. That hadn't allowed him time to be anything but serious.

This Caleb Hartz was too appealing for her own *gut*. Instead of thinking how enticing his smile was and how his laugh made her feel as delighted as Joey with a new toy, she had to figure out a way for him to act like this when Leanna was with him. There had to be a way, and Annie was determined to find it.

Caleb showed her the cramped closet with shelves on one side and space for crates on the other. It barely had room for a person to stand inside it and select something off the shelves. Its outer wall had once been a sliding door opening to the railroad tracks, but it was nailed shut.

"It's a shame this is a closet," Annie said. "This old door would give extra character to the front room."

"I can move it there. I need to insulate in there, and

putting in a regular wall would allow that." He flashed her another smile. "An excellent idea, Annie."

Her knees seemed to melt with the warmth of his expression. It was wrong to react like this if she wanted to make a match between him and her sister, but she couldn't stop the ripple of delight any more than she could have stopped a freight train on the tracks outside. When his gaze met hers, she wondered if she could remember how to breathe as time seemed to stutter to a standstill.

The moment shattered when the phone rang.

Caleb jumped to answer it, and she took a steadying breath. She held it as she waited to see if Becky Sue's family was calling.

"That's okay," he said, hanging up the phone. He sighed, disappointment lengthening his face. "Wrong number."

"Becky Sue's family will call."

"They should have by now."

"Maybe they didn't feel right leaving a message because they weren't sure who would hear it."

"Like Becky Sue?" He leaned against a crate, folding his arms over his chest. "I'd thought about that. A couple of the guys at the firehouse have offered to lend me a phone or let me use their number, so Becky Sue's folks can reach them at any time, day or night. I'd hate to miss their call because I'm not here. I spoke with Eli, and he agreed that having the cell phone for that purpose would be all right, so I'm going to borrow one when I go to the firehouse for our meeting tonight." He walked toward the door. "That's all there is to see. Tomorrow we'll get to work."

Staying where she was, Annie asked, "Have you thought about taking Becky Sue and Joey home?"

"I have." He faced her. "We could get a bus out of Saratoga to take us most of the way, but I'm not sure if bringing her home would make matters better or worse."

"You think she'll run away again?"

"*Ja.* Don't you?"

Annie breathed out before saying, "I do. Whatever set her to fleeing this time may not have been resolved. We can't know until she decides to tell us why she left."

Reaching for her coat, he smiled. "And can you imagine a bus trip with a *boppli* who sounds like a fire siren whenever I get within three feet of him?"

"You could sit at one end of the bus and have them sit at the other."

He started to retort, then burst into laughter. When she joined in, she couldn't keep from noticing how nice their laughter sounded mixed together.

"That feels so *gut*," he said. "Some days, I wonder if I've forgotten how to laugh."

"It's not that bad."

"No?"

"Not for you, at any rate. You don't have a recalcitrant teenager and a *boppli* who would like to be attached to my hem."

"Annie, I told you—"

"I was joking again," she said to halt him from apologizing for the Waglers taking in his cousin and her son. "Having them at the house isn't any trouble. Our house is always in chaos anyhow. If you ever get tired of peace and quiet, come over and get your fill of noise."

"I will." He held out her coat.

When she reached to take it, their fingers brushed. She was shocked when a powerful sensation sizzled along her skin as if his skin had set hers on fire. She held out her hand for her coat again, and he offered it to her at arm's length. Had he experienced the same unexpected spark?

She must erase the memory of that delightful feeling. How could she make a match for her sister if she was growing more attracted to Caleb every time they were together? She could ruin all their lives if she wasn't careful.

Chapter Six

Wishing for spring to hurry up and arrive so the sun would rise earlier in the morning, Annie lit the propane lamp in the kitchen before moving to the stove. She'd made breakfast every morning since they'd come to Harmony Creek, and the motions were automatic. Which was *gut* because she'd been up half the night. Joey was getting another tooth, and he wanted to make sure everyone knew how much pain he was suffering. He'd fallen asleep, exhausted, an hour before Annie had to get up.

After a week of trying to sleep in the same room with a fussy *kind* and dealing with his *mamm*, who was becoming more defiant as each day passed, Annie took each step as if sloshing through a knee-deep swamp. She measured out *kaffi* and mixed up batter for pancakes. Looking out the window, she saw the glass was etched with a delicate filigree of frost. The patterns reminded her of the ferns growing in the woods higher on the hill behind the barn.

Summer seemed forever away, but she pushed aside

the depressing thought as she reminded herself of how many times she'd been able to introduce Leanna's name into her conversation with Caleb at the bakery yesterday. He'd been a bit taken aback by the multitude of ideas she'd offered him, but he'd listened to her as Rolan had refused to…or, at least, she'd thought Rolan had.

Banishing Rolan from her thoughts, she couldn't help smiling. Had Caleb noticed her twin sister was a common denominator in the suggestions Annie had made? Trying to be subtle was proving to be harder than she'd imagined. It was so tempting to come right out and tell him Leanna would be the perfect match for him, but she always bit back the words.

Exactly as she tried to dampen how she was drawn to him and how a picture of his strong, hewed face filled her mind whenever she didn't keep it buried deep in her mind. That he'd asked her for her ideas had pleased her, though she'd scolded herself for sharing them.

During breakfast, while she listened to her siblings discuss their upcoming day and watched as Becky Sue fed Joey, Annie's thoughts battered her skull. She checked that Juanita and Kenny took their lunches with them to school. She offered to feed the goats because her twin had overslept and didn't want to be late for work.

Grossmammi Inez asked Becky Sue to help her with changing the beds upstairs and dusting. The girl started to protest, but a single glance in Annie's direction shut her down. Did she think Annie would kick her out of the house if she didn't assist with the housework?

Annie smiled as she fed the goats. Becky Sue shouldn't worry about Annie rescinding her invitation. In the Wagler house, *Grossmammi* Inez was the person who would make such decisions, and Annie couldn't imagine her softhearted *grossmammi* turning out anyone.

Hurrying into the house, she glanced at the wall clock in the empty kitchen. She had almost half an hour before Caleb was arriving to pick her up for work. She'd have enough time to…

Annie stared at what had previously been an open space by the table. A dark brown wooden high chair! Where had it come from?

She got the answer when the front door opened, and the other two members of the Harmony Hollow Spinsters' Club, Miriam and Sarah, walked in. They were bundled up from head to foot and carried laundry baskets filled with folded clothes.

"What's this?" Annie asked.

"Becky Sue and her *boppli* have to have things to wear, so we decided to surprise you by sneaking in the front door." Miriam unwrapped her scarf to reveal a broad grin and bright green eyes so much like Caleb's.

"Before you go on, how is everyone at your house? Caleb said you were sick."

"We were, but we're getting back on our feet. Having something to do helps. Sarah and I have been doing a door-to-door collection." She set her basket on the table. "With several *kinder* a bit older than Joey here, there are plenty of things people were willing to loan you for his visit."

Red-haired Sarah, who was a full head shorter than

blonde Miriam, grinned as she put a box on the floor in front of the sink and took her glasses off to wipe away the steam fogging them. "The Summerhays family had a bunch of clothing and toys to share, too. They always buy more than they need." She laughed, "I don't think that will ever change."

The *Englisch* family treated their former nanny as if she were one of them. They'd come to her wedding and always stepped up to help her or someone she knew. Annie was sure it'd been Sarah's suggestion that had led to Mr. and Mrs. Summerhays selling the appliances they'd bought for the canceled kitchen renovation to Caleb for his bakery.

Miriam pointed to the basket she'd brought in. "The bag on top is from the thrift shop by the old county courthouse in Salem. The clothing isn't plain, but a *boppli* can go through a lot of clothes some days. Nobody among the *Leit* is going to be upset if he wears *Englisch* overalls one day instead of plain ones. Those I spoke with hope *Mamm* and *boppli* feel welcome here so Becky Sue won't run away again."

"He does seem to drool on everything, so we go through a lot of clothing."

Sarah dug into another bag and pulled out a trio of bibs backed with plastic. "Try these. The younger Summerhays *kinder* had so many they never used these. They're brand-new and should keep Joey's shirts a bit drier."

"Please thank them for their generosity."

"I have. We're blessed to have such kind *Englisch* neighbors." She smiled at Miriam as she added, "They've volunteered to talk to other *Englischers* and ask them to drive more slowly through the hollow. I hope their words are heard before someone gets hurt."

That changed the topic of conversation. While Annie continued to unpack the *boppli* clothes and toys along with items for Becky Sue, she thanked God for the warm hearts in the community. She listened while her friends talked about the quandary with speeding cars along the twisting road. There had been several close calls, but so far nobody, either *Englisch* or plain, had been hurt. Annie prayed God would continue to look out for the foolish speeders and keep everyone, including other drivers, out of their paths.

Hearing footsteps behind her, Annie turned and waved to Becky Sue, who was carrying her son. "*Komm* and see what your cousin and Sarah have brought for you and Joey."

The girl took one look, burst into tears and crumpled to sit by the table as *Grossmammi* Inez came into the kitchen. She patted Becky Sue on the shoulder and nodded to Miriam and Sarah, a grateful smile rearranging the lines and crevices of her face.

"Now Annie won't have to look so sad about having to do laundry every day." Her *grossmammi*'s words brought laughs from her friends.

"I don't mind doing laundry," Becky Sue said through her tears. She rubbed them away after Miriam took Joey from her.

The little boy ran his fingers along Miriam's face and leaned into her as he had everyone but Caleb. He stuck a thumb in his mouth and relaxed against her.

Miriam smiled as she rested her cheek on his soft

hair. "Offer to help Annie with the laundry, Becky Sue, and you'll have a friend for life."

"You don't like doing laundry?" The teenager acted as if she couldn't believe what she was saying.

Annie laughed, "I despise it."

"Then let me take over the chore." The girl dimpled as she handed her son a stuffed rabbit from the stack on the table. After he'd held it close to his face and rubbed his hands over it, he began to chew on one of its pink ears. "It's the least I can do to repay you for taking us in."

"You don't have to repay us, but I won't say no to help with laundry." Annie looked at her hands and said with an emoted moan, "You won't be chapped all winter long."

Everyone laughed, then thanked her when she suggested hot chocolate to her guests, and *Grossmammi* Inez whispered that there were marshmallows in the pantry. By the time Annie came back with the bag, the table was cleared and Miriam was sitting next to her cousin and bouncing the *boppli* on her knee.

Her *grossmammi* and Sarah had moved into the living room to stack the clothing and other supplies to make it easier to put them away. Annie guessed they were giving Miriam and Becky Sue a chance to speak in private.

Annie went to the stove and clattered the pot and cups so she couldn't overhear the conversation at the table. She hoped Caleb's sister would do a better job convincing Becky Sue to divulge the truth than either she or Caleb had.

"Is everyone ready for a treat?" Annie asked as she

put the steaming cups on a tray and carried them toward the table. "Before anyone complains, I put the same number of marshmallows in each cup."

While everyone chuckled again, Miriam glanced at her and gave the slightest shake of her head as Becky Sue lifted cups off the tray.

Annie understood what Miriam hadn't said. Becky Sue had refused to share anything new with her cousin.

As Annie set the empty tray on the counter, she heard the rattle of wheels. She cut her eyes to the clock and realized Caleb must have arrived. She'd got so caught up in chatting with her friends that she hadn't noticed time scurrying past.

When she looked out, though, she didn't see Caleb's buggy. Instead a wagon was parked there. It wasn't Lyndon's, and the man stepping out of the driver's seat was so wrapped in scarves around his black wool hat and his coat of the same color that she couldn't guess which plain neighbor had arrived. He reached into the wagon bed and lifted out what appeared to be a section of stair railing or a gate. He turned toward the house.

She rushed to the door to open it and let the man inside. The merciless cold struck her like a fist, and she stepped aside.

"I didn't think it could get any colder" came Caleb's voice from beneath the layers of scarves.

He leaned the wooden piece against the wall before he stripped off his gloves and began to unwind the scarves. He draped each one over the chair at the foot of the table. He nodded to Sarah and his sister, who held Joey, before greeting *Grossmammi* Inez and his cousin.

"I don't remember it being this cold last winter," Annie said.

"I don't think it was." He gave a quick shudder. "I'll get the rest of the pieces once my fingers have thawed a bit."

"The rest of the pieces of what?"

"A crib."

"You found a crib for Joey?" She resisted the urge to throw her arms around him and thank him. The little boy might sleep better if he had a crib.

"*Ja.* Every *boppli* needs a sturdy crib."

"Where did you find it?" Miriam asked as she stood along with the others to study the section of railing. "It was the one thing we couldn't borrow. From the looks of the railing, it's never been used."

"Jeremiah had been hired to build it, but then no one ever came to pick it up. He said we might as well use it instead of have it sit there in his workshop taking up space."

Annie ran her fingers over the smooth, polished wood railing. The oak had been finished with a reddish-brown stain. Jeremiah, who lived next door to Caleb, was a skilled woodworker as well as a farmer.

"It's *wunderbaar*," Becky Sue crowed. "*Danki,* Caleb."

"Like I said, you can thank Jeremiah." He took a cup of hot chocolate from Annie, then looked at the *boppli,* who was staring at the crib and at him with a somber expression. "You'll find it more comfortable, little man, than a drawer, ain't so?" He bent toward the *kind.*

As he did every time Caleb got within a few feet of him, the *boppli* began to bellow. His voice seemed too big for his tiny frame, and thick tears rolled down his cheeks.

Silence dropped on the kitchen except for Joey's shrieks. Annie wished she had something to say, but as she looked from her friends' shocked faces to Becky Sue's pale features, she couldn't think of anything that wouldn't make matters worse. Then she saw Caleb's pain and wondered if there were any words that would ease the situation.

Caleb was acutely aware of Annie and his sister witnessing the unsettling scene. Though Annie had tried to reassure him that Joey's reaction was nothing but an idea the toddler had got into his head, Caleb wasn't certain. The *boppli*'s cries seemed to get louder each time Caleb approached him.

"I'll get the rest of the crib," he murmured.

Realizing he still held the cup of hot chocolate, he set it, untasted, on the table. His gaze was snagged by Annie's, and he wondered if he'd insulted her by not taking a sip. Seeing her sympathy, he realized she sensed how distressed he was. He wanted to thank her for being understanding, but hesitated to do so in front of the others. How could common words seem too intimate?

He rushed outside where the cold felt almost welcome…for a few seconds before it threatened to freeze his lungs. Grabbing the other pieces of the crib, he carried them into the house. On his final trip he brought the mattress, which he leaned against the wall.

"Lyndon will set it up later," Inez assured him when he offered to put the crib together. "Another nap in the drawer won't hurt Joey." She smiled at the other women. "God has blessed this community with many *gut* hearts."

He didn't look at the *boppli* as he picked up his scarves. He started to twist them into place, then paused as he glanced at where Annie stood, her fingers laced together in front of her.

Her cheeks became the same shade as her rose pink dress, and she lowered her eyes. Was she feeling unsettled as he was? Maybe she could explain to him why he was uncomfortable, as if he were the one keeping secrets instead of Becky Sue.

"I should go," he managed to say. "Annie, are you—"

"Get over to the bakery," Miriam replied. "I know you can't wait to get to work. We'll take care of things here."

He turned toward the door, then glanced at Annie in spite of his determination not to. She was supposed to work at the bakery with him today, but she might want to remain at the house to help with sorting out the largesse.

"We'll be fine," her *grossmammi* said, warning the old woman might be discerning more than either Annie or he wanted. "Go and do your job, Annie."

"Ja. Danki." She went to get her coat and bonnet. "I'll see you later." She squeezed Miriam's and Sarah's arms as she edged past them.

Caleb held the door for her as they went outside, warning her to watch out for a patch of ice near the wagon. He put his fingertips on her elbow to guide her around it, and the day seemed far warmer until he drew his hand back again.

As she climbed into the wagon, he berated himself. How many times had he made the promise—which he'd asked God to witness—that he wasn't going to let another woman get in the way of his plans to make his dream come true? He couldn't let his plans fall by the wayside because Annie Wagler touched a part of his soul he'd never guessed existed.

"You could have stayed behind today," he said when they were seated side by side on the narrow plank seat.

"No, I said I'd work for you, and I can't play hooky anytime something *gut* happens at home." Her eyes crinkled in a smile. "This way *Grossmammi* Inez and Becky Sue can have time to go through the donations."

"Which she couldn't do when I'm around because Joey would be too upset."

"Give him some time, Caleb. Think of what that little one has gone through. Assuming your cousin lived at home from his birth until they left, he has endured some big upheavals in recent days."

"True, but are you prepared for the gossip?"

Her brows lowered. "What gossip?"

"As I was warned before I bought my farm, everyone knows everything about everyone in Salem." He chuckled. "There's not a person in the village who hasn't heard my sister went to the thrift store and bought as many clothes for a *boppli* as she could find and brought them to your farm."

"Those gossips have heard about Becky Sue and Joey already, so they won't be surprised."

"You're right." He took his eyes off the road and

gave her a wink. "But you know as well as I do stories change when they're repeated, whether along the
Amish grapevine or among the *Englischers*. Who
knows what the tale might become?"

Annie smiled beneath her scarf, which was covered
in frost where her breath had turned to ice on the wool.
How kind of Caleb to try to make her feel better about
leaving when he was upset by how Joey reacted to him!
She had no idea how to help him, so she played along
with his silliness.

"I know too well about how things get distorted,"
she said as he steered the wagon around a rut. Though
riding in the open wagon was far colder than his buggy,
she didn't want to complain. It would take time to unhitch and rehitch his horse, time he wanted to spend
at the bakery. Shoving down another shiver, she went
on, "In my circle letter, sometimes I hear outrageous
things that the writer believes is true."

"I'm sure the rest of you set her straight."

"We try to, but by the time the letter gets back to
that person, the matter's been forgotten."

When he chuckled, she savored the sound. She'd
met Caleb in the living room at *Onkel* Myron's house
a little over a year ago. He'd laughed like that, too, with
her family. He'd come to talk about his plans for a settlement in northern New York. Many of the younger
people in their district couldn't afford a farm in ever
more crowded Lancaster County. To the north, they
would be able to purchase land and build a future for
themselves and their *kinder*.

Lyndon had been enthusiastic. He'd been working

at a meat-processing plant and had hated being stuck inside for most of each day. The opportunity to have a farm was too sweet for him to let it pass him by. He'd told Caleb he wanted to come before discussing it with his wife. Rhoda had been as excited about the prospect of having a farm of their own as Lyndon, and the *kinder* had looked forward to having their *daed* home throughout the day.

Annie had listened as well, delighted to see her brother look happy for the first time since he'd gone to work at the plant five years before. But then she'd noticed how her twin was more interested in Caleb than what he had to say. How Leanna's eyes had glowed when she gazed upon him! Annie hadn't seen such joy on her twin's face since the news had come of Gabriel Miller marrying someone else the previous week. From that point until Lyndon purchased land for them in Harmony Creek Hollow days later, Leanna hadn't talked of anything but Caleb's plans and how it was an opportunity for them to put the small inheritance left by their late parents into a farm that could provide them with a home of their own.

At that moment, a plan—one to help her sister—had blossomed in Annie's mind. She'd waited to see if Leanna would let Caleb know or if her twin had found someone else in the new settlement. Neither had happened, but when she concocted the idea, Annie hadn't guessed how she would be drawn to Caleb herself. She couldn't be happy if her sister was miserable, so she must…

"What did you say?" She realized Caleb had asked her a question while she was lost in her thoughts.

"I was wondering if Becky Sue has said anything about anyone in Iowa." He stopped the wagon beside the bakery and jumped out.

"Not that I recall," she replied as he came around to her side and held up his arms to assist her.

She put her hands on his shoulders. Leaning forward as he guided her to the ground, she found her eyes too close to his as his thick scarves brushed against hers. Her lips tingled as she imagined them on his without the wool between them. His gaze shredded her defenses. What would she discover if she were brave enough to explore the depths that were the color of deep green shadows?

Then her feet were on the ground, jolting her enough to break the connection between them. She thanked God for the pulse of common sense that had come in time.

"Why are you asking about Iowa?" Annie asked, focusing again on the mysteries surrounding Becky Sue.

"The day we found her at the bakery and I left a message for her family, I noticed there was an earlier call made to a number in the 319 area code. When I checked with Q yesterday, he looked online and found out the area code is in Iowa."

Annie recognized the nickname for the Salem Volunteer Fire Department's assistant fire chief, Robert Quartermaine. Caleb and Q had worked together to bring plain men in as volunteers. It'd been vital to the fire department because many of their members worked out of town, and there might not be enough to answer the siren and fight a fire. Because the Amish men worked at home, they were almost always available to respond.

"You think Becky Sue called someone?" Annie asked as Caleb opened the door and they went into the bakery.

"Who else?" He began unwrapping his scarves.

"The door was unlocked. Anyone could have wandered in and discovered the phone was working."

"That's true. I'd hoped it would be a clue to where she was heading." His face fell as hope dimmed in his eyes.

She regretted being blunt. Putting her fingertips on his sleeve, she said, "And it may be, Caleb. I wanted you to consider alternatives, but I've been wrong before. Plenty of times."

She was filled with the icy memories of how she'd been wrong to trust Rolan. As before, she tried to remind herself it was better she'd learned the truth before she'd risked her heart. That didn't help. His betrayal had seared her.

And she would never betray her sister the same way. Annie had to put aside her attraction for Caleb and help him see Leanna was perfect for him. She had to figure out how.

Chapter Seven

"I've told you everything, Caleb!" Becky Sue stood with her hands on her hips and her chin lifted in the pose she took whenever Caleb tried to probe into the secrets she refused to share.

He'd invited her to visit the bakery that morning on the pretense that he wanted to show her the recent changes, but she'd seen right through him. During the drive from the Waglers' farm to the main road, she'd repeated the story she'd told him and Annie when they'd discovered her hiding in the building. Not a fact changed, which made him more suspicious. Had she memorized what she was going to say ahead of time?

Caleb doubted his young cousin had any idea how difficult it was to keep his frustration from bursting forth. Only Annie's urging for him to let Becky Sue open to him in her own time kept him from demanding that she be honest right then.

"I'm willing to listen without judging," he said. "Whenever you want to talk, let me know."

"I want to talk without every conversation being about Joey." Tears blossomed in her eyes.

He looked at her standing in the half-finished kitchen. The appliances were connected and some of the cabinets hung. Supplies remained in crates, stacked almost to the ceiling. One wall was partially painted a fresh white, the project Annie had begun yesterday.

Among the large boxes and shining appliances, Becky Sue appeared so young, so vulnerable…so much in pain. Sympathy flooded him, and he nodded. Annie had been right. Becky Sue was deeply hurt and had left everything familiar in the hopes of escaping that pain. Pushing her further would only add to her grief.

"Not talking about Joey won't be easy," Caleb said, trying to make his voice sound carefree. "He does so many new things every day, and if you don't tell me about them, Annie does."

Becky Sue regarded him with suspicion. Did she think he was trying to coerce her into letting down her guard?

Ja, she did.

He sighed. If she mistrusted him so much, what hope was there of him convincing her to be honest? He wondered why she'd come to Harmony Creek Hollow. Maybe she'd thought he would welcome her and her son and ask no questions.

She'd miscalculated. And his curiosity was matched by Miriam's. His sister had asked him almost every time they spoke if he'd discovered the reason Becky Sue had traveled north from Pennsylvania, but Miriam hadn't got anything more from the girl.

"Annie doesn't focus every conversation on why I'm

here and what I plan to do next," Becky Sue retorted, her hands fisted at her waist. "She treats me like a person instead of a problem."

He flinched, remembering how he'd used the same word to describe Becky Sue and how Annie had chided him. Could they both be right? Had he got so accustomed to dealing with challenge after challenge with the new settlement that he'd lost sight of how people were involved? If so, it was *gut* he'd stepped aside as the district's leader. The *Leit* had been blessed by the lot when Eli Troyer had been chosen as their new minister and Jeremiah Stoltzfus as their deacon.

"You're right," he said. When Becky Sue stared at him in shock, he added, "I do admit when I'm wrong."

"Not something everyone in our family does."

At her bitter tone, he wanted to ask her to be specific, but guessed she would see his questions as another attempt to get the truth from her.

"Well, I'm one who admits when he's wrong. To do otherwise chances putting me on the road to *hochmut*." He sighed. "But I wish Joey would give me a chance. It's unsettling to hear him scream whenever I come near."

"Stay away from him, and he won't cry."

Again he had to bite back what he wanted to say. If her words were an attempt to infuriate him, he wasn't going to play her game.

Instead he said, "True, but I'd hoped for a different solution."

"I've got to get going." She edged toward the door. Opening the door, she was gone. A wave of cold washed into the bakery in the moment before the door closed again.

Caleb watched out the window as she climbed into his buggy. Slapping the reins on Dusty, she drove at a speed that made the back wheels bounce on the frozen ground. She hadn't asked if she could use his buggy, and he'd have to grab a ride home with Annie.

Glancing at the clock, he saw she should be arriving in about an hour. He'd arranged for her to drive herself that morning so he could have time with his cousin. Persuading Becky Sue to open up to him had failed.

He pushed away from the window as the buggy disappeared along the road. Jamming his hands into his pockets, he strode across the kitchen, maneuvering around the big boxes holding supplies.

Today, he had no interest in unpacking crates. He was making a mess of dealing with his cousin, and he wasn't sure what to do next. His self-doubts surged forward, eager to consume him.

Most of those doubts spoke to him in his ex's voice. Verba had insisted he give up his dream of opening a bakery, and she'd wanted to keep him under her thumb because she'd started dictating to whom he could speak and when.

Fool that he was, he hadn't seen the truth until she'd demanded he ignore one of his *gut* friends and sit with her at a youth event. He'd said he wanted to talk with his friend, and she'd flown into a rage. Embarrassed by the accusations filled with half-truths that she'd spewed in front of everyone gathered in the barn, he'd had his eyes opened.

So he'd set out to make his dreams come true. He'd

found the fallow farms along Harmony Creek Hollow that would make homes for others who shared his longing to own property and farm it. Now that the settlement was thriving, he'd turned to building a bakery where he could use products from his farm and others'.

What now, Lord?

Instead of an answer deep in his heart, leading him in the right direction, he heard the clip-clop of hooves. He glanced out the window and saw a buggy coming to a stop.

Why had Becky Sue returned? Had something gone wrong with the vehicle, or—and he prayed he was right—had she decided to be honest with him?

He reached for the knob, then froze when he saw Annie step out of the buggy. What was she doing here? She wasn't supposed to come until…

The wall clock chiming the hour startled him, and he realized Annie was on time. He'd spent the last hour lost in thought.

Wasted the last hour, his conscience reminded him. Instead of opening a box and wrestling out the contents so he could hang another cabinet in place to get him one step closer to being able to open his shop, he'd stewed about the past he couldn't change.

Annie breezed in along with another punch of cold air. She called a cheery greeting as she unwrapped her wool shawl. That he gave her no answer didn't seem to bother her because, as she hung the shawl, her heavy coat and her black bonnet up, she told him about Joey's latest antics.

Caleb's failure to laugh at her story seemed to cut through her chatter.

She halted in the middle of a sentence and stared at him before asking with her usual candor, "What's bothering you?"

"How little work I've got done today." It was the truth...or most of it.

"What would you like me to do?" She bustled across the kitchen to where she'd left off painting the previous day. "Keep going with the white? Or do you want this wall a different color? Customers will be able to see through the door to this wall. Maybe you'd like it to match or contrast with the color in the front section."

"Why?" For once, he was glad to let her keep talking. It would allow him to pretend his biggest worry was the color of the walls instead of the secrets his cousin was keeping from them.

She shrugged. "To pull their eyes toward the kitchen and the aromas emanating from it."

"I'll worry about those details after the bakery opens when I see if anyone comes to buy my goods."

Her eyes narrowed. "What's this depressing talk? Your bakery is going to be a success, Caleb."

"You sound sure."

"I am." She smiled, and the sunshine seemed to glitter more brightly on the snow. "You've considered the roadblocks for you and the bakery. You've mapped out the route you want to take."

"I thought I had until you made some excellent suggestions for things I hadn't considered."

Annie tried to ignore the warmth of his compliment washing over her and figure out what was bothering him, but it was impossible.

Caleb thought at least some of her ideas were *gut*. Did that mean he wanted her to keep offering them? Should she ask?

In the moment of her hesitation, he went on, "Don't ever get the idea I don't want to hear your ideas. I can't promise I'll agree with them or do anything with them."

"I appreciate your honesty."

"And I appreciate yours."

Her stiff shoulders sagged as she let her anxiety sift away. He was open to listening to her ideas. Even so, she shouldn't verbalize every thought in her head.

Yet she couldn't help herself from replying, "If you appreciate my honesty, tell me *honestly* what's going on with you. I don't know if I've ever heard you sound so glum."

While he explained his futile attempts to get to the truth of why his cousin had appeared in his bakery, she prayed again for the right words to remind him that everything that happened was in God's hands. In his frustration, he was forgetting that the One who knew everything wanted Becky Sue and Joey safe, too.

"I'm sorry."

"Don't be. Maybe by seeing how close your family is, Becky Sue will begin to miss her own enough to want to return home."

She laughed in spite of the tension lingering in the kitchen. "I don't know if she'll be able to pull Joey away from Penny. That *boppli* and puppy are never more than inches apart."

"Let's handle that obstacle when we get to it." He moved to a half-opened crate. As he bent to tear the cardboard away, he said, "*Danki* for listening to my troubles." He gave her an uneven smile. "*Danki* for listening to them again, I should say."

"I wish I could do more."

"You're doing more than you can guess. It should be our way to listen to each other and to learn from each other. Not just in our faith, but in the ways we decide to make our way while on this earth."

She pulled an extralarge shirt that had belonged to Lyndon over her clothes before reaching to reopen the paint can. "People are right, Caleb, when they say they know you would have done a *gut* job for us if your name had been drawn in the lot for minister or for deacon."

"It's time for others to lead the settlement."

"You don't miss it?"

When he didn't give her a quick answer, she perceived that, for Caleb, choosing whether or not to lead the settlement was a more complicated decision than she'd imagined. And why wouldn't it be? The settlement was something he'd worked very hard for, sacrificing his time and dreams to bring it to fruition.

"*Ja,*" he replied, "there are times when I miss being involved. There are plenty of other days when I thank God for giving me time to build my business and to allow me to spend time studying His word so I may grow closer to Him." He sighed. "And ask His advice on how to help Becky Sue and Joey. She's a stubborn *kind.*"

Pouring white paint into the roller tray, Annie glanced over her shoulder for a brief second. "She may seem like a *kind* to you, Caleb, but she's been thrust into adulthood by becoming a *mamm*."

"That doesn't mean she can withhold basic information from me when I'm trying to help her."

"Would you reveal everything you've experienced if she asked you to be honest with her?"

"It's not the same. I'm not a single parent who won't identify the other parent."

"We all have parts of our pasts we don't want to talk about." She selected each word with care, not wanting to turn his curiosity from Becky Sue to her. "She came to you."

"She said she didn't know this was the settlement I'd worked to build."

Annie grimaced as she picked up her roller and ran it in the tray. "You believe that thin tale? I might have believed it if she'd showed up on our doorstep or on the Troyers', but she looked for sanctuary in your bakery. Anyone in the area could have told her what this building was and who owned it."

"I didn't think of that."

"Neither did I. Not at first, but once my shock at her arrival wore off, I started to notice how she seems to know more about our settlement than she would have if she wandered into it by chance." She began to run the roller along the wall. "Have you heard anything from her parents?"

"Nothing."

"That's odd."

He wrestled the cabinet into place in an empty spot between the stove and refrigerator before he answered. "I think it's strange, too. Maybe I'd understand it if she'd be honest with me, but I'm getting nowhere with her."

"I knew that before you told me about your conversation with her this morning."

His brows pinched the skin over his nose as he frowned. "You did?"

"Of course. I'd have to be as unobservant as an infant not to notice how often you've tried to turn the conversation to the *boppli*'s *daed* and how every time Becky Sue has deflected your questions."

"Will you talk to her?"

"Me?" Her voice came out in a squeak as she paused with the roller against the wall. "But she barely knows me." Feeling paint trickle onto her hand, she moved the roller over the stream before setting it in the tray.

"She knows you better than she knows me. Will you help?"

"All right."

"All right?" He leaned against the cupboard as he faced her.

Breathing seemed as difficult as if she were under the clear, cool waters of a pond. His strong shoulders and narrow hips were emphasized by his long legs stretching toward her. There was an aura of strength surrounding him, but his heart, which made him determined to help his cousin, was gentle. A faint smile curved his lips and shimmered in his remarkable grass-green eyes.

"What?" she whispered, unable to speak louder.

"It's not like Annie Wagler to acquiesce so fast. I guess I don't know you any better than I know my cousin, ain't so?"

Ready to say she'd be happy to tell him anything he wanted to know, she halted herself. How could she tell him she treasured moments like this when the two of them were alone and spoke of important matters? Of how she sensed a sweet intimacy that urged her to abolish the walls around her heart and allow her to tell him how important he'd become to her in the past year?

She couldn't. She'd come to the bakery this morning, resolved to do what she must to help him discover how Leanna would make him a *gut* wife. Why hadn't he taken her joking suggestion to invite Leanna to do chores with him instead of insisting he'd persuade Annie to like working in the barn? There had to be a way to get her sister and Caleb to spend some time together.

Lowering her eyes, she said, "I'll talk with Becky Sue, but you have to be part of the conversation, too."

"Won't that defeat the purpose of having you talk to her?"

She shook her head. "If I speak with her alone, she might reveal something I won't recognize as a clue to the truth because, other than Miriam, I don't know much about your family."

"That's sensible. We'll have to work out where and when."

"Let's think about it. If she thinks we're conspiring against her, she'll refuse to talk to us." She bent to collect the roller again. She stared at the wall in front of her as she asked, "Now that's settled, will you do me a favor?"

He didn't falter. "Sure. I owe you big-time. What can I do for you?"

Chapter Eight

Annie was taken aback by Caleb's question. She hadn't expected him to agree so quickly. She'd figured he would ask what the favor was first.

Or maybe she shouldn't be surprised. He was a man of integrity. His steady, fair way of listening to everyone had smoothed rough edges as a diverse group from several different districts and states had merged into one.

Now he'd agreed to do her a favor. Without a single quibble. All she had to do was ask.

But it wasn't easy.

The words weren't difficult. Words had never been a problem for her.

Yet she hesitated. Once she told him what she'd practiced for hours last night when she should have been sleeping, and he agreed to do her the favor, her heart would take a sharp blow. She couldn't put her own happiness above her sister's. Dear Leanna had been so sad for too long, pretending to accept the fact that the man she loved had married another without bothering to tell her.

Taking a deep breath, she said, "The Salem Volunteer Fire Department is having a mud sale, which is coming up."

"I know. In about three weeks." He gave her a cheeky grin, and her heart skidded for a moment before regaining its beat. "I don't want to brag, but it was my idea to have the auction to raise money as they do in Lancaster County."

"So you're going."

He glanced around the kitchen. Boxes had been shoved into any possible space to allow room to work. As if he'd spoken his thoughts aloud, she guessed he was wondering if he could afford to take the day of the mud sale off because there was so much to be done in order for the bakery to open its doors in May.

"I don't think I should miss what was my idea, ain't so?" he asked.

"Probably not."

"Are you planning to go?"

"*Ja.* I mean… I assume I'll stop by at least part of the day."

She was making a mess of this. It should be simple. Ask for what she wanted. He'd already said he'd agree without finding out what she wanted.

How hard could it be?

Harder than she'd guessed.

Taking a deep breath, she put the paint roller into its tray. She stood straight and faced him. "Will you give Leanna a ride with you to the mud sale?" The words burst out of her in a rush.

He looked surprised. "Why? I'd assumed your family would be going together. Didn't you say something about Leanna donating a quilt?"

"I did, and I know she'd like to be there when it's auctioned off. With my *grossmammi* taking longer and longer to get ready to go anywhere, we might not be able to get to the firehouse before her quilt is sold."

"You don't have to worry. The quilts won't be sold until around noon. We want the biggest crowd possible for the quilt auction and for lunch itself."

Annie didn't want to say she'd known that. Why was it difficult to do what should be easy? She desperately wanted to see her sister happy. *Just say it!*

Before she could, Caleb's brow knit with concern. "Is Inez failing fast?"

"She has *gut* days and not-so-*gut* ones," Annie hedged. Why hadn't she devised some other excuse to persuade Caleb? "I don't want to take the chance Leanna will miss seeing who buys the quilt she made. Will you pick her up that morning?"

Puzzlement pulled at his face. "*Ja*, if that's what you want in exchange for helping me with Becky Sue."

"It's not a trade-off." Her voice sounded distant in her ears. Almost unrecognizable. Were those calm tones hers? How could they be when her stomach roiled and her heart, threatening to tear apart the weak patches she'd put on it, hammered like a cloudburst on a metal roof? "I was going to ask you anyhow."

"I made it easier for you by asking you to help me first."

"*Ja*, you did." She prayed God would forgive her for that half-truth. Everything about setting up this day between her twin and Caleb was tough because each word she spoke might be the very one that turned his thoughts to her sister forever. It was what she wanted. All of her except her heart.

But you can be friends with him when he's your brother-in-law, she tried to remind herself, but it was to no avail.

Then she told her to stop being selfish. If there was a chance—any chance at all—her sister could set aside her long months of grief and be happy again, it was well worth doing a bit of damage to her own heart.

It was, wasn't it?

The house was quiet because everyone else was either in bed or in their rooms preparing for the night. Annie was alone in the kitchen, and she was using the time to make some cookies for everyone to enjoy the next day. She'd doubled the recipe, planning to take a few extra to the bakery to share with Caleb when they had their midday break. For the first time since she'd got home, she felt as if she could draw a full breath. Spending time with her twin while preparing supper had made her so uncomfortable she'd thought everyone would notice.

Nobody had because Joey had been fussy. The *boppli* now had two teeth trying to break through, and he was miserable. Even the hard teething biscuits Annie had made for him, using an old family recipe, had failed to give him any comfort. They'd passed the little boy from one set of Wagler arms to the next. Each time, he would stop whining and crying for a few minutes as he patted each of them on the face, put his nose to theirs and gurgled his *boppli* talk to them. He had a name of sorts for each of them. "Wa-wa" for Juanita, "Lee" for Leanna and "Na-nee" for Annie. For Kenny, he said, "Ken." That delighted her brother, and Kenny and Joey laughed each time the *kind* said it.

Grossmammi Inez had made a concoction from herbs, lemon and sugar to put on his swollen gums. Rocking him to sleep, she'd given him to his *mamm* to take upstairs along with the rest of the paste to lather on if Joey woke in the night.

Annie sat at the kitchen table while the cookies baked. She enjoyed the aroma of the rich chocolate chips in the cookies while she let the quiet slip over her like a warm shawl. She read the circle letter that had been delivered in the morning's mail. Her momentary sense of peace had vanished by the time she read the five letters enclosed with the one she'd sent the last time the letter had come to her. She was supposed to pull that one out, throw it away and put in a new letter before posting the whole packet again to her cousin in Central Pennsylvania.

And she tried. In between putting trays in the oven and ten minutes later taking out the finished cookies, she'd pulled out a sheet of clean paper. While the latest batch cooked, her pen hovered over the paper. Each of the letters spread out on her table mentioned the writers' curiosity about whether anything had happened between Leanna and Caleb. Somehow, each of her friends had read between the lines to discern Annie believed her twin and the settlement's founder were attracted to each other.

She had news she could share, but she hesitated.

Writing the words that Caleb was escorting her twin to the upcoming mud sale would make it too real.

"But you want it to be real," she murmured.

"Talking to yourself can be a sign of losing your mind."

At *Grossmammi* Inez's jesting voice, Annie half turned in her chair, astonished because she'd thought her *grossmammi* had retired for the night. The old woman had her hair braided and hidden beneath a black kerchief. When *Grossmammi* Inez reached for one of the letters on the table, Annie wanted to snatch it from her hands. Instead she got up and took out a cookie sheet before putting the last one in to bake.

Scanning the letter she held, *Grossmammi* Inez sat at the table. Her breathing seemed more strained than yesterday.

"Did you make an appointment with the *doktor*?" Annie asked as she came to the table.

"Ja." Inez gestured toward the calendar hanging by the refrigerator. "For the first week in May."

"He didn't have anything sooner?"

"You know the *doktors* are at the clinic in Salem only a couple of days a week."

Annie bit her lower lip before she asked if her *grossmammi* had let the office know how much difficulty she was having breathing. Why ask? She already knew *Grossmammi* Inez would never complain like that, not even to medical staff.

"Maybe," Annie said, "we should go to Glens Falls or Bennington to one of the hospitals so you can be seen by a *doktor* there."

"I'd need to have an appointment with my *doktor* here first before they would see me."

Unless you went to the emergency room. Annie didn't want to say that aloud, because the suggestion would distress her *grossmammi*.

Grossmammi Inez patted Annie's hand. "You worry too much, Annie. Don't forget what was written in the eighth chapter of Romans. *And we know that all things work together for good to them that love God, to them who are the called according to His purpose.* Have faith everything will turn out right."

"I have faith, but…"

"You like to help things move a bit faster?" Inez tapped the letter she held.

Annie gave her *grossmammi* an ironic smile and hoped her cheeks weren't flushing. "You see me clearly."

"Eyes looking through love have a way of being clear-sighted."

"I wish that were true."

Grossmammi Inez put down the letter and folded her arms on the table. "So it's true."

"What's true?"

"You're matchmaking for your sister."

Annie was surprised the older woman didn't make it a question. "I want her to be happy."

"We all do." Her *grossmammi* sighed, her uneven breath breaking into it. "Who have you decided is the best match for your twin?"

Annie's gaze slipped toward the cookies cooling on the counter, then to the letters in front of her. A mistake, she knew, the instant her *grossmammi*'s followed.

"It's Caleb Hartz, ain't so?" *Grossmammi* Inez wagged a finger at her. "Don't look at me in shock, *kins-kind*. If you want to keep a secret, don't give yourself away by letting your eyes focus on these letters filled with such interesting questions about your twin sister and Caleb."

"I never could fool you, *Grossmammi*."

"True." Inez clasped her hands together as if in prayer. "But why Caleb, Annie? If anyone had asked me, I'd have said you're the one who likes Caleb Hartz."

"I do like him. He's a *gut* man." Annie pushed back her chair and went to open the oven door before the final batch of cookies burned. "After what happened to Leanna with Gabriel, she deserves a *gut* man in her life."

"Be that as it may, you're leaving out one important detail. The heart wants what it wants. I think that was written by an *Englisch* poet."

"Emily Dickinson," Annie said as she used a spatula to put the new cookies next to the others on the aluminum foil. "You're quoting many different sources tonight, *Grossmammi*."

"I didn't know who wrote those words. I saw them on a plaque in a store one time, and they've stayed with me."

"And I saw it in a gift shop when I was looking for a birthday card for Juanita." Annie smiled, hoping the time was right to change the subject. "Who would have guessed shopping was educational?"

"Educational? What did you learn from the quote, Annie?"

"That my heart wants my sister's heart to know happiness again."

"You can't choose how your sister feels, Annie. She has decided to mourn for what she couldn't have. *Ja*, the heart may want what it wants, but we can't be ruled by our hearts. The *gut* Lord gave us brains so we might remember His love flows through us. To turn our backs on it is what brings unhappiness. Once your sister recalls God loves her, no matter what happens, she can regain her joy with life and with Him."

Annie wished she could have her *grossmammi*'s strong faith. Maybe then she'd know what she was supposed to do.

Grossmammi Inez sighed again. "But you've already put your plans into motion, ain't so?"

"Ja."

"I'll pray God is using you as His tool, Annie, and it's not your impatience guiding you. And I'll pray it'll turn out as it should."

"I will, too." Annie wondered if she'd ever meant three words more seriously in her whole life.

Lyndon Wagler was washing the barn floor when Caleb walked in after dawn the following week. Annie's big brother was whistling tunelessly in time with his sweeping motions as he sent the water spraying across the concrete. Rivers flowed from under the stainless steel tank toward the drain beneath the sink hooked to the far wall.

"Gute mariye," Caleb called.

Lifting his thumb off the sprayer control, Lyndon

turned to face him. "I didn't expect to see you so early, Caleb. Figured you'd be milking at this hour, too."

"Just finished, so I thought I'd come and talk to you."

"Sounds important." Lyndon draped the end of the hose over the reel on the wall and bent to turn off the water. "Is it something with finalizing our *Ordnung*?"

"You're asking the wrong guy. You'd have to ask Eli."

Lyndon gave a snort. "Just because you aren't married and you couldn't have your name in the lot doesn't mean you're not involved any longer."

Caleb nodded. Everyone in the new settlement had had a voice—directly or indirectly—in the establishment of the rules under which they would live. That was the way a plain community was run.

"So what brings you over here before breakfast?"

"I wanted to let you know my plans before they went any further," he said.

"Plans? For the bakery?" Lyndon laughed. "Now *you* are talking to the wrong person. I can warm up soup and make toast, but that's the extent of my culinary skills."

"No, this has to do with the mud sale."

"Ah, looking for donations? Rhoda has been experimenting with some cheese she thought she might offer for the auction. We plan to be there to work. Anything else you need from us?"

"No, it's not about donations." Caleb launched into a very terse explanation of the favor Annie had asked of him. He finished with, "I wanted to let you know, Lyndon."

"So Annie asked you to take Leanna to the mud sale?" Lyndon pushed back his hat and scratched behind his left ear.

"Ja."

"Interesting..."

When Lyndon didn't say anything else, Caleb waited. Lyndon Wagler resembled his twin sisters. He was much taller than they were, and what was left of his hair was reddish brown, but he was like them in other ways. Sometimes he was as talkative and forthright as Annie. At other times he could be as reticent as Leanna. It seemed he was going to be the latter in the wake of hearing about the favor Annie had asked of Caleb.

Lyndon lifted two metal milk containers, and walked toward the door at the end of the open space. Caleb picked up a full milk can and followed. He hadn't planned on helping with the milking here after completing his own less than fifteen minutes ago. He'd assumed Lyndon would be done as well, then he noticed Kenny wasn't in the barn. The boy must not have helped that morning. Caleb remembered mornings, as a boy, when he'd stayed in bed so late he'd barely made it to school before the teacher rang the bell.

Caleb set the milk can next to the dairy tank. "I didn't want you to get the wrong idea."

"That you're interested in courting my sister?" Lyndon shook his head. "No, I suppose I shouldn't get that idea."

"Gut." Caleb went to the door opening into the barnyard, then paused. "It has nothing to do with any member of your family. I'm not looking for a wife."

"Got it."

Only later, when he was on his way to talk to Eli about helping load the bench wagon in preparation for the next service, did Caleb realize Lyndon hadn't specified which of his sisters he believed Caleb was talking about. Not that it made any difference. Caleb wasn't going to get involved with either Wagler twin. He'd learned his lesson about risking his heart and his dreams.

The hard way.

Chapter Nine

"I like to wash dishes," Becky Sue said with a laugh as she set a casserole pan in the drainer. "But I hate to dry and put them away."

"Most girls feel the opposite." Annie lifted a plate already half-dry from the stack in the drainer. During the past week, she and Becky Sue had got into the habit of doing the breakfast dishes together while *Gross-mammi* Inez and Becky Sue did the chore for dinner because it was only the two of them and Joey at home for the noon meal. Leanna and Juanita had taken over the task for supper. "They don't want to get their hands greasy or splatter water on their clothes."

"But the dish detergent makes my hands feel as soft as if I'd been rubbing them against a sheep."

"There's lanolin in detergent." Annie chuckled. "And in sheep's wool."

"Too bad it's not in goats' wool. Leanna would have the softest hands around. She loves taking care of those goats, ain't so?"

"*Ja.* Right now, she's letting the does she's been

milking go dry because the kids will be born in about two to three months. How Joey will love seeing them play! They're as inquisitive as he is."

Becky Sue scrubbed a plate as she stared out the window. "You're assuming we'll be here in two to three months."

"You know you're welcome."

"I know." She flashed a smile at Annie before rinsing the plate. "But I'm not sure how long we should stay."

"You won't leave without letting me know where you're going, will you?"

The girl looked at her again, in what Annie judged to be honest astonishment this time. "Why would you want to know?"

"Because this whole family cares about you and Joey. We won't force you to stay, but if you decide to leave, we'll want to know where you're bound so we can be assured you'll be okay."

"I didn't realize that."

"Look around. You and Joey are part of our family."

"Which makes Caleb part of your family, too. That's inconvenient, ain't so?" She shot a sly, sideways glance at Annie.

Without hesitation, Annie replied, "We're all family here in Harmony Creek Hollow."

"That's not what I'm talking about, and you know it."

Annie smiled. She wasn't going to get into a discussion of her relationship with Caleb. The sooner the teen figured that out, the better it would be.

"We have a *wunderbaar* community here," Annie said. "Not only the *Leit*, but our *Englisch* neighbors."

"My family would never accept an *Englischer* in any sort of relationship." Becky Sue glanced at Annie and then away, but didn't add anything else.

Had Becky Sue let slip that Joey's *daed* was an *Englischer*?

Annie wanted to ask, but finished the dishes in silence. By the time she put the last ones away, Becky Sue had already left to spend time with her son. Was the offhand comment a clue to the truth the girl had been hiding?

The day was flashing by, and Caleb was beginning to believe the kitchen would be done in time. The refrigerator and the freezer had been hooked up that morning, and the quartz counters were being delivered the next day. The butcher block for the island had been fabricated by his neighbor and friend Jeremiah. That would be in by week's end. After that, his attention would be on the front room where the baked goods would be sold.

Digging his fingers into his lower back, he stretched and tried not to groan at his tired muscles as he looked across the room to where Annie was unpacking paper supplies and putting them in the storage closet. He hadn't been certain how many bags and boxes to buy, but he'd know more once he saw how many customers came and, more important, how many returned.

"I thought about what you said about customers seeing the back wall," he called across the kitchen.

"You did?" She set a handful of flattened white

boxes on the lowest shelf and then straightened. Pressing one hand against her lower back in a motion that copied his, she faced him. Fatigue shadowed her eyes and dimmed her bright smile.

Guilt lashed at him. Was he insisting she work harder than she should? In addition to helping at the bakery, she had her chores at home and kept an eye on his cousin and the *boppli*. Though she hadn't said much, he knew she was worried about her *grossmammi*. At least he'd been able to ease her concern about her sister getting to the mud sale in time to see her quilt auctioned. However, it seemed there must be other ways he could have helped than offering her sister a ride to and home from the mud sale.

What if he was escorting Annie instead of her twin sister? His mind lingered there. He'd driven Annie to the bakery and home many times, but there would be something different about riding with her to the firehouse south of the village. And when he drove her home at the end of the long, exciting day…

Caleb halted the thought before it could take him where he shouldn't go. Not if he wanted to keep his dream moving forward. He was keeping the doubts planted by Verba out of his head, and he must be as vigilant about banishing thoughts of how *wunderbaar* it would be to slip his arm around Annie's shoulders as they rode through the late-winter twilight and…

Again he squashed the image in his mind. It wasn't easy when he was looking at her by the closet door, so he cut his eyes to the cupboards that soon would be filled with more supplies. He couldn't forget how relieved he'd been to set aside the burden of establishing the settlement. How much heavier were Annie's obligations? And she couldn't step away from her duties to her family.

No, it wasn't that she couldn't. She *wouldn't*.

Just as she'd keep working with him for as long as he needed her.

Lord, don't let me take her for granted again. Help guide me to show her I appreciate her efforts. But not by asking her to walk out with him when he couldn't offer her anything but friendship.

Discovering she was waiting with unusual patience for him to continue, Caleb said, "*Ja*, I've been thinking about the color for the wall."

"It should be bright."

"Bright? Why?"

Annie crossed the kitchen and stretched out her arms. She motioned for him to come stand beside her. When he did, hoping she didn't sense that his back was protesting again from long hours of work, she turned to face the front of the building. She tugged on his sleeves, so he copied her motion.

"See?" she asked. "If the color of the wall catches their attention, their eyes will be drawn right to the display in the cases. And once they see the goodies for sale, they won't be able to leave without buying something. Even a small order to sample your baking."

"What color do you suggest?"

"Yellow."

He gave her a wry grin. "You didn't hesitate on that."

"It's my favorite color. Reminds me of sunshine and daffodils and cake batter."

"Not chocolate cake batter?" he asked as he walked toward the door. Taking his hanging coat off the wall, he pulled it on, trying not to wince as he stretched.

"*Gut* to eat, but not a color I'd want on the wall." She smiled while she came toward the rear of the kitchen. For a moment, she turned and considered the room again. "If you don't like yellow, there are other nice colors like blue or green or purple that would grab customers' attention."

"You aren't planning on using them all, ain't so?"

"Like painting stripes?" she laughed. "Not if you want *me* to paint the wall. My skills aren't up to that task. However, we can paint some rectangles in different colors, so you can consider them and make your choice."

"Sounds like a plan. Let's go into Salem next week, and we can look at the color choices at the hardware store."

"You want me to go with you?"

He nodded, pleased to be the one to disconcert her for once. "I'm sure they have lots of colors. I could use your advice on which to pick."

"But what if you don't like what I do?"

"I'll let you know." He lifted her coat off its peg and held it out for her to slip her arms into it. "You aren't the only one who'll be working here. I'm going to be spending a lot of time in this kitchen, too, next winter when work on the farm is slower again. It'll help if I like the color on the walls."

"Okay. I'll go with you to the store." Several emotions scurried across her face, but she turned away to pull on her coat, preventing him from discerning what she was thinking.

Why was she making such a big deal out of an errand to get paint?

Why was he?

His gaze slid toward her as he reached for his hat. His fingers were awkward and groped for the peg while he found himself admiring the curve of her neck in the moment before she slid her bonnet into place, blocking his view. She and her sister were identical, but there was something unique about Annie Wagler. Something vital and vivacious, so alive that being near her seemed to bring life to parts of him he'd thought long dead: hope, as well as belief in the best in others and in himself.

Annie drew her shawl over her shoulders, and he looked away so she didn't catch him staring at her. That might lead her to believe he had time in his life for more than his work. He didn't.

Caleb closed up the bakery and locked the doors, wondering why he bothered. Nobody had tried to get inside since Becky Sue and Joey had taken shelter there. Each time he had someone come to work at the bakery, he had to make sure he was there to open up for them.

He went to get Dusty from the rickety barn owned by the bakery's neighbors. The old couple living next door wasn't using the space, so they'd accepted the offer he'd made last week to rent the barn from them. They also told him his horse could use the field connected to the barn, which would work well when the weather warmed.

After hitching his horse to the buggy, he climbed in along with Annie. He gave her one side of the thick wool blanket, and she tucked it in around herself. She had to shift to sit closer to him, but he didn't mind.

Be careful, he warned himself. *Keep everything between you business.*

She was his sister's friend. He'd already told her brother he considered the twins to be friends.

But he couldn't ignore the fact that far too often he found himself gazing in Annie's direction, losing track of time as he watched her graceful motions or when he listened to her latest idea for the bakery.

He was shaken out of his musings when Annie murmured, "Becky Sue said some things today you should know about."

"And you're telling me only now? Why?"

"Because I've been fighting the feeling I'm betraying her confidences by sharing them with anyone else."

"Did she ask you to keep what she said to yourself?"

"No, but if I want her to be open with me, I can't blab what she tells me."

He put his gloved hand on top of her thick mitten. "Annie, you aren't blabbing. You're confiding in her cousin who's worried about her."

"Don't try to befuddle me, Caleb Hartz!" She yanked her hand from beneath his and folded her arms in front of her. "I get enough of that from Becky Sue with her half answers."

"I wasn't trying to confuse you. I was trying to make you feel better about telling me what she said."

For a long minute, Annie didn't reply. "You're right," she said at last, and he wondered what she'd decided during her silent discussion with herself. "If she were my cousin, I'd want to know everything."

He listened while she shared what Becky Sue had let slip during their conversation. Asking Annie to repeat as much of the conversation as she could, he considered what his cousin had said and in what order.

"Something doesn't add up," he mused aloud when she finished.

"What?"

"I'm not sure, but something seems off."

"I think so, too."

He glanced at her and saw her relieved smile. "What do you think is off in her story?"

"If Joey's *daed* is an *Englischer* she met in Lancaster County, why did she come here? It seems unlikely to me she met an *Englisch* boy from Salem when she was in Pennsylvania." She raised her hands to halt his reply. "I know what you're going to say. *Englischers* travel farther than we do, but that's not why I'm finding her tale hard to believe. If the boy is here, why hasn't he come forward?"

"Maybe he doesn't want to admit to the truth. Or maybe he doesn't know she's here."

Annie sniffed her derision. "Everyone knows everything about everyone in Salem. Isn't that what you told me?"

"I did." He thought about the careful questions he'd asked at the fire department, wanting to get advice from his *Englisch* friends as well as his plain ones about what to do to help his cousin and her *boppli*. "And you're right. I would imagine everybody within twenty miles has heard about our discovery at the bakery. Maybe she was honest when she said it was a co-incidence she ended up here."

"Coincidence is, I believe, often God's way of giving us a second chance to right a wrong we may not have realized we did to someone else. Or to ourselves."

He gave her a half smile. "It sounds as if you've given this a lot of thought."

"I have since Becky Sue showed up."

"So have I." *And since I asked you to work for me when I intended to ask Leanna instead.*

"Give her a chance to be honest with you. If you keep pressing, you'll back her into a corner. That will make her distrust you more."

He nodded, knowing her advice was sound. They had to try to follow it in the hope the girl would finally be forthcoming about what had driven her from her home.

Chapter Ten

Sunday morning dawned with a hint of warmth, a promise winter wouldn't last forever. Caleb drove his buggy into the busy yard in front of James Streicher's house. The blacksmith had moved to the community late last summer, and he'd already become an integral part of the district.

Handing his buggy over to Eli Troyer's nephew, Kyle, who would put Dusty with the rest of the horses in a nearby meadow, Caleb walked to where the other members of the *Leit* were gathered by the house's front door.

The women and the men began to divide into two groups as he walked toward them along a narrow path cut into the deep snowbanks. He turned to his left to join the other men, but froze as if the temperature had dropped fifty degrees.

Only his eyes moved as he stared in painful astonishment when Joey, who was in Lyndon's arms, held up chubby arms to Jeremiah, babbling in excitement. The *boppli* had never seen Jeremiah before, but was eager for the man to take him. He batted Jeremiah's face, as he did the Waglers', and gave a deep chortle that rumbled beneath the conversations around them.

So Joey wasn't going through a stage where he didn't like men. He'd been content with Lyndon holding him and gone eagerly to Jeremiah. Yet he screamed in terror when Caleb came near. Had something changed? Caleb wasn't going to test that before services, so he avoided getting too close to the men and the *kind*.

Through the service, as he joined others in singing the long hymns and listened to Eli's sermon and prayed, he couldn't keep the questions quiet. Why had the little boy had such an instantaneous hatred of him? What could Caleb do to ease the little boy's fears?

Lord, give me some idea.

Church Sundays were always among Annie's favorite days of the month. She could spend time with her friends and catch up on their lives. Before Miriam and Sarah had married, they had joined her and Leanna for outings, like going grocery shopping or attending a charity dinner at the firehouse or special events in the village. Their Harmony Creek Spinsters' Club hadn't done anything together since before their weddings last fall. Or, as they'd decided when they started the group, the Harmony Creek Spinsters' and Newlyweds' Club, agreeing to change the name when one of them married. At the time, none of them had plans to marry, but Miriam and Sarah had in the past year.

Annie hoped it would soon be Leanna's turn to take marriage vows. But how would it be possible when

Caleb hadn't asked her sister to the mud sale as he'd promised to do a week ago?

"Do you see what I see?" asked Miriam as she came to stand by the door. Its window offered a view of the snowy driveway and the yard marked with footprints where the *kinder* had been chasing each other.

"What?" Annie asked.

"Your sister and my brother." Miriam chuckled. She pointed to the twosome, who were standing a few feet from the house. "I don't remember the last time I've seen the two of them talking to each other."

"They've been very busy with their work." Did her voice sound as strained to Miriam as it did to her?

Caleb and Leanna's conversation ended, and her sister rushed toward the house at the same time Caleb walked toward his buggy.

Miriam didn't wait until Leanna had taken off her bonnet before she asked, "So did he finally ask you to the mud sale?"

Annie was pierced by surprise. Why? Caleb talking to his sister and getting her advice on how to ask Leanna wasn't anything out of the ordinary. Her own brother had sought out her insight and Leanna's when he started walking out with Rhoda. They'd been no older than Becky Sue then, but he kept saying he wanted a female point of view.

"He did." Leanna kept her gaze on the floor as she lifted off her bonnet and put it on the table with the others. "He's being very kind because he knows how long it can take to get our family going in the morning."

"I'm glad you'll be there to see when your quilt comes up for bid," Annie said. And she was.

Yet, at the same time, she couldn't help the feeling she was sliding into a deep pit where not a hint of sunlight would ever reach. No, she wasn't going to let sorrow overwhelm her as it had Leanna. Rather, she was going to be grateful her sister might escape the darkness left in the wake of her heartbreak.

Half listening while her sister and Miriam talked about the mud sale, Annie was startled when she heard a hiss close to her left ear. She turned and saw Becky Sue crooking a finger toward her.

Annie excused herself, though Miriam and Leanna were so immersed in their conversation she wasn't sure they noticed her leaving, and walked to where Becky Sue stood near a closed door.

"Is it true?" the teen said.

"Is what true?" Annie wished—just once—Becky Sue would clarify what she was saying.

"Caleb is walking out with Leanna?"

"You know we don't talk about such things." Annie didn't like her stern tone any more than the girl did. Softening it, she said, "Caleb is giving Leanna a ride to the mud sale."

"And home?"

Annie shrugged. Would Caleb offer her twin a ride home, too? If none of the other Waglers got there, he would. However, at least Lyndon, who was also a volunteer firefighter, would be going and could bring her home.

"Are you okay with this?" Becky Sue persisted.

"It's nice of your cousin to be so thoughtful." She wasn't going to admit she'd set up the whole thing because she wasn't sure if Becky Sue would keep that to herself.

"I thought *you* liked him."

"I do. He's a nice man and a *gut* boss."

"You know that's not what I mean."

"I know what you mean, but I also know Caleb asked Leanna and I'm glad she's going to be there for the quilt auction."

The teen folded her arms over her chest and frowned. "He asked you to join him in doing chores in the barn."

"How do you know that?"

"I hear things." Becky Sue shrugged insolently. "Like everyone else does. Why haven't you accepted his invitation? Don't you like my cousin?"

"I like him. I don't like working in the barn."

Becky Sue glowered at her, then spun on her heel and stamped away.

Annie went in the opposite direction, avoiding where Miriam and Leanna were giggling together as if they were no older than Becky Sue. She paused to grab her coat, bonnet and mittens. Fresh air might help because the house suddenly felt as small as a *kind*'s shoebox.

The wind had risen again, and Annie ducked her head into it as she strode out into the cloud-darkened afternoon. Was another storm coming? She was beginning to doubt winter would ever end.

Snow clung to her boots, trying to halt her on every step, but she pushed forward until she bumped into someone. Raising her eyes, she nodded to her brother who was talking to some other men who were getting their buggies ready to leave. He started to ask a question, but she turned away before he could.

He didn't call after her but she heard assertive footsteps give chase. Looking over her shoulder, she saw Caleb behind her. She wanted to groan. He was the last person she wanted to talk to. What would she say to him when he let her know he'd done her the favor she'd asked for?

"Can I have a minute?" Caleb asked as he caught up with her.

"Ja." She'd be glad to give him more than a single minute, but he should focus on Leanna. *"Danki* for asking Leanna to go with you to the mud sale."

He waved that aside as if it didn't matter. She realized his face was drawn. What was wrong? It couldn't be because Leanna had agreed. If he hadn't wanted to ask her, he would have said as much to Annie. They were honest with each other…about most things.

"Joey let Jeremiah Stoltzfus hold him today before the service. He didn't make a peep." Caleb's words fell over one another in his hurry to speak them. "But he screams anytime I'm near him."

Her self-pity became sympathy for him. She didn't have any right to feel sorry for herself when events were unfolding as she'd arranged, but Caleb had been hurt over and over by the *boppli*'s response.

"It's impossible to know what's going on in a *boppli*'s head," she said, putting a solacing hand on his sleeve and trying to ignore the strong muscles beneath the layers of wool and cotton. "It may not have anything to do with what you've been doing. Think about how Becky Sue is so tense around you. Maybe Joey thinks she's frightened of you, so he is, too. A one-year-old isn't going to understand why his *mamm* feels as she does."

"I'd like to believe you're right, but it's clear Joey hates me."

"A *boppli* doesn't hate anyone or anything. He's scared for some reason."

"*Danki* for trying to make me feel better, but you're using different words to say the same thing."

"Stop it!"

Annie's sharp words jerked Caleb out of his morass of shame. He stared at her, wondering why he was startled she wasn't reacting as he'd expected. She seldom did.

Her voice softened. "I know it bothers you, Caleb, that Joey cries, but he's a *boppli*. Like I said, none of us can guess what goes on in his head. He's a loving *kind*, wanting to touch us whenever we hold him. He'll warm up to you when he sees you want to take care of him, too."

"I'd like to think—"

A sharp ring cut through the gray afternoon as his pocket vibrated against his leg. The sound and the sensation repeated before he could move. Maybe everyone didn't whirl to stare at him, but it sure felt that way. Fishing the cell phone out of his pocket, he strode away from Annie and the men gathered closer to the house. He tapped the phone screen the way he'd been shown and held it to his ear.

Nothing.

He'd missed the call.

Maybe it hadn't been important.

He looked at the screen, and his gut tightened as he recognized the number. It belonged to the phone shack that Becky Sue's family used!

He pushed another button to call back. He grimaced when he heard a busy signal. Giving himself to the count of twenty, he tried again with the same result. He waited another full minute—which felt like an eternity—and made another attempt. This time, he got the same answering machine he had before. Leaving a message to call him as soon as possible, he ended the call.

Walking to where Annie stood, he glowered at the phone. Why hadn't Becky Sue's family waited long enough for him to call back? It didn't make sense. He tightened his hold around the slender phone. It was almost as if they'd done their duty by calling and felt it wasn't necessary to do anything else.

But didn't they want to know where their daughter and *kins-kind* were? Weren't they worried about whether they were safe and had a place to sleep and food to eat?

He tried to remember what message he'd left. It had been bare-bones facts that the two had been found and Caleb would make sure they were okay until Becky Sue's family sent instructions about whether they wanted him to bring her home or they wanted to come to Harmony Creek Hollow for a reunion with the runaway teen and her *boppli*. But if they'd taken time to make arrangements, why hadn't they waited for him to call and find out what they were?

"Was that Becky Sue's parents?" Annie asked.

"Ja."

"Are they coming here?"

He lifted one shoulder in a half-hearted response. "I don't know. I didn't answer the call in time, and when I called back, I didn't get an answer."

She put consoling fingers on his arm as she had before, and he felt his frustration melt away beneath her warm touch. How did Annie manage to do that with a simple brush of her fingertips on his sleeve?

"The important thing is they called," she said.

"Ja." He looked at the phone as he added, "When I tried calling them back, the line was busy."

"A *gut* sign someone is in the phone shack."

How did she always see the best side of every circumstance? While he looked for problems so he could avoid them, she seemed to believe everything would be fine if she moved ahead.

"But then the answering machine picked up."

Her eyes widened, and he looked away before he lost himself in their enticing depths.

"That's strange," she said. "I would have guessed that they'd hang around long enough to wait for you to call."

"I thought so, too. But—"

Again he was interrupted by a sound from the phone. This time it was a chirping noise.

Caleb looked at the screen to see an announcement that there was a voice mail. Hoping he was remembering the correct way to retrieve it, because it'd been a few weeks since his friend had showed him how to use the various utilities on the cell phone, he tapped the screen before holding the device to his ear. He listened, then lowered it, shocked at what he'd heard. Pushing the buttons again, he held it to his other ear, hoping that what he thought he'd heard was a mistake.

It wasn't.

"Was that a message from Becky Sue's *mamm* or *daed*?" Annie asked.

Without a word, he handed her the phone. He motioned for her to activate the voice mail, and she followed his silent instructions.

He knew the moment she heard the words that had sent disgust rocketing through him. Her face flushed and tears filled her eyes as she looked at where Becky Sue was emerging from the house surrounded by the Waglers.

The words spoken in a man's clipped tones were seared into Caleb's brain. "You've got Becky Sue. Keep her. We don't want her or her *boppli* here."

Chapter Eleven

Annie frowned at the windows in the bakery's front room. Her fingers itched to dip a cloth into hot, soapy water so she could begin to wash the layers of grime from the glass. As soon as the cold weather broke, she intended to give the windows in both rooms a *gut* cleaning. She imagined how sunshine would glint off the polished glass cases where cakes and pies and cookies and other sweets would be displayed.

Each day, Caleb brought in a product he wanted to sell at the bakery and asked her opinion. She'd sampled whoopie pies as well as cookies and cake and cinnamon rolls. Every one had been delicious, a sure sign that the bakery would be a success.

For the past week, she and Caleb had been working on the main room of the shop. He'd repaired windows and started nailing down the loose floorboards, replacing some that would no longer fit into place. She suspected he was easing his frustration with Becky Sue's parents by slamming the hammer into the boards. Several times a day, he tried calling their number and he left dozens of messages.

None were returned.

How could parents wash their hands of their *kind* and *kins-kind* like that? Annie couldn't come up with an answer for that puzzling question.

She felt her own frustration fall from her shoulders when she drew in a deep breath. The astonishing aroma of chocolate chip cookies would, she decided, never grow old. She was eager to sample Caleb's recipe, which added a touch of maple syrup to the dough. He was baking them today to check the temperature in the double ovens and make sure he wouldn't burn products when he was ready to open the doors in a few weeks.

At the happy chirp of the timer, she went into the kitchen and grabbed a pot holder and the waiting trays of cookie dough he'd prepared before he went out to pick up some debris that had blown against the building during the previous night's storm. She opened the wide door on the ovens, which had more controls than she'd imagined any appliance could. Switching the two trays and resetting the timer, she let the enticing scent of baking cookies swirl around her.

She slid the cookies off the tray and put another batch in their places, so they could go in when the others were done. Feeling like a naughty child, she picked up a warm cookie. She took a bite and grinned. The rich flavor of maple syrup was subtle but enhanced the luxurious chocolate and pecan bits mixed into the dough.

Golden maple syrup...

Annie glanced at the kitchen wall that remained a

boring white. The plans to go to the hardware store to get paint had been pushed aside day after day while they finished tasks inside the building. Supplies had arrived and had to be unpacked. A couple of roof slats had been cracked by an ice dam, so Caleb had spent a day repairing the damage where water seeping past the broken slats had turned a section of the ceiling brown.

She looked at the calendar where Caleb crossed off each day. They had five weeks before opening day. Would they make it?

The door opened and Annie started to greet Caleb. She choked on the cookie when Leanna walked in.

"What are you doing here in the middle of the afternoon?" Annie asked after taking a gulp of water to wash down the crumbs. "Isn't today your day to work at Mrs. Beattie's house?"

Leanna untied her bonnet. "She asked me to skip this week because her daughter's visiting. I thought I'd stop by and see what's been keeping you so busy." She hung her bonnet by the door. Scanning the space, she whistled. "This is fancier than I expected."

Annie began to explain how Caleb had bought the appliances and extra cabinets from Mr. Summerhays. When her twin frowned, Annie realized how defensive she sounded.

"It was a blessing that the appliances were available," Annie said as she hurried to finish.

"I guess it would have been *dumm* not to take advantage of such an opportunity, ain't so?" Leanna stood in the center of the room so she could take in every inch of it. "How many bakers is he planning to hire?"

"I don't know."

"He can't intend to use all this by himself."

"I told him, though he hired me to run the cash register and deal with customers, I'd be willing to help with baking." Annie gave a careless shrug. "Of course, it's going to depend on how many customers he gets and what products they buy."

Leanna began to count on her fingers. "Whoopie pies, all sorts of cookies, fresh bread and biscuits, cakes and, of course, pies. Especially shoofly pie. That seems to be everyone's favorite plain treat."

"*Komm*, and I'll show you the front room where the customers will shop. We're still working on it."

As she led the way into the other space, Annie held her breath. Would Leanna see past the work still to be done? Annie no longer saw the stained walls or how the glass display cases needed their doors set into place. Instead she imagined the walls painted a soft shade, and tables and chairs on one side filled with happy people and others gazing at a chalkboard listing products along with their prices as more eager customers stood in a long line winding out the door.

"I didn't think it'd be this big," Leanna said. "The counter and display case don't take up much room."

"I suggested that Caleb put some tables in for customers."

"That would fill up the empty space, ain't so? Is he going to do it?"

"He's deciding."

"What's to decide? If people come in and the place looks empty, they'll think there's something wrong and go away."

"He'll make up his mind when it's the proper time," Annie said, though she agreed with her sister.

"I hope he doesn't wait too long. Isn't he opening at the beginning of May?"

"Ja." Why was she trying to justify Caleb's decisions to Leanna? He was her boss, and the choices he made for the bakery were his and his alone. "Want a cookie?"

"Sounds *gut.*"

Leading her twin back into the kitchen, Annie went to the ovens a second before the timer beeped. She exchanged the trays again, then motioned for her sister to select a cookie or two.

The door opened, and the icy wind swirled through the kitchen, making the May opening seem a long, long time off. Annie wrapped her arms around herself, but the motion couldn't stave off the cold.

Caleb knocked snow off his boots before he stepped into the kitchen. Above his scarf, his eyes crinkled with a smile. He yanked off the scarf, letting it fall over one shoulder.

"Leanna! What brings you here today?" Caleb's smile broadened as he walked past Annie, paying her no more attention than if she'd vanished.

Her twin brightened as she flung out her hands. "My curiosity got the better of me, and I couldn't wait for the bakery to open to see what has kept you and Annie so busy here."

He began to list the tasks they'd done as if her words hadn't affected him. A bright red flush rising from his shirt told Annie otherwise. He was flustered by her sister's comments.

When he began to repeat Annie's tour, Leanna shot her a glance warning not to interfere. Or was it meant to tell Annie to find something else to do so her twin could spend time alone with Caleb?

Annie hated how her happiness had vanished. She should be thrilled that her twin had come to the bakery to get a preview of the shop, but being ignored stung. Or was she being too sensitive because Caleb smiled at her when he asked her what she thought of his recipe for the chocolate chip cookies?

"They're delicious, Caleb. Once people taste them, they're going to fly off the shelves. If…" Her voice trailed away when she realized he wasn't listening to her as he strode with Leanna into the front of the shop.

Glancing at the timer and seeing she had a couple of minutes before the cookies were done, she rushed after them. Word had spread that Leanna was riding to the mud sale with Caleb. Thanks to Becky Sue, Annie was sure, but people would look at Leanna and Caleb differently if it was assumed they were walking out together. Though they were adults, long past teens on their *rumspringas*, there must be no question of impropriety.

Becoming a chaperone for Caleb and Leanna was something she hadn't considered, and she wondered if she'd ever been more uncomfortable than she was when she joined them in the front room. They were busy talking, Caleb repeating much of what Annie had already told her twin and Leanna acting as if she was hearing it for the first time.

Did they even notice she was there?

She flinched when she heard Caleb say her name, then realized he remained focused on her sister.

"Annie mentioned," he said as he smiled at Leanna, "that you might want to display some of your small quilts here. I'm hoping we'll get plenty of *Englisch* tourists on their journeys to and from Vermont."

"And *Englischers* love small quilts they can hang in their homes," Annie hurried to add so she couldn't be accused of sneaking into their conversation. "The colors would be pretty in the shop, as well."

Leanna looked at the graying floorboards. "That's true." Turning to Caleb, she said, "I've got some pieces that I could bring in when you're ready to open. Wall hangings and pot holders and other little items like that. If anyone is interested in any of them, then I can make more to replace the ones that sell."

"What about a full-size quilt?" Annie asked. "One to put on the wall behind the tables."

Caleb frowned. "I haven't made up my mind about having tables."

"I know, but I thought—"

"I said I'd think about it, and that's what I'm doing."

She opened her mouth to protest, but closed it when Leanna laid gentle fingers on her arm. How many times had her twin used the same motion to warn her to be silent before she spoke and got herself into trouble?

Mumbling some half-formed excuse, Annie went into the kitchen to start cleaning the baking pans and other dishes. She scraped off stuck-down pieces of cookie from the sheets before putting them in the dishwasher along with the mixing bowls. As she started the machine she'd learned to use, she heard laughter from the other room.

She felt more alone than she had in her whole life,

because she had to envision her life without Leanna being a big part of it. But worse was knowing everything was about to change between her and Caleb, too. She should have been beside herself with joy, but all she could feel was sadness and loss.

Caleb drove the last—or he hoped it was the last—nail into the floorboard closest to the front door. Sitting on his heels, he looked along the floor. It wasn't even near the trap door. Though he didn't want his customers to trip, he'd decided against nailing that shut until he decided if he'd have to use the storage space under it. He'd seen low-pile carpet at the hardware store, but it would show wear quickly. Until he had enough money to pay for several truckloads of gravel to cover the muddy parking lot, the carpet would be filthy within an hour of his opening the door each morning. This old floor would have to do until he could find the time and the money to put in a new one.

Pushing himself to his feet, he picked up the box of nails and his hammer. He carried them into the kitchen, where Annie was emptying the dishwasher. Because the state health inspector would require such a machine in a bakery kitchen, Caleb had had it installed. It was loud and made clouds of steam, but it made sure the dishes and utensils were sanitized before their next use.

"How's it going?" he asked when Annie didn't greet him.

She'd been strangely quiet since her sister left. He hoped they hadn't had an argument. He'd never seen them quarrel, but siblings had differences of opinions at times. Certainly he and Miriam had when they were growing up.

"The dishes are clean," she replied, "and I put the cookies in a sealed container so they won't go stale soon."

"Why don't you take them home? Leanna gave them her approval, and I'd like to hear what the rest of your family thinks."

"Okay."

What was going on? They might as well have been strangers for how little she was talking to him. If the problem was between her and her sister, he'd be wise not to get in the middle of it. Anytime Annie had had a problem with him, she hadn't been averse to letting him know right away.

"Caleb?" she called as he turned to put his tools away.

"Ja?"

"As we're going to use the dishwasher regularly, the detergent should be stored under the sink. Where did you put it?"

"Under the sink."

"It's not there now."

"No?" Baffled, he asked, "What did you use to clean those dishes?"

"There was a small cup with detergent in it. That's empty. Where else could the big container be?"

"I don't know. Maybe in the storage closet," he replied, though he wondered how the plastic container, which he remembered placing under the sink, had moved.

He didn't need enigmas. He must concentrate on

the dozens of tasks waiting for him. Catching a flash of motion out the window, he reminded himself that if he didn't order the blinds they wouldn't be ready for the bakery's opening. The front of the building faced west, and the afternoon sun would be pitiless on his customers and his products.

Annie went to the closet, opened the door and walked inside, holding out one hand to keep the door from slamming shut. A moment later, she shouted from the closet. "I see the detergent, but it's up too high for me to reach."

Knowing that there wasn't enough space for the step stool in the closet that was stacked high with unpacked boxes, he put down the hammer and crossed the kitchen. He motioned for her to move so they could exchange places.

She stepped into the kitchen, and he squeezed into the cramped space. He shifted a couple of the heavy cases into the kitchen before he could bump into them and knock them over. Nothing was breakable in them, because they contained napkins and other paper supplies, but he wanted to keep the cardboard boxes from breaking and spewing paper everywhere.

He ran his fingers along the topmost shelf, but didn't find the plastic bucket. When the cleaning supplies had been delivered, he'd put it against the right wall within easy reach for him. But then he'd moved it under the sink.

"Can you guide me to where it is?" he asked. "I can't see it from where I'm standing."

She slipped into the closet, letting the door close behind her. She pointed up. Her fingers were a bare inch from his nose, and she edged her arm away.

He realized she couldn't move more because there wasn't much space between him and the filled shelves and crates. Since he'd been depending on her to get supplies out of the cramped closet, he hadn't guessed how difficult it was to retrieve anything. He should build more storage space, but that would cut into the kitchen area. Something else to put on his to-consider list once the bakery was open and he had a better idea of how many customers would be stopping by each day.

"To your left," Annie directed.

"Left? It should be on the right."

"Maybe it should be, but it's on the left side. Second box in. A bit farther to your left," she added when he ran his fingers along the shelf again. "A little bit farther. There!"

He rose on tiptoe and closed his fingers around what he hoped was the correct container. "This one?"

"*Ja.* I think so. Your head is blocking my view."

"Sorry. I don't think it's removable."

When she laughed, he was delighted that his weak joke had shattered her coolness in the wake of her sister's visit. The sound made his heart hitch and then beat faster.

As he pulled the container off the shelf and lowered it between his chest and the shelves, he heard her turn the doorknob so she could get out of his way.

"Anything else you need?" he asked when she didn't open the door.

"The key."

"What?"

* * *

Annie tried the doorknob again. It refused to turn. She tried to jiggle the door, wondering if something had got stuck in the latch.

"What's going on?" Caleb asked as he eased away from the shelves. When he bumped into her, he repeated the question.

"The door is locked."

"What do you mean?"

She rolled her eyes. "I mean it's locked. The door won't open."

"Let me try."

Wanting to tell him she doubted he'd have different results, she edged aside, giving him room. She tried to make herself small so he could reach past her to grab the doorknob.

His bare forearm beneath his rolled-up sleeve stretched past her, touching hers. Her skin prickled where his brushed against her. His muted, quick intake of breath told her she wasn't the only one aware of the enticing sensation. She jerked her arm away, holding it close to her like a shield.

He didn't look at her as he yanked on the doorknob. It didn't move.

"Here." He handed her the bucket of dishwasher detergent. "Can you move back?"

"I don't think so."

Glancing everywhere but at her, he startled her as he grasped her by the waist. A squeak of surprise burst from her when he lifted her and sat her on one of the boxes as if she were no older than Joey.

"This might give us a bit more room," he said.

"Okay." Her voice shook with the tempest of emotions roiling through her like a summer storm.

As he turned to try the door again, Annie took a steadying breath. What was wrong with her? She'd witnessed him spending time with her sister and lavishing attention on Leanna. Anyone seeing them together would have assumed they were a couple. If all went as Annie planned, Caleb and Leanna soon would be walking out together.

She was saved from having to imagine a future with Caleb as her sister's husband when he slapped the door with his palm. It didn't open.

"How could it be locked?" he asked.

"I don't know."

He looked over his shoulder at her and gave her a half grin. "I didn't expect you did. That was my frustration talking. But the door shouldn't be able to lock on its own."

"True, and we've got to figure a way to get out of here." She rested her hands on her apron that was spotted with water from her work in the kitchen.

"If you don't show up for supper, someone will come here to look for you, ain't so?"

"I'm not worried about that. I'm worried about the kettle on the stove. I was going to make us some tea."

"You left it on?"

As if answer to his question, the whistle from the kettle announced the water was boiling.

When Caleb whirled to face her, she gave him a scowl to match his. "I wasn't planning to take more than a couple of seconds to get the detergent. I didn't think I needed to take the kettle off."

"Of course not." He sighed and rubbed his eyes. "We've got to get out."

"The kettle is pretty full, so it shouldn't boil dry for a while."

"Fifteen minutes?"

She nodded. "Do you have that cell phone you borrowed?"

"No. I returned it a couple of days ago."

"How about that pager thing you wear?"

He looked at his waist and the small device the volunteer firefighters wore. "It lets us know where there's an emergency. It doesn't call out."

"Pounding on the door won't get us anywhere."

He sighed as he looked around the cramped space that was lit by the faint light coming around the door. "If I had my tools, I could pop the pins out of the hinges and remove the door."

"But they're outside in the kitchen."

"Ja."

The kettle's whistle went up in pitch as if it sensed the urgency of the situation.

He eased past her knees, the momentary contact of his chest against them propelling the powerful awareness through her again. With a mumbled apology, he faced the outer wall. He pushed on one side of what once had been the sliding door, but it was securely nailed in place.

The kettle continued singing out its warning.

They had to get out.

"It's going to be okay," Caleb said.

Annie stared at her hands, knowing her distress

must have been visible on her face. "I should have taken the kettle off when I came to get the detergent."

"You couldn't have known, Annie. If you want to blame anyone, blame me for not checking the door's lock."

She shuddered when the kettle's whistle seemed to reach a higher pitch. Did that mean the water was boiling away faster?

"I'm sorry, Caleb," she whispered.

His hand under her chin tilted her face up so she couldn't avoid looking at him as he stood right in front of her. Whatever he'd intended to say was lost as his gaze locked with hers. Unlike ever before, they were on the same level, and she saw silvery flecks in his vivid green eyes.

Her breath caught when his fingers uncurled along her cheek, cupping it. All thought vanished but of how sweet his touch was. His eyes sought something in hers. What? She didn't know, but she was willing to let him discover every secret in her heart...even how much she longed for him to kiss her. She slanted toward him, not closing her eyes because she didn't want to break the connection between them.

Suddenly he pushed forward into her. His hands caught her by the waist, steadying her so she didn't tumble off the box. She grabbed his shoulders before her chin slammed into his.

Annie gasped as she looked past him and saw his cousin standing in the doorway. Becky Sue pushing the door open must have been what had shoved Caleb into her.

"What are you two doing in the closet?" the girl asked with a giggle.

Realizing it must look as if she and Caleb were embracing, Annie lifted her hands away from his shoulders. He stepped back, and she jumped off the box, straightening her clothing that had got mussed beneath her. Without a word to either of them, she rushed to the stove and turned off the burner. She took the kettle off it, wincing as the heat scorched her hand.

Caleb put the detergent container by the sink before facing his cousin and asking, "Did you lock the door, Becky Sue?"

"Why would I do anything like that?" She motioned toward where Annie was cradling her burnt hand in the other one. "I was out, so I stopped by to see what you two were up to. I heard the kettle screeching, then heard noise from the closet. I opened the door, and there you were." Her smile became sly. "Looking very comfortable together."

Shocked by her insinuation and worried that Becky Sue would carry the tale to Leanna and others, Annie said, "Comfortable was the last thing we were. Hearing the kettle, knowing the water was boiling away and the bakery could go up in flames doesn't make anyone *comfortable*."

The girl gave them a flippant shrug and then a wave before she left. As the door closed behind Becky Sue, Annie frowned. The teenager had said she was "out," but not where she'd been or where she was going or why. It was suspicious.

Saying the same to Caleb, Annie added, "She must have locked us in."

"I agree. I wish I had some idea why. My thought when I saw her on the other side of the door was she'd changed her mind about planning to use the time to slip away from Harmony Creek Hollow while we were shut in the closet."

"I've given up trying to figure out what she's thinking."

"I should, too." He gave Annie a smile that sent delight swirling through her middle again. "How about that cup of tea you had planned?"

There was so much Annie wanted to say about how his touch had thrilled her. So much she wanted to ask about whether or not he'd shared her feelings. Would he have kissed her if the door had remained shut a moment longer?

It was better, she told herself as she went to find tea bags, that she didn't know. Better for her matchmaking plans for her twin. Better for Caleb, who wouldn't be torn between them. Better for everything...except her aching heart.

Chapter Twelve

As Caleb's buggy reached the pair of stoplights at the very heart of the village, where Broadway and Main Street intersected, the light snow changed into a heavy fall. Caleb stopped for the red light. Going in the other direction, cars had slowed to a crawl, their windshield wipers fighting against the snow piling up on the glass. A couple of shopkeepers were already outside brushing snow off the stone steps leading up to their front doors. *Kinder* rushed along the sidewalk, hunched into their coats. Not even youngsters were excited any longer by snow after the hard winter.

"I remember when snow was fun and not something that gets in the way," Caleb said as he switched on the wiper on the front of his buggy.

"I still think snow is fun." Annie opened her door and ran her hand over the window to knock off the snow, so he could see any oncoming traffic to the left.

Thanking her, because they must take extra care that a car would be able to stop on the snow-covered road, he chuckled. "Why am I not surprised? You somehow always find something positive."

"Isn't that better than the alternative? Finding something depressing about every situation?"

"Are you saying I do that?"

She laughed, "No, but if the boot fits…"

"It doesn't fit well. Or, at least, I hope it doesn't."

When she chuckled again, he relaxed as he hadn't been able to since he'd picked her up at her house. She'd been as serious and quiet this morning as she'd been yesterday afternoon before they somehow got themselves locked into the closet…or were shut in with Becky Sue's help. It hadn't helped that Joey had launched into shrieks the moment Caleb walked into the Waglers' house. Annie had rushed him out so the others could calm the *boppli*, who wanted nothing to do with him.

Was he the only one the *boppli* reacted to like that? Annie, for once, had no suggestions other than to be patient. It was *gut* advice, but hard to follow when Caleb wanted to put the *kind* at ease.

Caleb turned the buggy north along Main Street toward the hardware store on the right side of the street. He'd hoped the snow would hold off until they got home from the long-postponed trip to get paint. Clouds covering the tops of the mountains had descended into the valley, bringing the storm with them. Already plowed snow blocked the wide parking lane beside the sidewalk, narrowing it until there was room for only a single car instead of the usual two.

He saw Annie's surprise and realized she'd expected

him to leave the buggy and horse by the hitching rail near the library.

Drawing in the reins to stop them closer to the hardware store, he said, "As fast as it's snowing, the plows will be out soon. Dusty will be safer here between cars than in the open where the spraying snow could strike him."

"I didn't think about that." She chuckled. "I thought that—for the first time ever—you were breaking the rules."

"I am. The village leaders have asked us to park the horses by the library or at the hitching rail in front of the grocery store."

"No, you're not breaking the rules. You're protecting Dusty."

"Isn't that the same thing?"

When he looked at her as the buggy rolled to a stop, he saw she was grinning and shaking her head. "Maybe for others. But for you, Caleb, breaking such rules is a big deal."

He decided the best answer was to laugh, so he did. As he got out and scaled the snowbank beside the buggy, he wondered what else she could discern about him. No other woman—or any man, to be truthful—had tried to look beyond the obvious to pick out the truth he kept close to his heart. Yet Annie had been able to do that almost from the moment they'd met. He recalled the questions she'd asked him when he came to talk to her family about the settlement he envisioned. Those questions had been insightful and demanded he be honest at the same time.

As he stepped onto the sidewalk that was littered

with snow, he realized her questions made him lower the barriers he kept up between the world and himself. And between his head and his heart, as if he didn't trust them to work together.

"Did you forget something?" Annie called as she climbed the steps to the hardware store's front door.

Shaking his head, and sending snow flying from the brim of his hat, Caleb hurried to catch up with her. He had to keep focused on making his dreams come true instead of daydreaming about Annie.

She led the way to where cans of paint flanked sample cards. The lighting in the hardware store wasn't strong, and shadows covered most of the displays of tools and equipment lining every wall. The long wooden counter at the rear of the store was deserted, but he knew Tuck, who owned the hardware store, would pop out when they were ready to buy something.

"What do you think?" she asked.

He stared at the array of colors. "I don't know where to begin."

She reached out and pulled a card with several shades of yellow on it. She tapped the middle one. "There's the color I was envisioning. You might want to look at it over by the window to see it better." She handed it to him.

For the very shortest possible moment, their fingertips touched. A spark as hot as if he'd grabbed a welding torch seared him. A buzzing sensation lingered as he fought not to fumble taking the card. His other hand rose toward her face, partially concealed by her black bonnet. He lowered it before he could give in to his longing to touch her as he had in the closet yesterday.

"You like this yellow?" he managed to ask, though his brain was urging him to step closer to her.

"It's bright and cheerful." She drew out another card. "Then there's this blue. It may go better with the wood on your display cases."

How could she sound so calm? He was sure he'd seen her pull back in shock, too. Then he noticed she was speaking at a rapid clip as she pulled out several more cards and outlined the pros and cons of each color. She wasn't as serene as she was trying to appear. Could she be drawn to him?

That was silly.

As she talked about painting sample patches on the wall and deciding which one was best after viewing several, he nodded, half listening. If Annie was interested in being more than his friend and employee, why had she asked him to take her sister to the mud sale instead of her? He must be missing something.

He wished he knew what.

Annie stepped back, being careful not to bump into the paint sample containers she'd put on the kitchen floor. Five large rectangles gleamed on the wall. Yellow, blue, green, tan and gray. She couldn't wait for them to dry so Caleb could choose which one he liked best.

She bent to screw on the gray sample's lid. She straightened with a gasp when the door opened, nearly hitting the container holding the yellow sample. Grabbing it, she jumped out of the way as Caleb rushed into the bakery.

She took one look at his face and asked, "What's wrong?"

"Becky Sue has disappeared!"

Staring at him, hoping she'd heard him wrong, she repeated, "Disappeared? Has she run away again?"

"It seems so." Pushing back his black hat that drooped toward his eyes with the melting snow on its brim, he said, "Miriam alerted me. Becky Sue stormed out when my sister insisted she help with some chores. Did she come here?"

"No." Annie sighed. At the Waglers' house, the tug-of-war between *Grossmammi* Inez and the girl had been growing more heated. She hadn't guessed that Becky Sue was being as obstinate with Miriam. "Did she go home...to our house?"

"No."

"Maybe she went into town."

"It would take her an hour on foot to go to Salem. She'd be foolish to make such a trip on a stormy day. Drivers wouldn't see her until they were almost upon her."

"Vanishing like this is already foolish." She whirled as the timer beeped. Rushing to the stove, she opened the door and pulled out the cookies. She didn't set the other tray inside to bake.

As she used the spatula to push the cookies onto the aluminum foil, she watched Caleb open the storage closet and look inside. He didn't doubt her assertion, she knew, but he had to see for himself that his cousin hadn't taken advantage of Annie's focus on her baking to slip past her.

"Do you think this has anything to do with where

she was the other day when we got locked in the closet? She said she was out, but didn't explain where she was going." She pulled off the pot holder and set it on the table beside the cookies.

He drew in a deep breath through clamped lips and then shook his head as he walked into the front room. "I don't have the slightest idea what that girl will do next."

"What about Joey?"

He bent and opened the trap door in the floor. Closing it, he answered, "She didn't take him."

Annie watched him stamp into the kitchen. "I don't believe Becky Sue has run away. She wouldn't leave him behind. Not when…"

He spun to face her. "Not when he's terrified of me."

"Caleb, this isn't the time for discussing the whims of a one-year-old. If your cousin has gone missing, something could be very wrong."

"Don't you think I know that?" He paced the kitchen, his boots striking the concrete floor as if he intended to drive his feet right through it. "Do you know who her friends are? Beyond our families, I mean."

"I don't think she has made any yet."

"There must be some clue to where she is."

Annie planted herself in front of him. When he started to go around her, she grasped his sleeves and forced him to halt before he dragged her off her feet. "Calm down, Caleb. We've got to think about this rationally."

"Even when she's not being logical?"

"It's more important *we* think clearly." She looked at the falling snow. "We need help. We might not be able to find her on our own."

The wild light dimmed in his eyes as he nodded. "*Danki*, Annie, for your *gut* sense." He shifted his arms so he could grip hers. "Wait here while I get help."

"No!" She reached for her coat.

"It's so cold, Annie, and I don't have my regular buggy."

"Where's your...?" She answered her own question. "Becky Sue took it, ain't so?"

"It's gone. She's gone. You do the math." He sighed. "You'd be better off staying inside."

"I'm going to get cold when I walk home, so what does it matter if I get cold now? We have to find Becky Sue before something happens to her."

He was torn. She could see that. He didn't want to miss a minute of them working on the bakery, but he was worried sick about his young cousin.

At last, he nodded and motioned for her to lead the way outside. She paused long enough to check that the stove and oven were off, then pulled on her coat and bonnet. She threw her shawl around her shoulders and took a deep breath before heading out with him into the storm.

She regretted her insistence the moment she stepped outside and the howling wind tried to suck her breath right out of her mouth. Why had Becky Sue chosen such a horrible day to disappear? Closing her lips, Annie bent her head and pressed forward into the storm's unrelenting wall. She climbed into the buggy on one side while Caleb jumped in from the other. A single glance from him told her what she already knew.

If they didn't find Becky Sue soon, it might be too late.

* * *

Two hours later, half-frozen and wondering if he'd ever get feeling back in his hands, Caleb turned the open buggy toward the bakery. The storm was getting worse, and he couldn't risk a hit-or-miss search any longer. He'd alerted his neighbors, but none had seen the girl.

"Where are we headed?" Annie asked as she huddled beneath the trio of blankets they'd piled on top of themselves.

"To the bakery."

"To call the police?"

He was no longer surprised their minds worked in tandem. "I don't have any other choice. I don't want to delay any longer, and it's going to take longer to get back because of the snow."

"That isn't snow. It's ice." She whipped her scarf off and half turned to wrap the bright blue scarf around him. Looping a finger beneath the top edge, she pulled it up enough to cover the bottom half of his face. "Does that help?"

His voice was muffled as he replied, "Me, but you don't have any protection against the storm."

"I do." She raised her shawl up over her bonnet and held it closed in front of her nose.

He was about to argue, then noticed how tight the stitches were in the thick wool shawl that reached almost to her knees. The wind would have to blow harder to drive the icy pellets past them.

"Did Leanna make your shawl?" he asked, to keep the conversation going. For some reason, it didn't feel as cold when they talked.

"No, I did."

"I didn't think you liked handicrafts."

"I don't like quilting, but I love to knit." Her laugh was muffled. "Last Christmas, I made scarves for everyone in the family. The *kinder* got ones with images of goats and ducks knit into them."

"They must have liked them."

"Rhoda says she doesn't have to insist on the *kinder* wearing their scarves when they go to school. They love wearing them."

He chuckled. "Sounds as if they were a great success. Maybe you should think of putting some out for sale at the bakery."

Her voice dropped to a near whisper. "I don't know if that's a *gut* idea."

"Why not?" He wondered why she always acted shy and withdrawn when he made a suggestion that would bring her more attention. "You've been talking about displaying Leanna's quilts. I think adding your scarves to the bakery's wares would add the color and interest to the space like you're always talking about." When she didn't reply, he kept his sigh silent. "Think about it. Okay?"

"Okay."

Why was she being so grudging? She'd offered him one idea after another, almost every one *gut*, and he was certain his customers would be interested in her hand-knit scarves.

When Annie remained silent, he put his arm around her shoulders and drew her closer so they could use each other's warmth to battle the wind. He was relieved to feel her shiver, because that meant she wasn't being overtaken by the cold yet. She was, he'd learned, far stronger than she looked.

Even so, she let him help her out when they got to the bakery. He left Dusty in a leeward spot, not wanting to unhitch the horse until he was sure when or if he'd be leaving the bakery tonight.

Keeping his arm around Annie, he lurched with her through the wind and into the bakery. They stopped inside the door, and Caleb reveled in taking a breath that wasn't snatched away by the storm.

He went to the phone and called 911. When someone picked up, it didn't take long to explain the situation. He was told the sheriff's department would send a deputy to the bakery as soon as possible.

"It may take a little longer than usual," the female dispatcher said. "Lots of accidents with the storm." She confirmed the bakery's address before hanging up.

Putting down the phone, he said, "Now we wait."

"The thing we hate most."

"Ja." There was nothing else he could say. She knew as well as he did how dangerous the weather was if Becky Sue hadn't been prepared for the storm.

Annie made hot chocolate while Caleb tested the fancy *kaffi* machine that he'd found in one of the crates delivered from the Summerhayses' house. He kept asking for her help to figure out the many buttons and attachments. She did her best to assist because she was grateful for anything to keep busy while they waited for the deputy to arrive. The ticking of the wall clock was a constant reminder of each passing minute. She kept listening for a vehicle to pull into the parking lot.

Even so, she recoiled when a heavy knock sounded on the front door. She went into the main room as Caleb hurried to answer the door. A man in a sheriff's department uniform stood on the other side.

The deputy sheriff thanked Caleb as he came inside. He wasn't as tall as Caleb, but his shaved head and grim expression warned he was all business. After a quick scan of the space, he introduced himself as Rick Flanagan. He nodded when Caleb gave him his name and hers. An offer of something warm to drink was waved aside by the deputy, and he got down to gathering information on why they'd called the sheriff's office.

The two men couldn't appear more different. Deputy Flanagan wore a uniform with a gun in a holster along with a myriad of other gadgets, and a radio and a camera hooked to his shoulder. Caleb's simple white shirt and black suspenders attached to his broadfall trousers announced he was a plain man who eschewed any sort of violence.

Yet both spoke with the same calm determination to resolve the problem. She wished she could be like them, but her heart was pounding as if trying to break out of her chest.

Could they find Becky Sue in time?

In silence, she watched. Deputy Flanagan listened to Caleb. The deputy nodded and wrote in a small notebook until Caleb said, "And that's all we know."

"A girl who's run away once will run again, I'm sorry to say. Miss Wagler, do you have anything to add?"

"No, sir. Other than I'm worried that she didn't run away."

"You believe someone may have forced her to go?"

"I can't believe she would leave her son behind if she'd had a choice."

The deputy nodded, but his face remained as free of emotion as the wall behind him. "You may have to make an official statement to that fact when we find her. Running away is very different from abandoning a child."

"She wouldn't do that," Annie asserted.

Deputy Flanagan unbent enough to give her a commiserating smile. "More kids who do stupid things need advocates like you in their corner. Let's find her and then we'll see what can be done to help her and her little boy." He flipped his notebook closed and stored it beneath his dark coat. "I know you plain folks don't keep photographs of each other, so I won't ask you for one. We'll go with the description you gave us."

Collecting their personal contact information, including the phone number for the bakery and when Caleb expected to be working there and when he'd be at his farm, Deputy Flanagan gave them each a card with his direct number on it.

"Don't hesitate to call," he said.

Caleb walked him to the door. After the deputy left, he turned off the *kaffi* machine.

Annie finished her hot chocolate and washed out the cup, looking over her shoulder when Caleb said, "It's beginning to snow harder, so we should get home."

"I wish there was more we could do," Annie said.

"We can pray for her safety. If we can't help, God can."

"I've already been doing that."

"Me, too." He smiled sadly. "I know this is upsetting for you, Annie, because it is for me. However, no matter how much we want to help, leaving Becky Sue in God's hands may be the best thing we can do."

"God and the sheriff's department."

"They work as part of His plan, too." He plucked her coat and black shawl off the peg and handed them to her. "Bundle up. If anything, it's got colder out."

"Impossible."

"I wish you were right."

She slipped her arms into her coat and hooked it closed before pulling the thick shawl over her shoulders.

"Do you think she knows that her parents don't want her to come home?" she asked as she watched him button his coat.

"She's a smart girl. She has to know about their disapproval." He gave an inelegant snort. "That's probably why she left."

"Will you insist she returns there after she's found?"

"It's my duty to see she's taken care of."

"And she's doing fine right here. Let's leave things the way they are until we've sorted out her story."

He shocked her by pulling her close and leaning his head against the top of her bonnet. She stiffened in astonishment, then softened against his firm chest as he murmured, "*Danki*, Annie. I don't know how I would have dealt with Becky Sue and Joey without you."

"You would have found a way. Caleb Hartz solves

every problem." She tilted her head to look at him as she grinned. "Isn't that what everyone says?"

"If they did, they were wrong, because I couldn't have managed any of this without your help."

And my family's, she should have added, but she leaned her cheek on his chest again, savoring the moment that would never come again if her twin started walking out with him after the mud sale.

Chapter Thirteen

The wind eased as Caleb turned the buggy onto the twisting road that followed Harmony Creek because trees lined the road along the farm fences. The cold deepened more. He peered through the falling snow. He hadn't expected so many storms this late in the winter. Last winter had been rough, but had begun easing before the middle of March.

"Caleb! Look!"

At Annie's call, he shook himself out of his lethargy. Had he been surrendering to the cold? A fearsome thought.

Caleb peered through the thick snow in the direction she pointed. At his house, he realized. No, not the house. The driveway.

A gray-topped buggy was parked there. His buggy, he realized, when he saw the shelves stacked in the back seat. He'd planned to take them to the bakery until Becky Sue and the buggy vanished.

Turning into his drive, he didn't wait for the open

buggy to stop before he jumped out. He raced through the fallen snow to his door.

He threw it open and stared at his young cousin, who was peeling an apple.

"Becky Sue, what are you doing here?"

"You said I could come here anytime I wanted," she replied, then waved as Annie came into the kitchen. "Hi, Annie! *Gut* to see you."

Caleb frowned. "But where have you been, Becky Sue? We've been looking everywhere for you."

"You were looking for me?" She kept her eyes on her task as she cut up the apple and dropped the slices onto others in a pie pan. "Why would you do that?"

"Because nobody knew where you were."

"You didn't?" She reached for a stick of butter and began to cut small slabs to put on top of the apples.

Annie stepped forward, pulling off her shawl. She dropped it on a chair. "You said you'd never leave without letting me or someone else know where you were going. You agreed to that, Becky Sue."

"I know, but we were talking about when I leave Harmony Creek."

He winced. How callously the girl spoke of walking away from the Waglers, who had welcomed her into their house and into their hearts!

"I thought," Annie said in a measured voice, "that you might have left Harmony Creek today."

"Without my son?"

"*Ja.*"

Annie's terse answer had startled his cousin. Enough to stop her from acting as if everything that had happened was nothing more than an inadvertent misunderstanding?

"I wouldn't leave my son like that," Becky Sue said. "I love him."

"We know you do," Caleb replied with care. "Anyone who sees the two of you together knows that you belong together."

His cousin made a soft sound. A gulp? A gasp? A smothered sob? He couldn't tell as she put the top crust on the pie.

"I left you a note on the table in the living room at your house, Annie." At last, Becky Sue looked at them. "Right by the books Leanna is always reading."

"But Leanna was at her job, and I was at the bakery."

"Oh," Becky Sue said with a flippant shrug. "I guess that's why you didn't see it. I thought you were home when I went out."

"Out where?" He regretted the question before Annie put a cautionary hand on his arm. The minute the words came out of his mouth, Becky Sue's face grew stony.

"We've been worried about you," Annie said. "If we sound angry, it's because we were scared you'd got lost in the storm."

"I know to stay in on a bad day like this." The girl waved the knife she was using to slice openings in the top crust. "I mean, I came over here, but it can't be a half mile from your house to here, Annie." Lowering the knife to the counter, she sighed. "Okay, I came over here to make a couple pies for you, Caleb. I thought if you sampled what I can bake, you might hire me to work in your bakery, too."

He hoped he was able to hide his shock. The last thing he wanted in his bakery was a recalcitrant teenager who seldom thought of anything but herself.

Again Annie saved him from saying something he'd regret. "Becky Sue, I'm sure once Caleb's bakery is the success it's going to be, he'll be looking to hire several more people. How wise of you to look toward the future like that!"

If there was sarcasm behind her comment, he didn't hear it. Neither did the girl, because she smiled and carried the pie to the oven.

He left the two in his house as he went to the phone shack between his house and Jeremiah's. A quick call to Deputy Flanagan put a halt to the search for Becky Sue. Yet Caleb remained bothered by something he couldn't explain.

After he'd dropped Annie off at her house and he was on his way home, Caleb realized what had been nettling him. If his cousin had left a note on the living room table by the books, one of the Waglers would have seen it. He couldn't imagine *Grossmammi* Inez's eagle eyes not picking up on something as unusual as a note left on a table in the living room.

Becky Sue had been lying...again.

Annie followed Caleb into the bakery the next morning. He'd told her on the ride from her house that he'd checked out the colors she'd painted on the wall, and he thought her idea of yellow would be the best. She listened to his comments, knowing he didn't want to talk about Becky Sue and what had happened yesterday. Like her, he didn't believe a note had been left at her house. There hadn't been any sign of it last night, and Becky Sue's excuse was that the *boppli* or the puppy might have taken it.

Caleb groaned as he halted right in front of her.

She squeezed past him and stared at the front room in shock. Paint was splattered over every surface and flowed across the floor, mixing together in puddles in the scraped boards. The whole space looked as if a rainbow had exploded in it.

"What happened?" he asked, shock straining his voice.

As if in answer to his question, Joey began to shriek from the other side of the display case.

Annie ran around the case to where the little boy stood. He held two paintbrushes, one in each hand. They dragged on the floor, adding another layer of paint to the worn wood. Blue and yellow were speckled across his clothing and in his hair.

She waved Caleb away, and he stepped into the kitchen. Once he was out of sight, the little boy's tears vanished. When she knelt beside him, Joey reached out to pat her face. He began to grin, his six teeth, including the new ones, visible.

"Jo-Jo. Pretty."

Annie picked up the *boppli* and stood before he could do more damage. She took the paintbrushes from him. When he started to screw up his face again to protest, she said, "It's very, very pretty, Joey, but it's finished."

"Fin-ish?"

She used the word he did at the end of every meal. "Done. You did a *gut* job."

That was the truth, she had to acknowledge. There weren't many surfaces he hadn't painted. The glass in the display case was covered with streaks of yellow, blue and green from the small sample bottles they'd got from the hardware store, and the front door had those colors as well as red—where had that paint come from?—which were marked on it with tiny fingerprints.

Puddles of paint marked any lower area in the floor. More paint oozed in slow streams around higher ridges in the wood, creating a crazy-quilt pattern.

She was relieved to see that the big window hadn't been splashed, but there was a spot of red on the ceiling near the door. How had the toddler managed to get paint up there?

Looking at the kitchen, she said nothing as she watched Caleb take in what one small boy had done in such a short time. It couldn't have taken him long because Becky Sue was an attentive *mamm*, keeping a close eye on her son.

At that thought, Annie asked, "Where's your *mamm*?"

The bathroom door opened and Becky Sue emerged. She stared around herself in disbelief. "Joey did this?"

Annie frowned. Was it possible for a single one-year-old *boppli* to make such a mess so quickly? She bit back her question as tears welled up in Becky's eyes.

"Oh, Caleb," the girl cried. "I'm sorry. I left him alone for just a moment while I was in the bathroom. I never guessed he could do this! I'll clean it up."

"No, get him out of here."

Her face crumbled. "Caleb, I'm so, so sorry. Please don't be angry."

"I'm not, but you need to get out of here."

Tears rolled down her cheeks. "We shouldn't have come to Harmony Creek Hollow. We've caused you nothing but trouble. I hope you can forgive me. You've got to forgive Joey."

"Becky Sue, you're misunderstanding me." His voice softened as he put a hand on his cousin's shoulder. "I don't want you to leave the settlement. I want you to get Joey out of the bakery because I don't know how old that red paint is. It might have lead in it. A little one shouldn't be near that stuff." He gave her a gentle smile. "There's nothing to forgive. As my teacher used to say, boys will be boys and nothing on God's green earth will ever change that."

Annie's heart swelled at how kind he was to the distraught girl. She hurried to add, "Don't worry, Becky Sue. Caleb and I will take care of this." She held out the little boy, making sure he didn't face his cousin and start crying again.

Taking him, Becky Sue said, "But it'll take you hours to clean this up."

"Which is why we must get started."

The girl nodded, gathered her son to her and, holding his face against his shoulder so he didn't see Caleb, hurried to get them into their coats and out of the bakery.

As soon as they were gone, Annie carried the paintbrushes to the bathroom so she could rinse them out in the old sink. Caleb called after her, and she halted.

"I couldn't hear everything she said from the kitchen," he said. "Did she explain why she was here?"

"No." She looked at the back door. "What do you think she's up to?"

Caleb found the top for the yellow paint container and twisted it on. Setting it on top of the green jar, he said, "I can't begin to guess what goes on in Becky Sue's head." He glanced around the mess the *boppli* had made. "To think I took so long making up my mind about what colors I wanted in my bakery."

A laugh burst out of Annie. She clamped her hand over her mouth, but whimsy continued to spark in her eyes. After putting the brushes in a cup in the sink and running water in it, she said, "I'm sorry, Caleb. I know it isn't funny."

"You're right. It isn't funny." He bent and ran his finger through a blob of yellow paint. "But this is." He tapped the end of her pert nose with his fingertip.

She yelped. "What did you do that for?"

"So your face matches your apron."

Looking at the splotches of color on her black apron, she laughed. She got a cloth and cleaned her nose. "You know, Caleb, the walls can be repainted, but..."

"But what?"

"What do you think of leaving the floor as it is? It looks so cheerful."

He had to agree. "But too fancy for a bakery run by plain folks. I doubt our leaders would think it's appropriate."

"You could ask Eli and Jeremiah." She got another clean rag and began to wipe the paint from the glass display case. "There's nothing in our *Ordnung* about a painted floor in a retail shop."

"True."

"And you can tell them that the design was Joey's idea."

"*A little child shall lead them*, it says in Isaiah, though that's not the intention of the verse."

"Why not?" She chuckled. "If we leave his fingerprints right next to the splatters, it'll be clear to everyone that youthful enthusiasm created this. Who knows? People may come from far and wide to take a look at your floor."

"I'd rather have them come for the baked goods."

"They'll come *back* for those." Rinsing out the cloth in the sink, she patted his arm as she walked past him to get a bucket from the kitchen. "You worry too much, Caleb. Trust God will see you through."

"I do trust God, but He has left the details to me."

"You worry too much," she repeated. "You should try to enjoy watching your dream come true."

Her words stung. Not because they weren't true, because her advice was sound. However, her words reminded him of Verba and her constant harping that he should be different from what he was. He hadn't guessed that Verba's meddling would still bother him, but it did. It took all his strength to submerge those feelings and not lash out with serrated words, because it wasn't Annie's fault he couldn't get over what Verba had done. Until he could, he must not consider walking out with any other woman.

Not even, he thought as he watched Annie fill the bucket in the kitchen sink, this one.

* * *

Why couldn't she guard her tongue and halt it from wagging before she had a chance to think?

Annie dumped yet another bucket of paint-filled water into the kitchen sink, being careful not to splash the dirty water onto the counter and cabinets. Her fingers clenched on its plastic side. How could she lecture Caleb, who was a man of great faith? So many people had hoped he would marry before the men in their settlement were ordained, because they'd hoped that he would go from their community leader to their spiritual leader. His ability to listen to both sides and find common ground was admired. By the *Leit* and *Englischers*, according to what she'd heard his fellow volunteer firemen say.

She tried to engage him in conversation while they worked to clean the cases, the ceiling and the walls. Every attempt failed. He'd respond with a few words, then go quiet. As the morning passed, she wondered if he'd said more than a dozen complete sentences to her.

When, a couple of hours after midday, Caleb said that they should return in the morning and start the repainting then, she was relieved. She rinsed out the cloths and bucket she'd used, as well as the paintbrushes Joey had. She hadn't seen where Caleb had put the paint containers. She guessed they were somewhere out of reach of the little boy.

How had Joey managed to open the containers? She was plagued by the niggling thought that he hadn't managed it on his own, but she couldn't guess why Becky Sue would help her son make such a mess.

Annie wished she and Caleb could discuss it, but

he'd raised a high wall between them with his curt answers and silences. She finished cleaning up before pulling on her coat and other outerwear.

The ride to her house was as uncomfortable as the work at the shop. When she got out of the buggy, she thanked Caleb as she did each day and told him she'd see him tomorrow. He nodded and turned the buggy toward the road.

Shouts rang through the air. Happy shouts. She glanced toward the far end of the hollow. It sounded like teenagers having a *gut* time. With a sigh, she walked toward the house.

Squealing tires and a scream vanished beneath a crash that reverberated through the winter afternoon. The huge snowbanks couldn't muffle it.

Annie whirled. A buggy was crumpled against a tree. Caleb's? No, he'd been going in the other direction. She ran toward it.

The cold lashed at her. She paid it no mind. She heard shouts from the barn behind her, but didn't slow as she ran out onto the road.

A car appeared over a hill, racing in her direction. She scrambled toward a snowbank. The car skidded right in front of her. She tumbled forward and stared at its out-of-control bumper coming toward her.

Hands grasped her arms. She was yanked up the bank and away from the car. Snow spurted from beneath the tires, pelting her. She heard a deep grunt and knew the icy shards had also struck the person who'd pulled her out of the way. They collapsed together into the softer snow on the far side of the snowbank.

"Are you hurt?" she heard from beside her.

Caleb!

She glanced toward the drive where his buggy stood just down the road, safe.

Caleb had pulled her away from the car. He'd saved her from injury, possibly from being killed.

She longed to throw her arms around him and press her face to his chest while she thanked him over and over for saving her life. She couldn't. For so many, many reasons, but the most important was that Lyndon and Juanita were hurrying at their best possible speed through the snow toward them.

"I'm fine." *Thanks to you.* She was surprised how the idea of saying those words made her feel so shy. "How are you?"

"I'm okay, Annie."

"What happened?" shouted Lyndon.

As one, she and Caleb stood and looked in the direction the shouts had come from.

Annie didn't wait to answer her brother's question. She slid over the snowbank and down to the road. Racing along it, she reached the broken buggy. The horse was being cut loose by a teenage boy, and the mare pressed against the snow as it raced past her, panicked but unhurt.

Two more boys were standing behind the buggy. They were staring at the snow. Not by the buggy, but by a tree several feet beyond it.

She gasped when she saw another boy lying in the snow next to the tree. She recognized the groan she'd heard too often when her younger brother didn't want to do chores.

Running up to him, she pushed past the boys. "Kenny, are you okay?"

"Ja." The word, spoken through his cracked and bleeding lips, wasn't reassuring, but he pushed himself to his feet. He winced when he bent to pick up what she realized were broken skis. Limping, he hobbled to where Caleb had reached the boys by the ruined buggy.

The boys let out a worried yell when Kenny's knees folded beneath him and he fell, face-first, into the snow.

Rolling Kenny onto his back, Caleb motioned the rest of them to stand aside. He swept snow off her brother's face before running his hands along Kenny's arms and legs, then his torso. Though unconscious, Kenny winced when Caleb touched his left side.

"I'd say he's cracked a rib or two." Caleb motioned to the boys. "Go to the nearest phone and call 911. Tell them to send an ambulance."

"Go!" Annie ordered when the boys seemed unable to move.

They rushed away.

Not wanting to leave Kenny in the snow and risk hypothermia, Caleb and Lyndon tore the seat out of the buggy and slid it beneath the boy. Annie dug in the broken buggy and found a blanket, which she draped over him, then she watched as they carried Kenny to the house.

The next two hours were a blur as the rescue squad came and the two EMTs checked over Kenny, who'd regained his senses by the time he was inside the house. The EMTs agreed with Caleb's diagnosis and suggested taking Kenny for X-rays. However, *Grossmammi* Inez decided that, because the emergency room was more than thirty miles away, it wasn't worth putting him through the uncomfortable ride on roads filled with potholes. They wrapped his ribs and suggested Kenny see the local *doktor* tomorrow.

One of the EMTs let Annie use his cell phone to make the appointment before they packed up their supplies and left, each with a bag of chocolate chip cookies and a jar of chowchow. Becky Sue had put together the food while everyone else hovered around Kenny's room.

The teen asked if she could see how he was doing, and Annie said, "You're going to have to wait. He's sleeping, but when he wakes he'll be bored. Maybe you can take Joey in and spend some time with him."

"Joey likes your brother."

"And my brother likes him." She smiled. "I think he's glad for once not to be the youngest guy around the house."

Becky Sue chuckled. "I'll put together some blocks and books for Joey. That way they can entertain each other."

"And give you some time to catch up on the mending you need to do."

The girl's nose wrinkled in disgust. "I hate mending."

"Me, too," she said, copying Becky Sue's expression.

Again the girl laughed, and Annie suspected she was seeing a bit of the person Becky Sue would have been if she didn't hide her true self among so many secrets.

Coming down the stairs, Annie saw Caleb pacing in

the kitchen. He'd remained there after bringing Kenny in, not wanting to upset Joey.

"Kenny is going to be fine," she said before he could ask. "*Danki* for helping."

He ignored her gratitude as she'd known he would. "Did he mention what happened?"

"They were buggy skiing." She shook her head in amazement. "One of the boys spent some time on the internet at the library and saw other plain kids skiing behind a buggy. They thought it would be fun, and I'm sure it was."

"Until a car came speeding along the road. Most likely, more kids out for what they considered fun."

"The driving is becoming more reckless. They're drag racing before it gets dark."

He sighed and reached for his hat. "We're going to have to talk with the sheriff's office again. Not that it'll do much *gut*. They'll patrol for a few weeks, and the kids will lie low. As soon as the patrols ease off, the drag racing begins again."

"It's all we can do. The rest is in God's hands."

"You have such a solid faith," he said with a smile.

"Some days. Others it's as wobbly as Kenny on his skis." She came around the table. "That's why we call it faith, ain't so? Because we have to depend on it no matter how sure we feel about anything."

"Are you okay?"

"I'm fine." She held up a finger. "And before you ask, everyone else is, too. Leanna is keeping a close eye on our *grossmammi*, and Becky Sue is going to sit with Kenny when he wakes up."

"The two of them alone?"

She laughed, "You sound like a suspicious *daed*, Caleb. Don't worry. To Kenny, your cousin is a much older woman. He's twelve, and the only females he's interested in spending time with are the calves he hopes to raise to add to our dairy herd." Her voice softened. "Don't look for trouble where there isn't any."

"You're right."

When he closed the distance between them with a couple of long steps, she knew she should back away, find an excuse to head upstairs before...

Before what?

Before he reached out to her, or before she stepped forward and drew his arms around herself? She yearned to feel the strength that had hefted her brother and carried him through the snow to their house. How much joy would there have been in that powerful, yet gentle, embrace?

The answers weren't for her to find. Leanna was the one who should be in his arms, not her. Pain rushed through her, so potent that a gasp slipped past her lips. When Caleb asked her what was wrong, she shook her head.

Was *this* what Leanna had been feeling since Gabriel Miller abandoned her to marry someone else?

No, that must be worse, because Leanna had been in love with Gabriel. What Annie felt for Caleb was... She didn't know, but she was certain of one thing. She would do whatever she could so her sister didn't have to feel such sorrow again.

Stepping away from him before she could no longer resist the invitation in his eyes, she bade him a *gut nacht* in a strangled voice.

"Annie, what's wrong?" he asked again.

She wouldn't lie and tell him that everything was fine. But she couldn't speak of the tempest within her, a storm pulling her this way and that like a maniacal tornado.

"Gut nacht," she said again.

He took the hint and left.

She sank to sit at the table, her face in her hands. How much longer could she bear being torn apart by her longings, which were in opposition to one another? She had to bring this to an end.

But how? Next week, Leanna would be spending the whole day with Caleb, and Annie would be as lost as she'd ever been. Because she couldn't pretend to herself any longer. She might not be joining her sister and Caleb, but her heart would be because somewhere, sometime, when she hadn't realized it, she'd given it to him.

Chapter Fourteen

Annie smiled when her twin sister came into the kitchen the morning of the mud sale. Breakfast wasn't ready yet. She'd been serving it later the past week. Until Kenny's ribs healed, he couldn't help in the barn. Lyndon was doing the milking alone, and he had twice as many cows as most plain farmers did. Other farmers and their *kinder* who were old enough to help came when they could. Leanna had pitched in, but not today when she didn't want to go to the mud sale smelling of animals and hay.

"Gute mariye," Leanna said. She couldn't hide her excitement about the day ahead. No wonder. Not only was she going to the Salem Volunteer Department's first ever mud sale—something that the firefighters already hoped would become an annual event—but she was going to spend the day with Caleb.

Though Annie wanted to thank God for offering her twin sister the chance to have time with a man she was attracted to, the words wouldn't come. She hoped her envy was hidden.

"You look lovely." Annie brushed a bit of lint from her sister's dark cranberry-colored sleeve. She wondered when Leanna had managed to make a new dress as well as finish up the quilt she'd donated.

"For a mud sale?" Leanna laughed. "They didn't get their name because we're expected to dress in our best."

"Then maybe I should have said you look as if you're anticipating having a great day."

"I hope for Caleb's sake—and for the sake of the firefighters—that it's going to be a great day. From what you and Lyndon have said, they've been working hard to make it the best mud sale ever."

"That's why Caleb's been exhausted the past week. Working on the mud sale and his farm and the bakery."

"That's opening soon, ain't so?"

"The first week of May."

Leanna plucked her bonnet off its peg. "So you'll be trading your paintbrush for cookie cutters."

"I don't know how much baking I'll be doing."

Caleb hadn't said, and she hadn't asked. Becky Sue had come to the bakery a few days ago and had prepared several more pies and batches of cookies to show him what she could do. The teen was an excellent baker, and though Caleb had said nothing, Annie suspected his cousin would be working at least part-time in the kitchen once the bakery opened its doors.

That would be for the best, she'd told herself over and over. With Becky Sue present, she and Caleb wouldn't be alone as they'd been for the past few weeks. The timing was perfect if he and Leanna started walking out after their day together. God knew what He was doing.

Oh, if only she did.

"Caleb's buggy's coming up the drive," Leanna said, breaking into Annie's thoughts as she opened the door. "I'll see you there."

"I hope so."

Leanna frowned. "I shouldn't go with Caleb. He'll understand."

"Go ahead. *Grossmammi* Inez seems to be in *gut* spirits and was breathing better yesterday. Maybe she's right, and her symptoms are just left over from her cold." Annie longed to believe that, but feared there was something else wrong with her *grossmammi*. "I don't want you to miss the quilt auction."

"Our *grossmammi* is more important than seeing who buys my quilt."

Annie made shooing motions. "Go! You don't want to make Caleb late."

Blowing her sister a kiss, Leanna rushed out the door.

As the door closed, Annie's smile fell away. She bit her lower lip, refusing to let the tears burning her eyes fall. Wasn't this what she'd been working for? Leanna had been smiling as she left. Annie hadn't seen her sister look so happy since the news of Gabriel's marriage.

"You should have gone with them" came her *grossmammi*'s voice from behind her.

Annie spun to assist *Grossmammi* Inez to the table. "I didn't realize you were up already."

"I've been awake for a couple of hours." She looked past Annie toward where a buggy was visible through the windows that gave a view of the road. "I hope you are sure of what you are doing."

"Doing?"

"Matchmaking." She sat at the table. "Be careful about matchmaking for your sister and Caleb. Your own heart is too involved, and it may keep you from seeing what's right in front of you."

"I know." Annie sat facing her *grossmammi*. "But if there's a chance Leanna will be happy again—"

"That is God's choice and hers."

At *Grossmammi* Inez's tone, Annie didn't argue further. What could she say? She was on a treacherous path, a path that might not be the one God had for her or for her sister, but she didn't know how to step off.

Annie smiled at Joey, who sat in the middle of the kitchen floor. When he dropped to his belly to crawl to a block that had fallen off the pile he was gathering, she tried not to laugh while he groped to grab it and pull it to where his toes touched the other blocks.

"You're a cute little worm," she said as she finished drying the last of the dishes from breakfast.

He looked at her with his grin that showed several more teeth that had popped up during the past week. After days of misery, he was content again. But he had sniffles, and Becky Sue hadn't wanted him to go to the mud sale. The teenager had been thrilled when Annie volunteered to stay home with the *boppli* while she joined the rest of the Waglers—including Kenny, who promised to sit quietly—at the mud sale.

Grossmammi Inez had aimed a knowing glance at Annie when she left with the others. The older woman thought that Annie was hiding at home so she didn't have to see her twin with Caleb. Again, it was something Annie couldn't argue with because it was the truth.

But spending time with the *boppli* had been delightful. Every time she looked at him she thought of how adorable he'd looked while covered with paint at the bakery. He was a *gut* little boy, willing to entertain himself. If only he didn't panic when he saw Caleb... Joey went to her brother and to Jeremiah and to Eli and to the Kuhns brothers. The list went on and on.

A pair of blocks tumbled away. Again Joey stretched out, keeping his foot on the pile while he reached for a block. He swept his hands along the floor, missing the other block.

Annie gasped as she watched the *boppli* reaching as far as he could, again running his hand along the floor. But he misjudged, and he missed the block a second time. Frustrated, he cradled the block he'd found.

Was it possible that the little boy couldn't see well? She thought of the times he'd touched her face as if confirming what his eyes failed to show him.

Tiptoeing around the *kind*, she picked up a ball with a bell in it. She kept it silent and knelt an arm's length away. She held up the ball to his left and rang it.

Joey's head swiveled toward it. To his right, she rocked his favorite blue bear. He didn't look at it. She shifted the bell to his right side and shook it again. His head shifted, but he didn't reach for his beloved bear though it was about eighteen inches from his face.

She moved it closer. When it was about two inches from his face, Joey chortled. "Bear-bear." He grabbed for it with such excitement she knew he hadn't seen it until then.

Annie handed him the bear and let her hands fall to her lap. She watched as he pressed his nose to it and repeated its name as he did each time one of them picked him up.

Her head spun. The little boy couldn't see past the end of his nose. That explained why he preferred to pull himself along on his belly than get up on his hands and knees or walk. So close to the floor, he was able to perceive what was right in front of him.

Was there a way for a *doktor* to test his ability to see? If it were possible, were there glasses small enough for a *boppli*?

But it wasn't her decision to make. She must talk to Becky Sue before she did anything. She hoped that this time the girl would listen to *gut* sense.

Again she gasped as she realized something else. None of the men Joey went to had hair as light as Caleb's. Was the *kind* confusing Caleb for someone else? She wrapped her arms around herself as she wondered if that other person was the reason Becky Sue had run away.

Annie must talk to Caleb and get his insight on how best to break the news to his cousin. None of this was going to be easy, but this was one secret they couldn't keep. Joey had to have help, and she guessed Becky Sue did, too.

Caleb took an appreciative bite of his second hot dog. There was almost as much relish as meat in the roll, and he savored it. Leanna sat beside him near one of the propane torches that fought back the cold outside the auction tent. She ate her hamburger much more delicately than he was wolfing down his lunch.

"How's your burger?" he asked.

"It's *gut*. I can tell you like hot dogs."

"Pretty obvious, ain't so?" He was pleased that she was beginning to get more comfortable with him. For the first hour, while they sat in the bleachers under the big white tent behind the fire station, she hadn't said a word.

He'd thought she'd voice her opinion of some of the animals being auctioned off, but she hadn't spoken. She'd watched as each lot was sold, though she'd leaned forward when two lots of goats came under the hammer.

The mud sale was going well, as far as he could see. There was a single auctioneer at a time instead of the usual two or three he'd seen at the mud sales in Lancaster County, where there were many more donations after years of the events. But the firefighters were pleased with the amount of goods they'd received and how much money was being raised. Several lots had been sold for more than they were worth, which meant there were many generous souls in the crowd that was bigger than Caleb had hoped because the temperature seemed more like mid-January than early April.

Leanna's intricate nine-square quilt, in shades of cranberry, green and off-white, had sold for almost two thousand dollars because a pair of *Englisch* women had pushed the price higher and higher until one gave up. As soon as the next item came up for bid, the loser sought out Leanna and asked if she could hire Leanna to make her a similar quilt. Leanna had agreed to do so for the price of the materials and a donation to the fire department of the same amount as the other woman had paid.

"That was generous of you to agree to make the second quilt," Caleb said, hoping to keep the conversation going. How could it be so easy to talk with Annie while it felt as if he had to wrest every word out of Leanna?

"I'm honored to be able to help the fire department." Leanna took another bite of her burger and dabbed her napkin at the ketchup clinging to her lips.

Caleb watched her motions. How could her mouth be so like her twin sister's, but he wasn't tempted to taste it as he was Annie's?

When she caught him staring at her, he rushed to say, "You know Chief Pulaski is going to hope you'll donate another quilt next year."

"I plan to. I enjoy putting the pieces together. There's something about a quilt pattern that brings sense to an otherwise chaotic world." She flushed as if she'd revealed too much. "Sorry. You don't want to hear about my quilting."

"Nonsense. I understand how you feel. Being in the kitchen gives me the same feeling of peace."

She smiled at last. "You do understand. I'm glad." She paused, then asked, "My sister talked you into bringing me here today, ain't so?"

"Why do you say that?"

"Because I know my sister better than I know anyone else in the world." Leanna's gentle laugh told him she wasn't upset by Annie's matchmaking. "I've seen how she looks at me when she thinks I don't see. She's determined to make me happy, no matter what."

"And you're not happy being here today?"

"I'm having a *wunderbaar* time, Caleb. Not as she'd hoped, though."

"What do you mean?"

"You're a very nice man, and your sister is one of my best friends in the whole world, but I know you don't have any interest in me beyond being friends."

"Or you in me?"

"That's a loaded question."

He shook his head. "Don't worry what you say will hurt my feelings because, to be honest, Leanna, you're a very nice woman, and my sister is also one of my best friends in the whole world."

When she didn't laugh as he'd anticipated, he wondered if, despite the forthrightness she seldom revealed, he'd insulted her. He realized he'd misinterpreted her silence when she spoke again after he put the papers from their food in a trash barrel.

"What about *my* sister?" she asked. "Do you consider her a friend, too?"

It was his turn to be silent. Friend? Was that how he'd describe what he felt about Annie? Friend seemed too tepid when he thought about the fiery woman. And he'd be a *dummkopf* to pretend he didn't want more with Annie.

But not now, he started to tell himself as he had so often. This time the words wouldn't come. He didn't want to lie to himself any longer. He wanted to put his past behind him and look to the future. A future with Annie.

Leanna chuckled, and when he looked at her, he saw she was grinning. His thoughts must have been visible, no surprise when such a big revelation struck him.

"You don't have to answer," Leanna said, patting his arm as she stood. "But I do have one important request. Please don't hurt my sister as her last boyfriend did."

"Last boyfriend?" He was amazed at the rush of anger that filled him at the thought of someone hurting Annie. "What did he do?"

"It's not my place to say. If Annie wants you to know, she'll tell you." With another smile, Leanna walked away toward where her *grossmammi* and brothers were talking with some *Englischers* he didn't recognize.

His heart thudded with anticipation; then he realized Annie wasn't with them. Hadn't she come to the mud sale? He stood and began to walk through the crowd. If she was there, he intended to find her. It was long past time that he spoke from his heart.

The kitchen door opening roused Annie, who was somewhere between awake and sleeping. Raising her head from her arms folded on the table, she smiled at her twin.

"Did I wake you?" Leanna asked.

"No. I was almost asleep, but not quite. Everyone else came home about two hours ago." Her words were interrupted by a wide yawn. "Did you have a *gut* time?"

"I did."

Annie almost mentioned what she'd discovered about Joey's sight, but halted herself. She must tell Caleb first so they could inform Becky Sue together.

After that, the rest of the family and the *Leit* would be told.

"I thought you were coming to the mud sale today, too."

"Didn't Becky Sue tell you why I stayed behind?"

"She did. That was kind of you, Annie."

Embarrassed by her sister's praise, she asked, "Did the auction go well?"

"From what Lyndon was told by the fire chief, they're guessing that the fire department made as much or more than they do from their annual Fourth of July carnival."

"That's so *gut* to hear."

"I saw several volunteers thanking Caleb for giving them the idea of holding the auction and sale."

"Did you have fun with him?"

"We did, but after lunch we went our own ways."

Shocked, Annie blurted, "You did? So, who brought you home?"

"Sarah's brothers."

Annie was astonished. Menno and Benjamin Kuhns were two of the most hardworking men among the *Leit*, running a sawmill and a Christmas tree farm while planting an apple orchard on another of the steep hills behind their house. She wondered if one or both were interested in her sister, but she was more curious why Leanna hadn't spent the whole day with Caleb.

Before she could ask, her sister went on, "We talked about having a skating party tomorrow night on their pond. Will you come, Annie?"

Ach, how she wished Caleb had been the one to ask,

but she would be a fool to keep hoping for something that wasn't going to happen.

"It sounds like fun," she said.

"Probably more fun than I had today with Caleb."

Annie sat straighter. "Did something go wrong?"

Pulling out a chair across from her, Leanna smiled. "Of course not. I had a nice day watching the sale and listening to Caleb talk about the bakery."

"He's so excited that it's going to open next month. Did he tell you about his plans for opening day?"

"No, because he spent most of our time together talking about you."

"Me?"

Leanna reached across the table and clasped Annie's hand in hers. "For someone who's so smart and has so many *wunderbaar* ideas, Annie, you don't have a clue to what's right in front of your eyes. He's not interested in walking out with me, and I'm not interested in walking out with him."

"He told you that?"

"Ja." She smiled. "You did us a favor, Annie. Today showed us—both of us—that we can be friends. Nothing more."

"Are you sure? I know he's not similar to Gabriel—"

"Gabriel has nothing to do with any of this."

Annie doubted that, but didn't want to quarrel with her sister.

"He's not interested in me, Annie, because he's interested in you."

"Me?" Her voice squeaked as she repeated the single word.

"Ja. You think I'm lost in my grief over losing Ga-

briel. It's true the hurt remains, but how many more years are you going to hide behind your betrayal after what Rolan did to you?" She squeezed Annie's hand, then stood. "You've always been the brave one, Annie, the one who dares to speak her mind. Do you have enough courage to take another chance on love?"

Chapter Fifteen

It should have been like any of the other days that Caleb had come to the Waglers' house to pick up Annie so they could ride together to work at the bakery.

It wasn't.

He was exhausted from tossing and turning, checking his bedside clock every few minutes in the hope that dawn was near. Leanna's voice echoed in his mind: *But I do have one important request. Please don't hurt my sister as her last boyfriend did.*

Doing Annie any injury was the last thing he wanted. Despite not knowing what her ex had done, he wanted to see Annie's scintillating smile and listen to her excitement when she offered up yet another idea. If he had his way, she'd never be sad ever again. That wasn't realistic, but his heart didn't care. Its yearning was to be given in to her care.

Was that why he felt as nervous as a new scholar on the first day of school when he jumped out of his buggy? Only the kitchen lights were on, and he guessed the family was sleeping later after a busy day at the mud sale. A glance at Lyndon's house showed it was dark, too, but the barn glowed. Milking couldn't be delayed because someone had had a long day the day before.

Walking into the kitchen, he started to greet Annie, who was reaching for a bowl on an upper shelf. Joey stood behind her, unsteady on his feet, groping toward the top of the stove where oatmeal bubbled in a pot.

Caleb exploded across the kitchen, scooping up the *boppli* and swinging him away from the stove before his little fingers were burned. Joey let out a cry of surprise as if he couldn't figure out how he went from standing on his own two feet to having them sway twice his height above the floor.

"Turn him around, Caleb!" Annie ordered.

"What?" Caleb looked at her.

"Turn him around, Caleb! Now!"

"He'll scream once he sees who's holding him."

"Turn him around and hold him nose to nose."

"What?"

Annie was usually so pragmatic. Why was she acting crazy?

"Do it, Caleb!"

Not sure what she meant, he shifted the *kind* so Joey was facing him.

"Nose to nose," Annie urged. "Do it, Caleb! Fast!"

Lifting the *boppli* higher, Caleb felt like a *dummkopf* when he put the tip of his nose against Joey's tiny one. He steeled himself for the screech that would batter his ears.

But the little boy didn't scream. Joey regarded him

with dark green eyes much like Caleb's own, then gave him a big grin.

When the *kind* reached up and ran his fingers along Caleb's face as he'd done to others, Caleb's breath hitched. Was the *boppli* accepting him? Tears blurred his distorted view of Joey's face as the toddler began to chortle as he repeated something that sounded like "Kay-eb" over and over.

"He's trying to say your name," Annie said.

"He's not crying." Caleb chuckled when the little boy continued to pat his face.

"Because he can see you."

He looked past the *kind* to where Annie stood by the stove. She wasn't smiling. When she outlined what she suspected about Joey's vision, he listened without comment until she mentioned that she believed the *boppli* had mistaken him for someone else, someone who had treated him poorly.

When she took Joey and put him in his high chair, where pieces of toast waited on the tray, Caleb struggled to dampen his rage. Who would have frightened a little *kind* so?

"Do you think it's why Becky Sue…?" He let his voice trail off when his cousin walked into the kitchen, rubbing sleep from her eyes.

"What about me?" she asked before looking from him to her son. "He's not crying!"

Annie put a hand on Caleb's shoulder as she said, "He knows Caleb isn't the person who's scared him."

The teenager shuddered before stiffening her shoulders. "I don't know what you mean."

Caleb went around the table to stand in front of his cousin. "I think you do, Becky Sue."

Behind him, Joey kept repeating his name in a sing-song voice before giggling with obvious joy.

Becky Sue moved to collect her son, but Annie stepped between her and the high chair.

"I don't know," Annie said quietly, "how to tell you this other than straight out. Joey should be examined by an eye *doktor*. He can't see more than an inch or two in front of his face."

The girl's face lost color. "No, that's impossible."

"It's possible, and it's true." Annie's voice remained gentle. "I discovered it yesterday while you were at the mud sale. It was confirmed when Caleb held Joey close enough so your son could see his face. We'll get him to see a *doktor* who can help him. *Doktors* can do marvelous things, so they should be able to help him."

Caleb interjected, "Say the word, Becky Sue, and I'll make an appointment for him. Once we know what's wrong and what can be done, then we can talk about the other issue."

With a brokenhearted cry, the girl snatched the *boppli* from the chair and sped out of the room.

"Let me," Caleb said as Becky Sue's footsteps pounded up the stairs.

"I'll show you where to go," Annie replied.

He followed her upstairs. When she pointed to the second door on the left, he nodded and walked toward it. He paused at the door, unsure if he should enter the room his cousin shared with Annie.

"Go ahead," Annie murmured from behind him. "You must talk with her. I'll wait out here."

He gave her a quick nod, took a deep breath and went into the room that didn't look so different from the one where he slept. Though there were two narrow beds instead of his broad one, they were covered with handmade quilts as his was. Joey's crib, where the little boy was cuddling a blue teddy bear and babbling to it as if it understood him, sat in a spot where, in his own room, Caleb had placed a dower chest that had been in his family since their arrival in America over two hundred and fifty years before. The same green shades as in his room could be drawn to keep out the sun, and rag rugs warmed the oak floors.

Becky Sue looked up at him from where she sat on the bed closer to the crib. She didn't say a word, but seemed to withdraw into herself like a turtle pulling into its shell.

Deciding to take a cue from Annie, he cut to the heart of the matter. "I don't know what I've done to make you distrust me so much."

"You haven't done anything."

"Then why are you upset that Joey didn't shriek today when I was holding him? I'd have thought you'd be glad, too, that he isn't terrified of me any longer. What's wrong?"

She stared at her folded hands. "I can't say."

"Can't or won't?"

"Isn't that the same?"

Not wanting to get into another discussion with her that would go in circles and never get to the point, he said, "You've been here over a month, Becky Sue. I thought you would have come to trust me."

"It's not a matter of trust."

"Then what is it?"

She didn't reply, only continued to look at her hands that were clasped so hard her knuckles were bleached.

He noticed how her fingers trembled, and he sighed. Confronting her like this wasn't getting him anywhere. She held on to her secrets as if they were as precious as her son.

No, he corrected himself when he saw her lips trembling harder than her fingers. She was terrified. Of revealing her secrets?

He knelt by her bed. "Becky Sue, whatever or whoever frightened you and Joey was wrong. I'm here and the Waglers are here—in fact the whole *Leit* in Harmony Creek Hollow is here—to help you and your son."

"Danki," she whispered, then added nothing else.

"Whenever you're ready," he said, praying she'd have a change of heart.

God must have had other plans for them, because she stared at her folded hands and added nothing more. When Caleb stood, she didn't move.

Walking out of the room, Caleb closed the door behind him. He shook his head when Annie's worried expression voiced a question she didn't have to ask.

They had no choice but to wait for Becky Sue to be honest with them.

He hoped it would be soon, and he prayed that the teenager wouldn't take it in her head to run away with her *boppli* again.

Annie was relieved when Becky Sue agreed to join her and her siblings at the pond down the hill from the Kuhns brothers' tree farm. Moonlight shone on the snow, making it look fresh. About thirty people, including some of their *Englisch* neighbors, had come together for the evening. Annie looked forward to sampling popcorn balls and the taffy that the youth group had made.

"I guess God does love us," she said as she sat beside Caleb on a hummock where the snow had been covered with tarps and blankets.

He laughed as he laced up his skate as she did. "You sound as if this is something you've just discovered."

"I've always known it, but it's a joy to rediscover the truth over and over again. The *gut* Lord may have given us a horrible winter, but he also gave us a frozen pond to enjoy."

"I'm glad I was able to find a pair of skates in the thrift shop by the old courthouse." Caleb pulled on his other skate after setting his boots next to each other beside the others left behind. "They had only one pair in my size."

"A skating party wouldn't be much fun without skates, ain't so?" She laced her skates with easy skill. "We had extras, so Becky Sue found a pair that fits."

"Has she said anything?"

"No." Tying off her skates, she wiggled her toes in two pairs of wool socks. "Let's not talk about that tonight."

"I agree. I hear you brought hot chocolate. Your famous recipe?"

She hoped the moonlight would wash out the blush climbing her cheeks. "I don't think it's famous."

"It should be. I've tasted your hot chocolate several

times, and you add delicious flavors to it. What did you bring tonight?"

"Chocolate and raspberry."

"Is that one of the flavors you suggested serving at the bakery?"

"One of them."

"What about the others? Are they this *gut*?"

"My favorite is the chocolate and raspberry, but others prefer vanilla or the one with *kaffi* flavoring."

He slid his hand over hers as he leaned toward her. "I think we need to talk more about serving hot chocolate. Your *grossmammi* was right when she told me how many *gut* ideas you have." He finished tying his skates as he said, "Business can wait, too. Let's have fun."

When he smiled as she stood on her blades, Annie could have believed spring had erupted around them. Happiness wrapped her in warmth. Could Leanna be right? Was it possible that Caleb, a man she trusted and loved, could have strong feelings about her, too?

Caleb stood and stepped past her, gliding along the ice. She grinned. She'd learned that anything he did he did well because he gave every bit of himself to the job.

As she put her feet, one at a time, on the ice, Becky Sue skidded toward her. Annie halted her before the teen knocked them both over.

"*Komm mol,*" called Becky Sue, holding out her hand. "Are you going to skate, or have you frozen yourself to this spot?"

With a chuckle, Annie took her hand. Becky Sue pulled her along the ice as Annie and Leanna had each other when they were little girls.

Impromptu games of snap-the-whip and races

among the younger boys and girls sent waves of excited voices through the crisp winter air. Annie was pulled into some games and joined others as the evening unfolded. She waved to Caleb when she passed him as he careened across the ice after being whipped off the line of skaters. She paused once to enjoy a popcorn ball and watch as her sister skated past with Benjamin Kuhns before they fell to the ice and slid into two other people. Soon the whole crowd was laughing together.

More than once, Becky Sue came looking for her. Each time, Annie agreed to skate with the girl and used the opportunity to introduce the teen to others closer to her age.

Abruptly, Becky Sue shoved her forward. Before Annie could ask what the girl was doing, she hit something hard. Hands grabbed her arms to steady her and keep her from falling.

"You should have signal lights to show where you're going, Annie."

At Caleb's laugh, she raised her eyes to see him standing wondrously close. His chuckles faded as the heat in his eyes deepened until she feared the ice would melt under their feet. Releasing her arms, he held out his hand.

She put hers on it, and his fingers closed around it. They began to skate in perfect unison. Neither of them spoke, and that was fine. The song of their skates matched the eager beat of her heart as the other voices vanished. Every inch of her being was focused on him…on them…on being together beneath the cool moonlight as they slid along the ice while their eyes were focused on each other.

When he stopped and drew her toward the shore, she wanted to protest. He shook his head, and she followed, waiting while he ladled out two servings of her hot chocolate for them. Then, holding her hand again, he led her up the hill through the trees to a spot where they could watch the rest of the skaters.

They sipped their hot chocolate in the same silence, not needing words. When she finished the last in her paper cup, he took it and put it inside his. He set them on the ground and looked at her.

She searched his shadowed face, knowing every inch of it from the hours they'd spent together in the bakery and so many of her dreams. She closed her eyes as his arm swept around her waist and he brought her to him as he bent to caress her lips. What she'd imagined about this moment was tepid compared to the thrill of his kiss.

Did the shivers racing along her belong to him or her? All she knew for sure was that they had nothing to do with the chilly night and everything to do with the delight tingling along her. She slid her hands up the strong muscles beneath his sleeves and curved her arms over his shoulders, surrendering to the kiss she hadn't dared to believe would ever happen.

Too soon, he drew back.

Again Annie was going to protest, but she heard what he must have while she was lost in the moment.

"Hey, Caleb!" came a man's shout from closer to the pond.

Caleb leaned his forehead against hers as he murmured, "That's Lyndon. I should go and see what he wants."

"You should."

"Okay." He didn't move.

Neither did she, except to meet his mouth for another quick kiss before he picked up their discarded cups and walked awkwardly down the hill on his skates.

She remained behind, not wanting the perfection to end, wanting to keep it close so it didn't ebb away like a dream in the light of dawn. As the cold sifted through her coat and nibbled at her toes, she stood still.

Annie wasn't sure how long she remained on the hill, but her feet felt half-frozen as she lumbered down. Maybe it was time to get her skates off and put on her warm boots. A glance at the moon that was setting over the mountains to the west told her that the party had been going on for more than two hours.

A clump of shadows in front of her were, she discovered as she drew near, a group of men leaning on the trees and sipping her hot chocolate. She was about to announce herself when she caught Caleb's voice.

"The plan is to have a full selection of drink choices." He laughed, "*Englischers* are always talking about taking time to stop and smell the roses. Maybe we can convince them to stop and smell the *kaffi* and the hot chocolate and maybe freshly squeezed lemonade in the summer. I've been looking around to find some more small tables. If they're set in one corner, we hope patrons will stay and have something to eat before they take more home with them."

"That's a *gut* idea." Her brother slapped Caleb's arm. "A really *gut* one. You've put a lot of thought into this."

Another man spoke. An *Englischer*. "I can tell that you've done your market research, Caleb. We've needed a café and a bakery in Salem since the last one was turned into a diner a few years ago." He paused, then said, "My wife will be your best customer, I'm sure, once she tastes this raspberry hot chocolate. She raves about the bread you sold last summer. That you'll be serving hot drinks at a place where she can get together with her friends will make her really happy."

"You'll get a bunch of guys in there before evening chores, too," said another *Englischer*. Chief Pulaski, Annie realized, as the fire chief continued, "I shouldn't be surprised that you've got so many good ideas. Your suggestion about having that Amish-style mud sale raised enough money to pay for a lot of training for our volunteers."

"Danki."

"Your bakery is sure to be a hit. When I was in to do the final inspection this morning, I couldn't believe the transformation of that dusty old depot into a bright and cheery shop. How did you come up with the idea of splashing color on the floor? I thought you Amish liked things plain."

She waited, holding her breath because she didn't want to miss a single word. *Now* Caleb would say some of the ideas had been hers.

"We do." He chuckled. "But when my cousin's little boy spilled paint, it seemed like the obvious solution when it would have taken so long to clean up those old floorboards."

"And that bright yellow wall in the kitchen?" Chief Pulaski chuckled. "I'd guess I won't be the only husband in Salem who'll be repainting a kitchen once your shop opens."

"When customers come in, the color of that wall will catch their attention. That will draw their eyes right to the displays in the cases."

Annie reeled a half step as she heard what she'd said, almost word for word, coming out of Caleb's mouth. He was taking credit for her ideas as Rolan had after they'd broken up. How could she have been foolish enough to let this happen again? She'd thought Caleb cared about her, but had he cared only about the ideas she brought him for his bakery?

Stop it! she told herself. It shouldn't matter who got credit for how the bakery had turned out. To expect to be acknowledged for her help was *hochmut*. She should be pleased that her hard work was paying off for Caleb.

But how could she when he'd taken her ideas for his own?

She should have been more careful. If she hadn't let flattery from her *grossmammi* and from Caleb turn her head, she might have thought before she let each idea burst out of her. Instead, she'd freed each one as it popped into her mind, so glad to be able to express them.

And the worst part was that he didn't seem to have any problem with taking credit for her ideas mere minutes after he'd wooed her lips with his. Rolan hadn't tried to keep her off-kilter like that when he stole her ideas.

Bending over, Annie loosened the laces on her skates. She tramped through the snow to where she'd left her boots. She yanked off her skates and pulled on her boots. She looked around and saw Leanna and

Becky Sue talking to Juanita and Kenny a short distance away.

"Let's go," Annie said as she approached them.

"But, Annie—"

She didn't give Becky Sue a chance to finish. Linking her arm through the teenager's, she marched toward the road that twisted through the hollow. A glance back told her that her siblings were hurrying to follow and that Caleb was striding in their direction.

Talking to him would be another mistake. If she did, she might say something she'd come to regret later.

She shot another look over her shoulder. Caleb had stopped, staring after them. Puzzlement was seared on his face.

He doesn't realize what he's done.

That thought should have been comforting.

It wasn't.

Her pain was too deep, her betrayal too raw. She couldn't think about the situation logically.

What a joke! Annie Wagler, the always-logical one, the twin who didn't lead with her emotions but worked well with everyone, was the one who refused to listen to her own rational thoughts. Instead she was wallowing in pain, a pain so deep it hurt to breathe.

No one spoke on the short walk home. Her younger sister and brother glanced at her again and again, but apparently the set of her taut lips told them it'd be wise not to ask questions. They and Becky Sue hurried up to their rooms, and she could hear the soft buzz of their confused voices.

Leanna stayed in the kitchen and watched as Annie tried to find something to do to vent her frustration.

After about fifteen minutes, she took Annie by the arm and steered her to the table.

"What's going on?" Leanna asked.

"Caleb Hartz isn't the man I thought he was." The words sprang out of her like soda from a shaken bottle.

Her twin frowned and tapped her foot on the floor. "I'm not going to ask you what happened between you, but I can tell you that pouting about it and going around crashing into things and cutting short the *kinder*'s fun won't change it."

"I'm not doing anything different from what you've been doing."

"Me?" Her twin looked shocked.

"*Ja*. You've been in mourning since Gabriel Miller got married."

Leanna recoiled as if Annie had struck her. "I have not!"

"You don't see it, but you've been acting as if you're attending a wake for months and months. You used to laugh and sing and delight in making your quilts. I don't think I've heard you sing, other than during services, in a year. Each time you pick up a needle, you act as if quilting is drudgery instead of the joy it used to be. You enjoy taking care of your goats, but you've handed the job to me a lot lately. It's as if you've forgotten how to be happy."

Her twin stared at Annie. More than once, she opened her mouth to speak, but didn't break the silence that clamped around them.

Leanna threw her arms around Annie. "I'm sorry. I have been so focused on what I didn't have that I've forgotten what I do have. I've been selfish and let you carry too much of the load of moving here and watching over the others. My sole excuse is that you do everything so well that I've been going along with whatever you say and do."

"I don't do everything well." She'd made a mess of her relationship with Caleb.

She admitted to herself what scared her most: that, after tonight, they couldn't even be friends any longer.

Chapter Sixteen

It was quiet.

Too quiet.

The last time Caleb had been smothered by such silence at the bakery was the day before he hired Annie to work for him. Since then, the space had been alive with her *gut* humor and lively questions and endless suggestions aimed at helping him make his dream come true.

It was coming true, but at what price? Last night, Annie had stormed away from the pond without explaining why she was upset. He'd stopped by the Waglers' house earlier to pick her up. Leanna had met him on the porch and informed him Annie wouldn't be coming to work that day.

"How about tomorrow?" he'd asked.

Leanna had deflected his question, and he'd realized he wasn't going to get a straight answer. Unwilling to storm into the house and demand Annie explain—though the idea was tempting—he'd thanked Leanna, got into his buggy and headed toward the bakery.

But the silence taunted him. The bright colors on the floor and the shining appliances and display cases were mute reminders of how hard she'd worked by his side.

Now she didn't want to see him.

Like Verba when he didn't do as she wanted. She'd dumped him because she told him that she was tired of being less important to him than his dream of a successful bakery. Had he made the same mistake again? No. Verba had ended their courtship because he refused to become the man she wanted for a husband, a man who met each of her very precise specifications.

After that, he'd vowed to himself and to God that he'd never put himself in such a situation again. And he hadn't, had he?

No, he hadn't.

Annie was, he realized with a start, the complete opposite of Verba. Instead of trying to change him, Annie had spent hours coming up with ideas to make his dream better than he could have devised on his own. She'd accepted his hopes for his future as if they were as integral a part of him as his hair color and his faith.

She'd enhanced those dreams, caring about them as much as if they were her own.

Every time he'd needed her help—even when he hadn't known he could use her assistance—she'd stepped up and offered to do what she could. It hadn't mattered that what she volunteered to do added to her already heavy burden of taking care of her family and their farm. She'd smiled and taken over the task and done it well.

Better than he could have many times.

Would he have thought about the color on the

kitchen wall and how it would draw customers' eyes to his baked goods on display in the front room?

Would he ever have conceived the idea of putting tables and chairs in the open space to one side of the display case so people would buy extra *kaffi*, other drinks and extra sweets from him? And turning the *boppli*'s splattering of paint on the floor from a disaster to something fun never would have entered his mind.

The bakery seemed like a dead thing. Annie was gone, and he didn't know why. Because he'd kissed her last night? He'd thought she was willing when she stepped into his arms. She must have had second thoughts after their kiss, but why hadn't she told him? She'd been honest about so much else, even when he hadn't liked her honesty.

Caleb flinched when he heard a knock on the door. Who could be there? He didn't want to see some chirpy salesman or curious neighbor. He wanted to be alone with his misery.

With a sigh, he went to the door and opened it. He didn't recognize the lanky teenager who stood in front of him. The lad was overdue for a haircut because dark bangs covered his eyes. He was dressed in plain clothing, though it wasn't the style worn in their district.

"Gute mariye," Caleb said.

The young man shuffled his worn boots. "My name is Elson Knepp. I'm looking for Becky Sue Hartz, and I've been told I might find her or her cousin Caleb here."

"I'm Caleb Hartz. Why are you looking for Becky Sue?"

The young man ducked his head, then squared his

shoulders and looked Caleb in the eye. "Because she's going to be my wife. We've got plans to build a life and a family together."

"Aren't you a bit late for that?"

Elson's brow threaded with confusion, and then dismay dimmed his eyes. "Late? Are you telling me that she's decided to marry someone else?"

"No, I'm telling you that she already has a family."

"Do you mean her family in Lancaster County?" His lip curled. "That's no family for her." His brows rose. "Or do you mean her cousins here? I'm not sure what you're trying to tell me."

Caleb scowled. "I'm trying to tell you that Becky Sue already has a family. She and her *boppli* are a family."

The young man swayed on his feet as he grew ashen.

Putting out a hand, because he feared Elson was about to faint, Caleb guided the younger man toward the tables he'd brought to the bakery. He took down a stacked chair and helped Elson sit.

"Do you want something to drink?" Caleb asked.

"No. I…" Elson's voice drifted away.

"Are you okay?"

"Did you say Becky Sue—Becky Sue Hartz—has a *boppli*? That I'm a *daed*?"

It was Caleb's turn to be shocked. He wasn't sure what plain community Elson was from, but he did know that the young man wasn't an *Englischer*. Even if one had decided to put on plain clothes and give himself a plain name, he couldn't speak *Deitsch* with the ease of someone who'd always used it.

But Becky Sue had told Annie that Joey's *daed* was

Englisch. Hadn't she? Or had she just implied that? Was it all another lie? Caleb was determined to find out.

After convincing the young man to have a cup of *kaffi* to warm him, though Caleb suspected shock more than the outside temperatures had more to do with Elson's shivering, Caleb got another chair and sat facing him.

"Start from the beginning," Caleb said as he stirred cream into his *kaffi* and watched Elson add several spoonfuls of sugar to his own cup.

"Becky Sue and I walked out together, and we discovered we loved each other and wanted to spend the rest of our lives together. She wasn't happy at home because her stepfather made her life miserable."

"Stepfather? I didn't know she had one."

"Her own *daed*'s brother, which is why they have the same last name, but he made it clear soon after his first son was born that he wished she didn't exist. He favored his own *kinder* over her. If money was tight, she was the last one to get new shoes or a coat that fitted. She and I agreed it would be for the best if we got married as soon as possible. I didn't have enough money to provide for us, so I took a job in Iowa. Out there, they need workers and don't ask a lot of questions." He flushed, his face becoming tomato red. "The night before I left, we... That is…"

Caleb took pity on the young man. "You don't have to go into detail. You and Becky Sue aren't the first to make that bad decision, and you won't be the last. Have you been in Iowa all this time?" He thought of the phone number with an Iowan area code that had been made before Annie and he had found Becky Sue at the bakery.

Had she been trying to get in touch with Elson so he'd know where she and his son were?

A rush of anger swept through him as he wondered how any man, even one as wet behind the ears as Elson, could abandon his family. Then he paused. Elson seemed genuinely shocked. Was it possible the young man hadn't known about his son?

"Caleb," the teenager said as if Caleb had asked that question aloud, "you've got to believe me. I wanted to earn enough money so I could provide for us. I love Becky Sue, but I had no idea when I left for Iowa that Becky Sue was pregnant. I wouldn't have left her by herself, if I'd known. There could have been other ways to earn enough to provide for her and me and the *boppli* right there in Lancaster County."

"Did you let her know where you were?"

"I wrote to her every other day right from the beginning, but she seldom wrote back. I'd get a letter from her about once a month. They were short."

"But you talked on the phone."

Again Elson shook his head. "Never, though as soon as I got a cell phone in Iowa, I sent her my number and urged her to call me collect. I missed hearing her voice and her laughter. I fell in love with her because of her laugh. Silly, ain't so?"

Caleb sighed. "No, it's not." Annie's laugh created special music in his soul.

Elson hung his head as he clenched his hands by his sides. "She never called, and she never wrote to me about being pregnant or having a *boppli*."

Though Caleb wanted to say that was hard to believe, he thought of how habit-forming secrets could be. He hadn't revealed to Annie anything about how Verba had shamed him...how he'd allowed her to make him question everything he held dear. And Annie hid something from him, something he could sense when he kissed her, but he couldn't guess what it was.

"Are she and the *boppli* okay?"

"They are. They're staying with friends of mine." At least, he hoped he could still say Annie was his friend. "Becky Sue is doing well, and so is Joey, though he has trouble seeing."

"Joey? I have a son?" Joy brought color to Elson's cheeks.

Looking at him, Caleb knew there was no doubt that the young man was being truthful. Becky Sue had kept him in the dark, never telling him that she had his *kind*.

"*Komm* with me," he said, getting up. He couldn't let his and Annie's problems get in the way of Elson meeting his son. He wasn't sure what reception he'd get at the Waglers, but he'd wait outside if he had to. Nothing must prevent a reunion between Becky Sue, Elson and their son.

"What is wrong with you today?" chided Becky Sue as she bent to pick up the pieces of the second cup Annie had dropped while they did the breakfast dishes together. "Is something wrong with you and Caleb?"

Annie shook her head. "No, there isn't any Caleb and me."

"But I thought..." Becky Sue looked to Leanna as

she added, "I thought by now you two were walking out together."

"I worked for him. Nothing more."

"No! Don't be false to us!" Leanna snapped.

"I told you last night—"

"You didn't tell me anything. You changed the subject to how I felt about Gabriel marrying someone else. You said Caleb wasn't the man you thought he was. That could mean anything. Anything at all!" Leanna stamped her foot, shocking Annie, who couldn't remember the last time her twin had been so assertive. "You can lie to yourself, but you've got to be honest to me, Annie. It's no more than you asked of me when you tried to make a match for me with Caleb."

Embarrassment heated her face. She *had* insisted that Leanna speak from the heart with her after attending the mud sale with Caleb.

"I worked so hard," Becky Sue groaned. "I knew you liked him and he liked you. When you were *dumm* enough to fix up Leanna with him, I decided you must be shown how wrong you are. Both of you."

Comprehension burst into Annie's mind. "When you locked us in the closet?"

"*Ja.* I hid in your horrible cellar beneath the trap door until you both went into the closet to get the dishwasher detergent I'd moved. When that didn't seem to convince you that you're right for each other, I *disappeared.*" She made air quotes. "It seemed to work, but then you'd get busy and I wasn't sure you were making time for each other. I came up with an idea to get you to spend time together." She glanced at the sleeping *boppli.* "Joey helped me that time."

"With all the paint mess?" Annie had had no idea that the teenager was so ingenious.

Becky Sue had taken advantage of the few tools she had to throw Annie and Caleb together, and she'd succeeded each time. At least for a while, until one of them stepped away, unsure about what their relationship might have become.

"And you kissed him last night," Becky Sue cried. "How could you do that if you don't like him?"

"You were spying on us?"

The girl didn't deny the accusation. "If you two can't see the truth, someone has to help you."

Annie threw the dish towel on the counter and turned to leave the kitchen. She paused when the door opened.

Her eyes widened, but her heart beat out a joyous song when Caleb stepped in. Her tears distorted his image, but his handsome face had been etched into her memory so she could recreate each angle as if he stood in the brightest sunshine. She looked away, startled when Becky Sue gasped before she said words almost identical to the ones Caleb had used the day they found her and Joey at the bakery.

"Elson, what are you doing *here*?"

A lanky young man she didn't know rushed into the kitchen and tugged Becky Sue into his arms. He buried his face in the side of her *kapp* as he kept repeating her name over and over. She pointed to the *boppli*, who was rousing with the uproar.

"Elson," she whispered, "there's your son. Our son."

Unabashed tears ran down the young man's face, and Annie's heart pushed aside the last of the wall she'd built around it. Here was true joy, the reunion of two hearts that belonged together. No matter what she did, she couldn't have found this for her sister. Only Leanna, with God's help, could find it for herself.

Grossmammi Inez tiptoed into the kitchen, putting a finger to her lips because she didn't want her arrival to disrupt what was happening.

"I'm sorry I wasn't honest with you, Caleb and the rest of you." Becky Sue looked toward Elson as she picked up Joey and cuddled him close. "I couldn't be honest with anyone else when I wasn't honest with myself. I thought you'd be better off without me...without us."

"How could you believe that?" Elson took a step toward her, then halted. "Or was it that you thought you were better off without *me*? I know your parents never liked me."

"Leo Hartz is not my parent, so I don't care what he thought. He's just the man my *mamm* married after my real *daed* died, and he always has let me know that he wished she hadn't had a daughter before they wedded. I was told I should call him by his given name while his *kinder* called him *daed*."

Annie drew in a sharp breath, trying to imagine her own *mamm*'s second husband treating her and Leanna and Lyndon cruelly. Bert Wagler had treated the three of them as he had his own son and daughter. He was the person she thought of when talking about her *daed* because her own had sickened when she was so young.

Becky Sue turned to Caleb. "I should have told you why Joey was scared of you. It's because you have similar coloring to Leo. From the day he was born, Joey has known that Leo wished he didn't exist. I tried to keep Joey away from him, but Leo yelled at Joey about the slightest thing. I know he hit Joey, too, though I never caught him doing it."

He put a hand on her shoulder. "I'm sorry to hear that, Becky Sue. And I'm sorry that I believed there was no *gut* reason for you to run away. I was wrong."

Tears glistened in the girl's eyes, and this time she didn't try to hold them in. "*Danki*, Caleb. I've wanted you to understand, but I wasn't sure if you'd listen when nobody else had."

"Though you came here for sanctuary."

"I'd heard from so many people what a *gut* guy you were."

"But you still couldn't trust me."

"No, because while I hoped you'd help me—and you did—I've been afraid that, if I told you the truth, you'd tell me the same thing others did." She blinked on more tears. "When I sought help from our ministers, they told me that while Joey and I lived with Leo, I had to heed his rules. They thought I was a disgruntled stepdaughter who was looking to cause trouble." Thick teardrops fell onto her apron. "I had been that girl when I was Kenny's age because I didn't know how to put in the proper words what was happening at our house." She looked up at him again. "I got the punishments I deserved, but Joey didn't do anything wrong other than being born."

"And even that wasn't his choice," Elson said as he put his arm around her.

"But you're happy about it, ain't so?" the girl asked, sounding younger.

"Happier than you can know. As soon as we can become baptized, I want us to marry and have a real family. The three of us to begin with and whoever God sends to us after that."

She handed him his son, telling him to hold Joey close to his face. When the *boppli* ran inquisitive hands along Elson's features, Becky Sue whispered, "This is *Daed*, Joey. *Daed*."

"Daed?" the little boy asked.

"Ja," Elson whispered. "And you are my dear, dear son."

Annie's eyes overflowed as she watched the family that had been separated for so long come together. She doubted anything on earth would pull them apart again, because Becky Sue stared at Elson as if she could never get enough of looking at him. And the young man did the same to her.

When a hand took hers, tugging her toward the door, she knew it belonged to Caleb. There was a sense, a sense with no name, that connected them in a way she'd never imagined. She was sure a storm raged along her skin that prickled as if she'd stood too close to a lightning bolt.

"Will you talk to me?" he whispered as he opened the door to the mud room.

She steeled herself against the cold, but how could that bother her when his touch was so warm?

"Ja," she whispered, unable to speak more loudly.

He turned her so they stood face-to-face as they had on the hill overlooking the pond. "I don't know what I did wrong, Annie, but I'm sorry. I don't ever want to do anything to hurt you."

"You have to understand what happened in the past." As she told him how Rolan had betrayed her, she saw anger spark in his eyes. Not at her, but at the man who'd used her so. "Last night, I heard…that is, I thought I heard while you were talking to Lyndon and your firefighter friends…"

"That I took credit for your ideas? That I let them think they were my ideas?" He framed her face with his work-worn hands. "If I did, it was by mistake."

"I know you're not like Rolan because you've been eager to make use of my ideas and include me, not steal them for yourself."

He thought for a few seconds, then asked, "Are you sure I let the others think the ideas were mine? I remember saying 'we' because we've worked together on the bakery."

Annie stepped away so she could think. She replayed the conversation she'd overheard—or as much as she could remember, examining every word. In amazement, she realized he was right. He hadn't let the others assume the ideas were his. In fact, he'd gone out of his way to avoid that. Her perceptions had led her to believe otherwise.

"How did you know I cared so much about my ideas?" she asked.

"Because I care that much about my dreams, and when someone tried to stand in my way, telling me those dreams were useless, I ended what I thought we shared."

"You did?"

"Ja." He took her hands and laced his fingers

through hers. "I've made a lot of mistakes, Annie, but there's one I'll never make again."

"What's that?"

"Not knowing if I was talking to you or Leanna." He lifted her right hand and pressed it to the center of his chest. "My heart will always be sure. It wants to belong to you, if you'll have it."

"Only if you take mine," she laughed. "Not that you have any choice. It refuses *not* to belong to you. *Ich liebe dich*, Caleb."

"And I love you, too. I want us to be partners in life as well as working at the bakery. Will you marry me?"

She flung her arms around his shoulders and answered him with a kiss. When she heard excited shouts behind her, she looked over her shoulder to see her family and his clustered in the doorway.

"I guess you've heard," Caleb said with a chuckle.

"We haven't heard her say *ja*," *Grossmammi* Inez replied.

"Ja!" Annie repeated about a half-dozen times until she and everyone else dissolved into laughter.

Caleb held up one finger. "However, I want you to witness that there's one more promise I need to hear Annie make."

"What's that?" she asked.

"That you'll like milking cows."

She laughed, "That's never going to happen."

"Never is a long time, Annie."

"How about this? I'll let you try to convince me for the rest of our lives."

"That sounds like a *wunderbaar* plan."

Epilogue

"Ready?" Caleb asked as he held out his left hand. In his right, he held a tray of apple pie squares. It would claim the last empty spot in the display cases.

"Ready." Annie smiled at him as she clasped his hand.

They walked together out of the kitchen and into the front room of the bakery. Everything glistened in the warm morning sunshine pouring through the pristine windows. The light danced on the quartet of black tables topped with containers of creamers and sugar, waiting for customers to sit and enjoy a cup of *kaffi*. It sparkled on the glass in the display cases and across the small refrigerator Caleb had installed the day before when they realized they wanted to have a place to store fresh milk, cream and whipped cream for the drinks and baked goods.

Yesterday, she'd joined him out front when he installed the sign that announced Hartz Bakery would soon be open for business. She treasured the memory of his smile when he finished patting down the dirt around the posts holding the sign in place. His dream was coming true, and so was hers.

She looked at the multicolored floorboards. A smile tilted her lips as it did each time she thought of the little boy and his *mamm* and *daed*, who had decided to remain in Harmony Creek Hollow. They were renting a small tenant house from the Bowmans, whose farm was about halfway between Caleb's house and Miriam's. Joey had been seen by a *doktor* who had several ideas for helping him see better. Elson had already begun work with her friend Sarah's brothers at their sawmill, and he and Becky Sue were attending baptism classes. A happy ending to a difficult story...

And Annie was relieved that her *grossmammi* was going to see a cardiac specialist next week. She prayed the *doktor* would be able to diagnosis what was causing *Grossmammi* Inez to be so short of breath.

"You look happy," Caleb said after placing the tray in the display case.

"How can I not be happy? Becky Sue and Joey are being taken care of and your bakery is opening today."

"*Our* bakery." He ran his fingers along her cheek. "I didn't realize how much better a dream coming true could be when it was a dream shared."

"As I didn't know that once an idea is brought to life, it can belong to both of us."

He glanced toward the window where a line snaked from the door all the way around the driveway. With a husky laugh, he pulled her to him and gave her a resounding kiss that sent delight racing from her lips to the very tips of her toes. He drew back enough to whisper, "We'll finish the kiss later."

"And start more."

Chuckling, he squeezed her. "I love how you think." He released her and walked to the door.

Annie positioned herself behind the counter where she'd take the orders from their customers. When he looked at her, she gave him a thumbs-up.

He threw the door open and said, with a flourish of his arm, "Welcome to the Hartz Bakery."

A cheer rose from outside, and Annie almost shivered with glee. Their hard work had brought this day. Not just working on the bakery, but the tougher task of learning to trust each other after being betrayed in the past.

Checking that her *kapp* hadn't shifted while she helped Caleb put the goods in the cases, she greeted their very first customer, "*Gute mariye*, Deputy Flanagan. What can I get for you today?"

The tall man selected two raspberry muffins and three oatmeal-raisin cookies. As Annie put them into a small box, she looked past the deputy to where Caleb was talking with some of his fellow firefighters who were waiting for their turn to place their orders. He smiled at her, and she wondered how her heart could hold so much happiness as his dream and her own came true. She had a lifetime with him to figure that out.

* * * * *

THEIR CONVENIENT
AMISH MARRIAGE

Cheryl Williford

This book is dedicated to God and to my two gifted oncologists: Dr. Dennis L. Rousseau, who performed my complex cancer surgery in October of 2015, and Dr. Edsel Lumbca Hesita, who successfully got me through five months of chemotherapy in early 2016. Your wisdom saved my life and kept me writing. God bless you both.

Judge not, and ye shall not be judged:
condemn not, and ye shall not be condemned:
forgive, and ye shall be forgiven.
—*Luke* 6:37

Chapter One

Thunder rumbled in the distance. A peek out the window showed another band of drenching rain coming in from the west.

Finished with a sink of dishes, Verity Schrock wiped the sweat from her face on the sleeve of her dress and hurried out of the steamy kitchen with several ladies following on her heel.

It seemed lately she rushed from one task to another, never finding time to sit down and enjoy a moment of the day.

Fanning her hot face, she quick-stepped down the hall, ready to join the cluster of singers regathering in the great room.

She'd been up since five, long before the old rooster had had a chance to give his first crow of the morning. An experienced cook, she enjoyed the task of making a tower of assorted shoofly pies, a chocolate cake with rich mocha icing, and for herself, a gooey pan of rich golden-brown apple crumble, her favorite dessert.

Taking in a calming breath and clearing her voice,

she surveyed the room for the soprano singer's section and found Bunhild, the community's seasonal match-maker standing in the place she usually occupied. Purposely avoiding the meddling old woman, she slipped into the end of the alto singer's section.

Acting as if she were listening to the song director's instructions, Verity situated herself closer to Clara Hilty, who was making a point of ignoring her best friend since childhood while holding back a fit of giggles behind her petite hand.

With her gaze straight ahead, Verity's finger searched for and found Clara's rib cage, and gave her very pregnant friend a playful poke.

Clara jumped, nearly knocking over the young lady standing in front of her.

Everyone in the lines turned and glared their way.

"Shame on you, Verity," Clara muttered out the side of her mouth.

Verity leaned in close to her friend's ear. "You should have warned me Bunhild showed up for singing practice. I could have hidden in the kitchen closet until she'd left." Putting on a heavy Pennsylvania Dutch accent, Verity held back her own giggles as she muttered in Clara's ear, "Those Lapp *bruders* are still marriage-minded, and looking for a pretty young woman like yourself to wed."

Clara laughed out loud, amused by Verity's rendition of Bunhild's heavy northern accent. Verity couldn't help but laugh with her. For as long as she'd known Clara, which was going on fifteen years, they'd both been consummate pranksters. Nothing had changed now that they were adults.

Still grinning, Clara's arms came up and rested on her rotund stomach. There would soon be a long-awaited first *boppli* for her and her husband, Solomon Hilty. Verity couldn't help but be excited for them—and a little envious. She loved children, especially tiny babies. She had hoped for a half-dozen *kinner* of her own, but *Gott* had other plans for her life and gave her and Mark just the one sweet *dochder*. But she wanted to ignore unhappy memories. Her excitement grew as she thought instead about a new *boppli* in the community to care for and cuddle.

Clara's giggles turned into a delighted smile. "I could have warned you, but it's so much fun watching you squirm under Bunhild's gaze." But then her expression went dead serious. "You know her matchmaking skills are known far and wide, and you being such a young widow makes the opportunity to play matchmaker too tempting for the old girl."

Verity pretended to adjust her *kapp* and readjust the pins holding down her bun, so she would have an excuse to lean in close to Clara again. "You'd better watch out. I could tell Solomon how much you really paid for that new sewing machine you bought off that *Englisch* woman."

Two spaces down, Pinecraft's best solo soprano hissed like a leaky gas valve and gave both women a disapproving glare before going back to listening to Sarah Beth's information on the upcoming fundraising frolic where they'd be singing at Benky Park.

When Verity looked back, Clara's playful smile was gone. "You wouldn't tell on me?"

"I might," Verity whispered, her eyebrow raised in a

mock threat. But she'd never say a word about the extra twenty dollars spent. The seller had kindly thrown in a sewing basket full of threads and four packs of machine needles. A real deal.

Known for his penny-pinching ways, Solomon Hilty would still grumble about the extra money spent. Verity wasn't about to blab, but she ought to. Determined to wed Verity off, Bunhild Yoder was no laughing matter, and now she had to deal with her as soon as singing practice was over.

Feeling eyes on her, Verity glanced up and released an irritated sigh. Bunhild was staring at her again from across the room and wearing that exasperating expression of eternal hope. Verity inwardly cringed. "You know I respect Bunhild's skills as much as everyone in the community, but if I must listen to one more of her sermons on how marriage is *Gott*'s plan for your life, I think I'll scream."

A loud knock at the front door sounded, redirecting Verity's attention. "Whoops! Excuse me." She slipped out of line and hurried to welcome the late singer at the front door. Working as Albert Hilty's live-in housekeeper the last few years had proven to be hard work, but she'd grown to love the aging widower she'd known most of her life and his growing family. Life ran smoothly on the orange grove, which brought a sense of peace to her and her young daughter Faith's lives.

Verity hurried, convinced it was Helen at the door. She often came late to practices, especially if her precious three-month-old *boppli* had once again kept her up with night colic.

"Well, it's about time you got..." Verity's playful

words died in her throat at the sight of a tall well-built *Englischer* standing on the porch. He wore tight faded jeans and a white T-shirt that strained to cover his broad chest. A baseball cap perched on his long dish-water-blond hair advertised some brand of soft drink she'd never heard of.

Her heart skipped a beat and then two. Overtly handsome men always made her nervous, like ants crawling all over her skin. This one made her extremely nervous. "Oh, I'm sorry… I thought you were Helen." She took a quick survey of his smiling face and then glanced down at the sleeping dark-haired toddler he held. The pink-cheeked *kind* looked completely out of place next to the man's firm biceps. "Are you looking for Albert or Solomon?"

"Both." He grinned. A dimple appeared in his cheek. "What are you doing here, Verity?"

A chill rushed down her spine. The man's words were spoken in the same husky voice that sometimes disturbed her dreams at night.

"Leviticus?" It didn't seem possible. Now that she took a good look he did seem slightly familiar, but nothing like the young Amish boy she'd loved and promised her heart to all those years ago. How many years had it been since Leviticus abandoned Pinecraft and their engagement plans? *Nine, maybe ten?* Yet here he was on his father's doorstep, activating the nerves in her stomach.

He flashed a full-blown smile at her, again revealing the familiar dimple near his left cheek. "No one's called me Leviticus in a long time. My *Englischer* friends call me Levi."

Her angst against the man revived, even though she thought she'd forgiven him a long time ago. "I'm not one of your *Englisch* friends, Leviticus." She tried hard but couldn't manage to take her eyes off his suntanned face and the way his blue eyes twinkled behind familiar thick brown lashes.

She detected an angry red scar running the length of his unshaven right cheek. Her gaze dropped to the blond stubble peppered with ginger covering his chin. When he'd left Pinecraft, there'd been no scar and not much stubble, for that matter. He'd left wearing the plain clothes associated with their strict faith. Today, the man he'd become seemed perfectly comfortable in his *Englischer* clothes and worn-out running shoes.

Averting her eyes, she let him pass through the front door. There were so many reasons why she didn't want him back in Pinecraft. Forefront in her mind was the way he'd broken her heart and abandoned their dream of a life together. *So why is he back?* She motioned him farther into the house. "*Komm.* Your *daed*'s in the garden. I'll fetch him for you." A slight tremble in her voice revealed more about her irritation toward him than she wanted. She made her way past her mother and several chatting women, ignoring their inquisitive expressions and quiet murmurs as they moved down a long hall that led to the great room.

"Verity, wait." Leviticus tugged at her arm, his fingers barely touching her skin.

Verity looked down at his tanned fingers pressed against the paleness of her arm and sent him a cautionary look. *Don't touch me. Don't you ever touch me again.*

He released his hold, his questioning expression carving lines in his forehead.

She forced herself to relax. It was just Leviticus come home, after all. He meant nothing to her anymore. "You'll find Albert next to the rose garden."

He nodded, and then glanced back at the collection of women clustered in the living room. "Have the women gathered to pray? Is someone sick?"

She shook her head, shoving her trembling hands into her apron pockets to keep her reaction to him hidden. "*Nee*, the church choir is having a singing frolic in the park this weekend. There's been so much destruction in Pinecraft since the hurricane. Some of the women have planned a dinner to raise much-needed funds. Clara was kind enough to offer the choir use of the farmhouse so we could practice."

Verity could still feel the gaze of several choir members on her, watching and wondering. Should she mention to Leviticus that his father had had a stroke less than a month ago and was still in a weakened condition? No. It was best she stayed out of the Hilty family business. She was the housekeeper, after all. Not family. She'd leave that conversation for Albert and his son.

"Who's Clara?" Leviticus's eyebrows knitted together.

She spoke over the sounds of the choir warming up again. "Clara is Solomon's *fraa*. Your brother was courting her when you left, but that was a long time ago. No wonder you've forgotten." *Like you forgot me*, she added silently.

The women began to sing in sweet harmony. The words to "Amazing Grace" filled the old house, reminding her that *Gott* had all things under control. Even this awkward situation with the man who had once been her beloved. She tried to sound casual, like someone who didn't care that the man standing next to her had torn her young heart into a million pieces. "Solomon and Clara are living here now, but it's temporary. Hurricane winds did some interior damage to their *haus* down the grove a few days ago and Albert took them in till it's repaired."

"And you? I guess you're married by now and have your own *haus* and *kinner*." His warm blue-eyed gaze pinned her down like a bug to cardboard.

She went cold inside. She spoke matter-of-factly but was anything but inwardly calm. "*Ya*, I was married to Mark Schrock, but I'm a widow now, with a young *dochder* named Faith. She's with my younger *schweschders* while I'm busy with the ladies." Her gaze dropped to the child sleeping in his arms.

"I'm sorry about the loss of your husband." His words sounded sincere enough, but in the past, his words had seemed sincere, too. Especially after his mother's funeral, when she was seventeen and he had tried explaining why he was leaving Pinecraft, setting her back on the shelf as if they'd meant nothing to each other. That day he'd rambled on without making a lick of sense, especially when he'd suggested his mother had been overworked by the church and his father until the day she dropped dead from exhaustion. Hadn't he realized women like his mother thrived on being needed and never complained?

The *kind* in his arms stirred and stretched, drawing his attention. Flushed with sleep, the little girl made grunting sounds and then settled down. His blue-eyed gaze roamed the child's face as he tucked a pink blanket in around her chubby legs. A long, slim finger ran lovingly down the side of her rosy cheek.

She caught a glimpse of the baby's pursed pink lips. A trickle of milk seeped from the side of her sweet mouth. At least Leviticus had become responsible enough to keep the child well fed. "I see time's brought changes to all our lives. Is your *fraa* with you?"

He looked her over, his expression calm. "*Nee.* I never married."

He seemed comfortable enough with his statement. Like having a child out of wedlock was an everyday occurrence for *Englisch* men like the one he'd become. "She's a cute *boppli.* What's her name?"

"Naomi, after my *mudder.*" He grinned, his beguiling dimple flashing again, tempting her to reach out and touch it as she had a hundred times in the distant past.

He laughed. "I tend to call her Trouble when it's three in the morning and she's screaming blue murder with a wet diaper." He remained warm and friendly, even though Verity knew she had to be frowning his way. His playful personality had always been so irritating, yet so appealing to her.

"Babies are known for waking at the worst times." Drawn in by his smile, she relaxed a tiny bit. She thought of Faith's first year and all the sleep she'd lost rocking her in the chair Mark had fashioned for her before the accident took his life. Sadness replaced her half smile with a frown. "*Komm,* you must be eager to see your *daed* after all these years."

"You don't have to come along with me. It hasn't been that long. I know where the garden is." His tone was gentle, but firm. He stepped past her and out the door without a backward glance.

"It's been longer than you think, Leviticus Hilty," she whispered, dealing with what felt like a dismissal. She watched his long stride eat up the distance between the porch and the wood gate surrounding the rose beds. To his retreating back, she muttered softly, "Much longer."

Clara was suddenly by her side, crowding her out of the doorway with her big belly. Her friend's brow arched as she asked, "Who's that?"

Leviticus strolled alongside the sheds beside the house, over to where his mother's rose garden bloomed in perfumed profusion. "That's your *bruder*-in-law, Leviticus Hilty."

"How can that be?" Clara's honey-colored eyes widened in surprise. Always nosy, she flicked her *kapp*'s ribbon behind her shoulder and inched closer to the screen door for a better look. "He's not anything like the Leviticus I remember. That man's an *Englischer*."

"*Ya*, he is, but he's Leviticus Hilty all the same." Verity strived to steady herself. Her nerves were jingling like the Christmas bells on Faith's shoes. Leviticus had returned. *So what if he's returned? He no longer means anything to me.*

Verity watched as Leviticus turned toward the backfield of blown-over citrus trees and moved on. His shoulders rounded, no doubt in reaction to the damage stretched out before him.

The grove had been slammed by high winds during

the recent late-season hurricane. Squalls of heavy rain had flooded field after field until they were all underwater. The house had been spared, for the most part, but the damage to the grove would be considerable, if not devastating, financially. Verity loved the fields of miniature orange trees, this old house, its family. *How will the grove survive?*

"Solomon's not going to like Leviticus's returning home an *Englischer*. Even now, when an extra hand is needed and appreciated." Clara patted her stomach, as if rubbing it would rid her of the concerns that might upset her *boppli*. "And Albert. Do you think he'll easily forgive his *soh* for leaving the faith and never joining the church?"

"He certain-sure missed him." Verity forced her fisted hands to relax at her sides. "As far as I'm concerned, Leviticus coming home is exactly what Albert *didn't* need. And bringing a *kind* with him, even though she'll be a blessing, will bring more problems. We've got thirty nosy women in the house, all of whom love to spread rumors. We've got to get rid of them as fast as we can. I can hear them now. Albert's *soh* is home and has brought shame to the community yet again." Verity smiled reassuringly at Clara. "You find a way to get rid of the ladies while I deal with this situation."

Verity opened the screen door and scooted past. Consternation put a frown on her face. *Why had Leviticus chosen now to come home?*

Leviticus hurried along, his thoughts scrambled by the funny games God seemed to allow people to play with their lives. His mother's sudden death, his leaving home, his time at the Amish rescue home, his enlistment into the army. Serving a six-month tour in Afghanistan and nearly dying just days before he was to leave had left him dealing with PTSD.

He would have never guessed Verity, one of the people he'd hurt the most, would be taking care of his aging father. She was no longer a girl, and he had to admit she looked good. Better than good.

She'll never take you back, no matter how forgiving an Amish woman she is. You don't deserve someone like her. Not after what you did.

He was still captivated by the spirited Plain woman with coppery red hair and green eyes that sparkled like jewels, but his leftover feelings would have to be crushed.

She would have been my fraa *if I hadn't left.*

Naomi fussed. His hand trembled as he shaded his daughter's face from the morning sun. A reminder that his PTSD was kicking up. He had to keep using the stress management techniques he learned in the hospital and take his pills regularly. Naomi was so young and vulnerable. Her whole life lay before her. She had only him. Would he be enough? Was he up to raising a daughter by himself?

Deep in thought, he ambled toward the rose garden. Memories of his happy childhood flooded in, tugging at his heartstrings. He visualized his *mamm* clipping off dead rose blooms with care. She'd loved all living things, even him, and he'd seldom earned a day of her devotion.

Perhaps she'd still be alive if he hadn't brought shame to their door with his wild ways. He should have joined the church young and been baptized as she'd asked him. But no. He'd had to live the life that suited him best.

Regret swamped his mind. His father had always held his mother accountable for his inappropriate behavior. Late at night, he'd often heard his parents argue. His older brother, Solomon, never caused tension. Leviticus shrugged in regret and continued to his father's favorite resting place.

It broke him to know his mother would never know he'd grown closer to the Lord, straightened out his ways and returned to Pinecraft, where he belonged. With a *dochder* to bring up, it was far better to return home with tremors from the war than to linger in the *Englischer* world.

He took in a deep breath, the scent of the roses reminding him of who he was meant to become. A Plain man, with Plain ways.

The thick grass underfoot was still marshy from days of torrential rains. He squinted from the bright sun peeking out beneath a cluster of storm clouds. Up ahead his father, Albert, sat in a wooden Adirondack chair, his back to him.

Leviticus walked up quietly, searching for the words he'd practiced repeatedly, but found he'd lost them to the nerves twisting his gut. *"Daed?"* he whispered. *If only speaking Pennsylvania Dutch would make me Amish again.*

A strong gust of wind carried his word and rushed it toward the sea. He stepped closer, fighting the urge to reach out a hand and touch his father's silver hair blowing in the breeze. He had no idea how he'd be received. Like the prodigal son, he'd lived with the pigs and eaten their slop for far too long. It was time he faced his past. But doubt crept in. Would he be forgiven? Could he live the Plain life? *"Daed."*

Albert Hilty's head twisted round, glancing over his shoulder. His smile melted away. A dazed expression crossed his weathered face. He rose with effort, staggering, then reaching out for the arm of his chair. His father's blue eyes blinked, his countenance growing incredulous. "It's you, Leviticus? This time I'm not dreaming?"

"No, *Daed.* You're not dreaming. It's me. Such as I am. I'm home for good if you'll have me." Leviticus waited. A sense of peace came over him, edging out the dread he'd felt at the thought of confessing his sins to his father and the bishop. He was glad to be home, glad he didn't have to deal with the remnants of PTSD alone. He'd needed his family and his growing faith more than he'd realized.

Albert stumbled forward, arms reaching out. He threw himself at his *soh* and clung to him in a warm embrace as he kissed his neck, murmuring, "At last you are home."

As Albert held him, Leviticus could feel his father's frail body trembling. A wave of love washed over him. This old man was more precious to him than he'd realized. For a moment, he couldn't let go. *It's been so long.* He'd been so angry. "I'm sorry I left so abruptly. I thought… Well, it doesn't matter what I thought back then." His head dropped with shame as his father's gaze sought his. "I should have come home sooner."

"*Ya*, you should have." His father nodded in agreement. "Ach, and who is this child between us?" Albert held on to Leviticus's arm for support, considering the face of his grandchild for the first time. The edges of his mouth turned up into a smile.

"This is my *dochder*, Naomi. She's come to see her *grossdaddi*."

Albert appeared bemused for a moment, his thin, graying brows arching down. His gaze locked with Leviticus's. "The *kind* has your *mamm*'s button nose and her name. This is *gut*." He nodded again. "You have a family now. I should have realized you would after all these years." The old man's next words rushed out. "*Welkom* home, Leviticus. You have been sorely missed."

"But not by everyone. I'm sure Otto and some of the elders were glad to see the back of me all those years ago."

Albert squeezed his son's arm. "*Nee*. They prayed for your soul and your safe return home, as I did. But let's forget all that for now. My *soh* is home. *Gott* in His mercy will forgive your past sins if you repent. He who was lost has returned. I care not what others think. Today is a *gut* day. *Komm*, let's go into the *haus*. I want to get better acquainted with my *kinskind*."

Albert shuffled forward, his steps unsure. Leviticus stayed close. *How had Daed gotten so weak in a matter of years?* When he'd left, his father had been a strong and able-bodied man.

Leviticus glanced up. Verity hurried to his father's side, supporting him as he took small steps. He leaned heavily on her for strength. How long had his *daed* needed help just to walk? Shame raced through him, burned his cheeks. While he'd been busy living his own life, he'd forgotten time hadn't stood still for his father, or for the grove. Gott *forgive me, I should have never left this place.*

"What happened to you, *Daed*?"

Verity supported his father by the arm. Her eyes surveyed Leviticus, saying, *It's too late to be concerned now. You should have stayed home.*

Her arm around his waist, Verity assisted Albert up the back steps and through the kitchen door. The old man shuffled over to the table and sat with a loud sigh, then wiped sweat off his face with the swipe of a bandanna he carried in his back pocket.

Verity stood by the sink, her hand pressed to her throat, a worried frown creasing her forehead. His gaze shifted between her and his father.

Albert smiled. He spoke, as much to himself as anyone. "That *Englischer* doctor said I had a stroke a while back." He shook his head. "*Nee.* I don't see how he could suggest such a thing. I can still walk and talk just fine."

Leviticus pulled out a chair at the kitchen table next to his father and lowered himself, watching the aged man's every move, seeing confusion cross his father's wrinkled face.

Albert's age-spotted hand smoothed the tablecloth in front of him. "I'm certain-sure most folks can't walk or talk after a stroke." He smiled Leviticus's way, one side of the old man's mouth slightly drooping. "Verity can tell you. I'm doing mighty fine for an old man of seventy plus years. Ain't so?"

Verity locked eyes with Leviticus and shook her

head, encouraging him not to correct his father's mis-conceptions. She reheated the coffee she'd made for herself a few minutes before and laced a cup with two scoops of sugar to ward off Albert's shock. "He's doing fine now that he's up and about." She placed her hand on Albert's shoulder and set a cup of sweet coffee in front of him.

"Would you like something hot to drink?"

"Sure." Coffee sounded good. Leviticus took off his billed cap and placed it on the table, revealing his windblown, long blond hair that grew down around his collar.

Verity's mouth pursed, her disapproval narrowing her green eyes. Once he changed his clothes to Amish and had his hair cut around his ears he'd fit in better.

There'd been a time when he'd fit in fine, be-longed...regardless of how rebellious he'd become. He was one of them. But now? The loss of who he could have been caused his heart to ache. *What must* Daed *be thinking?*

Verity poured another cup of coffee and set the steaming mug in front of him. As she went back to the stove, Leviticus could hear his new sister-in-law ushering the last of the singers out the front door. The pregnant woman's nervous giggles told him she was doing her best to avoid saying too much about his ap-pearance and the suddenly shortened choir practice.

A glance at the battery-run clock over the stove told him it was high noon. Solomon would probably be home soon for his lunch. Leviticus feared his re-turn wouldn't bode well with his hardworking *bruder*. There'd be enough gossip flying around the community about his homecoming without the ladies spreading tales of a heated argument between him and Solomon.

Verity swatted wisps of hair away from her forehead and then lowered her head, concentrating on making hearty roast beef sandwiches for the men. Albert slurped his coffee as he always did. Leviticus remained quiet for a moment, observing and remembering. Verity stole a glance his way as the *kind* in his arms began to fret. Naomi's pudgy bare feet kicked the air in agitation.

"She needs a diaper change. Any chance my old room's still available?"

"It is." Verity cut into a ripe tomato and took out all the seeds for Albert's sandwich.

Everything was different. Never in a million years had he imagined he would someday come home and have need of a cot for a *boppli*. Nothing had prepared him for the shock of seeing his father so emaciated. Not even the war.

"I've got a small porta-cot Faith used stored under my bed. I'll wipe it down and put it up in a minute, just in case she gets sleepy again."

Albert's head bobbed. "*Ya*. Use your old room, *soh*, but leave the *kind* and such things to Verity. She's had plenty of experience with *kinner* of all ages. Ain't so?"

Verity raised her chin and nodded.

He was sure she had taken care of many children, but this one was his and another woman's child. There'd been a time that fact would have hurt her beyond measure. From the glare she was giving him now, Leviticus could see he was no longer important to her.

"*Ya*, I'll see to the *boppli*, if that's all right with her *daed*."

Leviticus lifted his shoulders in a half shrug. "I had thought…"

Albert tugged at his beard, watching him as he shifted Naomi to his shoulder and soothed her.

"A woman knows what's best for *bopplis*. I'm surprised Naomi's *mamm*'s not here, seeing to her needs. Will she come later?"

Leviticus straightened out his daughter's pink collar. "*Nee*. Julie's not coming. She's a judge advocate of some importance. Her job keeps her busy in Washington. We're not married, *Daed*. When Naomi was born, Julie made it clear she wanted nothing further to do with me or our *dochder*."

His *daed*'s eyebrows shot up. The room became silent, as if time stood still. Albert sat soundlessly digesting Leviticus's disturbing words. "This woman, Julie. She is *Englisch*, *ya*?" He scratched at his beard, his deep-set eyes surveying Leviticus closely.

"She is."

"That explains the lack of a wedding." Albert took a sip of coffee. "*Nee* Plain woman would walk away from her *kind* and leave a *mann* to care for it. *Gut* thing you came home. Naomi will be well loved here on the grove." Albert twisted in his chair, his bony hand motioning Verity over. "*Komm*, lunch can wait. The *boppli* needs a woman's touch."

Leviticus's gaze locked with Verity's as she lifted the *kind* from his arms. She nodded, their silent conversation missed by Albert. She would take good care of his child. Naomi whimpered and pushed away as she was taken out of her father's arms. Without a backward glance, Verity made her way through the kitchen door, into the great room.

Albert followed his housekeeper with his eyes. "She's had a hard few years, Leviticus. I think a husband is what she needs. Someone to carry the load of parenting with her. You've been away a long time. People change. Just go easy if you have a mind to court her again."

Leviticus dropped his head. What his father said was true. He and Verity had been over for a long time. And in the condition he was in, she was off-limits to him. He'd make sure of that. She deserved someone whole. Not a man who fought night terrors and jumped every time he heard a loud noise.

He couldn't help but think about the way Verity used to look at him, like he was something special. Today that look had been replaced with indifference, but who could blame her? She had forgiven him for breaking her heart, but not forgotten. He was sure of that. True, it was her nature to forgive. But she wore her heart on her sleeve and always had.

Yet, it was evident by her disapproving expression that she had no feelings left for him. He was just someone to be tolerated now. He was Albert's son, but not her lost love.

Chapter Two

Leviticus finished the sandwiches Verity had started and served one to his father before settling down with his own. His thoughts stayed on Naomi as he chewed. She was in good hands, but had Verity noticed Naomi was a squirmer? Less than a year old, she needed to be closely watched or she'd be rolling off the bed and onto the floor.

"Danki, soh." Albert pulled the well-filled sandwich closer. "There's chips in the larder, if you have a taste for them."

"Nee. This is fine."

"My doctor said no more greasy foods for me, but Verity lets me have baked chips occasionally."

"She treats you well, then?" Leviticus's gaze focused on his father's pale skin, noticing the way his heart beat fast in a vein on his neck.

"Ya, Verity treats me special *gut."* Albert took a small bite of his sandwich and began to chew.

In truth, time hadn't stood still for either of them. His father's eyes were on him, too, judging what he saw and probably finding fault with his clothes, the scar running down his cheek that screamed violence. But if his father *was* disappointed, he said nothing as he ate several bites and then pushed his half-eaten sandwich away. "My appetite isn't what it used to be."

"*Nee*. Mine, either." Leviticus glanced around the sunny kitchen. Some things remained as he remembered them. The same pot rack held his *mamm*'s old cookware. The pot holders she'd made from spare quilting blocks hung from the same golden hooks. A familiar set of plastic canisters sat against the back wall on the counter. His *mamm*'s indecipherable handwriting labeled them as flour, sugar and coffee. Memories of her love and care caused him pain and added regret. She had been a woman of tiny stature, barely the size of a twelve-year-old child. But what she lacked in height, she made up for in spirit and determination.

He could still picture her scurrying around this room, preparing meals fit for a king. Her spunk kept him out of trouble with the elders during *rumspringa.* She'd always expected the best from everyone and gave back in kind. But he'd stolen, lied and drank too much during his time of running around, bringing her nothing but disgrace in the end. Shame ate at him, burned his throat. Had the stress been the reason she'd died so suddenly, and not hard work?

Leviticus stored away his memories. His father didn't need to see him cry on his first day home. "You want a glass of water?"

"*Ya*, sure. *Danki.* I need to take my pill." Albert opened one of the brown medicine bottles on the table and laughed. "I never thought I'd find myself pushing pills in my mouth morning and night, but Verity says she'll tell the doctor if I don't take them on time."

He turned toward his *soh*, his expression incredulous. "You know, the doctor put me in an *Englischer* nursing home for three whole days after my stroke. But Otto sent Verity along. She pulled me out and brought me home, just like a *gut dochder* would do. I had to laugh at all her bluster and spirit, her bright copper hair flying wild about her *kapp* like she was *Gott*'s emissary come to rescue me."

Albert guffawed. "Certain-sure she saved me from the grip of the enemy." His head bobbed. "*Ya*, for certain-sure." He set the bottle of pills he'd been holding on the table. "She's been my right hand since that day, and a fine housekeeper, too." He laughed again. "That girl has spunk. Just like your *mamm*. You should have married her while you had the chance."

Leviticus knew he should have. He should have done a lot of things better than he had. Some had paid too high a price for his having his own way. He desperately needed *Gott* to show him mercy, remove the horrific dreams of war, the remains of PTSD still plaguing his mind from time to time. Would redemption remove his every sin as his bishop had preached when he was young? For now, he would live with the guilt burning his insides until God removed the pain. His father's forgiveness would go a long way toward securing a measure of peace for his troubled mind.

Footsteps crossing the small wooden porch out back told him Solomon would soon be walking in through the back door. No doubt hungry and expecting Clara to be fixing his meal.

Leviticus prepared himself for their confrontation. Solomon had every right to be livid with him. A young man of twenty, he'd been left to deal with the grove, with a father set in his ways and growing feeble with age and illness. Had there been too little money to hire fruit pickers to help run the land, buy what was needed the last ten years?

The back door handle turned and Solomon stepped in. His brother had grown taller, put on a little weight and seemed fit under his traditional Amish garb. Brown hair, so much like their *mamm*'s, ran riot over his head. Windblown clusters of curls poked out from under the dirty straw work hat that he wore. Dried mud caked his boots up to his dark trouser cuffs.

Solomon stopped in his tracks, taking a long, hard look at Leviticus. His blue eyes narrowed as he realized who stood by his father's side.

"What's he doing here? Did you send for him?"

Albert accepted the glass of tap water from his younger son's hand and swallowed his pill. *"Danki."* His eyes cut to his oldest son. "Now, how could I have sent for Leviticus? I didn't know where he was any more than you did. *Gott* directed your *bruder*'s steps home."

Leviticus watched the exchange. Albert seemed calm and steady, but Solomon's face reddened, ready to explode with fury.

Leviticus stepped forward.

Solomon turned toward him, ignored Leviticus's outstretched hand. His finger jabbed toward the back door. "Get out! You're not *welkom* here."

Albert swayed to his feet. His face flushed a ruby

red. "I'm still alive and owner of this grove, Solomon Hilty. Leviticus is my youngest *bu*. He can stay as long as he chooses, and you have *nee* say in if he comes or goes."

Solomon banged his fist down hard on the wooden kitchen table, rattling their coffee mugs. "Where was your precious *soh* when the orange trees dropped fruit from fungus? Remember how we worked twelve-hour days to save that crop?"

Solomon's loudly spoken words echoed through the house, a verbal slap across Leviticus's face. He'd earned that slap…and more.

"Where was Leviticus when you almost died in the grove?" He pointed to his *bruder*. "Did he come and sit by your hospital bed for days? *Nee*. But I was there, *Daed*." Solomon's finger poked his own chest. His tone dropped, tears glistening in his eyes. "I was there the whole time."

"You were there and that was as it should be. But your *bruder* is home now. You should be happy Leviticus has come to make things right with *Gott*. Hasn't that always been our prayer?"

Looks were exchanged between brothers. Leviticus's frayed nerves shouted at him to run, leave all the drama behind and just go. Solomon didn't understand why he'd left, but now was not the time for explaining. He'd done enough damage to this family.

Solomon has a right to want me gone. If the roles were reversed, I'd be saying the same to him.

Two steps brought Solomon to his father's side. "Is that what he told you? That he's come home to give *Gott* and the Amish way of life a chance? Do his long hair, his *Englisch* clothes look like a *mann* ready to turn over a new leaf, *Daed*? Do they?"

"This will end now!" Verity stood in the doorway, her eyes wide and spitting fire. "Your *daed* has no need of this foolishness. I will not have him made upset."

Solomon flashed a look at Leviticus that spoke volumes. He slammed his work hat back on his head. "This is not over, little *bruder*. Not by a long shot. The bishop and I will talk and then you'll be gone." He slammed out the door, the glass pane trembling in his wake.

Barefoot, Clara entered the room from the hall and flashed past Leviticus, her advanced pregnancy evident by the round bulge pushing at the waistline of her plain blue dress. Tears ran down her face as she rushed out the back door behind Solomon.

Leviticus took a sip of his water, swallowed hard and poured the rest of it down the sink. He'd expected Solomon to be relentless with anger and he hadn't been far off the mark. Solomon's forgiveness might come, but not today. Maybe not ever.

Her face flushed, Verity patted Albert on the arm. "You'll be all right while I gather the eggs?"

"*Ya*, sure. Leviticus is here now. He can fetch and carry for me till you're back in."

She nodded but paused a step away and turned back. "You took your pill?"

"*Ya*. Just like you told me. One at lunch and the other at dinner."

"*Gut*." Verity grabbed the egg basket and then hurried out of the room, but not before sending Leviticus a warning glance over her shoulder that told him she wouldn't put up with any more foolishness from him around his father.

Leviticus raked his fingers through his tangled hair and let his arm drop to his side. Verity wasn't comfortable with him around, either. What had he expected? A happy homecoming? Like Solomon, she may never forgive him.

Albert motioned for him to sit. "Your *bruder*'s angry now, but he'll calm down. It may take time, but he'll see the error of his ways and repent. I taught you both how to forgive, as *Gott* forgives us." He smiled at his youngest *soh*, his eyes lighting up.

"Your *bruder* missed you. He's just bone tired and frustrated. The hurricane—it did terrible damage to the grove." Albert rubbed at the base of his neck. "We're not sure the grove can be saved. A big city buyer came round today, offering fifty cents on the dollar for the ground, but Solomon ran him off before I could." The old man thrust his fist in the air. "I'll die before I see this grove given away." He laid his hand on his son's arm. "Now that you are home, there is hope for the future of Hilty Groves."

"Don't put your faith in me, *Daed*. Trust in *Gott*. I'll disappoint you every time." Humiliation ripped at his gut. He hadn't earned his father's trust yet, but he would, given time. He didn't know if he had what it took to be the kind of *soh* his *daed* needed him to be, but he intended to try. *Can I become a Plain man and please* Gott?

Somewhere in the dark room, a baby was crying as if its heart were broken.

Verity woke disoriented, her jumbled thoughts convincing her it was Faith's lusty wails. She hurried out of bed, hoping she could calm the *boppli* before her cries woke Mark. He rose early each morning, before the sun's first rays. *The poor* mann *needs his rest.*

She frantically searched for her robe at the foot of the bed, then went on a hunt for her missing slipper. Kneeling, she found it just under the bed. Verity rushed to scoop the baby up, but the cot wasn't where it should be by the back window. She turned, looking about in the darkness. The whole room seemed off-kilter, everything out of place. Why wasn't the night-light glowing? She always left it on, so she could check the baby without disturbing Mark. Had the bulb burned out?

She located a lamp on the dresser and switched it on. Its golden glow flooded the room.

She glanced around. One side of the bed was rumpled. The other empty.

Reality returned like the jab of a knife. She let out a loud sigh, all the while her heart pounding in her throat. Mark was with the Lord, his broken body deep under the soggy ground, along with their tiny *soh*, who'd been born much too early due to her shock and grief.

The crying child was sweet Naomi, Leviticus's child.

Her house shoes made scuffing noises as she hurried across the hardwood floor and lifted the squirming child into her arms. Naomi was furious, her face red and splotched from crying. Her feet kicked the air in outrage. Verity cooed and softly talked to her, trying her best to calm the irate *kind*.

She and Leviticus could have had their own *dochder* if he hadn't walked away. But he had. Faith's birth had filled her with a mother's love, but what about Naomi? The child needed the care and love of a *mamm*. But could she care for Naomi and not feel resentment? A look into the baby's shimmering dark eyes told Verity all she needed to know. She would love Leviticus's child and show no grudge.

She hugged the child closer, even though Naomi protested and pushed away. All *kinner* needed to feel wanted. Especially this bundle, whose *mamm* thought more of her job than her own flesh and blood. Anger rose up. Her heart ached for Naomi. How could anyone disown such a sweet *boppli*?

Soaked from head to toe, Naomi was inconsolable. Her diaper, sheet and blanket would need changing. She'd have to put a fresh diaper and gown on the *kind* before she could get the chill off a bottle of milk.

She worked fast, stripping off the *Englischer* onesie covered in tiny orange giraffes and pink rabbits. Amish children slept in nightgowns made of soft cotton, as was the custom. She'd made all her daughter's gowns by hand and packed them up as Faith outgrew them. They'd been stored away for her next *kind*, but that *boppli*, a son she'd named Aaron, had lived but a few hours and then taken his last breath. Out of the dozens of gowns she'd sewed for him, he'd only worn one while alive. He'd been buried in a casket gown made by her hands, his little body swallowed up in the tiny garment painstakingly sewn while she'd cried a million tears in sorrow.

Aaron had never gazed into his mother's eyes or fed at her breast. The loss of Mark had left her broken, but the loss of Aaron had left her inconsolable. Almost crazy with grief, she'd shaken her fist at God the day they laid Aaron in the ground. She still asked how her *soh*'s loss could have been *Gott*'s will. Nothing good ever came from his death.

A tap sounded at her closed bedroom door. Bending over the foot of her bed, Verity quickly wrapped Naomi in a blanket and picked her up before cracking the door. *"Ya?"*

Leviticus stood just outside the semidarkness of her room. As if he'd dressed in a hurry, his shirt was buttoned incorrectly and thrown over wrinkled jeans. His long hair stood out wild around his sleep-creased face.

"I heard the baby crying and thought you might need my help."

"You could fix her bottle while I redress her." Her nerves tensed. *Leviticus shouldn't be in my bedroom while the others sleep on.* She edged back to her bed, drawing Naomi close to her as she went. The child squirmed, almost slipping out of her hands. Turning her back to Leviticus, she tried to still the child's body as she wiped her down with wipes and grabbed for a fresh diaper.

Leviticus stood over her. "She squirms a lot."

Uncomfortable with the closeness of their bodies, she dipped her head, her eyes on his *kind*. *"Ya."*

He stepped away. "You'll have to be extra cautious

when changing her near the edge of the bed. She's quick."

"That she is." Glad he'd moved toward the door, she couldn't help but grin. His *dochder*'s wiggling antics reminded her so much of Faith at this age.

"I'll be right back." And with that, Leviticus was gone, his shape melting into the darkness of the long hall.

After a moment, she could hear him in the kitchen, clanging pans and opening cupboards. Verity pondered his predicament. Leviticus seemed practiced in things pertaining to his *dochder*'s care. She had never met a man who could tend to a little one's needs. Not that Mark hadn't shown an interest in everything she had done for Faith. But to have expected him to go for a warm bottle or change her? She chuckled aloud at the thought. Amish men didn't do such things unless their *fraa* was ill and there was no one else to help, which was seldom the case in Pinecraft.

Before she could slip on and snap together Naomi's one-piece sleeper, Leviticus was by her side, shaking the warm baby bottle with gusto. "The nurse I hired said to shake the formula really well."

"*Ya*, but I don't think she meant you to make whipped cream of the milk." She held out her hand and took the bottle, avoiding his fingers, even though a secret part of her longed to touch him. She tested the warmth of the milk on her wrist before settling herself and the child in the small rocker in the corner.

Leviticus stood looking at them, his expression undecipherable in the shadowy room.

"You can go back to bed now. I can manage."

He reached back, blindly searching for the door-knob, and stepped out with a nod. Silence filled the room. The muted sounds of Naomi smacking down her milk brought calm to Verity's soul. She began to hum one of the songs she would sing to Faith. Movement caused Verity to look back toward the door. Leviticus had returned, partially hidden in the gloom. "Go. I'll take good care of her. There's no need for you to worry." *Would he ever go away?*

"I know you will, but it's hard for me to let go."

"You don't have to let go completely. Just trust me to see to her needs. To love her like she deserves to be loved."

"Why would you want to do this for me after the pain I've caused you?"

Verity rested her head back against the rocker, her eyes closed. The weight of the baby was a comfort to her empty arms. The soothing motion of the rocker brought needed peace. "My caring for Naomi has nothing to do with what went on between us. Naomi needs me. I'll see to her needs. Any woman would."

"Not every woman. Her own *mamm* wouldn't." He stepped out of the shadows, into the light. "How can a *mudder* feel nothing for her own flesh and blood?" Leviticus's expression was bleak.

Anger gripped her. She fought down the compassion she felt growing for him. She couldn't fathom any woman being so heartless. "I have no answers for you. You'll have to ask Naomi's *mudder* the next time you see her."

The lamp's muted glow turned his hair to spun gold. "Do you mind me asking what happened to your husband?" He leaned against the doorjamb, waiting for her reply.

She took in a quiet breath, prepared to tell the story once again. Each time she had to speak of her husband's death, her loss grew. "Mark was a hard worker, a *gut* man. New to Pinecraft, he took a job with a local arborist. He was still in training when he climbed up a tree and fell to his death." She sighed. "No one was at fault. He somehow managed to put on his harness incorrectly. It didn't hold when a rotten branch broke and fell on top of him."

"I'm sorry for your loss."

Verity nodded. She couldn't speak for a moment. Leviticus's words seemed sincere enough, but his regret didn't mean a thing to her. All those years ago, he'd sounded sincere when he'd told her he loved her, too. But he hadn't. Not really. He'd left her standing next to his *mamm*'s grave, with everyone looking on as he tenderly kissed her lips and walked away without so much as a backward glance.

Tears gathered in her eyes. "Morning comes early around here, Leviticus. Get to bed." Verity spoke carefully, keeping her tears from falling. When he finally shut the door behind him, she let her tears flow. She cried for Naomi's loss, for her loss of Mark and for her *soh*, who'd never known his *mamm*'s love. But she refused to cry for Leviticus. He'd earned his pain, even though something, that small voice, told her she was wrong.

Chapter Three

Golden rays of sunlight rose above the groves. The gray sky overhead had turned into a cloudless blue day.

Shredded palm fronds and broken tree branches littered the big fenced-in yard. Leviticus turned back toward the house. Roof tiles and tar paper added to the debris near the rambling dwelling he'd grown up in. There was a lot of work to be done and not many community hands available to help, thanks to the widespread damage around town.

He stepped inside the kitchen door, nodded at Verity, who was busy working at the end of the counter, and then smiled at his father, who was eating at the breakfast table.

"*Gut mariye*, Leviticus. Did you sleep well?"

"*Mariye, Daed.*" He knew he was breaking one of his *mamm*'s cardinal rules when he slathered his hands with dish soap and rinsed them in the sink meant only for washing dishes, subconsciously hoping she'd appear and scold him one more time for misbehaving. "I slept well enough, I guess." He dismissed the night terrors he'd endured that had woken him with muffled screams. Verity and his father didn't need to know about the remnants of PTSD that still haunted him night and day.

Verity gave him a disapproving glance for abusing the sink but went about her business, cutting fresh fruit into chunks. She didn't say a word of greeting. There were dark circles under her eyes. *Had Naomi kept her up crying?* The first weeks he'd cared for Naomi, he'd had his own share of sleepless nights. Google called the problem a mix-up of days and nights. He'd called exhaustion a miserable way to live.

Perhaps Naomi missed her mother. He thought of Julie, wondered how she was feeling now that the *boppli* was gone from her life forever. She'd had six months to bond with her own flesh and blood, even though the nanny seemed in charge of Naomi the day he'd been around. He'd never seen Julie pick up Naomi once or feed her, and she'd said no goodbyes to her when they'd left.

Leviticus grabbed a cereal bowl out of the cupboard and took a spoon from the freshly washed dishes on the drain board and then pulled out a chair and sat close to his hard-of-hearing father. He grimaced as he poured cereal from the plastic container and noticed moon-shaped, colored rainbows coated in sugar.

Verity stepped beside him carrying a cutting board of fruit. "You sure you don't want oatmeal?"

He shook his head. "*Nee*. This will do fine."

She put some of the fruit on his father's hot cereal. Leviticus's head lifted in surprise when Albert dug into the tan gooey mush with all the gusto of a small boy. Some things *had* seriously changed around the grove. When his mother was alive, his father had his oatmeal with brown sugar and lots of butter, but that was how she'd made it for her husband and his father never complained or asked for anything different.

Leviticus ate a crunchy bite of the sickeningly sweet cereal and held back a groan of disgust. A sugar rush was just what he didn't need, but he wasn't going to be a bother to Verity. She had enough to do; besides, she was rushing around like she was in a hurry. "Where's everyone?" He ate another bite of cereal, determined to make it through at least half the bowl.

Verity flipped over a perfectly fried egg. "Solomon left for the grove over an hour ago, and Clara's still sleeping. Solomon said she had a rough night of it. The *boppli* kept her up with all its movements."

His thoughts went back to Julie. He'd left for his six-month tour in Afghanistan right after she'd learned she was pregnant. While he was gone, he'd missed out on her strange cravings, the sight of her belly growing round with his child. He'd been cheated out of Naomi's first few months of life, too. He could thank his injuries and lengthy hospital stay for that.

Forget Julie. Naomi was home among family now. That was all that mattered.

Albert tipped his coffee mug and drained the last drops of his dark brew. "I thought we'd take the ATV out and inspect the grove's damage for ourselves. Solomon says it's extensive, but until I see it for myself I can't come up with a plan for how to fix it."

Verity cleared her throat and finished drying her hands as she spoke. "Solomon called Otto before he left. Seems the packing plant was flattened by the high winds. No one's sure if they'll be rebuilding it anytime soon."

Albert shoved back his chair and rose. "I'm certain-sure Thomas will do the right thing. He'll put the building up again with the help of the community." He edged toward the sink and put his bowl among the other dishes needing to be washed. "Amish and *Englisch* alike depend on him."

His shoulders dropped, his head shaking. "I don't know what we'll do if he chooses to close the business for *gut*." Staring into space, he tugged at his beard, using the kitchen counter as support.

Verity dusted down her apron and adjusted the cleaning scarf on her head. "Otto's going to see how many men he can gather but warned he might not find enough to make much of a difference. There's a lot of damage done to the houses in the district. Everyone's busy caring for their own *familye* needs first. Some Plain folk have hired *Englisch* laborers."

Her concern for Albert showed in the dark circles under her eyes, the way her shoulders sloped from the heavy weight of responsibility on her shoulders. Had she considered what would happen to her job if the grove closed? Who would be her mainstay if it did?

Albert grinned. "Don't underestimate that ole bishop's ability to gather a crowd. He can still be a persuasive man when the need arises." Albert used the sturdy kitchen table as a crutch as he maneuvered back to his chair. "You send Otto along to me when he gets here, Leviticus. We'll head out to the grove as soon as he comes."

Leviticus quickly finished the last spoonful of cereal he could stomach and rose, his eyes on Verity. "You'll have time to see to Naomi's needs?"

She dished up a bowl of oatmeal for herself and sat on the far side of the table across from his *daed*. "*Ya*, she'll be sleeping for a while yet. She took her bottle without a fuss at six and went straight back to sleep."

"I noticed you found the duffel bag of baby clothes I left by your bedroom door yesterday."

She poured milk over her oatmeal, added a heaping teaspoon of brown sugar and then tossed a handful of blueberries over the top. "I did. *Danki.*" She returned his gaze. "I hope the rain holds off. She'll need the cloth diapers I have dried. I've used up most all the disposable ones you had in the diaper bag, and the spare store-bought ones I had left over from Faith."

"Speaking of Faith, when's the *kind* coming home?" Albert poured himself a half-cup of coffee and splashed in milk.

"*Mamm* said she'd bring her back this morning, but I figure I'll see them later in the day." Verity smiled Albert's way. "Today's cherry vanilla day at Olaf's Creamery. It's Faith's favorite flavor. *Mamm*'s sure to get her a scoop before leaving town." Verity's smile brightened. "*Mamm*'s got a half-dozen grandkids and another on the way, but you'd think Faith was her only *kinskind* the way she spoils her."

Leviticus watched Verity's eyes light up as she spoke about her daughter, saw the worried lines vanish from her face. She was the old Verity in that moment. The girl he'd once loved and never deserved.

"Does your little girl like *bopplis*?" Would Verity

have enough energy to see to two active *kinner* after the difficult night with Naomi?

Verity sent a rare, genuine smile his way. "Faith loves *kinner* of any age. In fact, she's always asking when I'm going to get her a baby *schweschder*."

Albert guffawed into his tall mug as he slurped down the last of his coffee. "You've got to lower your standards and marry again for that to happen." His teasing expression was a welcomed sight, but he became serious once more. "No *kind* should grow up alone."

Rising, her hands on her hips, Verity looked poised to react negatively to Albert's words, but the sounds of several ATVs and an *Englischer* van pulling to a stop on the graveled driveway outside stymied her words.

Leviticus glanced out the window. Otto and Mose Fischer piled out of a black van and headed toward the house. Several men, some he didn't recognize, followed close behind. Solomon got off his ATV and walked over to the bishop. He jerked his head toward the house, his face pinched, no doubt still fuming. Was his *bruder* informing Otto of his homecoming? The aging bishop looked toward the back door and nodded, his steps lively as he approached. Mose trailed not far behind. There would be questions asked. Hard ones. He prayed he'd have the right answers for the man of God.

Albert slid out of his chair, his hand reaching for the door. He slipped outside just as the thump of their boots sounded on the porch. Pulling his gaze away from the window, Leviticus put his water glass in the sink and braced himself. As a young man, he'd gotten along with Mose Fischer, the bishop's son, just fine. But Otto, the local New Order bishop? Not so much. They'd had their run-ins, and Leviticus knew he would have been shunned if he'd been a member of the church during his restless time.

But he was different now, willing to accept the Amish way of life. With *Gott*'s help, he'd figure out what the Plain life meant for him.

The slam of the front door and sounds of muffled laughter sent Verity skittering past Leviticus, down the long hall that led to the great room, her bare feet slapping against the wooden slats of the floor as she hurried along. Faith was home, and she needed to tell the little girl about Leviticus's arrival and the *boppli* he had brought with him.

Her gaze sought out Faith. Dribbles of strawberry ice cream marked the skirt of her *dochder*'s pale pink dress. Verity smiled her welcome to her *mamm*, but her eyes were drawn back to her Faith. "I see someone got ice cream."

In her childish version of Pennsylvania Dutch, Faith exclaimed, "The ice cream was so *gut*. *Grossmammi* let me have two scoops." Verity kneeled, and Faith hugged her *mamm* round the neck, almost pulling Verity down with her excitement.

Verity accepted a shower of kisses from Faith while removing her slipping cape and outer *kapp*. "You must have been a special *gut* girl to get such a treat."

Faith's head bobbed up and down with enthusiasm, her messy bun at the base of her head bouncing, ready to fall without the support of her everyday *kapp* to keep it secured. "*Grossmammi* said I was so *gut* that we could go see the new puppies at Chicken John's after Thanksgiving. They're too little to touch just yet." Faith's big brown eyes grew wide with excitement and anticipation. "Can we go see them soon?" Verity's heart melted with love for her *dochder*, but she shot her *mamm* a frustrated glance. When would she have time to care for a small dog underfoot?

Verity's *mamm* laughed at Verity's serious expression and silent warning. "It's just to look, Verity. It's not like I promised Faith she could have one."

"Maybe your *grossmammi* and I should talk about your visit to Chicken Joe's while you go change your dress." Verity tucked Faith's lightweight winter cape and *kapp* under her arm, searched for and found her *dochder*'s white everyday *kapp* hanging from her small fingers. She quickly tidied Faith's bun but didn't attempt to replace the head covering. "There. Now, scoot. Change your dress. And mind you don't run…" Verity's last words became a whisper of frustration as Faith took off in a flash of pink down the hall, headed, no doubt, to the kitchen to find Albert.

Verity turned to her mother. "A puppy, *Mamm*? Seriously? That's the last thing I need right now. I'll have to be the one who tells her she can't have it. Not you."

"She doesn't ask for much, Verity."

Verity dropped her head, wishing she could relax her hold on life and enjoy it like she had when Mark was alive. "Leviticus has returned home, much to our surprise. I'd best go catch Faith before she starts giving him the third degree. You know how she is with strangers." Her trembling hands sought refuge in her apron pocket as she hurried off. Her mother was right. Faith didn't ask for much. Just love and a small fuzzy puppy.

Chapter Four

Waiting for his father to return to the house, Leviticus glanced toward the arch of the kitchen door as a petite, barefoot little girl ran into the room, her hair a cluster of wild ginger curls escaping from her bun, much like her *mamm*'s hair often did. Her big brown eyes sparkled in the sunlight streaming in through the kitchen window. The *kind* stopped abruptly and gave him a look of surprise and awe.

"Are you my new *daed*?" The child's gaze penetrated every fiber of his being, into his very soul. A sprinkling of honey-colored freckles disappeared when she scrunched up her nose and grinned impishly, exposing two missing bottom teeth. "I told *Gott* I wanted a blond-haired *daed*. He got that part right, but you've got blue eyes. I wanted a *daed* with brown eyes, like me." Her crinkled brow and piercing gaze suggested disappointment, but her smile returned quick enough.

Leviticus couldn't help but laugh out loud as the mixed emotions flashed across her face. He knew an imp when he saw one, and Faith Schrock was that and more. "I apologize. I do have blue eyes, but that's okay, because I'm sure *Gott*'s still debating on who's to be your new *daed*."

"*Nee*, he sent me you. He just got the eye color wrong." Bareheaded, the child wore a traditional pink Amish dress and apron, but her miniature *kapp* hung from her delicate fingertips.

"Shouldn't you be wearing that *kapp* on your head?"

"*Nee*, my *grossmammi* said it could stay off. She got tired of pinning it back on this morning." Her grin grew into a full-blown smile. "Do you think I'm hopeless?"

"No, I think you're adorable."

Her grin widened. "Did you bring my *boppli* with you?" Faith moved forward one step and then another, her hands busy situating a cloth doll under the crook of her arm.

"I'm assuming you asked *Gott* for a *boppli*, too?"

"Not a baby. A *boppli schweschder*. One like Beatrice has. She won't let me hold hers." Her bottom lip poked out in a pout. "She said I might break her, but I wouldn't."

Verity and a woman he recognized as her *mamm*, Miriam, came into the room. Verity reached for Faith's hand and pulled her to her side. Her troubled gaze pierced him. "I'm sorry. I should have warned you. My *dochder* is a real *blabbermaul*. She doesn't understand it's not okay to speak to strangers."

Faith buried her face in her mother's skirt for a moment and then laughed as she sprang forward, exposing her toothless grin again. "He's not a stranger, *Mamm*. *Gott* sent him to me. He's my new *daed*."

Verity flushed red. She knelt and spoke quietly, the smile she had for her *dochder* staying firmly in place. "A week ago you said *Gott* sent the garbage man to be your new *daed*. I'm confused. Which is it going to be?"

"Him," Faith declared with all the conviction a small child could muster and pointed Leviticus's way.

Emotions tore through him. What kind of father would he make if he was this *kind*'s *daed*? One day Naomi would be just like Verity's little girl. Full of life and silly questions. He'd have to step up. Find a way to be all Naomi needed him to be.

Longing tugged at his heart, and for a moment, he allowed himself to imagine parenting two delightful little girls with Verity. When they were teens, Verity had said she wanted a house full of children. Back then, he'd had everything a young man could want. They could have become a happy *familye*. But rebellion and grief had pushed him away and left him the shell of the man he was. Verity had been better off with the man she'd married, this Mark she spoke of in such high regard.

He took in a deep breath, watching the girl. He couldn't encourage her childish dreams. *Gott* would have to rebuild him if he was to be all he could be. Gott *grant me wisdom. Show me the way.*

Verity smiled at her daughter, her thoughts on Leviticus. Some might have missed the momentary flash of alarm that crossed Leviticus's face, but Verity hadn't. She had no intention of pursuing him as she had when she was young.

Kinner had a knack for coming up with the most

ridiculous ideas. If he didn't understand that yet, he would soon, now that he had a *dochder* of his own to raise. Verity squeezed her eyes shut for several seconds, gathering her thoughts, tempering her annoyance.

She concentrated on Faith, who was smiling bright and impatiently waiting for her *mamm*'s response. "*Nee*, I'm sorry, my *lieb*. Leviticus can't be your *daed*. Not today, or any other day. He already has a *familye*. He has a precious *dochder* named Naomi to raise."

Faith's face crumpled, prepared to cry. "But why can't I be his *dochder*, too?" She pulled away from her mother and jerked round to face Leviticus, her small hands placed on her slim hips. "Right? Your *boppli* can be my *schweschder*. We can be a *familye* just as I prayed?"

Leviticus approached the child slowly, his gaze touching on Verity and then back to Faith. His words were spoken soft and easy to the child as he kneeled in front of her. No doubt his words were said for Faith's benefit and hers. "I'm just starting to learn what it is to be a *daed*, Faith. I'm not very good at dealing with little ones yet. It would probably be best if you prayed some more. Ask *Gott* for someone with a bit more experience with *kinner*. You shouldn't have any problem finding your *mamm* a husband since she's so pretty."

The back door opened, the squeaky hinges heralding Otto Fischer's entrance.

"Leviticus?"

Verity took Faith's hand and hurried out of the kitchen. Leviticus had opened the floodgates of retribution on his own head. Let him deal with it alone.

* * *

Disturbed by Faith's comments, Leviticus tried to gather his thoughts as he stood with a nod directed toward the old man making his way around his father. A senior citizen now, the old bishop still moved with purpose and authority, like some of the generals Leviticus had served under. Otto always had a way of carrying himself with dignity, but without any of the pomp and ceremony used by the four-star generals. If he lived to be a hundred, Leviticus would never know the kind of veneration Otto and the officers had earned.

He recalled being a *bu* of ten and being called into Otto's study for stealing candy from Old Dog Troyer's five-and-dime store. He felt the same ripple of trepidation curl his stomach now as the Amish bishop's piercing blue-eyed gaze turned on him, hard and steely. A bad case of nerves had his hands shaking. More than anything, he didn't want to be sent away, back to the *Englisch* world.

Otto muttered something to Albert and Mose on the porch, and then quietly shut the door, leaving them alone in the kitchen.

Otto spoke, his accent still heavy with the same Pennsylvania Dutch inflection his father and many of the old ones used. "It is *gut* to see you, *soh*. I'd feared you were lost to us when you walked away." Otto pulled out a kitchen chair with a gnarled arthritic hand and motioned Leviticus over with a wave.

Habit almost had him saluting and clicking his heels together at attention. His respect for the man was that strong now that he'd matured into an adult. He lowered himself into a chair. "*Gott* taught me hard lessons and brought me home with my tail between my legs."

"Perhaps you were in the pigsty, bruised and battered for a time, but not harmed beyond repair. Ain't so? It is *gut* you came back when you did. Your *daed* grows frail and needs you more than ever. This grove needs you, too. Solomon is one man. He can only do so much." Otto tugged at his beard, gave Leviticus's *Englisch* clothes a thorough once-over. The man's hairy brows rose with disapproval. "Is it your intention to join the church and be baptized right away, or will you continue to fight the will of *Gott* and make your *familye* grieve further?"

The restrictions of military life had brought about much needed changes in Leviticus, but still, making the choice to be a Plain man wasn't coming easy to him. He was making the choice mainly for Naomi, he told himself, but deep inside he knew better.

He understood the need for rules and uniformity better now, but he still didn't like the feeling of being boxed in and held to guidelines he didn't always agree with. No doubt, he would find it hard to live by the community's strict *Ordnung*, but he could endure anything for his *dochder*. She'd need a stable *familye*, people to love her, and this tiny community could provide all that. "Yes. I realize the Amish way of life is best for me."

Otto's hand stilled on his beard. His eyes narrowed. "I'm told you have a *dochder*, but I see no *fraa* at your side."

"That's right." His mouth went dry, but he managed to hold Otto's piercing gaze. He had repented to

God for his relationship with Julie but refused to be ashamed of Naomi's existence.

"And is there a plan in motion? Someone you have in mind to marry, see to your *dochder*'s needs? Children can be a heavy burden for a *mann* with no *fraa*, no matter how much they love their *kinner*." Otto settled back in his chair, not giving Leviticus a chance to answer his questions before he started speaking again. "It makes me wonder if an arranged marriage would be the best solution. There will be several eligible women coming to the community during the winter season. Perhaps you've considered this yourself and have already thought of someone suitable?"

Leviticus worked his jaw, not sure what to say. He had assumed Verity would continue to see to Naomi while he worked with his father and brother in the grove. "Verity—"

"*Ya*, this is a *gut* plan. Verity will make a fine *fraa* for you. She is a broad-minded woman with spirit. And her *dochder* needs a *daed*." Otto nodded, a half smile curving his lips. "Verity was a *gut fraa* to Mark Schrock, and she will be faithful to you, too. Albert is already used to her ways, and content to have her around. You've made a *gut* choice." Otto nodded vigorously. "Wasn't there a time of walking about for you and Verity? An engagement, even? Perhaps bans were read in church?"

Alarms went off in Leviticus's head. Sure, he needed a babysitter or full-time nanny, but a *fraa*? He wasn't prepared to court *anyone* just yet. Not the way he was, and especially not Verity. It was apparent she still held a grudge against him for leaving her all those years ago. And who could blame her? He rose and shoved his trembling hands in his jeans pockets. "We did court for a time, but—"

"There's no need to be troubled about the lack of remaining emotional attachment, if that's what's concerning you. Love will return, given time. Once you're schooled, become a member of the church and are baptized, we can set the wedding date for December or sooner. With an immediate engagement, Verity's family will have no need to be concerned about her reputation."

"Her reputation? But Verity and I haven't picked up where we left off." His heart raced, almost thumping out of his chest. Things were moving too fast. He needed time to think, time to consider what would work for all involved. Certainly not this foolishness. What would Verity say?

Otto watched his every move and gesture, reading into it what he would. It was the man's nature to scrutinize people. He spoke firmly, his look fierce. "You can't expect Verity to live in this *haus* with you, a single *mann*, and not be touched by local gossip. She must stay. Albert can't do without her. Not with his health still so unpredictable. *Nee*, one of Verity's unmarried *bruders* must come and live on the grove until the wedding." Otto nodded, deep in thought. "*Ya*, this is all *gut*."

The sound of an ATV motor's revving brought Otto to his feet. He moved toward the back door. "*Komm*. We must go. We'll discuss this later in the day, after we've surveyed the damage to the grove." He clasped his hand on Leviticus's shoulder and squeezed. "I'm sure, given time, Verity will agree to a quick marriage of convenience and all will be settled."

Leviticus followed close behind Otto, his feet dragging and thoughts frantic. What *would* Verity think about this situation they found themselves in? Trapped in an Amish till-death-do-us-part trap. *Thanks to my big mouth.*

Chapter Five

Verity did her best to slip a clean cloth diaper under Naomi's bottom, but the *kind* squirmed and fought valiantly, insisting she be allowed to roll on her belly and crawl away. "You'd best be still, little *schatzi*, before we both get stuck by this pin."

She smiled and then laughed out loud as the *boppli* babbled and attempted conversation. Naomi's easy-to-read eyes expressed sheer joy at the trouble she was causing and resisted the distracting kisses Verity tried to rain down on the *kind*'s forehead and nose.

Clara came into the bedroom and inched in beside the cot. She helped hold the roly-poly *boppli* down long enough for Verity to close the big diaper pins and pull a tiny dress over the *kind*'s head. With a laugh in her voice, Clara asked, "Where's Faith?"

"Sulking in her room."

Her hip supported by the edge of Verity's double bed, Clara slipped off her shoes and sat, her swollen ankles crossed. "What did she do?"

"The usual. Got *lippy* with me and didn't want to take *nee* for an answer."

Verity lifted Naomi out of her bed, kissed the child's soft curls and then moved to the rocking chair.

Clara covered her toes with the hem of her long skirt and settled in for one of their girlie talks. "I expected to find you out of sorts and ready to explode."

Verity raised her chin, her forehead wrinkled. "Why would you think that? I've changed a million diapers in my life. What's one more?" Verity offered a warm bottle to Naomi and grinned as the *kind* reached out and jerked the food toward her rosebud mouth. Her pudgy fingers grasped the bottle and held on tight.

"So you're all for it?"

"For what?" Verity looked closely at her frowning friend. "Is this one of your jokes?"

Clara's expression turned perplexed. "You can take my word for it. I wouldn't kid about something as serious as this. Why in the world hasn't someone told you? I thought for sure the bishop, or at least Leviticus, would ask you if you were all right with the proposition."

Verity leaned forward, careful not to jostle Naomi, her interest piqued. "What proposition? I don't have a clue what you're talking about. It sounds like I need to be told about this scheme since it involves me."

Clara slipped off the bed and with some effort shoved her feet back into her plain black shoes. "Maybe it would be best if someone else explained it to you. I really didn't overhear everything, even though Otto does tend to talk loudly."

Clara tried to slip out of the room, but Verity latched

onto the hem of her friend's dress and tugged her back in. She loved Solomon's wife and Leviticus's sister-in-law as much as she loved her own sisters, but sometimes Clara's teasing and nosy ways drove her to distraction. "Sit! Tell me what you know."

Clara's eyes twinkled innocently. "Seriously. I didn't hear much of what was said. And besides, I could have gotten it wrong." She laughed, but the sound held a nervous edge. "You know how rattle-brained I am." She jerked her skirt away from Verity's grasp and inched toward the door.

"Please tell me."

Clara's pace slowed. She shrugged. "But… I'm not sure I should be the one to tell you."

Their gazes met and held. Verity's brows knitted.

Clara reluctantly shuffled back to the bed and sat on the edge with a bounce of defeat. She refused to meet Verity's hard stare. She thrust her hands into her apron pockets and they stayed there.

Verity rose and stood over her. "Once this *boppli* finishes her bottle I'm going to go find Otto and ask what all the excitement's about. He might be interested in hearing you're spreading gossip again." She wouldn't tell on Clara, knew her friend loved a good tongue wag, but one way or another she was going to find out what was up.

"*Nee*, don't do that! He'll know what I was doing. Solomon's warned me to stop listening in on other people's conversations. Otto's sure to preach on the sin of eavesdropping come Sunday service."

"Then tell me."

"Has anyone ever told you that you can be a very

hard woman, Verity Schrock?" Clara's pink lips pouted, but her eyes glowed with excitement as she began talking. "I was just standing by the door, minding my own business, innocently waiting for Albert to move away so I could go in the house." Slightly top-heavy with child, Clara slid a hand out of her pocket and placed it against her gyrating stomach.

"*Ya*, I think we've established you were snooping at the door, seeing what you could see and hearing what you could hear. So, go on."

Clara grunted her displeasure at Verity's less-than-gracious remark. "Otto found out about Naomi not having a *mamm*. Since Leviticus has no *fraa* to care for the *boppli*, Otto asked how he planned on managing the daily grind of the grove with a *kind* on his hip."

Nerves tingled up Verity's spine. She didn't like where this conversation was going. "And?"

Clara's eyes became liquid virtue. "Leviticus didn't seem to have a permanent solution and hem-hawed around a bit." The volume of her normally loud voice lowered to a whisper. "You know how fond Otto is of arranged marriages, especially since his and Theda's worked out so well."

"*Ya*, theirs was one of the blessed ones. But what has this got to do with me?" Verity took in a long, cleansing breath. Clara could test the patience of the Lord Himself. "Is this one of your jokes or another chance to spread gossip?"

Clara's shoulders stiffened. Her eyes narrowed with indignation.

I've hit a nerve.

"*Nee*, of course it's no joke. This really does concern you and if you'll be quiet long enough I'll tell you the rest."

"Seriously, Clara. Talk." Verity pulled the empty bottle from Naomi's damp lips and placed the child's chubby body against her shoulder. She patted and rubbed the *kind*'s back, hoping to lull her back to sleep. "Tell me *only* the parts of conversation that concern me."

Clara nodded, her grin mischievous. "Otto suggested an arranged marriage for Leviticus." She leaned forward. "You should have been there to see his face when Otto explained his plan. I thought Leviticus was going to swallow his own tongue."

A strange sensation gripped Verity's stomach. She sighed. Her impatience grew by the minute. "Please, repeat only the parts that involve me, Clara."

"If you'd stop interrupting I might be able to get to the good bits." Clara's brow arched. "Leviticus blurted out your name when pressured about a prospective *mamm* for Naomi, and Otto became as happy as a child on Christmas morn." Clara smiled. "I mean he smiled a really big, robust smile and nodded a lot, convinced Leviticus's plan was to marry you. By then, Leviticus looked ready to throw up, his eyes bulging like a fresh-caught catfish." A grin flashed at the corners of Clara's mouth, but she went back to nattering, then got serious again. "Otto asked if you two had courted back in the day."

"That was a long time ago." Verity's stomach clenched tighter, not liking what she was hearing. "I no longer have a romantic interest in Albert's *soh*."

"*Ya*, well, you might want to dig up some of those

old feelings, because Otto already has your wedding date planned for the month of December."

A trembling began in Verity's legs and crept up to her arms. It took every ounce of willpower she had to keep herself standing. "Are you sure of this? You couldn't have gotten my name mixed up with someone else's?"

"*Nee*, it was you, all right. Otto even mentioned what a sensible woman you've always been."

Verity's mouth became so dry she could barely get her words out. *Sensible. Ha! I'll show him sensible.* "And Leviticus agreed to this marriage arrangement?"

"Well, he didn't belabor the point, or say *nee*. They both walked past me a moment later, and I did notice Leviticus looked red in the face and flustered."

Verity fought for breath. Everyone in their small community knew about Otto's fondness for arranged marriages, but she'd never dreamed she'd become one of his victims. Hysteria rose and built to a crescendo pitch until she thought she'd scream out loud.

"Don't you utter a word of this to anyone else, you hear me, Clara Hilty?"

Clara chuckled, making Verity's tension grow. She gave up trying to make sense of what her friend had just said. Drawing in a deep breath, she looked down at Naomi. The child was sleeping peacefully in her arms. She felt compassion for the tiny girl, but not enough to get herself tangled up with a half *Englisch*, half Amish man. *We Amish marry forever. There would be no divorce.*

"I may be a sensible woman, but I won't be railroaded into a loveless marriage. Otto will just have to understand and make other arrangements."

"You *are* single and *do* need a *daed* for Faith. Otto may give you an argument."

Verity gave a dismissive wave of her hand. "He can argue all he wants. Unless *Gott* Himself sends a message from heaven, I won't be marrying Leviticus Hilty come December."

Verity jumped when the back door slammed shut and Mose Fischer began urgently calling her name. Leaving Naomi with Clara, she hurried through the hall but stopped short when she entered the kitchen and saw the washed-out look on the big man's face. "What's happened?"

"It's Albert. He's been rushed to the hospital."

Sitting behind the wheel, Leviticus waited for Mose to come out of the house and jump in the back after alerting Verity. The back door slammed, and Leviticus watched as Mose, followed by Verity, flew over to the passenger side where Albert sat slumped on the truck's bench seat, his head resting against Solomon's shoulder.

The truck rocked as Mose jumped into the back. Solomon took the time to roll the window down, so he could address Verity's fears. "I'm sorry but we have to go. There's no time for explanations. I'll call you as soon as I know something."

"But wait. What's happened? Is it another stroke?" Verity's voice was high with anxiety.

"We don't know. Leviticus and I were speaking and

Daed just slumped over. Now, *nee* more talk. We've got to go."

Leviticus glanced in his rearview mirror as they sped away, gravel flying from under the fast-spinning wheels of the truck. Verity stood alone in the distance, her skirt blowing in the wind. She needed someone to comfort her. He inwardly groaned. She'd have words to say when she found out he and Solomon had been arguing.

Leviticus pulled his attention back to driving and turned onto the main road. Tempted to speed, he made his way through the traffic, his eyes glancing over to Solomon from time to time. His *bruder* held up their dad's body as best he could. What fools they'd been for arguing over differing opinions in front of their frail father. Stress was the last thing Albert needed.

Regret tore at Leviticus. He couldn't seem to do anything right. Perhaps he'd come home too late to make peace with his brother. As *kinner* they'd been close, shared a strong bond. But now? Now they were strangers and he had no one to blame but himself. He'd been a fool to leave his family, his community. Especially his faith. *Gott* had taught him many lessons, all of them hard to stomach now that he saw the foolishness of his actions all those years ago. If he'd had issues with the way his *mamm* was treated, he should have spoken up, tried to change his father's mind-set. To Albert, hard work was expected of all Amish. Both men and women. It was their way. But his mother's failing health might have been avoided with rest and time to do what pleased her. He pictured his mother,

her face smiling in whatever task she took on. Had he been too young to see how content she was?

His time with the *Englisch* had taught him many things, some good, but most not. He'd talk to his father if given the chance. Clear the air between them. God willing, he'd have the opportunity. Another glance at his father's pallor warned him not to take too much for granted. There was no promise his *daed* would live through this latest heath scare. No promise at all.

Father, I release Daed*'s fate into Your hands. Forgive my doubt. Heal my mind. Give me strength to deal with whatever lies ahead.*

Chapter Six

The noxious scent of chemicals and disinfectant hung heavy in the air.

Leviticus could smell it, and wondered if Solomon could, too. He put his hands over his ears, trying to block out the sound of the nurse's squeaking shoes, the conversations all around him. Someone's heart monitor beeped loud and fast. It could have been hooked up to him, his heart was beating so hard. Hospitals brought back memories he'd buried deep and didn't want uncovered.

Slumped in a chair across the hallway, Solomon cleared his throat. Leviticus looked up. Blue eyes that had once sparkled with mischief as a *bu* now appeared gray and lifeless, his mouth an angry slash. Sand and mud stains covered his brother's trousers up to his bent knees. Leviticus looked down at his own casual pants, at his borrowed boots caked in mud. They'd brought the muck and mire of the flooded grove into the hospital with them after their father had fallen ill.

Solomon hadn't spoken a word since they'd arrived

with their *daed* in tow. Not even as they waited in ICU while Albert was being worked on. Hours passed and still the silence continued. Leviticus didn't have to be told that Solomon blamed him for their father's sudden attack.

Almost an hour later, Albert was moved from ICU and put into a room on the third floor. He and Solomon had been asked to wait outside the room while their *daed* was hooked up to a fresh IV and monitor. They'd been told there were more tests to be run before they could be sure whether it had been another ministroke.

Footsteps sounded down the hall. Solomon's head lifted.

Leviticus glanced up, expecting it to be Otto rejoining them. He'd gone downstairs for coffee. But when he looked, he saw Verity threading her way past a large family crowding the hallway. She appeared stressed, her usual tidy appearance forgotten. *Just what she needs. Something else to stress over.*

"I left the *kinner* with Clara and got a ride with Mose. Is there any news?"

She was pale and shaking. Leviticus could see Verity's nerves were stretched to the breaking point.

Always thoughtful, Solomon patted the chair next to him and slid his arm around Verity's shoulders when she sat.

Leviticus balled his fists, not liking the familiarity of his brother's touch. Verity was a widow; she was to be treated with respect. Strong feelings of protection washed over him, not that he had any claim on her. She was her own person, someone who'd forgotten him and married another man. Had he expected her to wait until he got his head screwed on tight?

He calmed himself. His brother was being compassionate, not flirtatious. Post-Traumatic Stress Disorder brought on strange and bewildering moods and added internal drama he had a hard time understanding.

Solomon spoke in hushed tones. "*Nee*, there's no news yet. But I've seen this before with *Daed*. He's had another stroke."

A tear trailing down Verity's cheek. She lifted her shoulders in a half shrug. "*Ya*, I thought as much. Mose Fischer said Albert was unable to use his right side. Was the damage to the grove so devastating that the sight shocked him?"

Leviticus waited for Solomon's reply. He knew their bickering back and forth was responsible for their father's sudden stroke.

"The crop's in a bad way." Solomon massaged the back of his neck with long fingers caked in mud. "But that's not what set *Daed* off. It was Leviticus and I arguing. We didn't agree on replanting trees." His forehead furrowed with emotion.

Rekindled regret? Leviticus was dealing with plenty of regrets of his own.

Leviticus spoke up. "*Daed* said the trees should come out and be replanted. I found fault in his wisdom and said so. I suggested we plow up the land and plant hay as some are doing around the state."

Verity rubbed her temples. "Is it possible your *daed* is right? Can the grove be saved?"

Leviticus didn't care if Solomon wanted to hear his opinion again or not. "*Ya*, *Daed* was probably right.

The grove could be replanted. It'll just take more work. Most of the serious damage is in the small grove on the east. Fresh dirt can be brought in to strengthen the roots and keep fungus away. We can plant peach and plumb trees where the soil's been eroded."

Solomon bristled. "Is this your *Englischer* wisdom, Leviticus? *Daed*'s plan is sound, but do you have any suggestions on how we'll pay for all this replanting and soil replacement?"

"I didn't tell *Daed* yet, but I have money saved."

"We don't need your *Englischer* money." Solomon's glare was challenging.

Overwrought, both men slipped out of their chairs and circled each other like birds of prey.

Verity rose and touched Leviticus on the shoulder. "If this is how you two acted today, no wonder your *daed* had another stroke." She pointed to the chairs behind them. "Both of you sit down and gather your wits."

Like a wayward child, Leviticus sat, and Solomon soon followed his lead. Verity was right. He and Solomon swiping at each other only compounded their problems. What fools they'd been. "I'm sorry, Solomon. Forgive me."

"Ask *Gott* to forgive you, *Englischer*. I have no pity for you. I only have pity for my *daed*. The grove is ours. Not yours. You never loved the land like *Daed* and I. We'll figure this out without you once you're gone and he's well enough. Go back to where you came from. There is no inheritance here for you, no one to cling to."

"Was ist letz?" Otto's brows snapped together as

he approached, his frustration showing in his tone and stance. He stood near them, feet planted wide apart. "Is it not enough that you put your *vadder* in the hospital? Do you want to kill him, too? No more squabbles." He threw up his arms in frustration. "Who is right and who is wrong? Such foolishness out of two grown men! Stay seated and be silent."

Leviticus buried his hands in his hair, struggling to pull himself together. Everything Solomon had said was true. How could he expect him to understand his restlessness back then? He couldn't understand it himself.

But he had changed since the war. Death all around had a way of making what was important crystal clear. His faith, his *familye* and the grove were important now. His newly found desire to put his faith in the Lord had pulled him home, and he was bound and determined to stay in God's will this time around. The grove would continue. "You're right, Otto. This is no time—"

"Albert is all that matters now," Otto interrupted. "Both of you must work together to keep his dream alive. He needs a reason to live." The old bishop shrugged, his broad shoulders drooping. "Once he's gone, you two can fight over the land and settle your difference any way you like. But for now, there will be peace." His tone was serious, his look penetrating.

Solomon held Otto's gaze, hostility draining from his face. "*Ya*, we both hear. No more fighting. This is a time for prayer and renewed hope. Forgive me."

Leviticus tugged at his collar, smoothed down the front of his dirt-smeared shirt. He watched tears well up in Verity's eyes, but then she turned away, displeasure for him written in the wrinkles on her forehead. He could always find a way to disappoint her without even trying. "I'm sorry for acting such a fool, Verity."

Otto gave both men a frosty appraisal. "Has the doctor returned with results?"

Verity turned back, her eyes glistening with tears. "*Nee*, there's no news."

"Then we sit and wait." Otto slid into a narrow chair and made himself comfortable.

Leviticus didn't need test results to know what was wrong with his father. He'd seen it before in Afghanistan. Stress did terrible things to a body. His father was under a burden too heavy for any man his age to carry. He'd had a stroke all right, but just how bad a stroke had yet to be proven.

The clock on the wall ticked off each passing second, though each seemed an hour long. Leviticus finally asked, "The children? How are they?"

"They're *gut*. Clara promised to take them to my *mudder* and *schweschders* to be seen to."

"*Danki.*" Leviticus bent his head low, listened to the heartbeat of the hospital. Were these his father's last hours? Only *Gott* knew for sure, and He was being very silent.

Have mercy on my father, Lord.

Verity slipped into Albert's dimly lit hospital room alone. She'd left Solomon and Leviticus to deal with the bishop's anger.

She paused just inside the hospital room, letting her eyes adjust before shutting the door behind her. One by one, she took halting steps toward the single bed in the middle of the room. The nurse had instructed her not to wake Albert if he was asleep. Was she prepared to see him paralyzed? Unable to walk and talk?

She took three more hesitant steps. Pale, his breath shallow, Albert lay on his back, deep in sleep under a white sheet and a lightweight blanket of pale blue cotton. The oxygen tube positioned under his nose hissed. He snored lightly, the familiar sounds giving her a measure of comfort. The monitor on the wall showed his heartbeat was strong, but sometimes erratic. He looked almost serene—but what did she know about recovering from strokes, heart attacks and such matters? Nothing. An hour ago, she'd read a pamphlet about heart disease and strokes, but its words did little to reassure her. Instead, they scared the life out of her.

She glanced around Albert's bed. He was connected to lines plugged into the machines that buzzed and clicked around him. *There must be a way to keep his blood pressure under control at home, so this won't happen again.* Her hand trembled as she touched his arm, the side of his face. He felt warm, not cold and clammy as she'd expected.

Years ago, her *mamm* had had problems with high blood pressure while pregnant with Mary, the fourth of her *mamm's dochders.* But her problems had been nothing as serious as this.

During that time Verity had become familiar with beeping heart monitors and at-the-ready call buttons that worked much like *Englischer* phones.

She sighed, longing to talk to Albert, needing to know he was all right.

Light from the hall momentarily flooded the room.

She glanced around and saw Leviticus slip in. She stepped deeper into the shadows. His gaze sought out his father. He moved forward, slow and steady. She couldn't tell what his expression was, but she heard him sniff, as if he was holding back tears.

Not wanting to intrude, she stayed at the foot of the bed and quietly lowered herself into the hardback chair against the wall. Had Leviticus seen her when he'd come in? She didn't think so. *Let him have his moment with his* daed. *He deserves that much.*

"I'm sorry, *Daed.*" His voice cracked and was barely audible. "Please don't die. I need you in my life...in Naomi's."

Verity's heart skipped a beat. As Leviticus moved to touch Albert, she rose, placing a hand on his arm. "Don't wake him. The nurse said he needs his sleep."

Leviticus whirled round, a hand reaching for his heart. "I didn't know you were in here."

"*Nee,* I didn't think so." She gave a half smile. She'd scared him like he used to scare her a hundred times a day as *kinner.* Their relationship had always been fraught with teasing words and battle cries. Today was no different.

"My words were private. Meant for my father."

Shame on you, her conscience murmured. She lost her smug, self-satisfied smile, ashamed. *He's dealing with his father almost dying, and here you are starting up a cat-and-mouse game from the past.* "I'm sorry. That was insensitive of me."

A scant smile turned up his lip. "It was, but it was so like the old Verity I knew." His expression turned serious again. "How does he look to you?"

She moved over to the head of the bed, leaving a gap between them. "He's a shade pale, but otherwise looks *gut* to me, like he's going to wake up at any moment and ask what all the fuss is about."

"I thought he looked *gut*, too. I wondered if it was just my wishful thinking." He chuckled ruefully, his hand rubbing at the rough stubble on his chin. "When do you think the doctor will be back?"

"Probably not until morning, unless the tests they just did reveal something sinister." She put her hand on Albert's bed. She needed to feel a connection to the sick old man.

"Do the nurses know we're still waiting for answers?"

She smoothed out the sheet under her fingers. "*Ya*, they know. Last time it took two days to finish all the tests and get back most of the results."

He took a step closer to be heard by Verity. "What exactly are they looking for?"

His breath brushed past her, tickling her neck. "They're trying to figure out why he keeps having strokes."

Leviticus moved away from her. "It's me coming home so suddenly, isn't it? I should go, find someplace else to raise Naomi."

"*Nee!*" Albert's word was soft and slightly slurred, but he managed to get his point across.

Leviticus bent, his fingers reaching for his father's limp hand.

"*Di u sell er?*" Albert pushed out the slurred words, his face contorted.

"No, *Daed*! Don't talk. The nurse wants you to remain quiet. You need rest. Go back to sleep." Tears rolled down Leviticus's face and dropped onto the front of his mud-spattered shirt.

"Ell er!" Albert lifted his left arm and let it drop.

"Tell me what?" Verity's heartbeat kicked up and began to race. *What could be so important that Albert demand she be told?*

Leviticus stiffened. "He's confused, doesn't know what he's saying."

Albert's hand lifted inches off the bed, his finger pointing Verity's way.

Verity tugged at Leviticus's arm. "Tell me what you're holding back. You're upsetting him."

"Are you sure, *Daed*?"

Albert blinked rapidly.

"Just remember I tried to stop this foolishness." Leviticus tugged at his shirt collar, undid a button at the neck of his throat. He didn't look directly at her as he spoke. "Otto has a plan and *Daed* agrees with him."

A funny sensation hit the pit of her stomach. Clara had heard correctly. She knew what Leviticus was about to say. "What plan?"

He cleared his throat, and then spoke loud enough for his father to hear, too. "Otto has decided it's best we marry for the children's sake."

"I can't believe you'd even consider…" She couldn't breathe, couldn't swallow. Dry mouthed, she forced her tongue to form the words screaming in her head. "There's no way I'm marrying you."

"Ya." Albert stumbled over the word, but it was clear this marriage was what he wanted for them.

Verity considered Leviticus's expression and saw

the same trapped emotions she was feeling. She became aware of her body trembling, rocking back and forth. Uncontrolled tears coursed down her face, into her ears. "This is your will for my life, Albert?" She held her breath. He nodded. Her heart sank.

Hysteria bubbled just under the surface. There was no way she would marry Leviticus Hilty. Not even for their *kinner*. She had her little girl's future to think of, and the man standing in front of her would have been her last choice. Leviticus hadn't changed. He'd never been dependable.

There had to be a way out. She went to speak, but nothing came out. She wasn't going to upset Albert. For now there was nothing to do but shut up and play along. At least until she found a way out of this insanity. Certainly, Albert wouldn't expect her to go through with the wedding once he was better and thinking clearly.

Breathless, she whispered, "If that is what you want, I'll marry your *soh*." Deep inside, she knew. Oh, yes. She knew. This marriage to Leviticus would never happen.

Chapter Seven

Albert's hospital door opened. Leviticus rose from the chair he'd retreated to. His gaze followed a tiny, dark-haired woman as she flipped on the overhead light and walked in the room with Otto by her side. A cream-colored chart tucked under her arm and a black stethoscope dangling from her oversize lab coat pocket told him who she was.

Solomon, who had slipped in moments before, appeared to be surprised, no doubt by the attending physician's gender. Leviticus's army experience had taught him women in the *Englischer* world could rise to high position and rank. He'd risk a guess the young, attractive woman standing a few feet away was the head cardiologist they'd all been waiting for.

Otto shuffled to the foot of the bed, his black hat in hand. The paleness of the old bishop's skin and the serious expression on the doctor's face told Leviticus more than he wanted to know. A trembling raced down his spine. The doctor must have told Otto the worst before coming in to talk with Albert. Tough as he was, Otto kept taking in deep breaths, like he was having trouble holding in his heartbreak.

Leviticus observed his father. Was the shrunken, blue-skinned old man of *Gott* ready to hear what was coming? *How could he be?* No one was prepared for bad news, no matter what their age.

His gaze swept to Verity. She stood tall and straight, and altogether too lovely for the heartache about to be heaped on her. A nerve ticked in her cheek, proving she was seething with anger. Without a doubt, the strong Amish woman would put a stop to Otto's wedding plans the first chance she got. She was no one's fool. Even he knew he wasn't good enough for her.

Solomon stepped forward, avoiding his brother's gaze. "Doctor Wendell?"

"Yes." She approached, her small-boned hand extended. "You must be Albert's youngest son, Leviticus. He's been asking for you."

Solomon's face blanched. With a scowl, he gestured his brother's way. "*Nee.* He'd be Leviticus."

"Doctor Wendell." Leviticus took the doctor's extended hand. Her grip was strong as any man's.

She glanced around, taking in the number of people in the small hospital room. "Perhaps I could have some privacy with you and your brother."

He looked at his father, waiting for a cue from him. Did he want everyone to know about the seriousness of his health? Albert lay still and quiet, his eyes opened and focused. Leviticus nodded. "We're all family here. You can speak freely."

Doctor Wendell directed her words to his father. "Our test results show you've recently had multiple ministrokes. There's also evidence of a past silent heart attack that's left one of your heart's ventricles slightly damaged."

He kept an eye on his father's facial expression as he took in her words. Optimism turned to resignation.

"I'm sorry, but we can't do bypass surgery on you. Your body's been weakened by undiagnosed type two diabetes and mild kidney failure, which we need to get under control before we make any further plans."

Solomon stood by their father's bed, his hand clutching Albert's. Leviticus thought he saw Verity sway, but she quickly righted herself.

He realized he'd been holding his breath and took in a raspy gulp of air. The room tilted. Tiny dots of light blurred his vision. *That's right, Sergeant. Faint at the foot of your father's bed.*

"I wish I had better news, Mr. Hilty, but I've consulted with several of the on-staff cardiologists. We all agree. Perhaps in time, six months or more, we can operate, but for now we want you to heal and become stable."

His father's throat worked. *"Danki."* His word was as clear as a bell, as if nothing the doctor had said had touched his frail mind.

But the reality of the doctor's words hit Leviticus hard. He had to sit, concentrate on keeping his knees from knocking together as he trembled uncontrollably. He'd come home to rekindle his relationship with his father, only to lose him again? Anger welled up. He had no one to blame but himself. This was *Gott*'s will for Albert's life. His father seemed resigned to his fate, be it death or surgery somewhere down the road. Somehow, he had to learn to trust *Gott* in the same way.

Help me, Lord. Show my vadder *favor.*

Verity peddled as fast as she could, her dress and apron soaked and sticking to her from another heavy downfall of rain. She regretted not accepting Otto Fischer's offer of a ride home from Memorial Hospital, where Albert lay fighting for his life.

Otto had said Mose had room for her in the cab of his furniture truck and that her bike could be stored in the back until they got to the grove. But no. It wasn't raining then so she'd stubbornly refused, convinced she needed time to think.

With the back of her hand, she wiped rain from her eyes. *What a fool I am. I would be home already.*

Clara would have picked up the children from her mother's by now. Faith would be waiting for her, wondering where she was. At five, the little girl wasn't old enough to really understand the seriousness of Albert's illness.

Verity shoved a wet strand of hair out of her eyes and sped up. Like all humans, Albert would someday die. She knew that. The problem was, she loved the kind old man almost as much as she loved her own father and didn't want to lose him. Mixed in with her own emotions, she didn't want Albert to die for Leviticus's sake, as well, and the feeling made her frustrated. He'd left Pinecraft on his own. If he'd come home too late, it was on him, not her.

Grief and anger added power to her legs.

Am I mad at Gott? Shaken, she had to admit she

was. She could lie to herself, but she wasn't fooling Him. The Father knew how she felt about Albert's poor health and the arranged marriage to Leviticus. She lowered her shoulders and sped on, almost blinded by the downpour. Sometimes life made no sense at all. *Gott* had taken Mark from her, as well as her tiny *soh*. Would Albert soon rest on that lonely hill on the grove where his wife lay?

She didn't bother to wipe the tears streaming down her face. The rain took away all traces of her anguish. She sniffed, stuffed down her bitterness and peddled on. Her damp skirt and the up-and-down motion of her knees made it hard to see eroding potholes in the unpaved road she had to travel back to the grove.

A vehicle honked behind her. Startled, she splashed through a deep pothole she normally would have seen and avoided. With a bump, she fell over.

Thanks to the rain pouring down in sheets, it took real effort to untangle herself from the bike and crawl to the edge of the road. Her knee hurt and her palm was bleeding.

She heard the vehicle door slam shut and looked up. *Probably the fool who honked and caused me to fall.*

A long-legged man walked over. "You all right?"

Ach. She didn't have to look up. She knew Leviticus's voice. Why did he have to drive past now? Couldn't it have been Ulla, or one of the other local *grossmammi* who often traveled down the lane to buy fruit from Albert or Solomon?

Thunder clapped overhead. A warning from *Gott* that He would not put up with any more of her pettiness about Leviticus? She rose like a phoenix out of the ashes, until the toe of her shoe caught one of the spokes of the bike wheel and caused her to fall on her already bloodied knee. Muddy water splashed up in her face, momentarily blinding her.

"Here. Let me help."

Under his drenched hat, was that a smirk on Leviticus's face? No, but his tone sounded much too amused for her liking. She would have expected him to mock her situation when he'd been a *bu*, but today? Back then, they'd teased each other mercilessly, but they were grown now.

She peeked at her grazed knee. Her skin was dotted with ground-in bits of tiny gravel. It was sure to hurt after the thorough cleaning it needed.

Leviticus extended his hand toward her. His fingertips dripped with rain. She pondered her dilemma. Surely, the sin of pride wouldn't keep her sitting in a mud puddle? Anger and frustration warmed her face, but she reached out and accepted his firm grip.

She'd ride in the old truck with him, but that didn't mean she had to talk to him. She had nothing to say. Not a word. *Gott* kept reminding her that He, in His loving mercy, required her to forgive Leviticus for the past, but He'd said nothing about her having to like the man.

"I thought you got a ride home with Otto." Leviticus hoisted her into the truck's front seat with a grunt.

"*Nee*, I'd ridden my bike into town and couldn't just leave it at the hospital." *You're beginning to lie much too easily.* "It wasn't raining when I started off." At least that much was true. She avoided his gaze, seething inside. Ya, *I know,* Gott. *I must find my way out of this mess without harming my walk with You.*

Leviticus deposited her bike in the truck's rusty bed with ease, as if the ancient bike weighed less than nothing.

The driver's side door opened, and he dashed in and buckled his seat belt. Rain and mud dripped off them both, and onto his truck seats and floor mats. Her grumpy mood allowed a measure of satisfaction at the mess being made. Thoughts totally unworthy of a Plain woman.

Busy buckling up, she imagined how disappointed *Gott* must be in her, especially when Leviticus handed her a soft white handkerchief and said, "Press that against your knee. It's clean."

"Danki." His kind act made her feel even more mean-spirited and worthy of *Gott*'s punishment. She sucked in her breath as the cloth touched her skin.

"If I were you, I'd clean that scrape really well when you get home."

"I will." Did he think her a *bensel*? She was a mother, after all. She'd become an expert at cleaning scrapes and bumps.

He's been nothing but nice to you since he came home. Did her conscience always have to be right? Couldn't she get away with one harsh thought without feeling petty?

"More rain is the last thing the grove needs." Leviticus clicked on the windshield wipers, flipped on the truck's turn signal and roared off down the road.

Pinecraft had experienced many hurricanes, but this last one seemed far worse than the others to her. It had lingered over the tiny community, demonstrating a will of its own while destroying property and people's lives without apology or signs of remorse. What the main brunt of the wind and downpours hadn't decimated, the residual rain bands forecasted for the next few days would finish off.

Leviticus pulled into the drive and stopped close to the farmhouse. He turned off the engine and unbuckled his seat belt as his head turned toward Verity.

Dealing with daunting thoughts, Verity watched the windshield wipers slow and then come to a stop before she realized they'd arrived at the farm. She needed to get inside, wanted to get away from Leviticus more than she'd ever wanted anything. The man kept her in a maelstrom of self-pity and bitter, confused emotions. But before she could reach for the door handle, he stopped her with the touch of his hand on her arm. "Wait. Before you go in, I need to talk to you in private."

Keeping her eyes straight ahead, she unpinned her drooping prayer *kapp* and laid it in her lap. "Our *dochders* haven't seen us since yesterday. Perhaps another time would be better."

He drew back his arm. "Give me five minutes, Verity. Please."

With a swipe of her hand, she pushed strands of wet hair off her face before daring a glance Leviticus's way. His hair was wet and plastered to his head like a pale skullcap. Holding his gaze, she was taken aback by the look of sincerity in his eyes. Her resolve to be distant and direct with him crumbled. It was early morning. Clara could handle Naomi's feeding.

Faith, most likely, was still asleep. "Five minutes," she agreed and waited for his words.

"I know you're upset by Otto's crazy plan."

"Upset? I think *revolted* is a far better word. Why did you suggest there might be a chance we'd court again?" *There's no reason to be cruel.* "I'm sorry. That was mean-spirited of me and totally unnecessary." She lowered her head. "I wasn't prepared…didn't imagine you'd mention my name to Otto and that he'd come up with such nonsense as a marriage of convenience. Do he and Albert really expect us to marry without so much as a private conversation between the two of us? There have to be far better choices."

"He misunderstood what I was trying to say when I spoke your name. He's growing older. Don't blame Otto for the mistake. I should have made my intent clear. Remember, he only wants what he feels is best for us."

"*Ya*, well, if someone had bothered to ask me, I would have told them I have no plans to ever remarry." Verity pulled her wet skirt away from her stinging knee. She yearned for a long hot bath. Sweet-smelling shampoo.

I'm not going to marry Leviticus Hilty. Not anyone. Period. If he needed a wife so badly, she could think of a half-dozen *maidals* and widows who were interested in marriage.

As if reading her thoughts, he spoke. "Otto wants *you* for my wife, plain and simple. If it makes you feel any better, I didn't have any say in the matter, either."

Verity could feel heat rising past her neck and into her cheeks. "And you? Am I not *gut* enough for you now that you've experienced the *Englischer* world?" Her fingernails cut into the palms of her hands. *Why did I say that?*

He rubbed the side of his nose. Remained silent. Finally, he spoke, his words coming slow. "I feel the same about marriage. I'm not ready, but it seems Otto's not going to accept any option but his own." He glanced her way. "But like you said, it won't work between us."

The words *why not?* almost came out of her mouth, but she stifled them and swallowed hard before she made another blunder. The last thing she needed was him thinking she wanted to be his *fraa*, and a *mamm* for his *kind*. "You must know my decision not to marry has nothing to do with Naomi. She's a lovely *kind*. Any woman would be blessed to have her as their *boppli*."

"Not every woman." His tone grew hard, his eyes narrowing. "Some women love their profession more than they love their own *kinner*."

That haunted look was back in his eyes. An aching ball in the pit of her stomach told Verity she didn't dislike Leviticus quite as much as she thought. In that moment, she hurt for him. Hurt for tiny Naomi… But certainly not enough to make them her *familye*. She'd help him find a wife. Someone who could love him. But that was all she'd do.

She took in a deep breath and prayed for guidance silently. "I've been thinking. Your *daed* is fond of me. Perhaps he suggested to Otto that we wed. Albert knows you'll need someone to help you through the difficult times if he passes and wants to tie you down to the grove, so you'll stay. Solomon loves the land. But you? I don't think Albert's so sure you'll stay unless you have a good reason." She tipped her head down, concentrating on the mud chunks and splatter on her plain black shoes. She couldn't look him in the face and say harsh words. Not with that hound dog expression in his eyes. "I'm sorry, but I won't marry you, Leviticus. I—I can't."

"Perhaps we could pretend to court. The pretense doesn't have to end in marriage. Lots of couples end their relationships before their wedding dates."

She raised her head. "I'll simply tell Albert I'm not ready to remarry and he'll understand."

"Will he?" Leviticus's frown made him look as doubtful as she felt. "He didn't seem to be thinking too clearly today. The stroke's affected his mind. And as for Otto, he always gets his way. If I'm willing to sacrifice a short period of time for *Daed* and pretend, why can't you?"

Verity all but sputtered, her annoyance growing with each word out of his mouth. "You make it sound like spending time with me would be a sacrifice you'd have to endure. A bitter pill to swallow."

"That's not exactly what I meant." He ran his hand through his pale wet hair, leaving plowed furrows.

"Not your exact words, but close enough." Verity clasped the door handle. "I'm the hired help, the paid housekeeper, remember? Nothing more." She opened the truck's door. Rain blew in, drenching her again. "I'll continue working until I'm no longer needed, and then Faith and I will leave."

"Where will you go?" he called after her. "Back to your parents' home just as they're ready to retire?"

Yes, she would have to go home. And her going home would disrupt her parents' future as they got older. They still had young *kinner* in an already crowded house. The reality of her situation didn't sit well with her, making her reply sharp. "My future is my business, Leviticus. Not yours." She stepped out of the muddy truck. "Find yourself another sacrificial lamb!"

As she trudged toward the door, she dealt with reality. She had no choice but to obey the community's *Ordnung* rule of obedience to authority, and Otto certainly was her authority.

She hurried in, wanting to be away from Leviticus. A strong gust of wind caught the door as she stepped into the house, slamming it behind her, right in Leviticus's face. At least he couldn't blame her for the gesture. Or would he?

Chapter Eight

Leviticus swung the door open and hurried in, the wind-driven rain wetting the great room's wooden floor. He worked on checking his rising temper. Waves of anger rolled over him. He'd had a hard time dealing with drama of any kind since the war. The smallest things could set him off, cause him to lose his temper. *Be calm. Don't say more than is needed.*

He understood where Verity was coming from. He didn't blame her. Not really. He had no right to expect her to go along with a pretend engagement or unwanted wedding. They were virtual strangers now, and marriage *was* forever for the Amish.

A troubling thought hit him. *Perhaps Verity has a reason for not wanting to court.* Did she already have someone she was fond of? But what difference did it make to him? He had no intentions of marrying, and certainly not Verity. He wasn't *gut* marriage material, and not fit for any woman for that matter. He was damaged goods. A life alone was what he deserved. But what about Naomi and her need for a *mamm*?

Wise up, Leviticus. Verity's a fine woman. Why wouldn't someone be interested in her by now? She's not for you. You gave up your chance long ago and now it's much too late.

He found Verity and an Amish teenage girl he didn't recognize standing by the table. Verity's expression had softened. Faith came running past him, her arms outstretched toward her mother. The child's blue eyes sparkled with joy. "*Mamm!* I thought you were gone forever."

Shut out, he watched as Verity knelt and scooped up her daughter, holding her close to her heart. Her rain-soaked clothes saturated Faith's plain cotton night-dress, but the *kind* didn't complain or pull away. She held on to her mother for dear life.

"I'd never leave you, *liebling.* You know that. I was with Albert. He's sick again and needed me."

"I don't want him to go live with Jesus." Faith's lip trembled, her blue eyes were big, round and earnest.

"Who told you such a thing?" Verity glanced over her shoulder, her gaze resting on the gangly, freckled-faced teenager standing a few feet away.

"*Aenti* Irene came to help with Naomi. A minute ago, I heard her tell Clara that Albert might die." The little girl clung to her mother's neck. "Is it true?"

Saying nothing, Leviticus bent to remove his filthy boots at the back door.

"I'm sorry for my *schweschder*'s foolish words, Leviticus. She had no right speaking to anyone about your *daed*'s condition. She's old enough to realize this kind of conversation is best left for adults."

"Faith would have overheard someone soon

enough," he stated matter-of-factly. Death had become black-and-white to him since the war.

Verity laid her *kapp* on the kitchen table and adjusted her bun once again. "*Ya*, sure. She probably would have, but in the right way and at the right time, from me." Verity shot another accusing look at her sister, who ducked her head in shame.

"Is there a good time to learn of a loved one's impending death?" Leviticus padded across the room in his rain-soaked socks, past Verity and the red-faced teen who was a younger blond-haired version of Verity. His mind was trying to concentrate on things eternal. He needed to pray, ask God to touch his father before he lost him forever. And he needed to pray for himself, too. And for Solomon, his *familye* and the grove. As for the foolish arrangements made by Otto? They'd figure something out eventually. "I'll be in my room if you need me."

A headache beginning, he rubbed his temples as he moved down the dark hall toward his bedroom. His *mamm*'s sewing room door stood open and a young man came strolling out, whistling, his bright red hair and freckled nose a sure sign he was another of Verity's kin, perhaps her younger brother. The teen wore traditional Amish garb, but his coppery hair was shorter than most Amish boys'. *Enjoying* rumspringa, *no doubt.* "You're kin to Verity, if I remember correctly. Your name's Joel?" He took the *bu*'s extended hand and they exchanged firm handshakes.

"*Ya*, I'm Joel, Verity's youngest *bruder*. And you're Leviticus, Albert's youngest, too."

"I am."

Joel placed a battered baseball cap on his head and shoved up the brim. "Mom told me about your *daed*'s illness. I hope he gets better soon. Albert's a *gut mann*. I got to know him when he coached our baseball team when I was a young *bu*."

Leviticus nodded. There were so many things he didn't remember about his father. The man's love of sports was one of them. He shoved his shaking hands in his pockets and cleared his throat, his stomach roiling, his head pounding. "*Ya*, he's a fine man."

Joel nodded toward the door he'd stepped out of. "I hope you don't mind me using your mom's old sewing room as a bedroom. I moved in while you were in the grove this morning. *Mamm* said I'd only be staying for a couple of weeks, at the most."

Stuck in his own misery, Leviticus struggled to maintain coherent thought. "Staying?"

"*Mamm* said Verity needed a chaperone until the wedding, and since I'm still on walkabout, I got picked." A half grin played on Joel's face, revealing his boyish, playful side. "You know how *mamms* are. Always protecting their *kinner*."

Leviticus ignored Joel's reference to the wedding that would never happen. Instead, he thought about his mother's smiling face. "Enjoy your *mamm* while you can, *soh*. They're precious and don't live forever."

"*Ya*, I know." Joel scratched his shoulder and stepped away. "I guess I should get out to the grove and help the men gather up as much of the rotting fruit as we can before nightfall." Joel patted Leviticus's upper arm in a brotherly fashion and said, "Don't worry too much. Albert's in *gut* hands."

Leviticus nodded his agreement. "Solomon's already home from the hospital?"

"He came in a few minutes ago and stayed just long enough to tell Clara their home repairs were almost complete and that they'd be moving back sooner than he'd thought. You want me to give him a message when I see him?"

Leviticus faked a smile. "That's okay. I'll catch up with him in a bit."

Joel lifted his hand in a friendly goodbye. "*Gut* meeting you. I'll tell your *bruder* you asked after him. You'll be coming out to help in a bit? Solomon's going to need every hand he can get."

"*Ya,*" Leviticus answered, but wasn't sure if he'd go to the grove today. His mind was a mess and his head still pounded with a growing migraine. "Hey, thanks for coming over and giving us a hand. I know Solomon appreciates the help."

Joel smiled. "I'm glad to do what I can." His deep voice cracked as only a teenager's could, and then he walked away.

Leviticus slumped against the doorjamb, tired in spirit and mind. *I should go work in the fields, contribute something more than drama.* He puffed out a fatigued breath. Today or tomorrow, he had to deal with Solomon's remaining fury sometime. He needed to settle things between them before another encounter caused their father's death, and not just a debilitating stroke. *Give me time, Lord. And the right words.*

He opened his bedroom door and the years fell away. The room had become a time capsule, everything the same as when he'd left. He fingered the wooden truck his brother, Solomon, had hand-whittled out of wood when he'd been only nine. They'd been close back then, done everything together like *bruders* should. But then he'd met the *Englischer* teens. They'd become his only friends just before eighth grade. He began to long for the things they bragged about. The big screen TVs and music videos. His rebellious attitude had eventually separated him from his *bruder*, who wanted nothing more than to be a good Amish *bu*.

Leviticus dropped his head, remembering how he'd become a disobedient loudmouth by the time he'd finished eighth grade and left school. He managed to make everyone around him miserable, especially Solomon. But Verity had fallen in love with him regardless.

Back then, Leviticus hadn't been sure he wanted to be Amish; he certainly hadn't wanted to obey the rules put in place for his own safekeeping. But his mother's sudden death shook him to his foundation, turned him against his father and his community and sealed his fate. He left broken and went to learn about the *Englischer* world. Like a fool, he'd gladly fought the *Englischers'* war, and ended up almost dying on their battlefield. Now he had to live with his messed-up head, the memories that made him want to throw up every time one of them flickered through his mind. For a time, it felt like death followed him around.

He pulled off his damp, soiled socks and lay back on his bed, his eyes closing, his head pressing into the softness of the pillow. Images of his father in the hospital bed followed him into his restless sleep, tormenting his mind.

* * *

Verity struggled to absorb the happenings of the day and failed miserably. She worked mechanically around the kitchen, wanting to keep herself busy so she wouldn't have time to think too deeply about what was going on around her.

White powdery puffs of flour rose to tickle her nose as she dusted cut-up chicken after dipping each piece in egg batter. She worked blindly, not really seeing anything but Albert's expression as the doctor spoke of his possible demise. She knew him well. He'd tried to hide his shock from all of them, but she'd seen it.

Minutes later, she washed glops of flour and egg off her hands as her *mamm* carefully dropped the coated chicken into hot grease. "You think anyone's going to want to eat?"

Verity's mother moved Faith away to keep the chicken from popping hot fat on her. "People don't stop eating just because they're tired and their hearts are troubled. Solomon's been working in the field most of the day. Leviticus joined him a few hours ago. They'll both be tired and looking for a good hearty dinner."

Verity finished cleaning her hands and then dried them with a dishcloth. She smiled at her daughter coloring at the table and then turned back to her mother. Her attempt at a genuine smile felt feeble, at best.

"We're all grieving Albert's diagnosis. You're not the only one who loves him." Her mother put a generous dab of butter into a pot of fresh, steaming green beans.

Verity nodded. "I know." She'd always had a good relationship with her *mamm*, even when she'd been a teen and as rebellious and mouthy as they came. When Leviticus had left her high and dry and her heart felt broken, it was her mother who soothed her, got her back on track, helped her find Mark, the one man who had truly loved her.

Memories of Mark, his dark hair, the way he showed his love for life when he smiled, moved her to tears. He'd been a *gut* husband and she couldn't even remember the sound of his voice anymore. She longed to hear him say he loved her just one more time.

She stared at her *mamm*'s back as the older woman took plates down from the cupboard. She couldn't imagine the pain that would come with losing one of her parents. She brushed away tears and stirred the creamed corn, her thoughts dark and broody from the day's events.

She could tell Leviticus had been devastated by the doctor's news. There was hope, but having so many sudden strokes could take him in a week or a year from now.

Leviticus had returned after a long spell away to be close to his *daed*. Stepping in his shoes for a moment, her heart became pained, as if a mule had kicked her in the chest. She could only imagine what he was going through, and she'd done so little to make things easier for him.

In a fog of regret, she mindlessly cut potatoes into wedges, placed them on a flat roasting pan, drizzled them with oil, salt and pepper, and put them in the hot oven to bake. "Otto wants me to marry Leviticus." Her words slipped out in a whisper so that Faith wouldn't hear.

"I know." Her *mamm*'s head bobbed as she placed a bowl on the counter and then pulled Verity into the privacy of the food pantry. "Your *daed* and I talked about the arrangement last night and can see wisdom in Otto's plan. Leviticus needs the love of a *gut* woman, someone to teach him how to be Amish again. You've been alone far too long and lonely. I see it in your eyes." She caught her daughter's hand. "You've become headstrong and bitter. Set in your ways." She glanced into the kitchen where Faith continued her coloring. "You have Faith's needs to consider, too."

Her *mamm* continued talking in the semidarkness, unaware that Verity stood transfixed like a wooden statue, her mouth open like a baby bird seeking food from its mother's beak.

"Faith needs a *schweschder* or *bruder*, and since Leviticus already has a *kind* of his own, your sweet *kind* won't have to wait long for that *schweschder* she keeps asking for. *Gott* will bless you and Leviticus with *kinner* of your own eventually." Releasing her hand, her *mamm* picked up a jar of pickles and one of olives, her mouth stretched into a full smile that quickly ebbed away as she turned and noticed Verity's disturbed expression.

"Am I the only one who doesn't get a vote on whom I marry?" Verity shoved her hands into her apron pockets.

"Don't be so dramatic, *dochder*. Naturally, you get a say in the matter, but we knew what you'd say if we asked you. You'd have said *nee*, even though Leviticus was your first love, the *mann* you picked to be your husband when you were young and impressionable.

Anyone with eyes can see you're still mooning over him now that he's back…changed or not."

Verity's hands fisted, her short nails pressing into her palms. "Have you or any of the others looked at Leviticus since he's returned? I mean really looked at him? He's an *Englischer*, from his long hair down to his Wrangler jeans. The *mann*'s no more Amish than I am *Englisch*, and yet you expect me to marry him, let him be Faith's *daed*?"

Her *mamm* straightened to her full height, which was little more than an inch taller than Verity. Her brows lowered, disapproval in her expression. "When did you become so hard, *dochder*? *Ya*, Leviticus left you and the community behind, abandoned his *familye*, but he has seen the error of his ways and returned to his roots, to the faith he was meant to embrace. He had not joined the church before he left, but Otto tells me Leviticus has asked for forgiveness and now seeks redemption from *Gott* in membership and baptism. What more do you require to forgive? Are your wants and needs more important than *Gott*'s will for your life?"

Her countenance softening, her *mamm* took Verity's hand again and whispered, "What would Mark think of this judgmental attitude you carry round like a yoke on your neck? The faithful have voted. Otto's given his approval. Leviticus will be allowed to join the church come Sunday service, and will get baptized that afternoon, as all good Amish men do once they come to a spiritual understanding with *Gott*. Are you so high and mighty that you see yourself as better than Leviticus? Is there no way that he can prove himself worthy of your love? Did I raise a woman who is proud, or are you hiding behind bruised feelings?"

Her *mamm*'s words cut into her soul and condemned her. Was she too proud to accept the bishop's plan? Was she being prideful, arrogant and haughty? She was repulsed by the thought. She had become *hochmut*.

She'd sought after the *demut* and *gelassenheit* all her adult life, and longed to be full of humility, composure and placidity. Did self-will hold her back, or was she resisting the arranged marriage because, deep down, it *was* what she really wanted? Could it be possible she was ashamed that she still had feelings left for Leviticus Hilty after he abandoned her?

"I'll consider your words and pray on this, *Mamm*. It's the best I can do. I'm sorry if I've disappointed you."

"Be more concerned how *Gott* feels about your expressions of distaste for one of His own *kinner*, Verity. *Gott* loves us all, both good and bad. He has a plan and we all must seek His will and be satisfied."

Verity accepted a warm hug from her *mamm* and wiped at the tears dampening her eyes.

"I wouldn't ask something of you that wouldn't benefit you, my *liebling*. I know the real you would gladly follow *Gott*'s direction, and our community's *Ordnung*. I believe this arrangement is *Gott*'s will for your life. Embrace it. Seek *Gott*'s face before you reject Leviticus, this marriage of convenience. Don't make a fool of yourself and go your own way. That's what Leviticus did. There's evil in this world and danger in that kind of thinking."

Verity drew in a deep breath. "I'm willing to ask

Gott for His will in my life." *But can I?* Could she dedicate her whole life to the man who'd walked away from her? Was this sacrifice too much to ask of her, or was she being stiff-necked and hardheaded?

"I know you love me and believe this marriage to Leviticus will bring Faith and me happiness." *Only time will tell if* Mamm *is right.* "Leviticus left for the grove hours ago, but first chance I get, I'll talk to him. But only after I pray."

Chapter Nine

Thick pork chops sizzled in the big frying pan and a cheesy casserole bubbled in the oven, ready for the noon meal. At the counter, Verity prepared fresh vegetables for a garden salad. Her eyes intermittently checked on the girls as they played across the room with a pile of pots and pans.

Shy when she'd first come to the grove, there was no holding Naomi back now, and with Faith's encouragement, the toddler was able to express herself with sentences of gibberish and lots of toothy grins.

Leviticus walked in the back door, his hand at his back as he squatted to greet his daughter first and then Faith. "So what kind of morning have you two had? I got to play in the mud all day. You would have loved the mess, Faith."

Faith took the time to hug Leviticus's neck, but was quickly back to "making dinner" with Naomi, who was busy sucking on a pot lid. "My *mamm* doesn't let me play in mud. She gets angry. Were you allowed to play in the mud when you were little?"

Verity sucked in her breath and held it, waiting for Leviticus to reply. He didn't like talking about his mother with her, or anyone else as far as she knew. In fact, she hadn't heard him mention his mother once since he'd been home.

"You can be certain-sure my *mamm* got mad, but she got over it quick enough. Kind of like your *mamm* does." He glanced up at Verity and smiled a tired smile, his lip barely inching up. They hadn't spoken more than a half-dozen words since they'd talked about a marriage of convenience. Naomi crawled over to her father and used handfuls of his shirt for support as she lifted herself on bowed legs and took tentative tiptoe steps around him. *"Dat, dat, dat,"* she chimed, her grin wide, expressing her love for the man covered in dry sandy loam.

"That's right. I'm your *dat*." Leviticus's face beamed. He lifted his gaze from his *dochder* and then centered it on Verity as he said, "She'll be walking soon. Ain't so?"

Verity placed the cooked chops on a platter and covered the golden-brown meat with foil. The cheesy casserole needed a bit more browning and then they'd be able to sit down for lunch. She found herself grinning like a silly fool, her pride in Naomi's accomplishments overwhelming her. "I'm already finding her walking around the couch and anything else she can pull up on." She patted sweat from her forehead on the sleeve of her dress and went back to dicing carrots.

"I'm filthy and ruining your clean floors. Do I have time for a quick shower?" Leviticus chucked first Faith and then Naomi under the chin and had them giggling in no time.

Verity nodded, avoiding looking at him as he left the room. She hid the flush on her face that had nothing to do with the heat of the kitchen. She couldn't help but notice how much of a *familye* they were becoming, each of them settling in their role as if it was the most natural thing in the world to do. *This is what it would have been like if Leviticus had stayed, and we'd married all those years ago.* Hard work, *kinner* and love, but the love was missing from this *familye* unit, save the *kinner's* affection for them both. If they married, would the love ever return? Could she love him again the way she had as a girl, with all her heart and soul? "I'll get the *kinner's* food."

Once she had Naomi in her high chair and Faith in her chair, the girls paused for prayer and began to eat without protest. It had been a long time since breakfast and they'd played hard all morning.

Verity prepared a warmed plate for Leviticus while keeping an eye on Naomi as the toddler made fast work of her bowl of cubed, cooked carrots. Verity had just set his plate on the table when Leviticus walked back in the kitchen, his hair damp and ruffled.

In his haste, he'd left his suspenders hanging at his sides like he used to do as a *bu*. Memories rushed in. Leviticus had told her he hated suspenders back then, and she wondered if he was any fonder of them now. Some things never changed. Just their love.

She took in a deep breath and pretended they had no past, that her heart hadn't been broken beyond repair by the man pulling out a chair and joining her for their noon meal.

Verity sat between the girls as she usually did, directly across from Leviticus. Together they bowed their heads in silent prayer. Leviticus lifted his head a moment later, his gaze catching hers. There was a look in his eyes, something unreadable, but she dared a guess he was thinking about the grove, all the work still left to do. She took a bite of pork and chewed, appreciating the tangy flavor of ginger. "Mmm, this pork is tender."

Leviticus nodded, even though he hadn't taken a bite of food. Much like Faith did when she wasn't hungry, he pushed his food around with his fork.

"I caught a butterfly today." Faith poked a chunk of meat in her mouth and spoke around it. "*Mamm* said it was the prettiest she ever saw."

Leviticus looked up. "I'm sure it was pretty, sweet girl." He smiled. "When I was a *bu* I used to catch butterflies and put them in a jar, but my *mamm* would find them in my bedroom and make me let them go. She said I was being mean by keeping them from their families in her rose garden."

Faith swallowed her meat and speared another piece. "Can your *mamm* come visit us sometime? She sounds nice."

Leviticus shoved his plate away and rose from the table. "*Nee, liebling.* My *mamm* went to live with Jesus a long time ago. Long before you were born."

"I'm sorry," Faith murmured, her eyes wide. "I'd miss my *mamm* if she went away."

"I'd miss your *mamm*, too," Leviticus answered,

and moved toward the door. "I'm going back out to the grove. There's a lot of work to be done."

"*Ya*, sure." Verity looked down at Leviticus's abandoned plate as the back door slammed. He hadn't eaten a thing. He needed nourishment for all the hard work he was doing, but he ate less than Albert did on a good day.

Had Faith's conversation about his *mamm* run him off? She never knew for sure what would upset him anymore. He'd changed, become more sensitive, hard to read.

Lord, help me to help him. I don't want to wed him, but I hate seeing him so unhappy. Like he doesn't have a friend to call his own.

Her own appetite gone, she cleared the table, wiped down the girls and sent them off to play at her feet as she washed the dishes. So much was going on. She couldn't keep her emotions steady. She looked at the girls, her heart swelling. One thing her mother was right about—these *kinner* needed both a *mamm* and a *dat. Gut*, loving parents was *Gott*'s plan for a *kind*'s life. They were to be raised in a home full of love. But there was no love between her and Leviticus. Wouldn't they be cheating the girls out of a loving environment if they married?

Leviticus was still gone as darkness shrouded the house and groves. Solomon left for the hospital, leaving Clara behind to help finish the supper dishes. Glad Clara and Solomon were still living in the house, Verity smiled as she bathed Naomi and fed her a bottle before bed. After a kiss on her head, she hummed low and sweet, her hand soothing the restless toddler with circular motions on her back. She chose to hum one of Faith's favorite songs, all the while thinking, *Where has Leviticus gone?*

Naomi soon fell asleep, her thumb stuck in her rosebud mouth, but Faith was another matter altogether. Just keeping her in bed was a nightly battle. The child needed a firm hand, a father to stand his ground and show her he meant business.

Minutes later, stars sparkled as Verity stepped out onto the porch. A fall moon hung heavy in the clear night sky, its beauty there for everyone willing to raise his or her head. Verity stepped farther into night, her old cotton dress glistening in the moonlight. She slipped into her favorite chair, the one Leviticus had made for his *mamm* before he'd escaped into the *Englischer* world.

She covered her bare feet and legs with the hand-crocheted throw Albert's *fraa* had made years ago. Tired, she eased back, her sigh soft. Why did life have to be so complicated?

Verity remained stationed in the rocker, thinking about Faith's need of a father. Since her daughter had been tiny, she'd fought bedtime. If only Mark were here to set down the law to the cranky little girl... But he wasn't. An ache tore through her. And he never would be again.

Through tears, she pushed away her pain and noticed the moon's glow shimmering on the rim of her tea mug. She lifted the drink and took a long, satisfying sip of the warm brew, then placed the mug on the arm of the wooden chair. She nestled back against the cushion, making another effort to get comfortable. She needed a bit of "me time," a moment to gather her thoughts and pray before she went to bed. Too much had gone on the last few days. Albert was better, but still ill. She and Leviticus's arranged marriage still hung in the air like a drifting black spider web ready to snare her.

Verity sucked in a long, calming breath, determined to find a measure of peace from the near-silent night. Moonlight pooled around her, placing her in a protective cocoon that would bring about a much-needed calm.

Her lashes dipped. She'd been up since five o'clock that morning. Naomi had woken her with the need of a clean diaper and warm milk. Her day had dragged on from there. There'd been so much drama since Leviticus's return and Albert's stroke. How long had it been since she'd slept through the night? She couldn't remember. Her normally calm nerves were stretched taut, almost to the point of breaking. Verity welcomed the solitude around her, the delicate sounds of the night creatures singing their lonely songs.

Earlier in the morning, her mother had come by the grove, inquiring about Albert and playing with the children while Verity washed tiny play clothes and a dress or two of her own. Her mother showing up had proven to be a blessing, but still Verity was glad when her mother had gone home to fix a meal for her own family.

Joel remained, still left behind to act as chaperone. Deep inside, she knew it was right he stayed. The *Ordnung* was clear. Single men and women did not share the same dwelling alone, and they would soon have to. Solomon was determined to dwell in his own home as soon as the damages from the storm were repaired.

A chill went through her. Thoughts of their proposed marriage sped up her already racing mind. She'd been hurt when he'd walked away from his life in Pinecraft. Walked away from her. Rejecting him came naturally to her, but somehow she couldn't honestly say she'd completely forgotten the love she'd once felt for him.

But if she'd wanted to remarry, she would have chosen a kind man of strong faith, someone older, who would make a good father for Faith. Someone completely opposite of Leviticus. Never would she have chosen a struggling *Englischer* who had to learn all over again what it meant to be Plain.

As if summoned up by her troubled thoughts, Leviticus pulled into the drive and the motor died. He ambled across the moonlit yard and up the stairs, his movements slow and easy. Was it her imagination or was he favoring his right leg a bit?

"You look comfortable." He sauntered past, making his way toward the closed screen door.

"I was." Her reply was out before she had time to correct herself. *That's right. Pick on the man while his daed lies sick in the hospital.* There had to be a way to curb her anger besides cutting out her own tongue.

Since a child, she'd been taught to be humble. Not act like some spitfire with a chip on her shoulder. But here she was, thinking bitter thoughts and speaking harshly again.

She pulled forward and rolled the taut muscles in

her neck and shoulders. Her mother's words came back to haunt her. She and Leviticus needed to talk, find a way to deal with this marriage situation once and for all.

"I'm sorry I disturbed you. I'll leave you to your peace and go look in on the girls." Leviticus's hand reached for the doorknob.

"*Nee*, wait. Don't go in just yet. Please." Gott, *You will have to put words in my mouth, because I don't have a clue what to say.* "We need to talk."

He remained silent but pulled a chair over and positioned himself next to her. He sat, his long legs stretched out in front of him, the dirty jeans he wore reminding her of who he still was. An *Englisch* man pretending to be Amish.

She swallowed hard. Even though her throat had gone dry, she began. "Did you see your *daed* tonight?" Her gaze drifted his way, but only for a moment. She wished she had time to figure out what to say. Forgiveness was required, and she had little to offer him. She could never marry him feeling this resentment.

She glanced back his way. He looked thin and restless, like he used to when he was young. His fingers tapped out a rhythm only he heard on the fabric of his jeans stretched across his thigh. All the changes in his life, his father's poor health had to be getting to him.

"*Ya*, I saw *Daed* earlier." He glanced up at the full moon and studied it like he'd just noticed its beauty. His face glowed, bathed in its light.

She nodded, even though he wasn't looking her way. She felt a need to acknowledge his words. Hope rose in her. Maybe Albert was thinking clearer now and realized what a foolish plan Otto had conjured up. "How does Albert look? Is he able to speak?"

"*Nee*, not much. Just a few words and they were almost unintelligible, but he looks better." He rubbed his hands up and down his arms, then massaged the muscles around his shoulder. "The nurse said this stroke did more damage than the last one, but his test results are improving a bit."

Verity finished her lukewarm tea, her eyes watching him over the rim of her cup. She found it impossible not to feel compassion for him, no matter how annoyed she was with him.

He turned toward her, as if he felt her eyes on him. He spoke casually. "Solomon came to see *Daed* just after I got there."

A cold breeze blew, ruffling the wispy hair at the side of her cleaning scarf. "Have you two been able to get past your differences? You know you're going to have to find a way to mend old fences." She smoothed out the throw across her legs. She didn't want to talk too much about Albert. If she did, she would cry, and she refused to cry in front of him. "Albert's going to need both of his *sohs*."

His blue-eyed gaze sought her gaze. "I know, but *Daed*'s heart problems have Solomon running scared. He's angry, and not prepared to deal with me coming home, bringing shame to the *familye* again, and I can't blame him."

"You didn't tell your *daed* what I said to you, did you?" Verity's fingers picked at the twisted yarn that made up the crocheted throw on her lap.

"About you not wanting to marry me?" He settled

back, his legs crossing at his ankles. "*Nee.* I didn't bring up the subject. It would just upset him. Come with me tomorrow and see *Daed.* We'll tell him our feelings together."

"We'll see," she murmured, the butterflies in her stomach fluttering. "I spoke with my *mudder.* About our marriage." She had to force her words out past raw nerves. She could have talked to young Leviticus about anything, but not this *Englischer* man. But they both had aged, changed. They were little more than strangers now. She tried to calm the pounding of her heart, but to no avail. As an Amish widow, she was expected to consider marriage offers after a suitable time and eventually marry but wouldn't be forced.

His laugh surprised her. It came out in a low rumble from deep inside his throat.

"I would have loved to have been a fly on the wall for that conversation." He leaned forward and looked directly at her. "What did she do? Threaten to take you home?" He laughed again. "She must think Otto's lost his mind...trying to match the two of us in holy matrimony."

She pulled up a strand of yarn from the throw and twisted it around her finger. He was the last person she wanted to admit this to, but it needed to be said. "She surprised me. She agrees with Otto. Said she and *Daed* think it's time I remarry. Seems I'm getting stodgy and set in my ways...like some *maidal.*" She nibbled the edge of her lip, wishing she hadn't added the last part. She wasn't an old maid. She was a widow in mourning.

He pulled up his legs and twisted his chair around

to face her. "Have you gotten stodgy?" he asked, a teasing tone entering his voice.

The flutter was back in her stomach, the moonlight and shadows cutting across his face, making him seem more appealing than she was comfortable with. "You don't want to know what I am." She tucked a wayward strand of hair in her scarf and continued. "But I'll tell you what I've decided to do."

He pulled off his baseball cap and laid it in his lap, his hand running through his fair hair. "Go on."

There's no turning back now. You opened this can of worms. "I will promise to court you, pretend to love you, but that's all for now." She sucked in air and pressed on. Watching him for his reaction, she slumped back against the cushion like all the stuffing had been pulled out of her when he grinned, his dimple reappearing. That confounded dimple melted her insides, brought about a longing in her she could never understand, even as a young girl.

"Your promise is good enough for me."

Moonlight glistened on his fair hair as he spoke, making him look wan and ethereal.

Verity sank deeper in the chair. She recognized his satisfied smirk. She remembered it from a long time ago. He'd gotten his way again and he knew it. Her eyes burned from held-back tears of frustration. She jumped up, her bare feet smacking against the porch as she made a beeline for the door. "I've got to go check on the girls."

She didn't wait for his reply. She didn't have time to listen to his smug retort. Tears splashed down her face and onto the front of her dress as the screen door slammed behind her. She hurried to her room, her heart pounding in her ears. She didn't have the energy to deal with Leviticus anymore tonight.

Chapter Ten

An early chill from the north spread down the Florida peninsula during the night. Verity was going into town to talk to Albert privately, before the lies began. The last thing she wanted was to court a man she didn't love.

Perched on her bike, Verity ignored the light drizzle falling. She waved to Clara and Faith, who stood under the covering of the porch. The picture of disappointment, Faith clutched Clara's skirt.

"Don't worry. She's just disappointed she can't go with you, but she'll get over it. Right, Faith?"

Faith nodded, an impish grin replacing her sulky frown.

Verity appreciated Clara understanding her predicament. "*Danki* for helping out the last few days."

Clara grinned. "You can return the gesture when the *boppli* comes."

"You have a deal." Verity inspected the darkening skies overhead. "I'd best get going. This drizzle is turning into rain." She gave one last wave and pushed off, ignoring the cool breeze blowing at her back as she headed down the lane toward town. In a hurry, her legs pumped up and down, the graveled private road slick under her narrow bike wheels.

Leviticus would be returning from the grove soon, prepared to take her to see Albert. She didn't want to ride with him. She needed a chance to talk privately to his *daed*, without Leviticus there. It was her only hope to end this ruse before things got out of hand. Albert would listen. *He must.*

Thunder rumbled at a distance. Her heart sank as she saw Leviticus's old truck turn down the grove's private lane. *When had he left that morning?* She hadn't heard him rumble past her bedroom window. It had to have been while she was bathing the *kinner*.

She dropped her head, peddling harder. The dark head covering and jacket she'd donned before leaving the house helped keep the rain off, and did a good job hiding her identity, too. Still, his truck slowed and came to a stop directly across from her.

As if she hadn't noticed him, she sped on, her bike tires slipping on the gravel from her sudden burst of speed. Rain pelted down, wetting the collar of her dress, dampening her hands and arms.

The truck reversed. Leviticus positioned himself alongside her. "Verity!" he called out through his partially opened truck window.

Her shoulders fell. She slowed to a stop, straddling the bike, her feet sinking into the gravel and mire. "I'll be back soon. I have a few things to do in town. Don't worry about Naomi. My sister Rose is caring for her, and Clara is there!" she shouted over the racket his old truck's motor was making.

"It's not Naomi I'm worried about. It's you."

"Me?" she questioned, her thumb jerking toward her chest. "Why in the world are you worried about me?" She had to look like a fool, straddling a bike in the middle of a downpour. "I'm perfectly fine." Her words were a lie. She wasn't perfectly fine. She'd always been afraid of lightning and Leviticus knew it. She worked hard at not squirming as rain ran in rivulets down her back, dampening her dress.

"Yeah. I can see how fine you are." His dimple flashed her way, even though rain hit him full in the face. "Let me throw that bike in the back and I'll take you where you need to go."

Rain dripped off the end of her nose. "*Nee*, that's all right. I've only got a short way to travel. But *danki* for your kindness."

"Do we have to go through this again? Just get in."

"*Nee*, seriously. I'm fine." She pushed off, but thunder rumbled overhead again. Her fear of lightning stalled her.

"You're being ridiculous, you know." His teasing tone set her teeth on edge.

Lightning split the sky, illuminating her as thunder growled overhead. "I'm sure—"

He opened his door, lifted her off the bike as effortlessly as he might have Faith and moved around to the back of the truck.

Her back plastered to his chest, she tried to protest. His feet crunched against the wet gravel. He ignored her objections like he would a sullen child. She spat rain from her mouth, her protests silenced by the downpour.

He stopped next to the passenger side door and lowered her to her feet. His hands free, he opened the truck door and gave her an encouraging prod forward.

Furious at being manhandled, at his arrogance and condescending comments, she whirled on him and instantly wished she hadn't. He hadn't stepped back, and now her face was planted in the center of his hard chest. He smelled of rain, damp fabric and good plain Amish soap. Her knees went weak. She lifted her gaze. Leviticus's eyebrow arched, his expression as frustrated as she was feeling. Was this to be her plight with him, constantly needing his help and him driving her home like a runaway *kind*?

Verity sighed. *Just get in the truck. Don't make yourself look more foolish than you already do.*

"I'm not kidnapping you, you know. I'm just trying to get you out of the storm."

She watched him walk away, pick up her bike and place it in the back. Oh, how she hated it when he was right. She was still being hardheaded and churlish with him, and she knew it. A nasty storm was brewing overhead. She had no business trying to make it into town on a metal bicycle.

She clambered into the truck, arranged her damp, limp skirt around her legs and then took the dry cloth he handed her from the glove compartment. *"Danki."* She patted at her face and then jerked off her waterlogged head covering. Her prayer *kapp* came away with it. The tight bun she'd placed at the nape of her neck that morning unraveled, the coil of sodden hair falling against her back before she could gather it up.

She reached to grab the hair, but he brushed her hands away, exposing the ginger mane few eyes had seen loose around her shoulders. His gaze shifted to her face. "I've always loved your hair. It's the color of a new penny."

"*Ya*, well, it's a shame you never learned to love the whole of me." She jerked away. With little regard for her tender scalp, her fingers worked at twisting a bun back into place on her damp neck. She used her one and only remaining pin to secure the knot. In haste, she positioned her *kapp* and tied the wet ribbon under her damp neck.

He turned away from her. "I did love you, you know."

She didn't believe a word of it. "You picked a strange way of showing it, leaving the way you did." Her words were barely audible.

Their eyes met and held for a long moment. "I had my reasons for leaving." He dropped his chin.

"I'm sure you did, but did you stop to think your father might need you? Your *mamm*, his *fraa* of many years, had just passed. All he had left were you and Solomon." *Did you consider I might have needed you, too?*

He thrust the key in the ignition and the truck roared back to life. "I'm not going to pretend that what I did was right. At the time, I didn't think about anyone but myself and the pain of losing my *mamm*. I was selfish. I know that now. I don't need to be reminded." He impatiently swiped rain off his forehead. His eyes closed for a moment. "Look. I admit I wanted to join the *Englisch* world. See what it was like before I settled down. I lived one day at a time, until I looked around and years had passed. After a while I thought I'd been gone too long to return and be welcomed."

Her words were whispered, barely heard over the roar of the motor and pounding rain. "What finally brought you back?"

"Naomi." He took off down the rutted road with a spray of gravel.

Bouncing along beside him, Verity wished he'd said *you*, but he hadn't. She noticed how white his knuckles were on the steering wheel. The young *mann* who'd left her standing, waiting for him all those years ago, never would have admitted he'd made a mistake, even a small one. He'd been too proud. He would have bluffed his way through, made excuses. Maybe he'd changed, but had he changed enough?

And maybe he's working you, like he used to work his mamm.

The truck had barely come to a stop when Verity jumped out and hurried out into the rain while holding up her skirt. She rushed in through the back door without a glance back.

Leviticus parked under a mossy oak tree and slammed the truck door behind him. He hadn't made a mistake coming home. He wanted his *dochder* to know his family, the grove, the Amish way of life. Time had brought about change, but he still resented how hard his mother had seemed to work. Certain-sure his foolishness and too little rest had killed her.

The responsibility for her being overworked, he laid at his *daed*'s feet.

The heavy rain bans on the edge of the retreating hurricane had left the ground soaked under his boots. He sloshed his way to the front yard, his mind whirling. Women liked choices, not mandates, even if they were Amish, like Verity, and raised to be subject to men's authority. He didn't have to be a mind reader to know she didn't want to marry him any more than he wanted to marry her, but he had a feeling she'd be fine being Naomi's mom…if he wasn't part of the deal. He could tell by the way Verity handled the child, especially when she thought no one was watching, that she loved Naomi. He'd seen the tiny kisses she'd placed on the child's cheeks. Somehow, he had to convince Otto to rethink his plan of them marrying. He wasn't ready for two *kinner*, and he sure wasn't fit to be a husband.

He trod through the rain, trying his best to ignore the lightning and endure the sudden bursts of thunder so reminiscent of the IEDs blowing up around him during the war. Sudden noises set off memories of bomb attacks in the dark Afghan nights. One thing the army doctors had taught him was to face his issues head-on, not delay the inevitable. It was time he and Verity talked, got everything out in the open about his tour overseas. About Julie.

He shut the old farmhouse door quietly behind him. The great room was empty, but he could hear Faith's excited squeals coming from the kitchen and Naomi's urgent cry for milk. He hadn't taken time to feed her or share a smile with the rosy-cheeked child all day. Guilt ate at him, reminding him why he questioned his ability to be a good father. Did he have what it took to bring up Naomi as Amish?

The kitchen door burst open, its hinges protesting as they announced Faith coming into the room. She wore a tiny dress of pale yellow, her shiny hair pulled back in a flyaway bun the size of a donut. She wore no prayer *kapp*; rather, it was clutched in her small hand. Her eyes were bright with excitement. She scurried over, her smile infectious. "Hello."

He found himself smiling back. "How are you, little one?"

She sidled up to him, almost touching. "My *mamm* said I'm not to bother you." Faith clutched her faceless doll under her arm. Mischievousness danced in her blue eyes. She plopped down on the floor, in front of the couch set back against the large picture window and cozied her doll among several square pillows. A square throw quilt, probably knitted by Verity, was draped casually across the doll's legs.

Apart from Naomi, he had little experience with children like Faith. He didn't know what to say, or what not to, but did his best to show she could trust him. "Did you have fun with Clara today?" He sat on the couch and saw the protective glance Faith gave her doll next to his leg. She didn't trust him fully, but he prayed she would in time.

Faith took her doll out from under the blanket and bounced it along the edge of the worn couch arm. "We made cupcakes. I ate two, but don't tell *Mamm*. She says I eat too much sugar."

In a surprise move, she opened her mouth wide and flashed tiny square molars. "Do you see any cavities?

If I get one, *Mamm* says I have to visit the *Englischer* dentist again." She batted her ginger lashes at him. "Does it hurt to have a filling? *Mamm* said it could. Have you had a tooth filled?"

Leviticus wasn't sure which question to answer first. He wasn't about to admit he'd often canceled dental appointments until extreme pain had him reaching for the phone. He had to set a good example for Faith and Naomi now. "I've seen the dentist lots of times. Brushing your teeth really good after eating sugar is the key."

"Your shirt is wet." She changed the subject. "Did it hurt?"

"What?" he asked, bemused. Like Verity, Faith had a way of delighting him, but kept him off-kilter with her rapid-fire way of talking.

Faith snickered. "The fillings? Did they hurt?" Her expectant gaze held his.

Hurt? Yes, it hurt. But a lot of things hurt in life.

He pulled his thoughts away from his problems, brought them back to the present, to Faith and the room they were in. Would his lack of concentration ever go away?

"Did it?" Faith asked again, her hands on her hips, waiting.

"Yes, sometimes it hurt, but just a bit. You look like a brave girl to me."

Faith looked guilty as Verity came into the room and took her by the hand, her forehead furrowed. "I told you not to bother Leviticus. He has a lot on his mind. Let's go see if we can help Clara fix a meal."

"You look brave to me," Faith called over her shoulder to Leviticus. Her skinny legs skipped alongside her mother, who flashed him a puzzled glance.

Leviticus watched as they disappeared down the hall. His chin dropped to his chest. *Brave. Ha!* If the little girl only knew what a coward he'd been in the war. He rose and moved toward his room, only to pause as his cell phone went off. "Hello."

The voice on the phone was formal and hurried. "Mr. Hilty. This is Janet Gaynor, your father's nurse. I'm afraid he's taken a turn for the worse. It's time you and the family get up here."

His vocal cords froze. He finally got out, "*Ya*, we'll be right there." His whole body went numb, his hand trembling so hard he almost dropped the cell phone.

"Oh, yes. Your brother said to bring Verity with you."

His brow creased in a deep V. He cleared his voice. "You sure he didn't say to bring Clara, his wife?"

"No. He didn't mention anyone named Clara. I distinctly remember him saying the name Verity."

"Okay." His heart pounded, almost deafening him. "We'll be right there." He ended the call and looked around the room, confusion clouding his mind. Why would Solomon want Verity to come? She was close to his father, but not family, not like Clara was.

He shoved his cell phone back in his pocket and tried to walk, but his legs failed to cooperate. He called out to Verity from where he stood, his voice strained. Was his father dying? On a shelf, the light overhead sent a spark of reflection flickering off his mother's favorite jug. He drew in a deep breath, remembering how strong she'd been as she lay dying and drew strength from her memory. He made another attempt to move and found himself able to hurry down the hall toward the kitchen. Time was wasting.

As he opened the kitchen door, Faith scurried past, her laughter filled with mischief, Verity following close behind the giggling child. Naomi took tiny steps while holding on to Verity's hands. As Naomi passed on tiptoe, she glanced up at her *daed*, her expression decidedly anxious, like being up on her feet made her feel unsure.

"I need to talk to you," he told Verity, his joy at seeing Naomi's first tentative steps pushed back by overwhelming fear of what they'd find at the hospital.

Something in his tone must have gotten Verity's attention. She slowed and then stopped to lift Naomi to her hip. Her gaze searched his face. "What's wrong?" She moved back toward him, her smile slipping.

"It's *Daed*. The nurse—" His voice broke, but he struggled on. "She said to come now."

She nodded. "Go. Quick. Don't worry about Naomi. I will take *gut* care of her." Wiping a tear from her cheek, Verity turned to follow Faith.

"No. Wait. You don't understand. You need to come. Clara will have to care for the *kinner*."

"But why? Clara should be going with you. Solomon will want her there with him." Verity repositioned Naomi on her hip, her hands holding on to the squirming *kind*.

"I have no idea why Solomon said to bring you, but he did. The nurse said to come now. There was no time for questions. You're needed."

"But—"

"Look, if you don't want to come, just say so."

She shook her head. Her face had gone pale. "*Nee*, it's not that. I just don't understand."

He finally noticed the tick of nerves in her jaw, saw fear in her eyes and became gentle. "We'll figure it out later, Verity, but for right now, let's get the kids situated and hit the road."

Chapter Eleven

❧

Verity's stomach roiled as she stared at the elevator. Until recently, she hadn't ridden in many and had hoped to keep it that way. They did unpleasant things to her stomach. Today would be no exception.

She stepped in, followed by Leviticus. He pushed a button and the doors swooshed closed behind them, her fate sealed. She reached back, blindly searching for the handrail to steady her footing.

A bell dinged somewhere on the silver panel. The door slid open with another whoosh, exposing polished cream-colored tiled floors and a brightly lit corridor. A man dressed in a janitorial uniform stepped on and nodded their way. His work shirt declared his name was Ralph.

Verity watched as he positioned his rake-thin body against the side of the elevator. Perhaps he didn't like riding in it any more than she did.

They rode up two floors together in total silence. With a will of its own, the shiny metal door swished open. At a distance, Verity noticed a crescent-shaped nurses' station. A cluster of nurses dressed in cheerful scrubs mingled close by. One hospital caregiver looked up and gazed at them. Verity had grown accustomed to *Englisch* curiosity.

Completely out of character, and something he hadn't done since their courting days, Leviticus grabbed her hand and pulled her out of the elevator. Surprised, she stumbled forward·and would have lost her footing if he hadn't pulled her close. "Are you all right?"

"Ya." Her face warmed. The man named Ralph slipped past and disappeared down a long hallway to their right.

Leviticus nodded, and together they moved forward, walking in unison.

If she remembered correctly, Albert's room was located two floors below. *So why did we get off on the fourth floor?*

Tethered to him by the warm grasp of his fingers, she hurried alongside him. "Wait!"

He paused abruptly, causing her to bump into his arm. He gazed down at her, one pale brow arched in curiosity. "You've changed your mind about seeing my *daed*?"

She had forgotten how tall he was, and handsome. She shook her head, ignoring the thrill tickling her stomach. *This foolishness must stop.* "*Nee*, of course I didn't change my mind." She glanced back at the elevator, toward the nurses. "Didn't we get off on the wrong floor?" She pulled her hand away from his and instantly regretted the loss of his touch.

After running his hand across his grizzled chin, he

shoved his hands in his pockets. "They moved *Daed* to this room early this morning. After fresh tests were run and his doctor examined him."

"Oh." She noticed how quiet the halls were, how silently the nurses interacted with each other. "Is this an ICU ward?"

"No. Not exactly. It's the hospice unit."

"Hospice?" Verity's chin wobbled. She was all too familiar with the medical term. Her *grossmudder* had lived out her last days hooked up to a morphine drip in a ward just like this one. The possibility of Albert's demise became very real to her in that moment. "I'm very sorry your father's worse."

"Ya." His shoulders rounded, his eyes bloodshot from lack of sleep. He looked exhausted. "I should have come back to Pinecraft sooner."

"Some will say you came home too late, but at least you *did* come home." She wished she could say any number of things that would make him feel less guilty. But the fact remained that he had taken off, left his father to worry about the fate of the family grove. And there wasn't a doubt in her mind that Leviticus had enjoyed his time in the *Englischer* world.

"Like anything I do can make a difference now." He cupped her elbow as he directed her down the short corridor to a room at the end of the hall.

"You have to know you coming home made a big difference to Albert."

He shrugged, his glace quick. "I guess it did." He rubbed his hand down his arm. "Don't be too alarmed when you see him." His expression became grim. *"Daed* might look pretty bad." His steps slowed and stopped in front of a door. "His heart's tired. Maybe giving out. We have to prepare ourselves for what might happen."

His words entered her brain, but their meaning didn't register. Time slipped away. Young Leviticus stood before her, vulnerable and grief stricken. She allowed herself to linger in the past, remembering the good times, when all that mattered was the color of the dress she wore to church and if Leviticus would approve of how she looked in it.

"Unless something changes, he could die tonight." His chin dropped, but then he looked up, his tear-filled eyes holding her gaze. "It's important we act strong." He wiped his big palm across his cheek, removing a trail of tears. "I don't know if I can pull it off." He laughed ruefully. "I've never been much of an actor." Immense pain showed clearly on his face.

Her heart raced. She read the signs of grief, saw the bags under his eyes. He was hurting badly.

Verity blinked back tears of sympathy. Her chest ached. These were the most honest words she'd heard him utter since he'd been a young man and walked out of her life. She mustered up every ounce of courage she possessed, her head nodding in unspoken encouragement. "*Ya*, you can pull it off, Leviticus. You have to."

She struggled inwardly for the right words, and suddenly they came. "We draw strength from the Lord. *Gott* promises to see us through hard times like these." She forgot about her anger bubbling just under the surface since he'd come home, about her anger at him for leaving and breaking her heart. Her resentment didn't seem so important now. Albert might be dying.

With a mind of their own, the tips of her fingers brushed across his cheek, the stubble growing on his chin scraping against their pads. Old emotions tried to flare back to life in a fire that would consume her heart forever if she let it.

She pulled her fingers away and forced a half grin. "Let's go see your *daed*. He's waiting."

Leviticus thought he'd prepared himself for his father's appearance, but he hadn't and evidently neither had Verity. He heard her shocked gasp. His *daed*'s body seemed to have shriveled overnight, his coloring so pale it looked translucent against the hospital bed's white sheets. His heart breaking, he listened to the sounds his father made as he gasped for air through dry, cracked lips. Someone had pushed his father's long gray hair off his forehead, exposing the old man's rawboned features. How had he lost so much weight so quickly?

He clutched Verity's arm, as much to support himself as to steady her. She was seeing what he saw, and yet she stood strong and unwavering. But he knew her bravado was just an act. Somehow, she always thought she had to be the strong one, to set a standard far too high for her to maintain for long. He acknowledged his brother standing at the foot of the bed, and then Otto seated next to him with a nod. "Sit here." He led Verity to the chair just vacated by Otto at the side of his father's bed.

Dressed smartly in pressed dark trousers, black suspenders and a white shirt good enough to be his Sunday best, Otto had aged during the years Leviticus had been away. But the short, stout man appeared sturdy and unyielding as he moved closer to Albert's side.

As best he could remember, Otto's finest official bishop's garb was reserved for special occasions, like weddings and social events of the highest caliber. If his father had awakened, he would have no doubt been honored by the man's display of respect and loyalty. Almost the same age, the men had been friends since *bus*. He knew Otto loved Albert, yet their competitive checker games at the park had often been loud and amusing. Still in shock over his father's declined health, Leviticus stumbled down to the foot of the bed.

Otto moved restlessly about the room, standing for a moment with Leviticus, only to relinquish the spot to Solomon and wander to a spare chair by the door. As the slightly bent man glanced around and observed their faces, he touched his beard, drawing his short, stubby fingers down the length of the bristled hair. He showed his edginess by stretching out the collar of his shirt with one finger, something Leviticus remembered seeing him do a thousand times while he would preach.

Albert suddenly opened his eyes and made a sound, surprising them all. He didn't move his head but sought to stare at Leviticus's face with eyes the color of a summer sky. Eyes so like his own. Deep emotions, feelings he thought he'd long forgotten, stirred, causing him to gasp for breath. This was the father he knew and loved as a child. Albert looked near death, but in his mind, his *daed* was still the strong, single-minded father he remembered all too well. It was as if he could read the old man's thoughts. Soh, *have you wed yet?*

He pulled his gaze away from his father's and

looked toward Verity. She had sidled up to him by the bed, hovering, her face twisted in concern. There was no doubt in his mind. She loved his father as much as her own. In that moment, he knew they would marry today and bring peace to the old man's mind before he passed. She would obey Otto's wishes. She was Amish raised, just like Albert. Their motto was God's will be done.

Her chin lifted, her eyes locking with his for a moment. Silent words were exchanged between them. There *would* be a wedding today, like it or not. The time to fight Otto had passed. They would become man and wife, here and now, in this hospital room. Verity nodded his way, silently like-minded. Her shoulders dropped, all resistance gone.

Reading their signs of resignation, Otto stepped forward, his Bible in hand. "For the love of Albert, I'm setting aside the rules of membership before marriage."

As minutes passed, Leviticus realized most of the formality of traditional Amish weddings was being set aside also. Leviticus looked into the eyes of his father's best friend. There would be a fuss raised among the congregation, but Otto stood steady on his feet, prepared to set aside whatever was needed for his life-long friend.

Amish marriages were till death do us part. This was a huge sacrifice from Verity. Come Sunday, he'd join the New Order Amish church and finally be in good standing with the community. But what would his standing with Verity be after today?

Traditional questions of loyalty to the church and

each other would be left unasked and unanswered for today. There were to be no cheerful songs sung, laced with *Gott*'s promise to the faithful. It didn't matter that he and Verity had no friends seated at their side, no wedding meal waiting for them at home. There'd be no family visits in other states, no days of visiting friends. *Will Verity feel cheated?* Naturally, she would.

Otto motioned Solomon over, cleared his voice and bowed his head. All in the room followed suit. Leviticus's fingers fumbled as he removed his baseball cap and tossed it on the floor. Why hadn't he cut his hair sooner, taken to wearing Amish garb before now? Verity would have wanted that for today.

Am I ready to be Amish? He reached out and took her cold hand in his. Her body quaked next to him. Marriage was forever. They both knew it. She was as terrified as he was. Maybe more.

Otto lifted his chin and spoke. "Before *Gott*, we are here to join this man and this woman in the bonds of holy matrimony."

Leviticus didn't know where to look. He fixed his eyes across from his father's bed, on a simple watercolor of rolling hills and meadows, where cows grazed in the bright sunshine. He forced his mind to go blank. Still, memories of his *mamm*'s last words to his *daed* screamed inside his head. *I love you, my husband. I always will.* Love was meant to be eternal. What they were doing was wrong. Marriage was sacred to Verity, something most woman went into after much consideration and prayer. Surely, she required a measure of love from the man standing next to her.

Did he love Verity? The *Englischer* life had taught

him to respect women, allow them to have a mind of their own, do what they thought best for themselves. He felt affection—but love her the way a man should love his woman? What did he know about that kind of love?

Albert and her family shouldn't be selling Verity off to him like a plot of land to be kept in the family. Especially to someone who had more mental issues than she knew about. *She has a right to know whom she's getting.* Would she have considered him worthy if she understood the depth of sins he'd committed? Not in a million years. She deserved a whole man, someone who could love her the way her first husband had loved her. She'd compare him to Mark. Who could blame her?

Solomon moved in closer, stood next to Verity as if to protect her from Leviticus. She might well need Solomon's protection. He thought of his remaining depression, his temper when riled, thanks to the remains of PTSD.

"Those *Gott* has joined together, let no man put asunder," Otto's words ended. They were man and wife, *Gott* help her.

The room echoed with silence. He looked down, saw Verity's true feelings written on her face. She was ashen, limp, her lips drooping at the corners. Her eyes swam with tears. She glanced up at him through pale lashes, her glassy-eyed stare unsettling him. *She's shut down.* He'd seen men shut down on the battlefield. Hadn't he done the same to keep what little sanity he had a year ago? He held tight to her fingers, fearing she'd pull away and reject him at the last moment.

Albert made a noise in his throat. Otto motioned her over. Verity hurried closer to his father's bed. Leviticus joined her, contemplating their situation. He looked at his father's face. His eyes were closed, but a peaceful smile tugged at the corners of his mouth. A knot in Leviticus's stomach grew. His father was still alive but could have easily slipped away as Otto spoke words of love and trust over them, joining them as one.

Otto stepped behind them. "Leave him for now. He needs rest."

Verity jerked her hand away and pressed it to her pale lips. She gasped for air and then rushed from the room, the skirt of her plain blue dress flying behind her. He made a move to follow, but Solomon's hand caught him roughly by the arm. "Let her go, *bruder*. She needs to be alone."

He jerked his arm away. "*Nee!* She needs me. She's my *fraa* now."

"*Ya*, she may be your *fraa*, but only because her love for *Daed* forced her into this union. She has no need of you. She needs time to gather her thoughts." Solomon's eyes burned with anger, his mouth an unforgiving line of contempt.

Leviticus hurried out the door and down the hall, all the way to the empty elevators. Verity was nowhere in sight. He looked back toward the hallway, beyond his father's room. Had she taken the stairs at the end of the short hall?

He stood on the edge of insanity, alone and without wisdom. He didn't know how to feel, what to think. He shook inwardly. His shoulders carried a heavy burden of guilt as he made his way back into his father's room.

This marriage arrangement had provided a mother for his tiny daughter, but what of Verity? What had she gained by it? An empty shell of a man.

Chapter Twelve

The toe of Verity's flip-flop caught on the top stair, sending her stumbling across the wooden porch of the old farmhouse. The sun had finally come out, making her walk from the hospital a long hot one. Sweat trickled down her neck, trailed down her spine.

Catching a ride on the back of Les Yoder's cart at the edge of Sarasota had been a true blessing. Her mind swirled from the events of the day. She'd remained silent when Les dropped her off at the grove gate and waved goodbye as he drove off. She told him about Albert's worsening condition, but not that she'd married his *soh*. The community would find out soon enough, and what would they think?

Leviticus and I married. How can it be?

Not willing to let her new husband fill her thoughts, she pictured Albert instead. His shallow, labored breathing still haunted her.

Will he live? Please, Gott. *Let him live.*

She'd learned death was a part of life, something she had to accept as the Lord's will, but losing the sweet old man was unthinkable. She had her strong faith to fall back on, but what about Leviticus? Was he truly a believer now or putting on an act just to please his father? Try as she would, she couldn't understand why *Gott* would want to snatch Albert away, especially now that Leviticus was home.

She'd never been close to her own father. Oh, he was kind to her and loving on occasion, but he was a hardworking man, someone who gave more of himself to his profession as a cabinetmaker than to his family. She'd been raised predominately by her *mamm*. As a child, she longed for a father who shared his wisdom and kind heart with her. She found those qualities in Albert when she came to work for him.

Now I'm tethered to Leviticus, a man who doesn't love me.

She entered the great room and called out to Clara. Silence greeted her. She breathed a sigh of relief. She needed a moment to collect her thoughts and calm down before she told Clara that she and Leviticus had married.

She moved through the familiar rooms of the house, toward her bedroom, and found a note attached to Albert's favorite chair with a large safety pin. She unfolded the slip of paper and recognized her mother's neat script. *I've got the girls with me and will return later in the day. Clara's gone to the hospital to be with Solomon.*

Perhaps she should have stayed with Leviticus. He was her husband after all. But the day had proven to be too much for her. Running away showed the weak side of her she wasn't proud of. Albert would have expected more of her now that she was his *soh*'s *fraa*.

Tears blurred her vision. She began to refold the paper and then noticed a scribble in purple marker just under her mother's message. A smiley face and Faith's name had been carefully drawn and printed at the bottom of the page. She half smiled. Her sweet girl might have her father's above-average intelligence, but she had Verity's terrible handwriting. She tucked the paper in her apron pocket and continued down the hall, past Albert's room, the back of her hand wiping a fresh tear from her cheek.

She shuffled through her bedroom door on rubbery legs. Inside, everything was neat and tidy as usual. Her bedroom window was open a crack, the lightweight curtains at her window dancing in the wind. It had been in the low sixties for days thanks to the hurricane, but now it had rained again, and the Florida humidity was back with a vengeance.

Moments later, a sound behind her made her turn and look. Leviticus stood just inside the dimly lit hall. "When did you come home?"

"Just now. You shouldn't leave the main door unlocked when you're alone."

Amish people seldom locked doors, but he was right. "*Ya*, times are changing. I'll have to form new habits now that Albert's not in the house." She dropped her voice, her words falling off into a deep dark well of misery. She was sure he wasn't ready to discuss their impromptu marriage or his father's worsening health any more than she was. She looked up, saw pain etched deep on his face.

He stood stoop-shouldered, as if he were an old man.

"Solomon and Clara are with you?" she asked. Inch by inch, she edged toward her bedroom door. Her bare toes curled under as she paused just outside the door.

"No. I left them comforting each other. Clara mentioned they'd soon be going back to their own place—in a week, perhaps more. The workers are almost finished with the repairs to their house. There was nothing I could say or do to help *Daed*." Leviticus looked hard at her, his eyes searching. "I had to come home, see if you were okay."

"Of course I am."

Their words echoed through the quiet house and died.

He said what she'd been thinking. "The place feels empty without him, doesn't it? Like *Daed* is the heart of this home and without him here there is no home." He wiped a tear from his cheek with the back of his hand, but it was replaced by a fresh one.

She took a step toward him and then another, compassion and her own pain drawing them together in misery. She grabbed his limp hand. It was cold and trembling. He'd left the grove when his *mamm* died. Would he leave the grove again if Albert passed?

Somehow, she found herself wrapped in his arms, his tears dampening her shoulder as he wept like a child. They swayed together as one, grief and concern for Albert tearing away all past angers in that moment in time.

Her ear pressed against his chest. She heard his heart beat as he took in quick, unsteady breaths. Moments passed. The old clock in the great room chimed.

He hadn't moved in minutes, but his arms were lax now, almost limp at his sides. She took in a deep breath, prepared to move.

"I'm sorry," he murmured, stepping away. "I don't know what came over me. I didn't mean to embarrass you." He rubbed at the gristle on his chin, his hand sliding down to grasp the back of his neck.

"Don't be silly. You didn't embarrass me," she insisted, even though she felt heat warming her face. "You needed comfort. We both did. I love Albert, too, you know." She cleared the roughness from her voice. "Let me get changed and I'll fix a quick meal."

He looked down the hall, toward his bedroom. "I'm not up to eating right now. I have a headache."

"I'll get you something to drink instead." She took another step back.

"Yeah, sure. That would be great." He ran his hand through his long, tangled hair, went to move down the hall and then turned back around. "I'll wait for you in the kitchen. Okay?"

Verity backed up against her door, her hand grasping the knob. "*Ya*, just give me a moment."

He nodded and then ambled off, his head down.

She hurried into her room, shut the door firmly behind her and slipped out of the old blue dress that had become her wedding dress. With little interest in what she wore, she grabbed one of her everyday dresses and left her apron and prayer *kapp* on the bed. Still barefoot, she hurried into the hallway. Albert would want her to see to his son's needs now that she was his wife.

The reality of her situation hit like a ton of bricks. She paused. The wedding… Everything had happened so fast. She hadn't had time to absorb any of it or come to terms with the new position she held in this household. A jumble of thoughts rushed in, more concerning than before. She turned back toward the opened bedroom door. Would he expect to share that bed with her tonight?

She shoved her shoulders back and marched away from the bedroom door. "*Ya*, well. He can think again," she whispered to the silent hall. "I'm not prepared for any such matters of the heart."

The kitchen still smelled faintly of bacon. Leviticus grabbed the pot of old coffee from that morning and placed it back on the gas burner to reheat. Blue flames licked around the bottom of the old metal pot. The brew would be bitter, but he didn't care. Military life had taught him to like his coffee strong.

As he moved around the room, he looked out the kitchen window. The wind was kicking up again, wildly blowing a set of white sheets someone had hung on the line earlier. He took down a thick mug from the cupboard, poured the dark steaming liquid in and then jerked out a wooden chair. The mug thumped loudly as he placed it in front of him. His hands were trembling again, his PTSD rearing its ugly head. He tried to relax, forced his breath to be deep and regulated.

But his mind would not stop racing, no matter how hard he tried to master the art of bringing every thought into captivity as the Bible suggested.

If only I had a breathing technique for that.

A headache at the base of his skull thumped hard, reminding him to take one of his little blue pills or he'd be sorry later. The headaches had started in Afghanistan, long before he'd been shot and almost killed.

Memories of the war flooded in. Running for cover during a barrage of gunfire, he'd taken a fall and hit his head on a rock. He'd seen stars but hadn't gotten the bleeding goose egg seen to. There was no time. The doctors were busy saving brave men's lives.

He stared down into the coffee and then slowly sipped, welcoming the unpleasant, bitter taste as something infinitely familiar. He'd experienced a lot of losses the last few years. The loss of his army buddies who never made it home, the loss of his way of life as part of a troop. He was glad when they released him from the army on a medical discharge. No more wars. No more moving. He could give Naomi the stable life she deserved as an Amish child with a mother by her side. But still, the ground didn't seem solid under his feet. He was attempting to live his old Amish way of life again, embrace old ways of thinking, and some days failing miserably.

He looked down at his jeans, tugged at the sleeve of his knit T-shirt. It was past time. All this garb would have to go. It was the behavioral changes that would challenge him most. He was a father now, *and* husband, too. His shoulders lifted and fell. Would *Gott* show him the way to complete redemption? Could he do right by Verity, their daughters? He pushed the coffee cup away, his stomach too acidic from nerves.

He ought to be able to relax about Naomi's future now, but what about Verity's and Faith's futures with him as head of the house? His daughter would have a loving mother, a big family who loved her. They'd meet her needs better than he could alone. He and Naomi profited from the marriage, but Verity and Faith had come out with the short end of the stick.

The kitchen door swung open with a squeak. Verity entered the room wearing a plain dark blue dress without an apron. She approached gingerly and set a stack of clothes on the table next to him.

"These were Solomon's things. Clara thought she'd help out and selected them for you a few days ago." She let her hand linger on the roughly sewn trousers on top of the pile. "The pants may be a bit short. Solomon's not as tall as you."

"Danki." Leviticus noticed a pair of suspenders tucked under the edge of the pants. They looked new, like Verity had bought them specially for him.

"Here, let me make you a fresh mug of coffee." She whisked his cup away and busied herself cleaning the coffeepot and filling it with fresh water and grinds. "You shouldn't have heated that coffee."

"I like it strong."

Verity made a sound with her tongue, like a mother duck clucking her disapproval at her foolish *kind*. "There's no need for you to drink stale coffee. You have a *fraa* now, someone to make sure you eat well and dress properly."

He set aside the suspenders and fingered the woven cotton shirt on the bottom of the pile of clothing. It was made of rough woven cotton, snaps instead of buttons closing the front. He favored knit T-shirts in warm weather. "Dress properly, as in Amish trousers and a plain shirt?" He smiled at her, trying to keep their conversation light. "You know I hate wearing suspenders."

She twisted around, her hands still busy adding soap shavings to the running dishwater. "But you are an Amish *mann* now. Plain. Love it or hate it, these are the clothes you'll need to wear to please your *daed* and the community. Did you think you could keep dressing like an *Englischer*? You're married, soon to be a member of this community. Changes have to be made."

"I know." His tone held more rancor than he'd intended. "I'd planned on buying suitable clothes the next time I went into town. I just never found the time."

Verity turned back, abandoning the cup she'd been washing. Her eyes narrowed. "Remember, clothes don't make the *mann*. You'll have to change your way of thinking, too, to become a true *mann* of faith."

He heard her sniff, saw her shoulders square as she turned back to the dishes. Was she fighting tears again? A tenderness came over him. Verity was a good woman. She should be sitting quietly, calming her frazzled nerves, not taking care of his needs. She'd been through a lot. Spirited or not, she had a gentle Amish heart. His guilt piled high, causing his head to pound harder.

"Take some ibuprofen. I can see your head is hurting again by the way you're squinting." She dried her hands and hung up the dishcloth. "There's a bottle of tablets on the table, next to the napkins." She pointed just past his hand.

"Thanks, but I've got something."

Why didn't she sit?

"I appreciate all you've done for me, for Naomi and for my *vadder*. You know that, right?"

She lifted the coffeepot, poured a steaming cup and

handed it to him. "Today, I didn't do any of it for you, Leviticus. I did it for Albert. He's been good to me and never asked for anything back but kindness. Marrying you was the least I could do for him."

Leviticus shook his head in regret. She was trapped in a loveless marriage thanks to his return. "I appreciate your sacrifice, Verity. I do. I promise I'll try to be a good husband and love Faith as if she were my own child."

Verity's chin quivered as she spoke. "I'll hold you to that promise. My *dochder* is not going to suffer because I made a pledge to an *Englischer* who's playing at being Amish for the sake of his father."

Her words stung, but he saw them as true. The main reason he had come home was to attempt a reunion with his father and brother, but his new awareness of God's love had spurred him on, too. Marrying Verity and being a father to Faith had never been part of his plans. But he'd keep his promise to her or die trying. He owed her that much.

Verity pulled out a kitchen chair and joined him at the table. She slumped back, as tired as he suspected.

"We have more to talk about." Her gaze didn't meet his. "From the beginning, I need to make something clear."

Her tone was much too serious for his liking. "Okay." He braced himself for her words. His hand moved, pushing away the cup of coffee untouched.

"Our union may be blessed by *Gott* and the church." She paused, took a deep breath and then continued on, "But I won't be sleeping in your bed. We are no love match. Not anymore." She smoothed out an imaginary wrinkle in the tablecloth in front of her, her gaze downward.

He understood her reluctance for intimacy only too well. "I didn't expect anything more from you, Verity. All I need is kindness for my daughter. I'm satisfied with our arrangement and see no need for change now, or in the future."

Her words didn't hurt him. He'd built too many walls around his heart to be wounded.

Chapter Thirteen

The next morning, the first signs of an early fall blew in on a brisk, cold wind from the far north. Verity woke from a fitful sleep, disoriented at first, but the aroma of coffee brewing had her slipping out of bed before the rooster crowed. She threw on her robe, changed Naomi's soaked diaper and then made her way to the kitchen for some much-needed caffeine and a bottle for Naomi.

Leviticus didn't look any better than she felt as he greeted her with an unsure smile. "*Guder mariye.* I see from the bags under your eyes, you slept about as well as I did."

Self-conscious, she silently nodded. She hadn't bothered to repair her braid. Her hand went straight to her hair, but she noticed his blond hair was as wild and uncombed as her own must be.

She smiled and nodded her thank-you when he set a hot cup of coffee on the table for her. Doing battle with a squirming Naomi, she slipped the soon-to-be one-year-old into the high chair and poured out a handful of dry oat cereal for her to eat while her bottle heated.

Faith hurried into the kitchen without house shoes on her feet and hugged her *mamm* from behind, rubbing sleep from her eyes as she made her way to a chair.

"Did you sleep well, *liebling*?"

"*Ya*, but Naomi woke me just now with her crying." Eyes as dark as Verity's coffee shot her new *schweschder* an accusing glance.

Verity coughed against her shoulder, her allergies kicking up from the brisk winds blowing outside. She downed a gulp of coffee as she made her way to the refrigerator for milk. "She's little, not quite a year old. You cried just like her when you were a *boppli*."

Today was Sunday, their first real day of married life and the grove's day to host members of the church for lunch. Word would spread, and she and Leviticus would be greeted as a married couple. Her nerves kicked up her stomach, but she fought down the urge to fall into dread.

It would be a cold breakfast for everyone, but first, Faith needed telling about the wedding before someone else informed her during the church service.

Leviticus worked on his own cup of steaming brew across from Faith while Verity downed the last of her coffee and gathered her courage to speak to her sleepy daughter.

"I have news I'm certain-sure you're going to like, Faith."

"*Ya?*" Faith said with about as much enthusiasm as Verity felt.

"Leviticus and I were married yesterday."

Leviticus looked up, seeking her gaze, his expression priceless. He hadn't been prepared for Faith's bellow of joy and neither had Verity. No doubt, Faith's explosion had woken Pinecraft and the outer edges of Sarasota proper.

Scared by Faith's ruckus, Naomi let loose a squall of her own. Verity lifted the child from the high chair, comforted her and watched as Leviticus squirmed as Faith rained kisses on his face and gave him hug after hug.

"I knew you two were in love. I could see it in your eyes," Faith said with a giggle.

Cool and controlled, Leviticus agreed. "*Ya*, it was love at first sight, ain't so, Verity? You knew best," he said to the child, with a forced smile he shared with Verity.

Calmed now, Naomi was set on a pallet near the table for her father to see to as Verity took down bowls and gathered her wits about her. All this talk of love unnerved her.

A secret glance back her husband's way had her breath catching in her throat. Glowing with confidence, Naomi grabbed hold of her *daed*'s pant leg and pulled herself up like she'd been doing it for weeks. Her first tentative steps were cautious but without assistance. A smile lifted Leviticus's mouth and brightened his eyes. Keeping guard, Leviticus's hands were there to catch Naomi when her tiny legs grew tired and she toppled over.

Leviticus cheered, but she held back a little of herself for fear she'd grow too fond of this normal setting of peaceful family life. *Lord, keep me ever faithful to Your will.*

Leviticus made a face, shaving under his nose and then critically examining the beginning of his pale beard. *Pathetic!* It would take some time for it to grow and even more time getting used to the look of it, but for now the itching on his chin was worse than the change in appearance. He dressed carefully, putting on one of the new homemade trousers and long-sleeved shirts he'd bought from Mose's wife, Sarah, the night before.

Just as he'd rinsed his face and toweled it dry, his phone went off. *Daed?* He lifted the small thin device and placed it next to his ear. "Hello."

"Good morning, Mr. Hilty. This is June Hillsborough, your dad's morning nurse. Do you have a moment to talk?"

Nerves curled in Leviticus's stomach. Each time the phone rang, and it was the hospital, he wondered if this was the call. Had his *daed* gotten worse? Perhaps even died?

"*Ya*, sure." The beat of his heart increased in his ears to a deafening roar.

"I'm sorry to be calling so early. I know you have young children. I didn't want to wake them, but I thought you'd be glad to know we're beginning to see some marked improvement in your father's lab work. He seems to be responding well to his new heart medication, and his diet is making a real difference in his kidney function. His kidney and liver functions are

much improved this morning. Also, his blood oxygen
levels are up. All good signs he's beginning to progress." The nurse cleared her throat. "Naturally we'll
be taking more blood through the day and continuing
to monitor his oxygen levels to make sure he remains
stable, but all and all we're seeing good reports and
plan to move him to a step-down room soon."

Leviticus took in a calming breath and pushed it
back out again. "*Danki* for calling me. Have you spoken to Solomon, my *bruder*, this morning?"

"Yes, I did just a moment ago. Like you, he seemed
relieved. Well, I'd best get back to my patients. You
have yourself a great day."

"You, too," Leviticus said, his relief laced in his
voice. Punching the red icon on his phone and hanging up, Leviticus leaned against the dresser he'd used
as a *kind* and groaned in relief, his head down, eyes
closed. A tear slipped from his eye, and then another.
He needed *gut* news. Needed something concrete like
a good report to hang on to. But would his father's
recovery have Verity regretting their marriage vows
already?

Five minutes later, after a moment of calming
prayer, he strolled into the kitchen and couldn't help
but laugh out loud as he watched Verity try to catch
Naomi, who was quickly crawling around on the
kitchen floor, doing her best to avoid being picked up.
Determination was written all over her chubby face,
and his *dochder*'s dark curls and eyes shone bright in
the early-morning sun. She scurried along toward him
in an awkward crab-like crawl, her tiny body clad in

the violet-colored dress he had watched Verity complete sewing the night before.

"If you'll just catch her and hold her, I'll finish dressing her," Verity said, doing her best to place the *kind*'s *kapp* on Naomi's head.

Holding the squirming *boppli* while Verity slipped on the child's tiny apron, he grinned Verity's way as she fought a mighty battle to hold Naomi's twisting head as she adjusted her prayer *kapp*. He was surprised to see Verity putting small dabs of sticky molasses on each side of the child's head before the final adjustment was made.

Verity grinned at him. "What? You thought *kapps* stayed on *bopplis* without a little help? She doesn't have enough hair for pins."

"A *mamm* always knows best," he muttered and then nodded his approval as Faith came prancing in, fully dressed, proclaiming she'd gotten herself ready. Her apron was tied in a messy knot at the back, but Verity was obviously proud of her daughter's accomplishments and let it be. "You did a *gut* job, Faith. Ain't so, Leviticus?"

He nodded like a proud *daed* would, amazed at how well their first morning as a family was going. He'd expected… Well, he didn't know what he'd expected, but not this feeling of delight.

"I'm the big *schweschder* now. I don't need help dressing anymore."

He sidled up to Verity as she poured round dry cereal in a bag for Naomi. "There was a call from the hospital."

Verity froze in motion, her eyes searching his, brows knitting. "Is Albert all right?"

"It's *gut* news, *fraa*. Calm yourself. His bloodwork is showing improvement and the nurse was decidedly more positive this call." Leviticus watched the stress ease from Verity's face and smiled. "*Gott*'s will for Albert's life, ain't so?"

"*Ya, Gott*'s will." A smile blossomed on her face.

A few moments later, warm capes and *kapps* were put on and then Leviticus shut the back door behind them. He led the way down the stairs with Naomi squirming in his arms, finally feeling like an Amish family *mann*.

"Are you nervous?" Verity asked, walking close to his side along the gravel road.

"About?" he asked, and then realized what she meant. He was joining the church today. His stomach flopped, but he smiled anyway. "*Nee*, not nervous. More like relieved. I should have done this a long time ago." What he was doing this morning felt right to him. Just like holding Faith's hand when Verity took over the care of Naomi as they strolled along.

She hadn't had time to digest the fact that his *daed* was improving. Soon enough he'd see if their marriage of convenience would work out or not. The thought of Verity tied to him all her life and regretting it worked on his nerves, but he knew how to pray nowadays. Prayer made a difference. Probably it always had, and he'd been too stupid to realize it.

Lines of men were already forming at the door of the church as they approached. He left Verity and the children with the ladies gathered on the grass and strolled up behind several married men in line.

Otto greeted him with a firm handshake, as he did all the men and women standing around, but while he held on to Leviticus's hand he asked, "Is all well? A lot of changes have taken place in a short period of time for you, ain't so?"

Leviticus nodded.

"Albert is better?"

"*Ya*, much better than we'd hoped. The nurse called while I was dressing. *Daed*'s improved. She said they would be moving him to a step-down room sometime today, but still watching his vitals closely."

"*Gut*, this is progress." Otto smiled his approval. "And Verity? She is well?"

"She and the children are fine."

With a nod, Otto slipped to the next man in line and greeted him, leaving Leviticus with his thoughts. Happiness filled him. His father was improving, and Verity showed her relief at the news by being easygoing all morning. If someone had been watching them interact, they would have thought them a normal Amish family. But he had noticed Verity watching him with wary eyes a moment before, as if she expected him to morph back into the man he'd been when he'd first come home.

Keep me learning and growing, Gott. *Bless my father with* gut *health. Return him to us.*

Her mind dwelling on Albert's improvement, Verity pushed away the jumble of nerves that had been eating at her. She peered out the kitchen door, and like a longtime married woman, looked around for her husband's help. There were tables to be moved and benches to be put in their place. She'd been busy after they'd walked home from church and lost track of him in the growing crowd of hungry people. *Where had he disappeared to?*

She shut the door and skirted around several volunteers who'd come to help arrange food platters and containers of peanut butter brought for the after-service meal. "Excuse me." Her mind was full of things still needing to be done. There were cold drinks to be made, a vegetable platter to be put together. But deep inside she was smiling like a silly *bensel*, content the *kinner* were happy and all was well. Albert was better, and Leviticus had finally become a member of the church.

A dark thought crept in, overshadowing her joy. What about the trap of marriage she'd stepped into? Would happiness remain? Content or not, she'd have to accept her lot in life until the day she died. *Please, Lord, Your will for my life and for Leviticus.*

It had been a while since she'd been able to check on Naomi. She hurried over to the corner and found the *boppli* still fast asleep in her mesh playpen cluttered with toys and a snuggle blanket.

Back at the kitchen sink a moment later, Verity washed dishes as her mind slipped away to that morning. Faith had been so thrilled to learn Leviticus was her *daed*. She smiled at the memory as she looked out the window and noticed Leviticus walking up the hill with one of the church pastors, deep in conversation.

A warm flush settled over her. Maybe it wasn't contentment she was feeling. How could it be? She was married to a man she didn't love. Didn't really know. She fought to fight down the stress eating at her. Her mother had always told her to find something to be grateful for and she settled on, *I'm grateful for my life as a* mamm.

"Hand me a stack of those paper plates?" Sarah Fischer asked, bringing Verity back to the present. A moment later, her hands busy washing cutting boards and utensils, she returned to her musing. As they'd walked home from church, Leviticus had smiled so attentively at Faith as the *kinner* chattered on, telling him all about the swings she'd swung on the day before and how, now that they were a *familye*, they could go to the park and have a swinging contest of their own.

Leviticus enjoyed Faith's run-on sentences and loud laughter. She was used to her daughter's exuberance. The child had been a chatterbox since she'd started uttering single syllable words, but for Leviticus to be so kind and patient with Faith gave her hope for their future.

Again, she was pulled out of her reverie by Sarah, who was busy working circles around her. "Your potato salad looks good. Mose is sure to eat more than his share of yours."

They laughed together, and Verity sighed. No one seemed to notice her up-and-down moods. Maybe they expected her to be happier than usual. She was a new *fraa*. It was only natural for her to be happy. She'd have to work harder at keeping her dark thoughts at bay and smile more.

"Congratulations on your marriage."

Verity placed a delicious-looking pineapple upside-down cake on the dessert table. *"Danki."* She smiled at Sarah, who was just beginning to show with yet another blessing from *Gott.* She wanted to confide in Sarah about the truth of her new marriage but ignored the urge. No need to spoil Sarah's good mood that washed her in a warm glow.

Verity accepted her friend's congratulations as if she were the happiest woman in Pinecraft. Truth be told, she was confused by her moments of joy while living a lie. Leviticus didn't love her, but she was trying to make do for Albert's sake. Perhaps Leviticus was going through the same states of confusion.

Time slipped past. The men started filing in, one by one. The faithful of Pinecraft seemed to be accepting her union with Leviticus as nothing more than a marriage brought on by renewed love.

But gossip was a staple in a town full of women in *kapps.* She'd heard snippets of conversation regarding Leviticus's sudden church membership, whispers about their quickie marriage while the women filed out of the church earlier. Most of the faithful, the important ones, seemed willing enough to accept Leviticus was home for good, and that was all that mattered. Albert was healing, and the girls had a *familye,* not just single parents. Their joy counted for something.

She wiped down the edge of the sink for the hundredth time as men continued to come inside in waves, eat and then slip back out to the yard, where they talked about needed repairs in the community. As she waited to eat with the other ladies, her mind roamed over the unusual circumstances of the last few days. Leviticus seemed to be trying hard to obey *Ordnung* rules, be the man his father wanted him to be since he had taken another turn for the better.

She was genuinely glad Leviticus had been allowed to re-embrace his Amish destiny, but what about Solomon's resentment toward Leviticus? And surely there were memories Leviticus brought home with him from the *Englisch* world he'd have to forget. Did he miss the *Englischer* way of doing things? Was he going to be content as an Amish man for the rest of his life?

Thankfully, the gentle part of him she'd grown to love as a girl was still there just under the surface. She'd seen glimpses of it and longed for a complete return of the old Leviticus.

Just as she'd collected the last of the men's dishes and added fresh bowls of food for the ladies, he sauntered in mud-streaked and sweaty, like the rest of the men who'd gone with him out into the grove to look at the damage.

She'd smiled at him as he stepped past, watched his face as he took the plate of food she'd made him and grinned back when he flashed his dimple at her. Had the smile been forced? He seemed tense, like something was bothering him. Was it the condition of the grove?

While she served food to several ladies already seated, he lurked in the corner of the kitchen and then disappeared like a puff of smoke when she looked back. She dropped her gaze and silently prayed, *Help me to trust the future. Give Leviticus what he needs to be a Plain man.*

Ten minutes later, a silent prayer said by Theda

Fischer, Otto's wife, ended the ladies' meal. Her head still bowed, she glanced over and witnessed Leviticus walking in through the back door. He looked across the kitchen, found her gaze and held it. She motioned for him to take the chair next to her.

Leviticus shook his head, grabbed a half sandwich off a plate stacked high, took a bite and threw it in the trash as he turned away from her.

"Ach," she muttered to herself. Often, she had to encourage him to eat. This morning, after hearing Leviticus's report about what the doctors had said about Albert's improvement, she'd gained hope that Albert's hard battle for life had been won. And Leviticus had seemed to believe it, as well. He'd relaxed. They'd had a good time walking to church, Faith on his shoulders and Naomi asleep in her arms. To her, they'd been the typical Amish family, but what had Leviticus thought? And there'd been no additional news about his father this afternoon, no reason to affirm her and Leviticus's continued hope.

She continued to study Leviticus when he wasn't aware, saw a haunted look on his face. At times, she noticed he clung to Naomi like a lifeline, as if his tiny daughter's love could save him from his own inner misery.

The kitchen still humming with the last of the women finishing their meals, Leviticus appeared, speaking to Mose, who hovered near his wife with a toddler in his arms. Leviticus again excused himself and shouldered his way out the back door once more. Was he going out to talk to the other men milling around, slapping each other on the back and laughing at things only men could understand? Or was he going to his mother's grave, or out to the garage to tinker with his old truck?

In this restless mood he seemed to be in, she didn't know. She prayed once more for Albert's healing and for the man who was now her husband. Encouraging herself, she went through her litany of reminders. *He's changed since he's returned. Obeys community rules. Acts more mature.*

But as she washed plastic forks and spoons, she wondered, would Leviticus ever grow to love her? Only God knew the answer to that question. She knew her angry feelings toward him were still hanging between them. She cared about the man's concerns for his father, but it was pity she felt for him, wasn't it? That and nothing more?

Right? It had to be.

Chapter Fourteen

The last of the men headed out the back door with their wives in tow, leaving a capable handful of women to clean up the last of the mess in the kitchen. Verity plunged platters into the big kitchen sink filled with hot sudsy water, silent, her thoughts roaming.

Leviticus's sudden mood swings unnerved Verity when they came, but he'd never been mean-spirited to her or the girls. While he was silent and withdrawn, he seemed jumpier and more depressed than angry. But wasn't that to be expected? His father was ill. He felt guilty he'd stayed away so long. Albert might make it, but the hospital staff still offered no promises. She clung to each positive report from the doctors as a sign from *Gott*. He had heard her prayers. Albert would live.

Deep in thought as she scrubbed another big dish, curiosity got the better of her. What had happened to Leviticus during his life in the *Englisch* world?

She turned her head, watching again through the kitchen window as Leviticus slowly made his way down the hill toward the shed. Faith and Naomi seemed to be the only ones who could reach him whenever he was silent like this, so deep in thought.

On impulse, she turned Faith over to her younger sister's care and straddled Naomi on her hip as she followed where her new husband had gone, out the door and down the grassy slope. But she hesitated just feet away from the porch steps as Otto began to sing the words to Albert's favorite hymn. She stayed, singing the words to "In the Garden," one of the songs she'd often sung with Albert, their voices blending well in harmony.

Otto's eyes lifted, speaking to the people of the community lingering around the back steps. "*Gott* is all knowing. In His wisdom, He may see fit to take Albert home or leave him here fit and back to health. Who here can question His motives?"

The old bishop fingered his gray beard, his head lowering in respect for the man he called his friend. "We rejoice in the majesty of the Lord and carry on as we always do, as any loved one prepares to go home." A tear glistened in the old bishop's eye and was quickly blinked away, but to Verity they revealed his true level of pain. "Now, let's be on our way to our homes and return tomorrow to work this grove back into shape. It's been a long day of worship and food. Clara and Verity both look ready to drop with fatigue."

Her knitting bag in hand, Theda sidled up to Verity. She nodded toward Naomi, who squirmed in Verity's arms. "That *boppli* is growing so fast. It won't be long before she's starting school, like Faith. You wait and see. Time has a way of flying past. Enjoy her young years while you can."

Naomi smiled a toothless grin and reached out her arms to Theda. Verity handed her over.

"This one is an added blessing to your family. She already has joy in her eyes. You are a blessed woman, Verity. Not everyone gets a second chance with first love."

Verity smiled at the older woman. Leviticus had come home nothing like the boy she'd known, but she didn't have to tell Theda that. He'd come home an *Englischer* in actions and dress, but day by day she was seeing subtle changes in him, and all for the better. Would the changes last? He would never be the Amish *mann* she'd fallen hard for as a teen, but he was a good man now. "Naomi is my *dochder*, too. I love her with all my heart, just as I love Faith."

Squirming to get away from Theda, Naomi stretched out her chubby arms and spoke a new word Verity's way. *"Mamm, mamm."*

The look of love in the child's eyes and her words pushed back the last of the protective walls she had built around her heart. "I am your *mudder*, little one. I always will be."

Theda studied Verity's face. "And Leviticus? What of him, child?" The older, wiser woman reached for her hand and patted it. "He is your husband now. Is he in your heart to stay? Will you let him be the husband you longed for all those years ago?"

Verity had to be honest. She couldn't be a Plain woman of faith and continually lie. "I'm ashamed to say my heart is still closed to him, even in this time of stress."

"It makes me to wonder if Albert's regained health and time won't heal the problems you two are dealing with. Leviticus's past life is over, sweet one. It's time to move on. You both have *kinner* depending on you. Find your way back to each other. There is much to be done on the grove. Leviticus will need your support and affection to make it through these hard times."

Verity lowered her head, condemned. She meant it when she promised, "I will pray for *Gott* to put a strong love in my heart for Leviticus. I promise."

"You know we're all praying *Gott*'s will for Albert." She released Verity's hand. "Accept His will, child. What will be, will be...no matter how much you want otherwise." Theda's smile deepened. "Now, get some rest and make sure you keep an eye on Clara. She's walking like she's ready to drop that *boppli* any moment."

"I will." She took Naomi from Theda's arms and snuggled her close as she walked back to the house, leaving Leviticus to his own devices. Her head on Verity's shoulder, Naomi took a long, deep breath and closed her eyes, whispering, *"Mamm."*

"Ya, boppli. I am your *mamm. Gott* has brought us together. We are a *familye."*

The last of family and friends said their goodbyes, leaving Verity alone in the house with Clara and the children. She didn't have a clue where Leviticus was at that moment. She knew he was upset about something. She silently prayed for him, asking *Gott* to bring peace to his mind.

Ten minutes later, Verity eased into a kitchen chair, her fingers reaching into her hair and pulling out the pins securely holding her prayer covering in place. It had been a long, grueling day. She needed a moment to herself. Time to think about what Theda had said.

Smiling, Clara placed her hand on the small of her back as she leaned against the kitchen's worn porcelain sink. "The girls drift off?"

"*Ya.* Finally." Verity observed her sister-in-law, looking for signs of labor. Seeing none, she eased back in her chair and took in a calming breath. "Faith wanted to stay up and wait for her new *daed*'s return, but I persuaded her tomorrow morning would be soon enough." She stretched out her legs, wishing she was in a nice hot bath full of scented bubbles, one of her secret indulgences. "That child's so excited to have Leviticus in her life. She loves having him as her new *daed*."

Her hand still pressed to her back, Clara's brow crinkled into a heavy frown. "Makes me wonder where he could be. Ain't so? It's coming on dark. Why isn't he home with his *familye*?" She finished drying her hands on the tea towel as she spoke and then placed the cloth by the sink.

Verity didn't want to admit it, but she knew Clara was right. Where had Leviticus gone? He did have a family who needed him home. "His leaving like this happens too often. He becomes so quiet and distant at times, especially since Albert fell ill, and now that Albert is showing remarkable signs of improvement he's still too quiet." She smiled over at Clara. "Oh, I know he has a lot on his mind, but I'm concerned whatever is troubling him is more than just rebuilding the grove."

"He didn't take the truck or any of his things, did he?" Clara pulled out a chair across from Verity and eased down into it. She slipped off her shoes, arched her swollen feet and splayed out her toes in relief. With gusto, she fanned her face with her apron, the movement causing damp wisps of hair around her face to dance.

Verity struggled to keep her composure. They'd had such a *gut* morning. What could have happened? "*Nee*, I checked a moment ago." Her finger traced the shape of a rose imprinted on the tablecloth. "The vehicle is where he left it last night, his clothes in the drawers." Images of Leviticus walking away from his Amish life minutes after the dirt was shoveled on his mother's simple casket snaked through her again. *What if Albert dies? Will he run again? Faith will be devastated.* And how would she feel? "Only *Gott* knows where he is." Verity managed to hold the threatening tears in check.

Clara sucked in her breath and paused a moment before pushing in the kitchen chair she'd been sitting in. Its legs scraping against the wood floor brought Verity back to the present.

Clara sighed and put her arm around Verity's shoulders. "I'll be praying for you, my dearest friend." She glanced at the clock on the wall. "But I really must go. Now that we're moving back into our own home, Solomon expects me to be there, waiting for him to finish arranging furniture back into its place. A half hour ago, I told him I was only coming back into the *haus* to collect my dishes." Her gentle smile turned into laugher. She slipped her swollen feet back into her church shoes and touched Verity once more on the shoulder. "You're sure you are all right?"

"Yes, I'm sure." Verity rose.

"*Gut*. Now try to get some rest. You look worse than I do and I'm nine months gone." Clara chuckled, lines mapping her forehead. "Those circles under your eyes get darker every time I see you. You mustn't let the children run you ragged. You know I'm only a phone call away."

Verity wanted to blurt out it wasn't the children keeping her awake and overwrought at night. It was Leviticus, too, their sudden arranged marriage…her growing feelings for him. But she kept silent. Tonight would be soon enough to cry into her pillow if Leviticus didn't return. "God's will be done, *ya*?"

Clara nodded with a smile, lifting her basket containing ovenware. A second in time and she was slumped over, the basket dropped back on the counter with a clatter.

Verity hurried over. "What's wrong? Are you in pain?"

A smile danced on Clara's lips. "I think my labor's finally started. I've been feeling nagging little twinges all day. They're getting stronger and more painful."

"This is one of your pranks, isn't it? You're just saying that to get my mind off Leviticus."

Clara sucked in her breath. "*Nee*, these pains are no joke. This is the real thing."

"And you said nothing to me? Does Solomon know?" Verity led Clara over to the chair she'd just vacated and eased her down.

"*Nee*, I didn't tell him. He was needed at Chicken John's and I let him go. This is our first *kind*. There's plenty of time to fetch him." Clara sucked in a breath and grimaced, her pains renewed.

Verity glanced at the clock, prepared to time the next onset of birthing pains. She hovered, unsure what to do, but knowing she had better get in touch with Solomon, and fast. She didn't want to scare Clara, but if her pains had been coming regularly all day, she might well need to reach the midwife urgently. "He'd want to know you might be in labor."

"I thought there was plenty of time and Chicken John really needed his help. They're growing old, he and Ulla." Clara flashed a quick smile at Verity that fast turned into a painful scowl. Clara didn't have a chance to comment further. Her head dropped, a groan emanating from her dry lips. She bent forward, her arms encircling her middle in misery.

"Does Solomon have his work phone with him?"

Clara's head bobbed. Her back rose slightly as she took in a long, deep cleansing breath as the pain receded. "I saw him slip it in his trouser pocket this morning."

Verity searched for the grove's business phone in the kitchen drawer. "Stay calm. I'm calling him and then the midwife." Thinking back to Faith's birth, Verity remembered how her precious *boppli* arrived with little fanfare.

"Please let him answer," she prayed aloud as she dialed on the small black cell phone kept for emergencies.

A light in the kitchen told Leviticus that Verity was still up. He slowed his steps, considered what kind of mood she might be in since he'd walked off hours ago. He'd needed time to himself, time to pray and confess his hidden sins.

Ready to face whatever she had waiting for him, he sprang up the steps, opened the back door, only to stop midstep. Verity had her arms around Clara, assisting her across the kitchen floor.

"What's happened? Is she okay?" He took off his sweaty straw hat and tossed it on the kitchen table.

Verity glanced his way, her expression a mixture of stark terror and relief. "She's in labor. Solomon's across town at Chicken John's. No one's answering their phones." A quick glance directed at Clara had Verity moving again. "I called the midwife, but she can't come. She's busy birthing another *boppli*, so Clara's going to have to go to the hospital."

"Give her to me." Leviticus's big hands visibly shook as he reached out for Clara. "Keep trying to reach Solomon. I've got my truck outside. I'll take her to the hospital."

"But you're covered in mud." Verity shielded Clara from him like the pregnant woman had no say in the matter.

He paused and watched Verity vacillate between relief that he'd offered an immediate solution and revulsion at the thought of Clara riding in his bumpy truck all the way to Memorial hospital.

"If you have a better idea, spit it out."

Clara made a valiant attempt to stifle a groan, but they both heard her cry.

"Look, it's me and my truck, or you're delivering this baby. What's it going to be?"

Verity flinched at his words. "Do you want to go with him?"

Clara nodded. "I'll go." And then her face flushed a bright red. "I think my water just broke."

Three heads looked down at the kitchen floor. A puddle of pink liquid formed around their feet.

"Let's get going." Leviticus lifted Clara into his arms. "Tell Solomon to meet us at the hospital." He hurried for the back door with Clara in tow.

Am I crazy? He'd never delivered a baby before but could if he had to. He'd delivered a breech-birthed goat while in Afghanistan, but he wasn't thinking about *that* birth right now. He was thinking about what Solomon would do to him if he let anything happen to his beloved Clara and their first child.

Verity turned on the porch light and held the screen door open wide, but she didn't speak again until he ran down the wooden steps with Clara bouncing as he took them two at a time. "Be gentle with her, but hurry. I don't think she has much time to spare."

He turned his head. Concern strained Verity's face, but she managed a sweet smile for him. He held her gaze for a heartbeat, longing to reassure her. Tucking Clara into the front seat, he slammed the door and hurried up the steps to Verity. "I promise you, she and the baby will be all right." He pulled her close, felt her trembling body and put a light kiss on her cheek. "Don't fret, *fraa*. Clara will be fine. Trust me."

Verity held his gaze, her eyes sparkling as he let her go and she moved toward the door. "I do trust you." Her words came out firm and clear, convincing him she meant it, but then he noticed her right hand. It gripped the screen door so hard all the blood had drained from her fingers. She didn't trust him. Not with Clara, and certainly never with her heart.

Ignoring his own misery, he called out, "Make that call to Solomon." His boots crunched on the gravel as he rushed back toward the truck, but he heard his *fraa*'s encouraging words.

"Go with *Gott*, Leviticus. Trust in Him. He'll see you through."

Chapter Fifteen

Even with his heavy trousers and long-sleeved shirt, the cold hospital air swept around him like an arctic breeze, chilling him to the bone. He knew they kept the temperature down to keep germs at bay, but he was miserably cold, his hands like ice.

The plastic chair he sat in creaked as he shoved his hands under his thighs, seeking a measure of warmth. No doubt Solomon would find a reason to make all this his fault, even though he had no control over Clara's labor or when it started.

She'd been in a lot of pain when they'd first arrived at the hospital. A nurse had whisked her up to labor and delivery. He'd hurried along behind the stretcher, forgotten by both chattering nurses until they had reached their destination.

One nurse turned toward him, blocking his entrance. Her name tag read Jessica. "You're the father?"

"No, the brother-in-law."

"You can't come in." A grimace lifted her narrow lips.

"But—"

She pointed to a chair just outside the door. "Sit there. We'll call for you if you're needed," and then firmly shut the door in his face.

Leviticus looked around for a men's magazine or local newspaper. Nothing, though he had plenty to read if he enjoyed women's magazines.

Bored, his thoughts wandered to places normally forbidden. He regretted he hadn't been at Naomi's birth. His unit had been on a six-month deployment to Afghanistan while Julie was still pregnant. No one had asked him if it was convenient or still fit into his life's plan. He'd had to go and ended up making do with Julie's housekeeper Skyping him about his child's birth. She'd muttered he had a daughter. When he asked questions, he got little more than "She's doing well." Her last sentence to him had been, "Do you have a name picked out for your daughter?" He'd replied, "Naomi," but wasn't sure she'd even heard him before the connection was severed.

He scrubbed at the itchy growth on his chin, changed position and crossed his legs. There were a lot of things he'd done wrong in his life, but Julie's pregnancy had been his biggest mess-up yet. He'd enjoyed his army life and all the perks that had come with it, like most young men did when they were irresponsible. Not that he would change anything if he could. Naomi was his blood, his heart.

And look at me now. Married to a woman who doesn't want to be married to me and forced to watch her make the best of a bad situation. What a fool you are, Leviticus Hilty. Ruining first your life and now Verity's.

In the past, always pleasant and in control of her emotions, Verity hadn't tried to hide her contempt for him his first few days home. And he didn't blame her for objecting to Otto's marriage plans. No woman, Amish or *Englisch*, liked the prospect of marrying a man they hadn't chosen. *Certainly not someone like me.* Amish women expected their husbands to be in charge. Strong. Men of faith. He had to admit, after their quick wedding, her attitude had softened some for appearance's sake, but moments alone with her convinced him she resented the marriage.

He huffed, then remembered he had things to be grateful for, too. This evening when he'd checked in on his *daed*, his father had been pink-skinned and looked stronger. They'd taken him off oxygen, were feeding him more than just Jell-O and watery soup. The nurse explained the doctors expected him to live and make a reasonable recovery, but she had made it clear he would need in-home care when he left the hospital. Verity couldn't manage Albert on her own with two children to see to. Leviticus would need to find an agency who provided twenty-four-hour care or ask the community for help.

He chewed at his nail, a habit he thought he'd gotten rid of months after leaving Afghanistan, but it periodically resurfaced thanks to his remaining PTSD.

He glanced at the clock on the wall. It showed only a half hour had passed since he'd last looked at it.

He saw movement in his peripheral vision and witnessed Solomon's arrival and interaction with the desk nurse. Their eyes met. His brother's weary expression, the way the man's body was bent over told him Solomon's day had been a hard one.

"She's in there." He pointed to the door across the hall where he'd been keeping sentry.

Solomon nodded. "*Danki* for bringing her, Leviticus. And for keeping watch."

Without another word, Solomon rushed into his wife's room and shut the door behind him.

Clara had her beloved Solomon with her now. He'd best be heading home. He needed to let Verity know everything was under control, and that his father was better. He rose and stretched his aching body. He looked down first one length of the hall and then the other.

Clara's door opened, and Solomon shuffled out. "They ran me off. Said they'd call me back in when it was time." He gave a mirthless laugh. "I think they thought I would pass out on them or something."

Solomon did look decidedly green. Leviticus sat and patted the seat next to him. "I'm not surprised they would think that. You look awful, ready to fall."

Solomon crossed the hall and took the chair Leviticus offered him, his knees splayed out, elbows braced on the armrests. "I am tired. There's so much to be done on the grove, but Chicken John's place is devastated. Ulla went to stay with Mose and Sarah." He rubbed his eyes, lifted his head. "The whole community felt the punch of the storm."

"Otto said people will be coming down from the North to help."

"*Ya*, there'll be a busload tonight and more able-bodied men on their way tomorrow." He finally looked Leviticus in the eye. "We need all the help we can get on the grove." He raked his hand, covered in mud, through his mussed brown hair. "He really wants you to stay, Leviticus."

"I know. I'm a married man now, with responsibilities. I need the grove to support my family as much as you do." He placed his hand on his brother's thigh. "You have to know…things are different now. I want to succeed and come to trust *Gott*, be a *bruder* you can be proud of."

Solomon shook his head, confusion lowering his brows. "I've never understood why you left. Why abandon *Daed* and the grove when they needed you most? *Mamm*'s death almost finished *Daed* off ten years ago. He really struggled with both those losses. Time and age have worn him down. His first stroke took a lot out of him. I thought this second big one would kill him." Solomon's piercing gaze seemed to look deep inside Leviticus's soul, searching out the truth.

Talking about his mother's death, about the stress he'd put on her, was a subject Leviticus always avoided. But giving Solomon an explanation for his leaving was long overdue. "When *Mamm* died, I guess a piece of me died with her." Leviticus shifted uncomfortably in the plastic chair.

Only his father knew what was in his heart, why he'd left, and even then, not all the truth had come out as they'd talked. "I watched Mom kill herself with hard work. She took care of everyone but herself." He rubbed his hand across the stubble growing on his chin. "*Daed* let her die from hard work, and I helped kill her by acting like a fool and shaming her." He blinked back a tear. "I should have stopped my running around. *Daed* should have made her slow down."

Solomon sat up straight in his chair, his expression bemused, eyebrows knitting together. "Your childish shenanigans and hard work didn't kill her, *bruder*. Cancer did."

It was the first time Leviticus had heard the word *cancer* associated with his mother. Even his *dat* had kept silent. *She'd had cancer?* "What do you mean she had cancer? Someone would have told me."

"*Nee, bruder.* I only know because I overheard *Mamm* and *Daed* talking about the doctors' diagnosis when they thought we were out doing chores. Years later, I admitted to *Daed* I knew about the cancer. It pained him that I knew. He explained the illness wasn't allowed to be talked about to anyone. It was *Mamm* who insisted it remain a secret, and *Daed* complied." Solomon wiped a tear from his cheek. "Her kind of cancer was terrible, cruel and aggressive. She'd ignored the signs, left it too long."

Fury rose up. Leviticus wrung his hands, flexing his fingers that felt stiff with rage. "I should have been told. You were my *bruder*. You could have told me sooner."

"I was afraid of how you'd react. You were just a *bu*, her youngest. I wasn't much older. She tried to spare us. Don't go looking for someone to blame."

Leviticus ducked his head. His mother had tried to shield him every day of his life. Was that why it had taken a war, the horror of battle to screw his head on right, to bring him to a full understanding of what was important and what could be easily set aside?

Leviticus looked hard at Solomon, needing to be angry with someone. "You should have told me when I came home."

"Maybe. But I did as she asked. Not even the community knew. When she passed suddenly, people thought it was from a heart attack or stroke. No one asked. Her secret was kept to the end."

Leviticus shook his head, tears running down his face. His brother's embrace came out of nowhere. Leviticus held on for dear life and cried like a child as they rocked together, all the bitterness and strife between them ebbing away.

A woman in scrubs stood just outside Clara's room. "Mr. Hilty! Your wife is calling for you. She's ready to push." She disappeared again, leaving the door slightly ajar.

Leviticus pulled away, sniffed. "Sounds like that baby's wanting to meet his *daed.*"

Solomon scrubbed the last tears from his eyes. "I best be getting back." He rose, hesitated and then turned back to Leviticus. "You'll be going home to Verity? She must be a basket of nerves by now. She could use a strong shoulder to lean on."

"*Ya,* I'm going home."

Solomon disappeared behind the shut door, but not before he shot a big grin Leviticus's way.

Cancer? Leviticus sat for a moment, thinking about what he'd just learned about their mother's passing, about the man he needed to become now that he knew the truth. He could change. *Lord, for Verity's sake, help me be the best husband I can be.* Even as he thought the words, he wondered, would Verity ever forgive him for leaving her? Could he be Amish Plain for the rest of his life, or would he keep running from life's hard trials? He shrugged. Now things were different. He wanted to change. To be Amish in mind and deed, but only time would tell if that was possible.

Verity vigorously washed her two daughters' late-night milk glass and sippy cup and placed both upside down on the drain-cloth next to the sink. The stray cat she'd brought into the house knocked one of Faith's books off the children's tiny table and chair set, making her jump.

Why was Clara's labor taking so long? Word should have come by now. The woman was young, healthy. Complications in childbirth were rare these days, especially when a doctor was in attendance, but they did happen. *Nothing's impossible.*

Verity dried her hands, chastising herself. *That's foolish talk. Clara's fine. The boppli's fine. You're just a worrier.*

The roar of Leviticus's old truck coming to a stop in the side yard had Verity abandoning the cup of coffee she'd picked up. She rushed to the back door and flipped on the outside light. A yellow glow lit the darkness. *He's taking a long time coming in.*

As though she had wings on her feet, she rushed out onto the back porch and watched as he turned the corner of the house and strolled toward her. *Does he have to walk so slow?* His head down, she couldn't search his face for a hint of news. Illuminated by the porch light now, his mud-splattered clothes reminded her that he'd had a hard day. A long night. *Had he eaten supper? He must be bone tired.*

Instead of bounding up the steps, he took them one by one. Her heart beat faster. Pumped hard. Adrenaline coursed through her body. But then she saw his wide smile, the look of joy in his eyes. *Hallelujah! All is well. The* boppli *is here.*

He reached the top step and she grabbed for his hand, yanking him up onto the porch with her excitement. "Well. Don't just stand there with a silly grin. Tell me. Is it a *bu* or girl? What does it weigh? Does it favor Clara or Solomon?"

He laughed at her, the sound of his joy deep and robust.

A thrill rushed through her. She remembered that laugh from years ago. *Best not think of those times.* "Talk to me, before I wring the facts from your scrawny neck."

He laughed, but remained quiet until he stepped into the kitchen, leaving the door open for Verity to pass through. "I hung around for a while in case Solomon needed me, and then a nurse finally told me Clara was fine and that I had a niece. I have no idea who she looks like or how much she weighs. I didn't stick around once I caught a peek of the baby being pushed to the nursery in a plastic cart. You'll have to wait till tomorrow and see for yourself."

"A girl!" Verity's face lifted toward the heavens. "Thank You, Jesus, for the answered prayer." She couldn't hold back the wave of laughter that swept over her. In her joy, Verity forgot to be reserved. She squeezed Leviticus's hand hard. His eyes enlarged with what had to be surprise. Tonight, she was deliriously happy, brave enough to touch him again. She longed to be held in his arms, so they could rejoice together as a husband and wife would.

"Did she say what they were calling the *boppli*? Did she have an easy time of it?" She didn't wait for him to answer her questions. "A girl! Oh, I'm so glad," she repeated, joyously laughing at her own foolish behavior. Renewed hope coursed through her for the first time in weeks. "Clara wanted a girl so much. She can show her off at the Thanksgiving dinner."

Verity remembered she was holding Leviticus's hand and dropped it. She stepped back, letting him slip past. "Come, sit. Have coffee with me while you tell me everything you know."

Pulling out a chair, he obediently accepted her offer of a hot drink. "There's not much to tell. I sat in a hard chair for hours. It was cold enough in that hospital to hang meat. No one spoke—"

Verity whirled around from the kitchen counter, the spoon of sugar she'd been about to add to his coffee mug suspended in midair. "Just tell me what you know. What you saw. I want to hear everything…about Clara, the *boppli*." She would never understand men if she lived to be a hundred. Why were they so close-mouthed?

Leviticus scooted over to a plate of freshly baked chocolate-chip cookies and shoved one in his mouth. Another quickly followed.

He hasn't eaten. I should have offered to heat him a plate of food. Guilt plagued her, but first she wanted information. She'd feed the silent man once he'd told her everything.

Eating a third cookie, he spoke around it. "No one told me if there was a problem." He shoved another cookie in his mouth.

Verity moved to the refrigerator and pulled out cold chops and sweet potato casserole. Leviticus hated marshmallows. She grinned at the thought of him having to eat around them. "Now, tell me about the *kind*. Is she dirty-blond like Solomon or brown-haired like Clara? Is she plump or all legs and arms?" She put a fat chop on his plate and scooped out a heaping serving of sweet potato casserole.

"From what I could see, she didn't seem to have much meat on her, and not much hair for that matter. All I know is...the *boppli* looked like a *boppli* swaddled in a blanket. You have to remember, I've never seen one as young as this before, and the nurse had her wrapped tight, like a mummy in a blanket."

Verity's brow arched in surprise. "But surely you were at Naomi's birth. Don't you remember how she looked?" Verity slid the plate of food into the heated oven and then yanked out a chair across from him to wait for the food to heat.

When he didn't respond, she looked his way. His hands clenched the back of the kitchen chair, and she noticed his face had blanched paper white. *I knew it. Something is wrong.* "What is it? There's something you're not telling me." She touched his shoulder. His body was trembling.

"Sit down, Verity." He cleared his voice, took a gulp of the coffee she'd handed him moments before.

Her eyes held him captive. She didn't want to sit. She wanted to scream. "Is it Clara? The *boppli*?"

A frown pinched his forehead. "No. It's not them. I told you. They're fine." His Adam's apple bobbed as he swallowed hard. "It's me. There are things you don't know about me. It's time you did."

Verity remained standing, but her legs suddenly threatened to buckle under her. "What kinds of things, Leviticus? You're scaring me."

His shoulders stiffened. "I wasn't at Naomi's birth. I didn't see her until she was almost six months old."

"But you said—"

"No, I never said I was there. You assumed I was." His eyes turned a dark blue. So dark she could see her own reflection in them. "Look. We're both tired. It's late. Tonight's not the right time to talk about all this. I should have seen it was the wrong time to dump this on you." He moved away from the table, his head down. "I'll see you in the morning."

Verity watched her new husband leave the room, his meal forgotten. What secrets was he holding on to? Would he ever confide in her? She ran her hand across the table, brushed a few cookie crumbs into her hand. She'd wait awhile, approach him about this conversation when things were more settled.

Lord, I need Your help reaching Leviticus. Please bless me with the right words when he does talk to me. Don't let me mess up our future. I want to be a gut fraa.

Chapter Sixteen

Both busy with their own work, two days slipped past uneventfully. Life went on. Leviticus said nothing about the night Clara's *boppli* was born. She held her questions about his past for another occasion. Verity looked at the back door for the third time in five minutes and forced herself to stop.

Get a grip on yourself, bensel. *He'll come in from the grove when he's hungry, and not a moment sooner.*

Her stomach went all funny at the thought of seeing him, talking to him, like there was a hive of honeybees taking up residence in her insides.

Her resentment toward him was changing subtly but it was still there, just not as intense. He'd been trapped into this loveless marriage, too. Little by little, she'd begun to make allowances when he grew quiet, to show kindness instead of anger, even though she knew he was as frustrated as her. He'd responded in kind and treated her fairly. Showed affection to her, not just to the *kinner*. He smiled more, the sound of his laugh thrilling her unexpectedly at times.

The day before, she worked in the yard and found herself seeking him out like some lovesick teen.

Verity jumped back when the bacon she'd been cooking spit hot grease her way. It had never been in her nature to distrust, but she wouldn't be fooled by Leviticus again. She was a grown woman now, fully aware of how real love felt. A man who loves his *fraa* shows his love. His emotions made him smile a certain way at his woman.

But he smiled at you that way this morning. You'd be lying if you said he hadn't.

She shrugged her shoulders, refocusing on turning the last thick slice of bacon and transferring it to an absorbent stack of paper towels. She wasn't going to let her growing interest in Leviticus cause her to have a bad day. Nee, *never again. My joy is in the Lord.*

Breaking a dozen eggs for scrambling, she found herself smiling at the sound of Naomi's giggles, enjoying the way her young *kind* chattered away in her own mysterious language to Faith.

She jumped and dropped the serving fork when the back door suddenly opened. Leviticus trudged in, dirt covering his face and hands. The straw hat on his sweaty head sat at a jaunty angle, like the wind had caught and displaced it.

He glanced her way, half smiled and then kissed both girls on the cheek. Naomi gave him a toothy grin, but Faith giggled and snuck in a kiss of her own on his grizzled face.

Verity watched as he turned on his heel, not speaking a word to her. Showers were predicted again, but later in the day. Had the news put him in a foul mood?

It didn't take much to make him moody since he'd returned.

He moved over to the kitchen sink and splashed water on his face and neck. She stifled a gasp as he used her clean dish towel to dry himself off. If his *mamm* had been alive, she would have sent him away from the table for such disrespect, but Verity didn't have the heart to utter a complaint. The man looked too worn out to say a word. *Had he and Solomon had words again?*

"The *kinner* ate oatmeal and blueberries, but if you want fresh eggs, there's some made."

He looked at her, nodded and ruffled Faith's hair as he took his seat. "*Ya*, eggs sound fine."

She poured him a mug of coffee and set it down in front of him. He grabbed the cup and downed the drink—black and bitter, without a drop of milk or sugar. Her shoulders shuddered in distaste. She wasn't sure what to say to him in his mood. "How's the grove coming along?"

"We need more workers." His words were crisp, with an edge that had nothing to do with her. He was worried, tired and hungry for a hot meal.

Verity dished up a plate of freshly made toast, scrambled eggs and crispy bacon and tried to remember how to use the small microwave Leviticus had brought home the night before. She concentrated on how to start the newfangled gadget. She didn't hear him walk up behind her until he spoke close to her ear.

"Just put the plate in, cover the food with a paper towel and punch in the amount of warming time you want. Heating this shouldn't take more than a few seconds." His finger pointed to a red square button that screamed *START*.

She thought she'd remembered his instructions from the night before, but suddenly his hand was next to hers, moving it away, punching in numbers. She jerked at his touch. *Why does he have lightning in his fingers?* Frustrated, she flushed. *Does he notice how prickly I am when he touches me?*

His smile at her was easy. "If you cook the food too long, it gets rock hard or burns." A bell went off and he opened the microwave door. "Look, thirty seconds was all the eggs needed."

"Are you sure Otto will approve of this contraption? I know of no other Amish who have one."

"Ach. Do you think Otto cares if you have an added convenience? He's bought one for his office."

Faith pushed in close, gawking at the steaming plate of eggs and bacon. "Can you warm mine, too?"

"*Ya*, sure. Hand it to me." She looked back toward Leviticus, who was pulling out a chair to sit in.

"*Danki*," she muttered and then pressed her mouth shut. It was obvious Leviticus needed peace and quiet. The beeper sounded again, and she opened the microwave door, surprised her plate wasn't hot to the touch. Being introduced to new *Englischer* contraptions always made Verity edgy and feel a bit stupid. She tucked the dirty hand towel in her apron band and scooted away.

Leviticus took a huge bite of his eggs and shoved a whole slice of bacon into his mouth.

She sat at the table, her nervous fingers smoothing

out her apron, avoiding Leviticus's gaze. "Otto told me your church classes began last week."

"*Ya*, kind of the cart before the horse. I've got another session with Mose this afternoon." He picked up his fork and shoveled in another mouthful of eggs. "He gave me some pamphlets to look at. They were interesting."

"So you're ready?"

"Ready?"

She grabbed Naomi's hand as it reached out to grab a handful of bacon. "*Ya*, to become a Plain man in every sense of the word?"

His head bobbed. "As ready as I'll ever be."

Verity pushed her food around the plate. *I certain-sure hope so.*

"I forgot to tell you. I bought you something else."

Verity glanced over at Leviticus as he polished off the last of his food. His eyes sparkled with something akin to mischief. "What is it? Not another microwave." She forced a laugh. What was the man up to?

Leviticus returned her smile. "*Nee*. Just something you've been needing with two children to raise." He put out his hand toward her and she hesitantly took it, enjoying the feel of the calluses on his palm that he'd earned from hard work on the grove. His fingers wrapped tight around her hand for a quick moment, making her breath quicken. She pulled her hand away and lifted Naomi out of her high chair and motioned for Faith to follow. "*Komm!*" Leviticus took her hand again.

Out the kitchen and across the back porch he held her hand. Faith jumped each step, singing as she swung about her big gray bunny that her new *daed* had brought her home days before.

The door of the shed creaked as Leviticus opened it, then pulled the light string as he went. Light flooded the small storage room. Verity gasped when she saw the white washing machine and matching dryer bathed in artificial light. "You bought me *Englischer* appliances?" Her heart beat against her chest. What would *Gott* think? What would Otto have to say?

Reading her expression, Leviticus said, "Otto knows all about the purchase. I asked his permission and he liked the idea so much he bought a set for Theda the same day."

"But these things are for *Englisch*, not us Amish."

"They're for whoever needs them, Verity. And you need one. That old contraption you wash on needs to be slung on the metal heap. I don't see how it's lasted this long."

"But—"

"There's no shame in using what is provided to us by *Gott*'s ingenuity. Our community *Ordnung* rules allow for the use of electricity in Pinecraft." Leviticus opened the lid of the washer and motioned for her to come look.

"But a washer?" Verity peered in. A massive tub waited for clothes to be thrown in. "Doesn't this thing need water to work?"

"It does. The plumber is coming in an hour or so, and so is the electrician. You should be able to use these by tomorrow at the latest."

"I don't know what to say," she muttered. And she didn't. She didn't know how she felt with such an *Eng-*

lischer machine to do her washing. And what would others in the community say? Would there be suggestions that Leviticus was dragging her into the *Englischer* world?

Leviticus pulled out a booklet and several papers from the inside of the machine and began flipping through its pages. "Let's see how this thing works."

Reading out loud to himself, Leviticus made his way back to the porch, Faith running by his heels. Verity shut the shed door, her mind in a whirl. She was used to the simple life. This machine felt like an intrusion into her way of living, but if Otto had bought one for Theda, how could she complain? Cell phones, microwaves and now washers. Where would it all end?

She followed Leviticus into the house, Naomi riding on her hip. She marched on, perplexed and fighting down the joy bubbling up in her. Not for the washer, but that Leviticus had thought of her, considered her needs. She wasn't used to this new man she called her husband, but she wasn't complaining, either. Not for a moment. Joining the church, committing to *Ordnung* classes proved to her that Leviticus was dedicated to change. Now, if they could just learn to love and trust one another.

Tired, Leviticus held the door for Otto and Mose Fischer, and then followed them into the church. He'd dealt with two long days and nights working in the grove but made time for his condensed *Ordnung* classes to please Verity, like joining the church and being baptized the Sunday after they'd been married had managed to do. The community's *Ordnung* rules were important to her, so they were important to him now, too.

His first session with Mose had been surprisingly interesting. Why hadn't he seen that the *Ordnung* rules were fair back when he was young, that they were put in place to help the people of Pinecraft, not control them? *Was I too young? Too rebellious?* Rules kept the faithful prospering. He'd have no problem living within the boundaries set down by Bishop Otto Fischer and the pastors.

As they walked out of the church together, Mose rubbed at the bridge of his nose. He paused. "There'll be another group of men coming to the grove tomorrow. Seven thirty too early for your family?"

Leviticus laughed. "*Nee.* Verity and I are up before the chickens nowadays. With all your kids, I'm pretty sure you and Sarah know all about early-morning feedings and messy breakfast tables."

"Sarah and I have six rambunctious *kinner.*" Mose looked down and picked at a dried clump of dirt on his trousers. "She's been feeling poorly of late. This pregnancy's been hard on her."

Seven children! How did Sarah manage? Yet, every time he saw Mose's *fraa* she looked happy, fresh as a spring flower and not in the least stressed.

Verity came to mind. He pictured her heavy with his *kind.* How would she feel about having *kinner* in the future? Not that there was much of a chance of that happening. Their marriage was in name only.

For a while now, he'd known he still had serious feelings for Verity. Feelings that went far beyond appreciation and friendship. Being realistic, he also knew there was no way she would feel the same about him after she learned what he'd done during the war. And he planned to tell her someday soon. He had to.

"You two getting along okay?" Mose climbed onto his bike and straddled it, distracting Leviticus's daydreaming.

"We're getting there. Ours was an arranged marriage, you know. It'll probably take time to get to know each other again. Eventually, all the kinks will be ironed out."

Mose smiled. "I know what you mean. My marriage was one of convenience, too." He laughed, his head thrown back as he hooted. "I quickly learned my Sarah, the mildest woman you can find, has a sharp tongue when riled." He nodded, lifting his suspender strap as it slipped off his shoulder. "She's a *gut* woman, and the best *mamm*, especially to Beatrice, our strong-willed *dochder*. Sarah's smart and knows just how to handle that tiny replica of Ulla."

Mose and Leviticus snorted at the reference to Ulla. Most men in Pinecraft felt sorry for Chicken John, but Leviticus had noticed the man seemed happy enough with his choice of wife.

"What's so funny?" Otto came out of the church and locked the door behind them.

"My comment about Ulla," Mose said with a smile for his father, and got a knowing grin back.

"Like us, Chicken John can't live without his woman, but enough of this silly chitchat about the womenfolk. My supper's waiting in the oven and a man needs his nourishment if he's to get a good night's sleep."

After waving the two men off, Leviticus rode his bike slow and easy through the streets of Pinecraft, becoming familiar with the houses going up, the new hotel being built in the center of the community.

A brisk wind almost blew him off his bike. Fall was here, and Thanksgiving would be coming soon. All the vacant-rooms and for-rent signs would disappear quickly enough. Spare rooms always filled up fast during the fall and winter months, when the snowbirds and Northern Amish began to come down to enjoy a bit of warm Florida sunshine.

Leviticus was disappointed to still see plenty of damage that had been caused by the hurricane. It would take months, maybe years, for Pinecraft to get back to what it had been, but the community was hard at work, preparing as best they could for the crowd of visitors arriving by bus daily.

Turning down the gravel road to the grove, his *daed*'s improved health came to mind.

He hoped his *daed* would be pleasantly pleased at how much work he and Solomon had been able to agree on and get done. The doctors were promising Albert would be home as early as Thanksgiving week. He smiled, picking up speed. *I hope they're right.*

His stress level was down to a manageable number of late. He had Verity's kindness and good humor to thank for being able to settle down into a calm routine. The only time his hands shook now was when he and Verity momentarily disagreed, which hadn't been as often lately and was always his fault. In fact, there were times Verity seemed almost friendly, like she'd stopped resenting their marriage quite so much.

Sometimes he caught her looking at him, her gaze still elusive, but warmer and hopefully full of unspoken promises.

He still needed to talk to her about the war, his PTSD and what all that entailed, but he was in no hurry to bring up the subjects and spoil what progress they'd made. Her knowing about his fighting in the war might put a rift between them, and he didn't want that. Would she trust him around the girls after she learned what a fool he'd been? Her questions would be hard to answer, reminders of what he'd done. What would she think of him once she'd heard everything?

Chapter Seventeen

Still apprehensive but thrilled with Leviticus's surprise of a new washer and dryer, Verity waited for the *Englisch* men to install water and electricity to the shed before she'd go out with a basket of dirty clothes. Sitting down with a cup of leftover coffee, Verity glanced over the machine's manuals one more time, shaking her head in confusion.

The *Englischers*' new technology was mind-blowing. What in the world had he brought home? Mixed emotions curled her toes in her shoes.

There was no agitator? How would the clothes get clean with nothing to swish them around?

Leviticus came into the kitchen wearing a smile. He had a kiss for the girls and a cheerful wave in her direction as she mulled over her predicament. "Would you like another cup of coffee? There's at least a cup left," she offered as she watched him and Naomi play tug-of-war with the *kind*'s favorite toy. His hug for Naomi was, as always, long and loving. It was plain to see the child meant the world to him.

He glanced her way as he ruffled Faith's already messy head of hair. "*Nee*, but thanks. I've got a lot to do today."

She waved him off with a smile, but her thoughts remained on her new husband. He seemed calm this morning, had a slight spring to his step. Almost as if he were happy. Like he'd finally found contentment. Watching as he plodded along, she waved at him as he turned back around and sent the girls a hand-blown kiss. She tried hard to hold down the spurt of joy warming her soul. Leviticus was becoming the man she'd been promised to all those years ago. She wasn't sure if and when she should reveal how much their new friendship meant to her.

Naomi asleep and Faith coloring on the porch, Verity made her way to the shed and upturned a basket of children's clothes into the big machine's tub. Her thoughts were on Leviticus.

Clara followed her out into the shed, kicking a basket of laundry along with her bare foot, her baby safely tucked in her arms. "What's the matter? You're wearing the strangest expression. If I didn't know better, I'd say you were a lovesick fool."

Not ready to confess her growing feelings for Leviticus and how they kept her perplexed, Verity avoided the subject. "Maybe I should use the homemade soap on the *kinner*'s clothes. I keep looking at these funny liquid washing cubes." She held up one of the colorful squares she'd found in a small cardboard box at the bottom of the washer.

"Leviticus would have warned you against them if he thought they were dangerous." Clara took the tiny soap square from Verity and examined it. Her brows raised, just as confused as Verity. "You know, we'll look complete *bensels* if we break the machine the first week. Best use this soap. It came with the machine."

"You're bound to be right." But still, Verity's stomach gyrated with nerves. *Englischer* things unnerved her, even though Otto had given his consent. *What if the soap doesn't clean well or gives both* kinner *a rash?*

Taking a deep breath, she took the cube back from Clara and dropped it in the slot marked soap that she'd accidently found a moment before. She shut the lid and punched the button for delicate clothes, reserving judgment until the children's clothes were washed. If all went well, she'd allow herself to feel confident with Leviticus's trousers and her dresses next.

Two hours later, after refusing to use the dryer on such a pretty day, she lifted another sheet from her wicker basket, snapped it out and pegged it on the wire line stretching from the garage wall to a T-shaped post stuck in the ground.

The wind caught the damp sheet and smacked her in the face. Placing her *kapp* back in place, she worked her way down the wire clothesline, pegging and grumbling to herself as she went. She missed her old wringer washer. Albert had been kind when she'd first come to work for him and bought it for her convenience, not that the machine ever performed that well. *Why hadn't Leviticus just gotten it fixed?* She would have hung on to the old machine for sentimental reasons, which was silly, considering its flaws, but she was sentimental. She smiled, remembering how many times she'd smashed her finger in the wringer before she got the hang of its peculiarities, but it had run faithfully...until Monday morning, when she'd tried to start it and nothing happened but a terrible groaning and shaking.

Verity sniffed at another damp sheet ready to be hung. The abnormal smell of store-bought soap tickled her nose. The clothes coming out of the washer seemed clean enough, but still she doubted.

She peeped through the two sheets blowing in the wind. Beyond the concrete sidewalk, Faith rode her bike, her head down like the race-kart driver they'd seen at the community fair the day before.

Naomi squealed in delight, pulling Verity's attention to her youngest daughter playing in the playpen with a pile of old pots and pans. Drool dampened her terry cloth bib and lightweight sweater. There were plenty of soft dolls and cloth blocks in the toy box the girls shared, but the *kind* learning to walk around the playpen preferred kitchenware and mixing bowls as toys. *A born cook?* Perhaps, but she doubted the talent came from Leviticus. He couldn't boil water, much less make a meal. If Naomi had a bent toward culinary arts, it would have had to come from Julie, her birth mother.

Pegging down a pair of Naomi's store-bought onesies, she allowed her thoughts to wander back to Julie, the woman who'd caught Leviticus's eye while he was away. Was it jealously eating at her? He hadn't said much about Naomi's *mamm* other than she was a professional woman who worked an important job for the military. But what he had said didn't make her sound the type who might be found in a hot kitchen, cooking for her family.

Verity's lip curled. *Unless she was cooking one of those fancy gourmet meals I read about at the pediatrician's office.*

After waving at Clara, who stood at the window watching the children's antics, Verity pressed a hand to her back. She was glad her sister-in-law had dropped in to chat this morning. For some reason, Verity had woken in a melancholy mood. She missed Albert. Missed their comradery and friendship. Clara's teasing and laughter was just what she had needed to cheer up and think positive.

She snatched up the last cloth diaper from her wicker basket. Pegs in her mouth, she looked up, the sounds of a car speeding down the gravel road leading to the compound drawing her interest. Dust and tiny rocks flew behind a fancy red sports car.

"Faith. Quick! Go tell your *Aenti* Clara someone's coming."

Who in the world could this be?

Solomon and Leviticus strolled toward the farmhouse in companionable silence. It had been a long, arduous day. Dirt had been brought in and spread in the small grove where the most damage had been done. The planting of new midsize peach trees was almost finished. They both agreed they would have never gotten this far along if it hadn't been for the local men's continued help. To say they were grateful would have been an understatement.

"*Daed*'s home day after tomorrow."

Solomon nodded, his smile reaching his eyes. "*Ya,* I know. I'm certain-sure he's going to be happy when he sees all the progress made."

A flash of red shining through a row of small orange trees caught Leviticus's eye. He didn't think it probable, but he asked the question anyway. "You know someone who drives a red sports car?"

Solomon stretched his neck, peering over a row of miniature trees. "*Nee,* that's no one I know."

Leviticus shrugged, no longer interested in the car or its driver. Shoulder to shoulder, the brothers walked on, past Verity's line of clothes flapping in the breeze.

Leviticus pulled off his work hat and wiped perspiration from his brow with the sleeve of his sweat-drenched shirt. One of the few things he missed about his *Englischer* clothes was his beat-up baseball cap. It had a built-in sweatband that really worked.

Solomon reached out and playfully popped one of the black suspenders holding up Leviticus's hand-me-down trousers.

"Two can play that game, *bruder,*" Leviticus called as he chased Solomon down, both men having to avoid a doll carriage and Faith's swing suspended from a tree limb as they ran. Inches from his target, Leviticus reached out and missed the black elastic suspender stretched taut against his brother's left shoulder.

Laughing, both men ran up the steps and burst through the kitchen's back door, much as they had as boys. Solomon dodged his brother's hand. Leviticus pursued him, not giving up the chase.

If only Mamm *were still alive.* He and Solomon had always gotten into trouble for their exuberant play. He pictured his *mamm* in front of the old range, her face red from the late-summer heat. He could almost hear her voice as she scolded them for running into the house like they were *kinner* again.

His feet still slick with mud, Leviticus skidded to a halt. A man wearing a suit sat at the breakfast table, in a chair nearest the sink. Verity stood transfixed a foot away, her eyes round, her irises a dark shade of emerald green. *Something is wrong.*

The tall man rose, his forehead creased, expressing his disapproval at their behavior. Leviticus approached. Their eyes met and held. This was no country bumpkin. An air of authority clung to the man like the scent of his expensive cologne. Leviticus had seen men like him before in big cities up north. He'd avoided them like the plague.

"Who's this?" he asked Verity. She remained dumbstruck. Silence vibrated through the room until he heard the wail of a young *boppli* crying in earnest at the back of the house. Was it Naomi? *Nee.* The child sounded too young. Perhaps Clara's new daughter, Rose? *But where are Faith and Naomi?*

His hand outstretched, an obligatory smile twisted the stranger's lips. His smart, well-fitted suit told Leviticus their visitor had money—and lots of it.

Verity cleared her throat, fighting to regain her composure. "This is Maxwell Horthorn. He's come to speak to you about Naomi."

Leviticus continued to ignore the man's outstretched hand. It took a moment for him to take in the ramifications of what Verity had said.

"Where are the *kinner*?"

Verity swallowed hard. "Faith is with Clara and her *boppli*." The tone of her voice was too high. Something was very wrong.

Solomon's shoes scuffed the floor as he moved out of the kitchen toward the bedroom, where his wife and child waited.

Leviticus stepped forward. He pulled a kitchen chair out and sat, his legs stretched out in front of him. He knew how to deflate pompous fools. He'd done it enough in the army. *Act like you're not intimidated.* "What about Naomi? Where is she?" His words were for Verity, but his scowling glare never left Maxwell Horthorn's face.

Horthorn lowered his hand but remained standing. "She's with her mother." The man's accent spoke of the islands to the south. Perhaps Jamaica. "I represent the Miami law firm of Zamora, Smith, Landers and Espinoza."

"I'm sure you do."

Leviticus's eyes cut back to Verity. She stood twisting a dishcloth in her hands, her fingers working the fabric, her tortured gaze fixed on the man. He could hear Naomi now. She had begun to whimper and cry out, *"Mamm!"* Her wail of fear sucked the air from his lungs. He stiffened. The floral scent was unmistakable. Chanel. Julie always wore too much.

High heels clicking on hardwood signaled her arrival in the kitchen. He pulled his gaze away from Verity. The one woman in the world who could ruin his daughter's life stood just inside the kitchen. Julie Hernandez. She hadn't changed in the months since he'd seen her. She was still rakish thin.

There was no smile of greeting between the two, just her usual petulant frown and pouting red mouth. She held Naomi in her arms much like a *kind* might carry a rag doll. Not the way a mother should hold her desperately unhappy child.

Naomi reached out her chubby arms to Verity. *"Mamm... Mamm!"*

Verity took a step forward and then stopped as if held by an invisible string. She stood motionless, her arms dropping limp to her sides. Gentle as a lamb, Verity was no match for Julie's annoyed glare.

"What do you want?" He looked her up and down. Out of her military uniform, she wore her usual business attire: a dark slim pencil skirt and lacy blouse meant to give an air of big-city sophistication. Like the fool he had been, he'd fallen for her gentle Southern charm and delicate features, but he'd finally seen through her, though too late. She had already been pregnant with Naomi by the time he was ready to pack his bags.

His hands clenched into fists. He'd take them both on...and the Miami court system if it meant saving his daughter from the likes of Julie. His thoughts swirled with ugly possibilities, making him sick to his stomach. *This isn't supposed to be happening.* Julie had wanted nothing to do with Naomi when she was a baby. What had changed? For the millionth time, he regretted not getting a signed legal document from her relinquishing custody before he'd left Washington with his daughter.

"Still not warm and welcoming, I see." Contempt laced Julie's soft words. Her smile might have turned up her lips, but her eyes were bright and shiny with rage. She'd always liked power games, playing with people like they were bugs until she squashed them under her heel.

"For some reason, I don't feel friendly today." Anger laced Leviticus's voice.

Naomi continued to cry. Julie put the squirming child on her shoulder and rubbed her back, only making the child cry harder.

"She doesn't know you, Julie. Let Verity hold her for a moment and comfort her."

Julie threw back her head and hooted. "Don't be silly. She's fine with me." Her eyes sought out Verity's gaze. "After all, I'm her mother." Julie looked down at the child in her arms with ownership, seeking to intimidate Verity further.

He saw an ugly glimmer of determination in Julie's eyes as she lifted her head and looked directly at Verity. "The kid's just tired. It's probably past her bedtime. Isn't that right, sweet girl?"

Naomi pushed away from Julie, stretching toward Leviticus, sobbing her heart out. But Julie wasn't finished with them yet. He could see it in the set of her mouth, the way her eyes watched Leviticus and Verity's reactions to her being there.

Julie hiked Naomi up higher on her hip and turned toward Leviticus. "Now, before we end this family reunion, let me ask. Does your little Amish wifey know about you joining the army and going to Afghanistan?"

Verity gasped, her hand flying to her mouth.

Julie smiled. "I didn't think so. Shame you weren't honest with her. You think she's going to be okay with you killing all those men and that young kid while you were over there?"

Pale and shaking uncontrollably, Verity looked as if she was going into shock. Leviticus walked over to her and tried to guide her to a chair, but Verity jerked her arm away, her gaze condemning, her stance rigid.

A manila folder of papers slid across the table and hit Leviticus on the arm. A pen marked with a law office's logo lay on top.

Julie spoke up, satisfaction etched on her face. "They're legal documents. Sign them and I won't call the police and report you for kidnapping."

"I'm not signing anything." Leviticus advanced toward Julie, reaching for Naomi.

"Look, Huckleberry. You can either sign or go to jail." The lawyer jumped up and sidestepped in front of Leviticus. "It's your choice." He smiled at Julie. "Miss Hernandez has every right to see her daughter, spend time with her as often as she likes. You took the child known as Naomi out of the state illegally, without her mother's consent. Unless you have a court decree granting you full custody from the state of Washington, DC, and a psychiatrist saying you're of sound mind, I strongly suggest you sign the papers and let us be on our way."

The urge to break the nose on Maxwell Horthorn's long, wrinkled face rose to a screaming crescendo in his head. He struggled to forget the ways he'd been taught to kill a man with one blow. He sought Julie's gaze. "Leave Naomi with me as we agreed and get out of this house. Make sure you take your pretty boy with you."

"Oh, honey. I plan on leaving, but not alone. Naomi goes with me. Women are prone to changing their minds. You ought to know that by now." Julie smiled sweetly at Naomi. "I want Naomi. We belong together, don't we, sugar?"

Leviticus rubbed his hands down his pant legs. *Be calm. Breathe.* He could see it in her eyes. Julie wanted him to put hands on Horthorn, kick them both out with brute strength and fury. She'd love having him arrested for violence. It was part of her plan. But he wouldn't play along. He didn't play those games anymore.

He walked toward her, hoping his angry expression might intimidate her. "I've enjoyed seeing you about as much as having a root canal. Now, give me Naomi and get out."

Clutching the whimpering child closer, Julie turned to her lawyer. "Come on. Let's go. I have what I came for."

Leviticus stood firm, not moving. "I mean it, Julie. You're not taking my daughter."

"Watch me." Her brow rose, perfectly arched. Furrows of rage marred her perfectly made-up face. "I know you better than you think. You're not man enough to deal with the threat of prison hanging over your head. You stop me and there'll be no chance of you ever seeing the kid again."

"The child's name is Naomi."

Julie handed her bulky purse to Horthorn and took a step forward and then another, testing the waters. "That old-fashioned name's not going to last long. I let you call her Naomi at first, but I'm having her name changed on Monday. I think Izzy's a pretty name. Don't you?"

"You can't do that!" Verity cried out.

Naomi recaptured Verity's gaze. Tears darkened the Amish woman's thick lashes.

Julie moved toward Leviticus, her assured smile piercing him to the bone. "I can and will take her. Without your name on the birth certificate, you don't have a leg to stand on and you know it."

Reality punched him hard in the chest, robbing him of air. "But you said you didn't want her, that your job—" He hated the way his voice trembled, exposing his doubt, giving her the edge she wanted.

Julie's eyes narrowed to slits. "You know me better than that, sugar. I said a lot of things I didn't mean while we were together." Laughing, she thrust out her left hand, showing off an engagement ring clustered with sparkling diamonds and rubies. "My fiancé really wants kids. He'll like this one."

She glanced around at the simple dinner table, at the old cookstove. "Look at this place. Can you really say you want our little girl raised in this hovel, around Amish people who don't have a clue what the real world's all about? I'll get custody one way or the other. It doesn't matter how. I'm happy to fight dirty. It's the way I like to win." She hitched Naomi higher on her slim hip. "Now get out of my way. We want to be on the road before the traffic gets heavy."

"I could just take her from you, you know." He continued to hold his ground, rigid and unwavering.

"I'm sure the pictures of you tearing a crying child

from her mother's arms would be very revealing to the judge. You got your phone handy, Max?"

"Right here."

Leviticus's legs tried to give way under him. "This isn't the end. We'll have our day in court and you'll lose."

Her dark eyes sparkled with victory. "We'll see." She brushed past him, her heels clicking, her head held high.

He swallowed a lump the size of a fist restricting his throat. "You can count on me being there."

Naomi reached out her arms to Verity. *"Mamm!"* But then she and Julie disappeared through the back door and into the shadows of dusk.

Calm and collected, Maxwell Horthorn sauntered past and through the door. He paused, one foot still in the kitchen. "Don't fight Julie on this. Her mind is made up and you know what she's like when her back's up. She always wins. She'd love to have you arrested for kidnapping."

The screen door slammed shut in Leviticus's face.

Bewildered, his anxiety building, Leviticus stumbled over to the kitchen window and watched as Julie deftly snapped his howling child into an expensive-looking car seat wedged into the back of the car and slipped in beside her. Determination strengthened his resolve. He'd get Naomi back. He didn't know how, but he'd find a way with *Gott*'s help.

He turned to Verity, but she was already out of the room, moving fast down the hall.

He reached out for her, tried to grab her arm, but she evaded him, her back against the door of his father's bedroom. "Don't you touch me. Nothing you can say will explain away what I've just heard. Our little girl is gone because of you. You should have protected her, made sure she was safe from the likes of her."

Leviticus let his hand drop, watched as Verity turned and ran, using the walls to hold her up until she slipped into her room. As soon as the door slammed shut, he heard her wail, heard her banging her fist against the door. "My *boppli*!"

Leviticus shook all over, his heart ripped from his chest.

"*Gott*, help me. What have I done?"

Chapter Eighteen

Only a few people were on the beach. Most who weren't clearing away rubble from the storm stood in line at small food trucks, waiting on burgers to fry or ice cream to be topped with chunks of chocolate or sugar-covered licorice. Desperate to be away from the grove for a few hours, Verity found a clean spot and settled herself and Faith on a homemade quilt.

"When's my new *daed* coming home?" The sun straight overhead beat down on them. Faith let sand run through her fingers as she squinted up, waiting for her mother's reply.

Verity smiled down at her, adjusted the *kapp* on her daughter's head. How should she answer the child? She stared out and watched an ocean wave as it raced onshore, piled high with froth, only to stop inches from her bare feet. "Soon, I'm sure." But she wasn't sure. The only thing she was sure of was that she missed Naomi with all her heart and couldn't understand how Leviticus could let something so horrific happen to their little girl.

She'd been forced to lie about where Naomi was at bedtime and again this morning. It broke her heart, but the lie was better than trying to explain the truth. There was no explanation that made sense.

"He and Naomi have been gone a long time. Days and days."

Verity fought tears threatening to flow. "Not so long, bumpkin. Just overnight." Verity held back her true feelings. She was glad Leviticus had still been gone when she got up, hoped he'd left Pinecraft. Leviticus had kept so many secrets. Done so many horrible things, and now the child paid the price.

She sighed, drew salty air into her lungs. As far as Faith knew, Naomi was still visiting *familye* so the two of them could have a special day on the beach. It had been the best she could come up with in the moment. Her mind still whirled with the harsh realities of life. Naomi could be gone forever. What would she tell Faith as time slipped past and Naomi never came back?

And Leviticus's past. What was she to think? What did *Gott* think of his past actions? Killing was a sin. He'd killed a child, if Julie was telling the truth. All this misery was Leviticus's fault. If only he'd confessed, told her what had been troubling him. But she was tired of thinking about his lack of forethought concerning Naomi, about the war he'd fought in. She wouldn't wonder about the circumstances surrounding the killings that had taken place during the war. She had tormented herself enough last night with what-ifs and if-onlys.

A brisk wind blew, kicking up sand in Faith's face. Verity smiled as her *dochder* fanned it away, her young *kind*'s frown expressing irritation at being distracted from the sandcastle she was building with a shovel and bucket. But then Faith smiled and scrambled up. "Theda! I didn't know you were coming to our day at the beach."

Theda Fischer strolled up arm in arm with Otto, who looked like an *Englischer* in his rolled-up pant legs and bare feet, the straw hat on his head and his beard the only giveaway that he was truly Amish.

"*Guder mariye*, Verity. You're looking very rosy-cheeked under the warm morning sun." Theda accepted Otto's arm as he helped his wife settle next to Verity.

Otto offered Faith his hand and helped her to her feet. "Let's you and I go chase seagulls while the ladies talk about all things Thanksgiving. That subject is much too boring for us, ain't so?"

Faith nodded and then waved goodbye and scurried along beside Otto, her small bare feet kicking up sand.

"I would have thought you'd be home preparing pie for tomorrow." Theda reverted to her native tongue of Pennsylvania Dutch, the language she'd first learned at her mother's knee.

Verity used her hand to shield her eyes from the sun. Dressed in a plain blue dress with an apron of starched white cotton, the older woman looked her over with compassionate eyes. This was no chance meeting. Clara must have gotten word to Theda about Naomi being whisked away by her birth mother. She needed help understanding why *Gott* would let such a thing happen.

"The pies are ready. I cooked most of them through the night."

"No sleep for the weary?"

"Nee." Verity brushed sand from the edge of her dress, doing her best to avoid Theda's scrutiny.

The older woman grasped Verity's hand and held on tight. "I'm told all is not well on the grove."

Humiliation flushed her cheeks hot. She'd been such a fool.

Theda patted Verity's hand. A sweet smile curved her lips. "You're not mad at Leviticus, are you? You should be angry at the situation you and Leviticus find yourselves in. Ain't so?"

Verity watched Faith running ahead of Otto as they headed for the ice-cream shack. No doubt the *kind* had convinced Otto an ice-cream cone would make the day special.

"I'm angry at Leviticus and the woman who birthed Naomi, but mostly at myself for being such a *bensel* and believing his lies."

"True enough he didn't talk to you about his past, but he didn't cause Naomi's mother to come and get her."

"No, but lies of omission are still lies. There were things I should have known, things that would have made a difference to Otto's decision making about marriage. He would have never asked me to get into an arranged marriage with Leviticus if he had known about the things that man has done in the past."

"Otto did know."

Verity pulled her hand away, putting space between them.

From a distance, Verity heard Faith's burst of laughter. She looked down the shoreline, searching among the few children playing in the surf. His legs as short as a boy's, Otto ran after a scurrying seagull and managed to miss its tail feathers by inches. "Otto knew and didn't tell me my future husband was a murderer?"

Gray clouds gathered overhead. The wind picked up. Red riotous curls peppered with gray danced under the *kapp* Theda had tied with her ribbons to keep it on. Her sagging jowls reminded Verity how old Theda was as she kept her gaze on her.

"Yes, he knew. Before Albert had his last stroke, Leviticus came to see us late one night. He was perplexed about the future, concerned he'd done more harm than good by returning home. Otto gave him sound advice. Prayed with him and sent him home."

Verity sat up very straight, her mind racing. How could it be? Leviticus had confessed his sins to Otto, and still her bishop arranged a marriage of convenience between them? "He knew about everything?"

"*Nee*, not everything. But the most important aspects of Leviticus's life with the *Englisch*. I heard a portion of the conversation, but not enough to form an opinion of my own. As I usually do, I trusted Otto to know what was best."

"Faith and I deserved better than a man who carried a gun and used it when he deemed necessary. Lives were lost. He played at being *Gott*."

"*Ya*, lives might have been lost. Leviticus could have died from his wounds, too."

Verity sucked in her breath, her heart pounding

against her ribs. "Another fact he kept from me. I didn't know he'd been injured."

"Would you have rather he stayed in the *Englisch* world, died from his wounds without *Gott*'s forgiveness?"

"Of course not. I wish for no man to meet *Gott* with sin in his heart."

"*Gott* in His mercy saved Leviticus for another purpose. Perhaps the purpose of bringing joy and love back into your life. It is time for Leviticus to come back to the *Leit*, be forgiven for sins committed while a foolhardy *bu*."

"He's not a *bu* any longer. He's a man. A very foolish man."

Theda shook her head, disappointment creasing her forehead. "And you are too *gut* to forgive him, even though *Gott* saw fit to forgive it all?"

Verity did nothing to hold back the tears. Shame made her face flame. "I've prayed for *Gott* to help me forgive and forget, spent hours last night trying to understand, make concessions for Leviticus, but nothing makes sense to me. How could he take lives in a war that wasn't his, put his *dochder* at risk? There were no legal papers drawn up. Only a verbal agreement with Julie. He's smarter than that. And now that woman has every right to take Naomi, and there is nothing we can do to keep her with us."

"You have never made impulsive moves, never sinned, never told a lie? I'm certain-sure I have, no matter how hard I try to stay true to the *Ordnung* and stand blameless before *Gott*. A *fraa*'s job is to be always by her husband's side. You didn't stand by Leviticus when he needed you the most. Perhaps you know better than *Gott*, Verity? Perhaps your *mamm* failed to teach you that forgiveness is blessed? Are you too proud to be married to a man who has sinned in the past and asked forgiveness of his community, his *Gott*? Perhaps you see yourself as too important for a man such as this. Do you hold Leviticus to a higher standard because he disappointed you all those years ago?"

Faith came running up to her mother and thrust out her hand. "Look. We found a sand dollar. It's a little broken, but Otto said *Gott* loves broken things."

That small voice deep inside her head spoke so clearly as she held the less-than-perfect sand dollar. *Leviticus is like this sea creature. He's broken but precious to* Gott.

Otto gave Theda a hand up.

"Think on the things we spoke about," she said, brushing down her skirt and apron.

Verity nodded, too ashamed to look up. She wiped a tear from her eye and then two.

"Are you crying, *Mamm*?" Faith hugged her mother around the shoulders.

"*Nee*, my precious. I'm not crying. There's sand in my eyes. Now let's go home and get ready for Albert's return. There's a meal to cook and I'm going to need your help with the salad."

The plush chair was the most comfortable he'd ever sat in, but still Leviticus squirmed. A lot rode on this visit to Otto's lawyer. Verity sat across from him, her legs crossed at the ankles, head down, as she stared unseeing at a magazine cover turned wrong side up.

They'd spoken briefly when he'd returned home the night before but said nothing about the previous night or how she felt about the things she'd learned that he'd done or hadn't done. He had no idea where things stood between them, but if he took a guess, he'd probably be more heartsick than he was already.

Otto roamed the large office, glancing at pictures of horses in meadows, of wildflowers and ladies in sun bonnets on rugs in green meadows.

Seated behind a large wooden desk littered with cream-colored files and legal books, the middle-aged secretary, who'd been ignoring them for the last hour, fanned herself with a folder and then suddenly jumped from her swivel chair like a bee had just stung her on her backside. "Mr. Glass can see you now."

She curtly acknowledged Otto with a nod as he approached, then promptly turned her back on him, her concentration now on the silver laptop screen in front of her.

Verity sprang up and led the way across the carpeted room. Leviticus hesitated, his throat restricting his breathing. His stomach clenched as he took Verity's elbow and accompanied her toward the office door, doing his best to reach Otto before they went in. *Am I doing the right thing?* Leaning in close to Otto's ear, he whispered, "You certain-sure I can trust Sam Glass with the whole truth?"

Otto guffawed. "*Ya*, sure you can. He's been a real help to the community over the years." The tips of his fingers scratched his gray-speckled beard while opening the lawyer's office door.

Otto with a nervous tic? Not a good sign.

Otto cleared his throat, glanced past Leviticus to Verity, who flashed a brave smile. "Believe it or not, even we Amish have the need of a lawyer on occasion."

Otto turned the knob on the door and it swung open wide. A tall balding man rose from a plush leather chair. "Well, look who the wind's blown in." He smiled, exposing straight white teeth that were obviously fake. His hand extended, he greeted Otto with a friendly smile and warm handshake.

Otto returned the man's smile. "*Danki* for seeing us on such short notice, Sam. It's been too long."

"Too long indeed." The two older men slapped each other on the back affectionately, giving Leviticus the impression that they had been friends for a long time. They chatted robustly about family matters and then shifted their friendly banter to the lousy weather they'd been having, and the cost of the city cleanup.

Leviticus thought of the dwindling amount in his bank account. The grove was fast becoming a money pit and he didn't have a clue what this meeting was going to cost him, but it had been two days since Julie had shown up and snatched away his daughter. He'd get Naomi back no matter the cost or what he had to do. He rolled his shoulders, trying to ease some of the tension building in his upper back and neck.

Otto pointed Leviticus's way. "This here is Leviticus Hilty, one of Pinecraft's faithful."

Leviticus took the lawyer's extended hand.

"You must be Albert's son."

"I am." He accepted Sam's friendly pat on the back.

"Your father and I go way back. I heard he'd been ill. Is he doing better?"

Relief about Albert coming home had Leviticus grinning from ear to ear. "He is. Mose is bringing him home this afternoon while we're out."

Sam Glass smiled. "Just in time for Thanksgiving. Good, good. And this pretty lady must be your wife."

"Ya." It was the first time he'd had the opportunity to claim Verity as his own. Pride made his chest swell as he watched her delicate hand be engulfed by Sam's tanned paw.

Sam's smile was polite as he pointed toward three empty chairs near the big desk in the center of the room. "Let's all get comfortable. Anyone want a cup of coffee or bottle of water before we get started?" Sam's alert brown eyes focused on Verity and then Leviticus.

Otto answered for them. *"Nee,* nothing for us. But you go ahead. I know how much you like your coffee."

Grabbing a disposable cup of hot brew from the coffee maker behind him, Sam once again made himself comfortable in his chair and refocused his attention back on them. "So, what's up? Sale of a house go wrong?"

Leviticus leaned forward, sitting on the edge of the plush leather chair he'd settled in. "It's my daughter… our daughter Naomi. Her birth mother, Julie Hernandez, came and took her and we want her back."

"You two have primary custody of the child?" Sam scribbled on the pad in front of him.

Leviticus dropped his chin. He hated that Verity had to hear all the stupid things he had done before coming home. "No, but I had a verbal agreement with Julie. When she found out she was pregnant, she agreed not to give the child up for adoption if I promised to raise it without her.

"When I returned from my tour in Afghanistan, Naomi had been born and was being cared for by a full-time nanny. Julie came home two days later and seemed glad to relinquish custody of Naomi to me without complaint or hesitation. I came down to Pinecraft with my *dochder*, so she could be raised Amish and get to know my family."

"Before that, had this woman always kept her word to you?"

"More or less. I had no reason to think she wasn't serious about not wanting the *kind*...until yesterday when she showed up at our door with an attorney."

"I assume you made sure your name was on the child's birth certificate?"

Leviticus glanced at Verity. Her head was down, her hands neatly folded in her lap. Where did she get her strength? "I thought it was. When I asked to see the document, she made up some excuse about Naomi's name being spelled wrong and how she'd send me a copy. Yesterday was the first time I saw the amended copy. My name was nowhere on it, and the lawyer said I could easily be charged with kidnapping." He cleared his throat, repositioned himself in his seat. He took a nervous glance Verity's way. She sat looking straight ahead, as if she'd rather be anywhere than this office hearing what a fool he had been.

"There was no short-term marriage between you and this woman?"

Leviticus answered. *"Nee."*

Sam's informal demeanor evaporated. He was all

business now. "I thought Amish folk married before they started a family."

Otto cleared his throat, his fingers tugging at his beard. Verity slumped in her chair as if in pain. "We usually do, but Leviticus wasn't a member of the church at the time the *kind* was conceived."

"Ah."

Leviticus loathed what he was about to admit, especially with Verity listening. "Julie and I were sharing an apartment, living together, but only for a short time."

"You live with her for more than six months? Ever refer to her as your wife?"

"*Nee*. Our relationship wasn't like that."

"What was it like?"

If the floor had opened and swallowed him, Leviticus would have been happy to fall in the hole.

Otto sat grim-faced, listening to Leviticus's words, disapproval washing out his complexion. He'd been told the bare facts weeks ago, but now the whole story of Naomi's conception was coming out. He tapped his fingers against the leather arm of his chair.

"I was in the army at the time and living the life, if you know what I mean."

Sam's head bobbed. "I do. These things happen. But you were honorably discharged?"

"*Ya.*"

"Good. That's a plus. You supported your child?"

"I did while I was away, and during the time I was in the hospital recuperating from my wounds." Leviticus saw Verity's head turn away from him. "Once I picked Naomi up, I stopped paying the nanny's wages.

There was no agreement put down on paper about child support from Julie. I thought she got on with her life. Forgot about me and the *kind* until yesterday."

"Okay." Sam scribbled several lines of information down before he spoke again. "Let me consider Florida laws and see what's going to make or break this case." He rose and gave Leviticus another bone-crunching handshake and then turned and patted Verity affectionately on the back. "Wish I had better news for you," he told Leviticus. "But you're going to have to prove paternity with a DNA test and then we'll have to fight this in courts. Parental rights cases can be messy and take a long time." Brows raised, his sympathetic gaze redirected solely on Leviticus. "As I see it, you don't have a leg to stand on, but if we can get something on this Hernandez woman, we might stand a chance."

"It's best we leave that. Julie's Naomi's birth mother. I won't slander her in public."

Sam cleared his throat. "She's happy to smear you. Why not go in for the kill? She's taken your child, lied, implied she'd have you arrested for kidnapping. But maybe you still have feelings for this woman?"

"*Nee*, nothing like that. It's just not our way." For the first time in a long time, Leviticus meant it when he said *our way*. He was a Plain man now. A man of faith. He'd put his trust in *Gott*. Plain men didn't slander women, even if they had ripped their heart out by stealing their *kinner*.

Sam walked them out, bear-hugged Otto, shook Leviticus's hand again and nodded at Verity.

Leviticus put his straw hat back on his head as he headed for the door, Verity by his side, his legs weak and trembling. "You'll let me know when you find something out?"

"Sure will."

Otto, Verity and Leviticus were silent as they strolled to the elevator. Verity hurried ahead, as if what she had heard was more than she could handle. Leviticus's heart broke for her, but then his mind went into overdrive. There was so much they needed to talk about. Why had he waited so long to confide in her? He rubbed the back of his neck. And there was Julie to contend with. She wasn't cut out to be a *mamm*. He had to find a way to get Naomi back.

Otto slowed his step. "You okay?"

Leviticus rubbed the stubble growing on his chin. *Am I okay?*

"*Nee.* I keep seeing Naomi reaching out to Verity, crying *mamm*." He threaded a hand through his hair and replaced his straw hat. He glanced up at Verity waiting for the elevator to arrive. "She loves that child as much as I do. Losing her has ripped the heart out of her. Faith doesn't understand where her little *schwe-schder* went and keeps asking for her." His shoulders slumped. "Julie's selfish, dedicated to her job. I can't understand her marrying a man who wants *kinner*. I had to beg her to keep the *boppli* when she found out she was pregnant. She wanted no part of being a *mamm* back then."

"Maybe she woke up to what she'd done. There has to be some good in her."

Moments later, Leviticus stepped off the elevator with Verity following close behind. He massaged the constant ache in the back of his neck. "I keep praying for *Gott*'s will, asking Him to show me what to do, but all I hear back is deafening silence."

"*Gott* has a plan for Naomi's life." Otto tugged at his beard.

"I'm trying to find peace, but I'm new at this thing called faith." And he *was* trying to be strong, for Verity's sake as much as his own.

Seconds later, they stepped into bright sunlight and meandered down the sidewalk. Leviticus, afraid to ask the bishop, spoke anyway. "What if it's not *Gott*'s will for me to have Naomi back?"

His heart pounded in his ears. Was it possible? Could the *Gott* he now served ask such a thing of him, of Verity? He chewed at his nail. Could he live without his daughter and still serve a *Gott* who allowed such a thing to happen?

"The *Ordnung* requires we trust *Gott*. It also reminds us we are His beloved children."

Leviticus's hands tightened into fists at his sides; he wished he could reach out and take Verity's hand. This situation was his fault, but she suffered for his mistakes. He couldn't fault her in any way. Naomi had become her daughter as much as his own. But somehow, they'd have to learn to accept *Gott*'s will. Were his blunders too much for her to forgive? Was he asking too much?

"You sure you two are okay?"

"*Ya*, we're okay," Leviticus said, hopeful Albert's being home would distract Verity from her worry for Naomi.

Please, Gott. Help us find a way to accept Your will for our lives, our child's life. Don't let my growing faith veer to the right or to the left. And, Gott, help Verity to forgive me and find a way to love me as much as I've grown to love her.

Chapter Nineteen

Four long tables had been pushed close together to accommodate the crowd of family and friends who'd come to celebrate Albert's blessed homecoming and Thanksgiving Day meal.

Verity seated herself in between Clara and Leviticus with a sigh. There had been a lot of last-minute things to do. Lack of sleep and more work than she could handle had her tired and not just a little grumpy.

"Verity." Leviticus nudged her. "Would you pass along the sweet potato casserole?"

"I'm sorry. Did you say something?" Verity redirected her attention her husband's way. Leviticus's arm was extended, patiently waiting, the sticky casserole dish held out for her to take. She did as she was asked, smiling her apology to Clara.

I haven't said a single word to Leviticus the whole meal. She really hadn't talked at length to anyone. She glanced down at the head of the table. Albert was seated in his place of honor, looking fit as a man could look after days of hospital care.

Verity couldn't help but notice how lackluster her husband's expression was. Like her, his thoughts were no doubt on Naomi. He was putting on a show of normalcy for his *daed*. Verity lowered her head, pushed round a slice of turkey, her appetite poor. Since learning the truth about Leviticus's past she'd spent so much time searching for understanding, for a way to forgive his secret life as a soldier and the painful loss of Naomi. Some way she had to be able to trust him again. But being Amish had taught her to forgive, helped her finally find a measure of peace. It was *Gott*'s job to deal with Leviticus's past and to bring Naomi home. Not hers. She had to lean on her faith, believe for the child's return.

Gott's will be done.

From time to time, as the meal progressed, Verity heard Albert laughing out loud at the head of the table. No doubt at something one of his old cronies had said about his inability to successfully get food to his mouth. Albert's stroke might be impeding his use of a fork and his speech, but he wasn't letting his disabilities ruin his good mood or his Thanksgiving meal.

Having her father-in-law home filled her heart with joy, but for the life of her, she couldn't stop fretting over Naomi. Where was the tiny child this Thanksgiving Day?

She glanced down at Albert again, noticed how pale he still looked, but refrained from suggesting he lie down for a while. That afternoon he'd raised a fuss when he heard the day nurse's suggestion that he stay in bed during the meal. Feisty as always, he'd made it clear he was not eating turkey and dressing without his family and friends around him. He would eat at the table or not eat at all.

Not being able to use his fork properly hadn't slowed the thin old man down one bit. What didn't hit his mouth hit the floor, but she didn't care a whit about the mess he was making. She could clean up under his chair later. He was home and happy. That was all that mattered.

Albert hooted his approval when the sweet potato dish was passed his way around the table a second time. He didn't say a word, but his lopsided smile expressed his appreciation to Verity. Clara scooped a small portion of the sticky goo onto her beloved father-in-law's plate and then went back to her chair and started chatting with Solomon.

A loud knock came at the door. At the end of his table, Joe Muller, Albert's cousin, shifted in his chair. "You want me to open it?"

His mouth full of food, Albert nodded his approval.

Joe scooted out of his chair and eased the door open. His expression became confused as he spoke to whoever was at the door. He stepped back inside and closed the door most of the way. "There's a fancy *Englischer* out there, insisting on speaking to you, Leviticus."

Verity laid down her napkin, her stomach quivering, watching as Leviticus excused himself and made his way through the maze of tables and over to the door. He slipped out quickly and shut it behind him.

A chill went down Verity's spine, the memory of the last unexpected visitor at the grove haunting her.

Forks clattered against plates, the hum of the room drowning out whatever was being said on the porch.

Minutes turned into what seemed a half hour. The sound of a car motor starting up drew her attention to the window.

Joe scooted away from the door as it opened wide.

Her hand raised to her mouth, Verity smothered a gasp as Leviticus stepped across the door's threshold, holding Naomi in his arms. His gaze sought hers, tears glistening in his eyes. A genuine smile creased dimples into his face.

Verity rose, excitement filling her to overflowing. Naomi was home!

"We've got a sleepy girl here. Verity, would you help me get her ready for her nap?"

"*Ya*, sure," she muttered, pushing back her chair and almost knocking it over as she hurried to reach Leviticus's side.

Albert waved his hand, trying to utter words.

Leviticus grinned his father's way. "We'll be right back, *Daed*. You keep eating."

Verity fell over her own feet as she scurried beside Leviticus, her hand on the small child's arm. Gott *has heard our prayers. Naomi is home!*

With the push of his shoulder, Leviticus eased the children's bedroom door shut behind them.

Verity's eyes sought his, perplexed and wide with wonder. "Our *boppli* is home for *gut*?"

Leviticus nodded, his hands trembling as he laid the child in her cot. Verity reached out and lovingly touched Naomi's dark curls, her rosy cheek. Verity's shoulder leaned into Leviticus's chest for support. "I don't understand. What's happened?"

The feel of Naomi cuddled up close to him had moved him beyond any joy he'd ever experienced. "I honestly can't say what changed. All I know for sure is Maxwell Horthorn brought our *dochder* back." Leviticus picked up the folder of papers the lawyer had given him and handed them to Verity. "He gave these papers to me and assured me they were legal. Look for yourself. He said they're signed by Julie and stamped by the local magistrate. The most important paper acknowledges me as Naomi's natural father and gives you permission to adopt Naomi as your own. Julie has relinquished all parental rights to her."

"But that woman was determined to lay claim to Naomi."

Joy rushed through him. "I know. But Horthorn said Julie changed her mind. Seems her future husband dumped her, and she had no further need of Naomi." Leviticus slid his arm around Verity's shoulders, and side by side, they stood watching their *dochder* sleep. Naomi's lips puckered, her mouth nursing on an imaginary bottle.

Leviticus laughed. "Look at her. It's like she never was gone."

He watched the darkness leave Verity's eyes, saw pure joy replace it.

"I can't believe she's ours once again." She snuggled close, her face pressed against his chest.

"I need to ask your forgiveness, even though I know I don't deserve it. I've given you every reason to distrust me, but I've changed and will continue to become the man you need in your life. *Gott* has forgiven me for my transgressions, helped me to see what is important and what's not. I need your love."

"I forgive you your past, Leviticus."

He was so grateful that her Amish faith was stronger than his, and that she'd found a way to forgive him. "As far as I'm concerned, we've been a family since we said our vows." He pulled Verity closer, wrapping his arms around her waist and sighing with relief when she didn't resist his overture of affection.

Verity's eyes sought his, her look of confusion gone as he bent to softly kiss her lips.

Leviticus lifted her chin. "Please believe me when I tell you that you mean the world to me, and not just as a *mamm* for Naomi. My feelings for you go deep, so much deeper than I knew possible." He held her gaze, allowed all the love he felt for her to shine to the surface for her to see. "You and the girls have shown me what true love is. You're precious to me. I promise to never hurt you again."

Her brow furrowed, ashamed she had to ask. "The *Englischer* world? Does it still beckon to you?"

"*Nee*, not anymore. I am a Plain Amish man now. My desire is to serve the Lord, be a *gut* husband and *dat*."

Verity rested her forehead against his chest, her arms circling his waist. "I've dreamed of this moment, been too afraid to dare hope for fear you'd slip away again."

Leviticus could feel Verity's body trembling. "Ten years ago, I was a fool. Forgive me for leaving. Say you'll be my love once again."

Verity lifted her head, her love revealed in her eyes,

in the sweet smile on her face. "I've loved you most of my life. How could that change now?"

Leviticus smiled. He'd dreamed of this moment, as well, longed for it for so long. "I promise you will always come first, that I will be a good husband and *daed* to our girls. But most of all, I promise to love you until my last breath and beyond."

Their kiss was warm and promising. They had time now, time to be the *familye* they both longed for. But his father awaited. "We have so much to talk about, but first we'd best get back to *Daed*. He'll be wondering."

Verity nodded, her smile bringing a glow to her face. "Do you think anyone will notice the difference in us? I feel as if our love is shining like diamonds all around us."

Leviticus laughed. "Let them wonder. This joy is ours and ours alone."

* * * * *